REDEMPTION'S ECHO

CATHY MCINTOSH

©2024 by Cathy McIntosh

Published by hope*books
2217 Matthews Township Pkwy
Suite D302
Matthews, NC 28105
www.hopebooks.com

hope*books is a division of hope*media

Printed in the United States of America

All rights reserved. Without limiting the rights under copyrights reserved above, no part of this publication may be scanned, uploaded, reproduced, distributed, or transmitted in any form or by any means whatsoever without express prior written permission from both the author and publisher of this book—except in the case of brief quotations embodied in critical articles and reviews.

Thank you for supporting the author's rights.

First paperback edition.
Paperback ISBN: 979-8-89185-109-2
Hardcover ISBN: 979-8-89185-110-8
Ebook ISBN: 979-8-89185-111-5
Library of Congress Number: 2024945666

This is a work of fiction. Names, characters, places, and incidents either are products of the author's imagination or are used fictitiously. Any resemblance to actual persons, living or dead, events, or locales is entirely coincidental.

CONTENTS

PROLOGUE – Dahlia, 1995 ix

PART-ONE

CHAPTER 1 – Abby, 2023.. 3

CHAPTER 2 – Abby, 2023.. 13

CHAPTER 3 – Abby, 2023.. 21

CHAPTER 4 – Abby, 2023.. 29

CHAPTER 5 – Abby 2023 35

CHAPTER 6 – Abby, 2023.. 41

CHAPTER 7 – Abby, 2023.. 47

CHAPTER 8 – Abby, 2023.. 53

CHAPTER 9 – Dahlia, 1997 63

CHAPTER 10 – Dahlia, 2004 71

CHAPTER 11 – Dahlia, 2004 77

CHAPTER 12 – Beth, 2004 83

CHAPTER 13 – Dahlia, 2004 89

CHAPTER 14 – Dahlia, 2004 97

CHAPTER 15 – Dahlia, 2004 103

CHAPTER 16 – Dahlia, 2004 109

CHAPTER 17 – Dahlia, 2005 115

PART-TWO

CHAPTER 18 – Turo, 2005 127

CHAPTER 19 – Turo, 2005 133

CHAPTER 20 – Turo, 2005 141

CHAPTER 21 – Turo, 2005 147

CHAPTER 22 – Turo, 2005 159

CHAPTER 23 – Turo, 2005 167

CHAPTER 24 – Abby, 2023 171

CHAPTER 25 – Abby, 2023 179

CHAPTER 26 – Turo, 2005 187

CHAPTER 27 – Abby, 2023 197

CHAPTER 28 – Abby, 2023 203

CHAPTER 29 – Abby, 2023 211

CHAPTER 30 – Abby, 2023 219

CHAPTER 31 – Abby, 2023 225

CHAPTER 32 – Abby, 2023 231

PART-THREE

CHAPTER 33 – Abby, 2023 241

CHAPTER 34 – Abby, 2023 251

CHAPTER 35 – Abby, 2023 259

CHAPTER 36 – Abby, 2023 265

CHAPTER 37 – Abby, 2023 273

CHAPTER 38 – Abby, 2023 279

CHAPTER 39 – Abby, 2023 291

CHAPTER 40 – Abby, 2023 297

CHAPTER 41 – Abby, 2023 301

CHAPTER 42 – Abby, 2023 305

CHAPTER 43 – Abby, 2023 315

CHAPTER 44 – Abby, 2023 321

CHAPTER 45 – Abby, 2023 329

CHAPTER 46 – Abby, 2023 335

Acknowledgments 341

About the Author 345

For Mom.

DAHLIA, 1995

Nearly half the bristles were shed, and those remaining were splayed and split. Still, she scrubbed with vigor, trying to rid her mouth of the lingering taste of his cigarettes. There was another awful taste she couldn't identify, too, and she wished for toothpaste. No matter how hard she squeezed and twisted, the empty tube wouldn't yield even the tiniest bit more.

This was the third time she'd brushed since meeting the man named Jerry this afternoon at Walmart. Her tears trickled past her lips and mixed with water from the tap.

She spat into the sink and looked into the eyes of the reflection staring back, her frame too small to see below her shoulders. Her blonde braids had loosened since Mama had carefully plaited them yesterday morning. Dust covered her cheeks. She knew she needed a bath but could only think about getting the nasty taste out of her mouth.

She'd been standing in Walmart's back-to-school section, surrounded by shelves filled with glue sticks and markers, adding up how much money she'd need for her little sister Bebee's supplies. His deep, raspy voice startled her.

"There are so many colors to choose from," he'd said.

"Yes," Dahlia crinkled her eyebrows together, still focused on tallying the prices in her head.

"I'm Jerry," he said with a smile. "What's your name?"

"Dahlia," she replied, immediately feeling bad that she hadn't looked him in the eye like Mama taught her.

"You look worried," he'd said. Dahlia remembered gazing upward, seeing him mimic the scowl of her facial expression. "You're only nine, maybe ten. What's got you so concerned?"

He looked nice, and once she recovered from her initial start, she chattered on as one never short on words, explaining how Bebee was about to start first grade and needed a lot of supplies. Knowing there was only a little bit of money, Dahlia had decided she could get by with the supplies she'd saved from last year, but Bebee needed new ones.

Kids were mean when someone seemed different, and she wanted Bebee to fit in. Dahlia longed for her little sister to find a real friend and enjoy school like a normal kid. New school supplies would help, but they were so expensive. She had some of the money saved, but where would she find the extra money to get everything on the list?

Jerry's smile seemed friendly. She hadn't thought much of it when he'd glanced up and down the store aisle, then whispered that he'd give her $20 if she'd kiss him on the cheek and promise not to tell anyone.

He'd picked up a small box of crayons and, glancing at the price, said, "You're right. These are expensive," drawing out the words into long, dramatic syllables. "I can see why you're so worried."

Jerry had asked for a kiss, and Mama said gentlemen ask first, so Dahlia believed she could trust him. But he was no gentleman. She recalled his snake-like whisper as he'd squatted down to look her in the eye. "Now, how about that kiss, honey?" His words still reverberated in her chest.

His odor repulsed Dahlia as she leaned in for a polite peck on his cheek. Without warning, he'd turned his face and took far more than she'd offered. She'd never felt someone's tongue in her mouth. It felt like a rock covered with sandpaper. The young girl wondered why anyone would kiss like that on purpose.

"If you need anything more," he'd said as he held out a crisp $20 bill, "there's more where that came from." The look in his eye had made her skin crawl, so she'd accepted the money and shied away, nearly tripping over a display of Post-it notes. The man abruptly turned and disappeared into the next aisle.

Dahlia gathered the supplies Bebee needed and hurried toward the cash registers, too intent on getting out of the store to notice the concerned customers who saw the terrified look on her face. Choosing the first available cashier, she'd emptied the plastic shopping basket onto the check-out belt then paid as fast as she could. Nearly running out of the store with her shopping bag in hand, Dahlia covered the three blocks as fast as her tiny legs would carry her home.

Though still repulsed when she let herself into the apartment, thoughts of Jerry had momentarily faded as Bebee shared her excitement. Her younger sister was overjoyed when presented with the collection of crayons, paints, pencils, and colorful folders. After accepting her sister's hugs and squeals of delight, Dahlia barely reached the privacy of the bathroom before melting into tears, the frightening scene at Walmart replaying in her thoughts.

After tucking Bebee into Mama's bed where she slept, Dahlia changed into the oversized t-shirt she usually wore to bed. Her clothes lay in a pile near her feet, covering the narrow section of floor tiles between the bathtub and sink.

Dahlia heard the familiar click of the front door, spit into the sink once more for good measure, hastily dried her face from the tears that refused to stop, then darted across the hall to her room.

Mama was home from her night job and would not be happy to find her awake at this hour. She leaped into bed, pulled the threadbare blanket to her chin, and tried to breathe slowly.

Her bedroom door opened with a slight creak as it did every night when Mama checked in on her, but tonight, the petite woman stood in the doorway for a few extra seconds before moving toward the room she shared with Bebee.

Does she know I'm still awake? Dahlia wondered. Mama didn't get mad often, but it happened sometimes. More troubling than Mama's anger was the thought of disappointing her. Since Daddy left, the woman worked two jobs all winter—three in the summer. The least Dahlia could do was hold down the fort and watch over her sister while Mama was away, even if it meant doing some things she didn't like.

She couldn't help thinking that she'd have never had to kiss Jerry if Daddy were here. She buried her face in her pillow and tried to push away the emptiness that threatened to swallow her since he'd been gone. The last day he was home, he'd played with her, laughed, and made the world feel safe. But she hadn't seen him since, and no matter how she pestered for answers, Mama wouldn't tell her why.

PART ONE

CHAPTER 1

ABBY, 2023

Sergeant Abigail Carter felt an undercurrent of dread tugging at her spirit. A subtle restlessness had stirred within her for several days as if something troubling and unforeseen waited in the shadows.

As was her practice before every shift, she sat alone in the briefing room of the Adams County Sheriff's Office, her head bowed as she silently prayed for wisdom and the protection of the team of deputies she supervised on "B Platoon."

The original mid-century substation located in Commerce City, Colorado, had been torn down and rebuilt on the same piece of ground in the early 2000s. The old brick building had been bursting at the seams, too small for the ever-expanding roster of personnel. The building had been crumbling with age and on the verge of condemnation. New construction escorted the Sheriff's Office into the modern era, transforming its presence into an expansive two-story structure with open floor plans and large glass panels that flooded its new offices in natural light.

Two decades later, the building now served as headquarters for the Sheriff's Office, home to modern forensic facilities, administrative operations, and the chief law enforcement officer, Sheriff Micah Adler. He was elected to serve the major metro county that was home to more than half a million people and abutted Denver to the north.

Abby didn't remember those days of renovation, having been hired on well after its completion. The new building was the only location she'd ever known, and it never lost its nickname. It was simply called "The Sub."

The first seeds of her law enforcement career took root after two detectives had visited her home and shattered her world into a million unrecognizable pieces. They'd delivered the news that her only sister, Dahlia, had been found murdered. Though it had been nearly twenty years ago, the grief remained as fresh as it had been in those first shocking moments.

Over time, one of the detectives, Turo Torres, checked in on their family often, and they welcomed his calming, authoritative presence. As they grappled with their pain, his compassion and loyal care ignited a fire within Abby.

In high school, she'd reached out to him to research a profession she'd consider pursuing. Conversations that began for a school assignment slowly developed into a mentoring friendship. When it became time to declare a major in college, criminal justice was an easy and natural choice.

More than a way to avenge her sister's death, for Abby, becoming a deputy stemmed from a driving need to protect the weak and support those who were hurting. The trauma she'd experienced and the care she'd received fueled her ambition to give back. After graduation, Turo had recruited her to join the ranks of the Adams County Sheriff's Office, where he'd served his entire career. She'd worked under his leadership for more than a decade and, like many of her peers, believed her career was more of a calling than a job.

Recently, however, something felt off. She couldn't describe the sensation if she had to, but she'd experienced it twice before in her 35 years. Each occurrence brought a tectonic shift in the events of her future.

The first time, at just sixteen, she'd received the devastating news about Dahlia. The next, her husband of only two months had confessed his perpetual infidelity, stemming back to the first night they'd met.

Now, the heaviness was back, and she perceived it as a divine signal to hold on tight while her ship sailed through another relentless storm. Change was coming, and she hoped she had the strength to face the challenges it would bring.

When she raised her head and opened her eyes, she saw Deputy Brunson tiptoeing into the briefing room. He stashed something on a chair and covered it with his jacket. His lips were twisted into a sly yet playful smirk.

"Whatcha got there?" Abby tilted her head slightly.

He gave a secretive wink. "You'll know when it's time to know."

Ten additional patrol deputies would soon fill the room and await her direction. She knew each of them well and had instructed most of them during academy training.

Abby was well respected throughout the agency as an instructor and as a supervisor. She'd been promoted to sergeant just over a year ago but struggled to shed the insecurity that plagued her thoughts.

Time and again, she'd proved her mettle while on the job, relying on training and skills she worked hard to develop. She took her fitness seriously, caring for her body like a blacksmith forging steel. Through relentless hammering—which for Abby was a consistent routine of weight training and kickboxing—she honed her body so it was strong and ready to conquer nearly any challenge.

Still, her small frame of just 5'4" and 120 pounds with her boots on gave some of her colleagues pause. To compensate for what some saw as physical limitations, she succumbed to perfectionism and was over-prepared for everything. That included shift briefings.

Within minutes, the remaining shift members began filing into the room one by one. The silence she enjoyed earlier was replaced with the lively buzz of camaraderie. Abby noticed nearly every deputy tried to look nonchalant while suppressing a smile that threatened to break through their tough veneer. She could see right through the charade and decided to confront it head-on. "All right, everyone. What's going on?"

Brunson spoke for the group. "We're here for briefing. You've been on us to come earlier, so here we are!"

Abby played along with whatever antics the deputies were up to and scanned the room as they took their seats. "Looks like we're missing Mulligan and Taylor. When they get here, we'll start." Glancing toward the door, she added with a hint of sarcasm, "And here they are now. *All* of you are early? Now I seriously suspect something!"

Brunson gently removed his jacket from atop the item he set on the chair, exposing a small cake with white frosting and a careful arrangement of candles. "The truth is, we're here early to celebrate the best sergeant in the department. Happy birthday, Sergeant Carter!"

Abby touched her hand to her heart. She was speechless. A smile tugged at the corners of her mouth, and she blurted out, "But it's not my birthday!"

"We know we're a few days early," Deputy Mulligan said. "But since it's a Wednesday, both platoons are working. We thought we could afford to take a few minutes for cake!"

He fished a lighter from his pocket and lit the candles while leading the group in an ear-shattering rendition of "Happy Birthday." Inside, Abby was aglow.

While on a call for service or investigating a case, she could push her doubts away and keep her mind firmly cemented in the work zone. It was when she was face-to-face with her peers and even her subordinates that she was most vulnerable to negative self-talk. She wanted to please them all, to feel like she was worthy of being one of them. In her mind, she often fell short.

To Abby, the small birthday celebration showed respect. It demonstrated that her shift genuinely cared and liked to spend time with her. Abby didn't let the statement *"best sergeant in the department"* go unnoticed. She hid the compliment in her heart, intending to hold it there for the days when she could use an extra dose of reassurance.

The group devoured the cake, and Abby scooted sideways between tables to collect used paper plates and plastic forks. Brunson stopped her, presenting her with a gift card to a local spa. A smattering of white frosting clung to his dark mustache. Abby grinned and decided to leave it unmentioned. "Everyone pitched in," he explained.

In the months since her divorce, Abby tried to be more intentional about self-care, and the gift was perfect. "You're all the best," she beamed, hoping the moisture she felt in her eyes didn't show. "Thanks again." Getting back to the business at hand, she stood before the group, looked down at her notes, cleared her throat, and said, "Now, here's what's on tap for swing shift tonight—"

Her B-side swing shift team walked as a group through the hallway, out the exit doors to the secured parking lot where they would load into their assigned patrol cars. Some carried small coolers filled with food for their lunch breaks. The 4:00 pm to 2:00 am swing shift was often chaotic, and uninterrupted breaks were hard to come by. It was nice to have a sandwich or two to munch on as the overnight hours stretched.

As was her habit, Abby carried a small, reusable zipper pouch filled with comfort items: lip balm, a few pieces of hard candy, and a travel-sized tube of hand lotion to combat Colorado's dry climate. She tossed the pouch into the cubby of her door panel, set her Stanley cup filled to the brim with ice water in the cup holder, and then nestled in behind the wheel of her patrol car.

Swings usually kicked off with fast-paced action that continued through the end of the shift. Today was no exception. The first several calls went without a hitch, and the deputies went from call to call as if executing a well-choreographed dance.

The rough neighborhoods of western Adams County became a flurry of activity. Incoming calls for service were stacking up. The night was busy, but the incidents were routine. Still, Abby couldn't shake the feeling of dread that seemed to foretell a coming storm.

A few minutes after midnight, dispatchers issued a tone alert indicating an urgent situation. There was a disturbance at Roughriders Saloon, a biker bar with a hellacious reputation a few blocks north of Denver's city limits on Pecos Street. Loyal patrons of the bar subscribed to several tenets: capacity limits were merely a suggestion, they could handle disruptions themselves, and cops had no business entering the establishment.

Bartenders were known to serve more than just alcohol, which often ramped up tensions. The use of recreational marijuana was legal in Colorado but not in public settings. Though other controlled substances remained illegal, enforcing those laws was a challenge for the ages.

Deputies throughout the county knew better than to walk into Roughriders without backup. The saloon was in District 1, which was Deputy Jackson's assigned patrol area. When the tone alert aired, Jackson immediately turned his car and made headway toward the bar. Abby was roughly a mile away from the bar and spoke into her radio handset, "Adam 20 en route."

The situation involved a man accused of using a weapon to threaten the owner of the bar, known by everyone as Buck. He let the bikers take things only so far and took a firm stand when he needed to. Abby had talked to him multiple times during the bar's off hours and knew tensions were already escalating if Buck called for help.

As she arrived on the scene, Deputy Jackson was addressing a loud confrontation in the parking lot. Buck stood nearby, surrounded by Harley Davidsons parked haphazardly, littering the pothole-covered asphalt. The air around the saloon carried the distinct aroma of soured yeast and alcohol.

A Pabst Blue Ribbon neon sign blinked in the window. Floodlights, attached to the building and dimmed with age, pointed into the parking lot along with the glowing headlights and emergency lights from the two patrol cars. Still, shadowy darkness cloaked the surroundings into obscurity.

By Abby's estimation, about forty bikers began to form a wide circle around the accused patron, who was now shouting in protest. Buck and Deputy Jackson were in the center of the circle, surrounded by the crowd who seemed antsy to see what would happen next. Abby surmised they were also eager to defend their turf from deputy intervention.

Her eyes trained on a man she hadn't initially noticed in the circling crowd. He towered over the others and took a purposeful step toward the center of the circle every few seconds. The rest of the crowd followed his lead, and the group of drunk, angry bikers tightened around Deputy Jackson.

She calmly pushed her way into the center of the circle and stood in front of the tallest patron, whom she silently dubbed, 'Tower Guy.'

"We don't need you cops here!" Tower Guy shouted, looking at her as if she were a sack lunch he intended to devour. His fitted white t-shirt looked grungy beneath his black leather vest. A red bandana served as a headband and kept his sweaty, tousled hair out of his eyes. Cuffed sleeves exposed tight biceps the size of cantaloupes, and colorful tattoos covered both arms. When he snarled at her, she noticed several missing teeth.

Years of sun exposure left his skin leathery and wrinkled. Tower Guy clenched and unclenched his fists, and Abby noticed several misshapen fingers. *He's a fighter,* she thought, then firmly planted her feet, holding her position before him. "Step back, sir."

"Get out of the way, little girl," Tower Guy growled through his teeth.

"I asked you to step back." Her voice was firmer now, intense as she stared into his steely eyes.

Without warning, Tower Guy bounced twice on the balls of his feet, formed a fist, then swung hard at Abby's face. She barely saw the punch coming but managed to duck and pull herself backward just in time to avoid his blow.

His narrow miss threw his bulky body off balance. Abby instinctively knew she needed to redirect his focus and make him think of anything other than annihilating her. She reacted and quickly countered his missed punch with a right uppercut that landed squarely beneath his chin.

His menacing smile revealed tobacco-stained teeth now covered in blood from his lower lip, pierced from being shoved into his upper teeth. Tower Guy was intoxicated, and she guessed there were other substances in his system as well. Biting through your own lip had to be excruciating, but this guy didn't seem to feel a thing.

"That's the way it's gonna be?" he roared. Just then, he reached to his side, grabbed a bright yellow helmet from a nearby motorcycle, and tried to knock Abby off her feet by smashing it into her left knee. As she absorbed the forceful impact, she heard the sickening sound of her bones popping, breaking out of joint.

Abby's knee buckled, but she maintained her stance with the help of an adrenaline surge and utter determination. Though her knee throbbed in protest, her mind blocked the pain and zeroed in on the urgent need to neutralize this mountainous threat. In one smooth and well-practiced maneuver, she drew her TASER and fired. It discharged an electric current strong enough to drop Tower Guy to the asphalt.

Deputy Braxton, newly arrived on scene, rushed toward Abby by pushing his way through the crowd, then handcuffed the large, fallen tower of a man. Abby shouted, her tone elevated through a keen awareness of escalating pain, "You're under arrest for assault on a police officer!"

Clicking the cuffs tighter and jerking Tower Guy upright, Braxton muttered sarcastically, "She should also cite you for excessive body odor." He led him to his patrol car, which would soon transport him to the county detention facility.

Abby glanced across the parking lot. Deputies had uncovered a concealed knife on the suspect and were leading him away.

With two suspects in handcuffs, the environment calmed rapidly. Once-circling onlookers returned to the inside of the bar a few at a time, presumably to line up for their next round of beers. The deputies congregated near Abby's car to talk the incident through.

Standing with all of her weight on her right leg, Abby pressed the radio mic clipped to her epaulet. "Adam 20, we're Code 4. Send medical and the investigations team." When she was sure the patrons were out of earshot, she said to Deputy Mulligan, "Dean, will you call someone to drive my car back to the substation? We'll see what the paramedics say, but I think that guy liquified my knee."

CHAPTER 2

ABBY, 2023

Abby clumsily made her way into the office of a workman's-comp-assigned orthopedic surgeon. The unfamiliar crutches were a struggle, and she felt a rush of embarrassment when she accidentally bumped into the reception counter while hobbling by.

After the bar incident, she'd spent several hours in the Emergency Department, where she was grateful for visits by most of the deputies on her shift. She was sent home with a heavy brace, crutches, instructions to keep her leg elevated, and a bottle of painkillers. Surgery was unavoidable, and she was directed to see an orthopedic doctor as soon as possible.

The first week away from work was enough to make her stir crazy. Abby read books from her ever-growing must-read list. She watched far too many Instagram reels and threw off her sleep patterns with unscheduled naps. She couldn't imagine how she'd make it through a lengthy injury leave. Without the freedom to drive her car, she felt trapped in her home, as if the recent pandemic—still lingering in everyone's memories—were happening all over again. Only this time, there was a bustle of activity just outside her window, making her feel restless and left out.

When she'd been home about a week, she received a surprise visit from Tim and Pasha Kline, good friends from church, who delivered homemade meals prepared by several families and frozen into individual portions.

To their credit, Tim and Pasha didn't draw attention to her disheveled appearance. Most of her blonde hair had fallen out of the hairband meant to grip a messy bun on top of her head. It was her third day in a buttery soft, oversized t-shirt emblazoned with the logo of a nonprofit she once donated to. It was wrinkled and likely smelled, but those details went without mention.

As they gathered in her small kitchen, she rested her armpits on her crutches and used both hands to push her coffee maker and toaster aside, making room for the plentiful assortment of plastic containers. The outpouring of support and generosity meant a lot, but the volume of food only emphasized the long recovery she faced. She'd have to figure out how to make room in her freezer to hold it all.

Abby shared the story of the bar fight with her curious friends, who responded with a chorus of "We're glad you're okay!" and "You're so brave!" After the encouragement and the laughter of friendship went on for several minutes, Tim and Pasha said goodbye and hurried out the door to let Abby rest. She thanked them profusely as they promised to pray for her, check in often, and help keep Abby's routine running smoothly.

After their unannounced visit, Abby stopped assuming she'd be alone all day. The strategy of keeping herself more presentable paid off when co-workers randomly appeared on her front stoop with Door-Dash gift cards and a few small bouquets of flowers.

One get-well card included a generous Amazon gift card from the members of the Adams County Board of Commissioners, who provided financial and administrative oversight for the county government. She was surprised by the gesture, having never spoken directly to anyone on the five-member board. She assumed it was protocol for work-related injuries. Still, the gift felt a bit like Christmas.

Deputy James Jackson, who was at Roughriders when Abby was injured, lived just a few blocks away and graciously drove Abby to her first orthopedic appointment. With James, silence was comfortable. He didn't need to fill awkward pauses with idle chit-chat. While she usually found it a challenge to lure him into conversation, today, she appreciated his quiet demeanor. She was anxious about this appointment, lost in her thoughts, and afraid that she may never recover from her injury or make it back to work.

As they drove a lengthy stretch of congested highway to the doctor's office, James shared bits of information instead of asking questions. He was a great reader of people and seemed to know exactly what Abby needed.

Receiving work updates, no matter how brief, brought the first genuine smile to cross Abby's lips in days. James shared happenings in each patrol district, unusual calls they'd covered, and how great Deputy Brunson was doing as acting sergeant in her absence. "He's following your lead and repping our shift well."

When he'd pulled the car close to the medical building entrance, Abby suggested he grab a coffee while she was at her appointment. Instead, he parked the car and sat quietly beside her in the overlit waiting room, silently swiping through content on his phone.

At last, Abby's name was called, and James stood to help her rise to her feet. She could feel his eyes on her as she clunked with her awkward crutches toward the examination room.

A nurse introduced herself as Emily. She wore blue scrubs that looked wonderfully comfortable, and Abby felt a twinge of jealousy over her white Crocs shoes adorned with colorful Disney charms. Sometimes, she thought it would be fun to bring some personality to the masculine sheriff's department uniform she wore every day. Emily led her to a small room, asked a few questions, and carefully examined the work of the ER team.

"I'm so sorry," Abby said. "This brace makes me sweat like crazy and stinks to high heaven. I know I smell awful."

"Oh, girl," Emily laughed. "You're a cop, and I used to be a paramedic. You and I have both smelled far worse. Odors are nothing to worry about." Abby winced as Emily gently probed her leg. "But we do need another X-ray. You can leave your personal items here; we're just going to the next room."

Small tasks took a monumental effort, and Abby was keenly aware of her sloth-like speed. Emily picked up on her frustration and winked as she spoke extra slowly. "The. X-ray. Machine. Is. Right. This. Way."

Abby couldn't hold back a laugh.

"The jokes are all new to you," Emily shared, "but believe me, I use them every day."

Manipulating her body into position for the X-ray brought tears to her eyes. She was afraid she would not stop the floodgates should any of those tears escape their borders. Abby knew she was stressed, but now that news of her prognosis was imminent, she realized she'd underestimated her level of concern about her future. Losing the job she loved and felt called to do was a realistic outcome of her injury. She was thankful as Emily kept the conversation light and sprinkled in several knee puns, even calling Abby a "mil-le-*knee*-al" when she typed a few notes from their conversation into her phone.

"Make yourself as comfortable as you can. Dr. Patrick will be with you soon." Emily left with an encouraging smile. She paused in the doorway and said, "You're in great hands, Abby. Dr. Patrick is the best."

Once the doctor had reviewed the X-rays, he came in to deliver unpleasant news.

"You have a displaced patellar fracture." Dr. Patrick explained. "In layman's terms, there are multiple broken bones in your knee, and they have shifted out of place. What we can't see from the X-ray is whether or not we'll need to reattach your tendons. I'll order a CT scan at our office in Englewood, which will tell us more so we're better prepared for your operation. They'll call you to get it all set up."

Dr. Patrick slid his rolling stool toward the computer and mumbled under his breath as he made several attempts to log in. On the third try, he nodded his head and began typing notes into the system.

"Let's schedule your surgical procedure for two weeks from today. We'll put your knee back together, realign the bones, and stabilize it with pins and screws. Then, if needed, we'll reattach tendons and basically rebuild your joint."

Abby's face scrunched with disappointment. "Pins and screws don't sound good. Those are permanent?"

"Yes, they are." Dr. Patrick turned toward Abby and held eye contact. His graying eyebrows were a mismatch to the obviously dyed hair on his head. Still, compassion flowed through his dark eyes, and Abby trusted his expertise.

"And that's a better option than a knee replacement?"

"From what I can see, there's enough knee still in place to make the repairs. You may need a knee replacement in another ten years or so, but the longer we can keep your natural bones, the better off you'll be."

Abby paused and then tried to keep her voice steady as she asked the scariest question. "How long before I can be cleared for full duty?"

"I can't know how your body will respond, but I'd estimate six to eight months, maybe up to a year. We might be able to clear you for a desk position in four to six weeks. That, of course, will depend on your police agency and the openings they have available." He typed a few additional notes into the computer then asked, "Any other questions I can answer?"

"What about driving?" She braced herself.

"It's usually four to six weeks post-surgery, the same as returning to work in a non-physical capacity. I'd ask for Uber gift cards if I were you." He continued to give her his full attention and waited patiently for her next question.

Tears threatened as she asked, "Will I ever be 100% again?"

"You're young and in good shape. With hard work and intense physical therapy, I'd say your chances of a full recovery are exceptional. It won't be an easy road, but I've seen people with your condition return to ski slopes and even run marathons." Seeing the distressed look in her eyes, Dr. Patrick patted her shoulder gently and added, "You're in good hands, Abby. Don't let the mental game take you down."

"That's easier said than done," she replied.

When she arrived home and hobbled into the house, she called her best friend, Mack. When it went straight to voicemail, Abby did her best to keep her voice from breaking. "Hey, it's me with big news to share. Call me when you get this." She doubted that her cheerful mask would fool Mack for a millisecond.

Feeling exhausted from the doctor's appointment and the stress of disappointing news, Abby eyed the spare bedroom. When she and her ex-husband, Kevin, were house shopping, they'd wanted a two-story with a spare bedroom on the main floor. Kevin had dreamed of starting a work-from-home business and envisioned the room as a remote office.

Abby's thoughts, however, ventured in a different direction. The idea of relocating to the Denver area from Grand Junction felt incomplete without the promise of a cozy guest room for her aunt and uncle. The very notion of sending the couple who had practically raised her to a hotel filled her with an inexplicable sense of unease.

It's funny, Abby thought. *I can take down a towering bad guy in a bar fight, but imagining unknowns in my own future can nearly paralyze me.* The contrast was not lost on her, and she shook her head at her complex tapestry of emotions.

Sadly, her marriage hadn't lasted long enough for Kevin to launch a business, but in recent months, Abby had purchased a new bed and coordinating accessories to make the room feel homey and comfortable. Now, this room would have to be her home base for a while. Not having to climb the stairs in a brace and on crutches was a huge blessing.

Abby made a quick call to Lieutenant MacDonald to fill him in on the next steps in her recovery. He listened intently, then asked her to call the Department's HR Manager and give her the details as well. She did so, then stretched across the queen-sized bed. The sunlight filtered through the blinds, and exhaustion caught up with her. She was sound asleep within seconds.

She woke to the theme song from *Friends*, the ringtone she'd assigned to Mack.

Abby had met Macaylie Thomas, better known as Mack, in her first year of college at Colorado Mesa University. They were both in the criminal justice program and hit it off immediately. Mack was spontaneous and a playful prankster, while Abby was cautious and a meticulous planner. Yet their personalities fit together like a hand in a glove.

After the first semester, the two became roommates and cemented a lifelong friendship. Mack knew everything about Abby, and Abby knew all there was to know about Macaylie. While they now lived on opposite sides of the Rocky Mountains, they'd maintained a close relationship that spanned the miles.

The two women talked at least weekly. They had full permission to speak boldly and truthfully at all times, having established a rock-solid foundation of trust.

"Mack!" she said, not bothering to first clear the sleep frogs from her throat.

"Were you sleeping, Bebee?" Mack asked. The playful nickname, a relic from Abby's childhood, sounded almost foreign coming from someone outside her family. Mack had picked it up during a college weekend home visit and occasionally used it with a teasing tone. "It's the middle of the afternoon!"

"Yeah, I'm on injury leave and caught a quick nap."

"What?! What happened? You okay?"

"Hopefully," she knew Mack would discern the apprehension in her voice, even from across the state. "Are you at a place where you can talk? Do you want the long version or the short version?"

"I'm on my days off, so tell me everything."

Abby relayed the story, adding details she hadn't shared with anyone, like the level of pain, the anxiety she felt before seeing the surgeon, and the way she dreaded losing her independence, particularly with the inability to drive. She hadn't yet cried over the incident but now let her emotions flow freely. This was a no-judgment zone, a safe place where she could release all the churning feelings that were beginning to dam up inside of her. Abby took full advantage and let it all out.

The pair spent years practicing the art of connecting with one another as friends and setting their law enforcement natures aside. That gave them the freedom to listen and offer compassion without trying to step in and solve one another's problems. They'd created and protected the boundaries of a friend zone where they were free to be themselves, no pretense allowed.

"Here's where I hope you can come in." Abby took a deep breath, knowing she was asking a huge favor of her best friend. "Could you come stay with me for a few days after my surgery? I'll need a ride to and from the hospital; then it would be amazing to have someone to run ridiculous errands and make sure I eat every now and again."

Mack didn't hesitate. "Absolutely! I'll take some vacation days and stick by you so closely you'll beg me to leave."

"You're the best, Mack. Surgery is scheduled for two weeks from today. I don't know what time I'll check into the hospital yet, so if you can get here the night before, that's best. Whatever you can work out with your days off will be great. Come as early as you want and stay as long as you can. Someday, I'll make it up to you."

"Hey. This is the kind of stuff we do for each other. Now rest up, and I'll see you soon!"

CHAPTER 3

ABBY, 2023

Neatly tucked into Mack's suitcase when she arrived was a collection of more than one hundred dime-sized resin ducks in a rainbow of colors. She hid the ducks throughout the house, supposing it would take Abby several months to find them all. She put one in the front pocket of Abby's uniform and another inside the tank of the toilet. Others rested inside the paper towel tube, inside pillowcases, dropped into coffee mugs in the cabinets, and under the cushions on the sofa. Some were hidden in Abby's car—in the glove box, center console, under the floor mat, and in the cup holder.

While Abby slept, Mack stocked up on groceries, adding extra paper products to the cart to cut down on washing dishes. She washed and folded laundry that had piled up, placing them in a laundry basket in the spare room so there was no need for Abby to traverse the stairs.

Together, the friends binge-watched Rom-Coms, talked about novels they'd enjoyed, and laughed about pranks they'd played in college. "You were always so prim and proper," Mack teased. The worst thing you did was stick googly eyes on the produce in Walmart. Remember that? You laughed so hard as you walked from bin to bin, making little veggie humans by giving them sight!"

"At least I didn't nearly get kicked out of the dorm because of all the shaving cream antics you played!"

Then, one night, as Mack stacked sandwiches on paper plates and set them on the table for dinner, Abby got a faraway look in her eye. "Mack, what if?"

Instinctively, Mack knew where Abby's mind was taking her. They'd spent hours in college talking about why law enforcement was such an important career for each of them. She knew for Abby, it wasn't about settling scores or exacting revenge. Her passion stemmed from the need to protect others from the kind of heartache she had experienced.

For Mack, the calling was rooted in a strong sense of duty. Her family was three generations deep in the city of Grand Junction. She wanted to serve her community and saw policing as a way to make a positive difference in her hometown. She tried to cut Abby's anxiety off before it could fully erupt.

"*What if* is not a thing, Abby. Don't you think it's a little soon to go there?"

"I can't help it. What if I can't go back to work? What if I'm out for good—"

"You can overthink all of this until you're consumed by the abyss," Mack interrupted her. "There's no way to know your future right now, so don't dwell on things that may never come to be. What's that you're always saying to me? 'Don't worry about tomorrow because today is hard enough'?"

"I just want to be realistic. Yes, there's a chance I'll heal. But my knee feels like a jar of marbles with everything sliding around in there instead of staying where it belongs."

Mack grimaced at her sandwich, stepped into the kitchen for more mayonnaise, then returned to the table and sat down. "I'll take you back to the doctor in a few days. He'll X-ray your knee again and be able to show you how you're starting to mend. You said people run marathons after this surgery!"

"Running a marathon is different from being cleared for duty. I have to pass the obstacle course again. How can I jump from the top of a fence? I can't even imagine planting on this knee ever again."

"It's got to feel like a stretch; I'll give you that. But no one's asking you to be superhuman. You have plenty of time to get better before you have to do any of the physical stuff."

"You're right," Abby said, staring at her plate. "But it's the junk that runs through my head when it hits the pillow. I obsess over everything that could go wrong. You understand more than anyone how important my job is to me."

"I know it's all you've ever wanted to do. And I know you're consumed with the fear of quitting. It's why you still feel guilty about your divorce, even though Kevin was unfaithful from your first date. I know working for justice helps you reconcile everything that's happened to you and your sister. But you know what, Bebee? Your job doesn't define you. It's what you *do*, not who you *are*."

It wasn't unusual for Abby to latch on to nagging thoughts without letting go. Like a mental itch demanding her attention, her worries made it difficult to focus on anything else.

"Remember when I didn't get hired by the Grand Junction Police Department?" Mack began. "It was all I wanted. I applied and thought I'd be a top candidate, but they turned me down. It was devastating, and I thought my law enforcement career was over before it began. I started down the *what if* trail, and you talked me through it. Remember?"

"Of course I do." Abby was quiet for a long time, mulling over her friend's words.

"I'll never forget what you said to me," Mack's voice broke into her thoughts with a tone of authority, and Abby hung on to every word. "You said we sometimes have to let go of expectations and trust God to finish creating the bigger picture. Things happen for a reason, you said, and God might play out the details in a way we never imagined."

Abby opened her mouth to speak, but Mack held up her hand to stop her. "I scoffed at you that day, Abby. You never knew it, but I thought all the talk about God and the way He was working out details in *my* career were nonsense. *I'm* the one who worked hard. *I'm* the one who nearly killed myself in college to prove *I* could do it. What did any of that have to do with God?"

"I had no idea you felt that way," Abby murmured.

"I know," Mack softened. "It would have crushed you if I'd argued. But I didn't agree. You encouraged me to keep trying and apply to other agencies. When I was hired by Mesa County, it was so much better than anything I'd imagined. They covered the cost of the academy, they have more chances for advancement, and I got a better shift assignment right from the start."

Mack fidgeted, pushing her chips around on her plate. "It made me think back to what you'd said. And for the first time, I saw a glimpse of God. I may never be a good Christian girl like you, Abby, but you helped me see there is a God, and He is involved in my life. And you were 100% right. The details look different than what I expected, but they're better than I dreamed."

Tears welled up in Abby's eyes, and her voice trembled as she responded to Mack's heartfelt confession. She blinked rapidly, trying to hold back the emotions that threatened to overflow.

"You have no idea how much that means to me, Mack," Abby whispered, her voice quivering with emotion. She reached for her napkin and dabbed at the corners of her eyes, hoping to conceal the tears that had escaped. With a small smile, Abby raised her glass in a silent toast to the beauty of unexpected revelations and the honesty of friendship.

Mack cleared her throat and waved her hand in front of her face as if to brush away the emotions. "So play this out with me. Let's say you can't go back to work. What happens then?"

"That's easy. Without my job, I can't pay my bills. I'll lose my car and my house. Basically, everything I've worked for."

Growing up in poverty made holding the deed to her own house an empowering accomplishment. Abby built aspirations for her career, her autonomy, and the control she held over her life on the foundation of owning a home. Rational or not, losing her home would be like losing a huge part of herself.

Mack kept her tone light. "So you'll come live with me until you're back on your feet. What other horrendous thing will happen?"

"I think you're in fixing mode. It's forbidden." Abby scolded.

"I'm not cop-kind-of-fixing. I'm just helping you with brainstorming. There's a big difference."

Abby mustered a smile. "And you're very good at it."

"You'd return the favor in a heartbeat."

"You're right. I would." Abby finally took a bite of her sandwich.

"What other jobs have you ever been curious about?"

She paused while she thought. "I admire our victim's advocates and the way they help people who have experienced trauma."

"You'd be a natural at that," Mack nodded. "What else?"

"I love the instruction side of law enforcement. Maybe they could use me in the academy as a civilian somehow?"

"See, you might not even have to move out of law enforcement entirely. So there's no need to lose sleep over this. Tell me, though," Mack swallowed her bite before asking, "What's up with your obsession over never quitting anything? Where does that come from?"

"My counselor and I have talked a ton about that." Abby reflected for a moment, then finally broke the silence that had fallen between them. "It stems from my dad. He was the first person I felt quit on me. He quit on all of us."

Abby let her eyes drift and focused on the clouds she saw through the window pane. "He was there one day, making me believe he was the greatest human alive, but the next day, he was gone. Not because something bad happened to him but because he chose to do something bad to someone else and then went to prison. It was his choice, and that hurt a lot. He destroyed our family. My mom carried all the stress of him being locked away, and because of that, she died way too young."

She turned to face Mack. "Of course, you know the whole story about my sister. I lost everything that mattered to me because my dad quit. I promised myself I'd never quit something I started. I'd go all the way."

"Have you ever talked to him about it?" Mack asked.

"To my Dad? No way. I've thought about it a bunch of times. And my counselor thinks it would be a good idea, but I've never made it happen. I can't bear the thought of even looking at him."

"I'm no counselor, but I think you should go see him. At least look online and see what it would take to set up a prison visit. You have the time right now, and who knows? Maybe if you heard his side of things, it would help change your perspective."

"Wait!" Abby raised her eyebrows in mock surprise. "Are you saying I have issues?"

"Yes, you have issues." Mack laughed and rolled her eyes. "But you work harder than anyone to take care of your mind as much as your body. You're more together than most people on this planet." She took a long sip of her lemonade. "I admire you, you know?"

"What in the world for?" Abby reached into the bag lying on the table and grabbed a handful of Doritos.

"Because you have worked so hard on being yourself. If I went through all the trauma you have, I'd need to be locked away in a rubber room. But you've made yourself better in spite of it all. You're never afraid to look life straight in the eye and confront every challenge that comes your way."

Mack reached across the table and squeezed Abby's hand. "Look at you. You're a female sergeant in a man's world. And you hold your own. You're no 'token promotion,' either. You've stood on your own merit and earned the respect of your peers. No knee injury is going to hold you back."

"You only think I have respect because I tell you I do," Abby chuckled.

"Oh, okay. I guess that's why our female deputies clear over on the Western Slope know exactly who you are. They want to be like you, Abby. Truthfully, there's a part of me that does too."

"Only a part?" Abby said with her mouth full.

"Just a wee little bit." Mack made a tight pinching motion with her fingers. "The rest of me likes being me."

—

After a few weeks, Abby's pain was beginning to taper off, and she could sleep without the help of her pain meds. Her knee slowly started to feel more solid, her armpits were building tolerance for the crutches, and she was gaining mobility. Dr. Patrick still didn't want her driving for another week or two but said he'd clear her for light duty at the same time. Those words were music to Abby's ears.

But since she and Mack had that talk over dinner, her thoughts had snapped back to her father like a magnet to iron. There'd been no doubt Mack was right—she felt it deep in her gut. Abby needed to talk to him for her own good. She wanted freedom from her fear of quitting. But when she thought of seeing her dad face to face, she could only imagine pain.

Would she see her sister when she looked into his eyes? Would she feel the pain and betrayal he'd put their mother through? Would she see parts of herself that she wanted to keep buried and hidden?

For most of her life, she'd blamed him for the massive void in her life. Their family had disintegrated because he'd quit being the dad he was supposed to be. Would hearing his side of the story shine new light into the dark places of her heart? Or would it justify all of the bitterness she held inside? Around and around, her thoughts tumbled, her questions unanswered.

She'd once read that refusing to forgive was like swallowing poison but expecting the other person to die. Finding forgiveness could only come through a decision to release her dad from any obligation to fix things or make up for all she'd lost. Only then could she let go of the hold he still had on her. She knew this in her head, but it was nearly unbearable to *do*. After praying once more for God's direction and peace, her fear and nervousness hadn't dissolved, but she found new resolve to move forward.

Abby reached for her MacBook and typed *Colorado Department of Corrections* into the internet search bar. While staring at her laptop, her emotions surged like a tumultuous storm that she struggled to navigate. The past clashed with the present, and the weight of years of silence pressed heavily.

Curiosity tugged at her heartstrings. She longed to unravel the mysteries of her father's actions and the choices he had made. But beneath her curiosity, anger simmered for the years lost, their shattered family, and the unanswered questions that she could never quite let go.

Fear also reared its head, whispering doubts into her ear. What if he rejected her, or worse, showed indifference? What if their conversation only opened old wounds and left her more fractured than before?

After a deep breath, Abby typed the required details into an application for an online prison visit. The wrestling match within her heart was far from over, but she took a brave step forward toward confronting the complexities of her past.

She hit 'submit' and snapped her computer shut. Now, all she could do was wait.

CHAPTER 4

ABBY, 2023

Abby stepped outside for a short walk to release some of her nervous energy, the fresh air greeting her like an old friend. The warmth of the sun on her cheeks was a comforting change from resting inside, and she lifted her face to the sky.

The world outside seemed both familiar and new. The sound of the breeze in the trees was a trademark of springtime, and the distant sound of chirping birds raised her spirits.

She noticed little things. A new truck with temporary plates was parked in the driveway next door. The lady who lived two houses down was out walking her dog. Abby felt a sense of accomplishment, doing something that felt somewhat normal. It was a tangible sign of progress and an important reminder to be patient in her healing journey. After only a few minutes, her strength was spent, and she returned home.

Once inside, she plopped onto the sofa and reached for her laptop, her hands visibly trembling as she logged on to the internet.

The last time she'd seen her dad was a memory tinged with bittersweet nostalgia, a steadfast reminder of the love they once shared and the void his absence would leave in their lives. Abby had been a mere five years old, a tiny sprite filled with boundless energy and innocence. He'd surprised the family by renting *The Little Mermaid* on his way home from work, a special treat that set the sisters aflutter with excitement and anticipation.

The girls bounced and wiggled in their chairs as they sat through dinner. When he'd finally inserted the movie cassette into the VCR, the satisfying click signaled the start of their magical journey, and Abby and Dahlia scrambled to claim their rightful places.

Abby had snuggled onto one side of his lap, her tiny form fitting perfectly against his sturdy frame, while Dahlia mirrored her on the other side. Their father's arms encircled them both, creating what seemed an indestructible cocoon of love.

Mama had delivered small bowls of popcorn to complete the cozy scene. She then settled onto the sofa next to the armchair, which overflowed with the people she cherished most in this world. It was a picture-perfect moment, a snapshot that would be etched into Abby's memory forever.

As the movie unfolded, their eyes remained glued to the television, mesmerized by the colorful, musical underwater world and the enchanting mermaid who longed for a life beyond the sea. Little did Abby know that this tender moment, snuggled in her father's lap with her sister by her side, would be the last time she'd feel his comforting presence.

The next morning, Mama was crying as she poured breakfast cereal for her daughters. Daddy was gone, and Mama never told them why he left or when he would come home.

That's when Uncle Rol started hanging around more. Mama said that as Daddy's brother, he was there to help, but being near him made Abby's stomach hurt. He smelled of sweat and liquor. Like her dad, Uncle Rol had a blonde ponytail and wore a leather vest, but his angry eruptions and coarse language frightened her. Whenever Uncle Rol visited, Dahlia had always seemed to lead her to another part of their small house to escape his abrasive air.

Years later, after Mama passed away and Abby went to live with Auntie Beth, she learned more about the story. After watching The Little Mermaid, the girls went to bed, and her dad had gone to the bar. The police said he'd killed a man and would never come home because he was serving a life sentence in prison.

She and Dahlia had never heard from their father again—no cards, letters, or phone calls were offered to soothe their hurting hearts. He'd left nothing of himself behind except for an empty chasm they would spend their lifetimes trying to fill.

Now, she was logging into a portal for the Colorado Department of Corrections for a virtual visit with the man who'd abandoned her three decades earlier. Her mind felt almost numb, having released any feelings she'd had for him nearly a lifetime ago. Several sips of water did nothing to soothe her dry mouth, so she unwrapped a piece of hard candy and set it on her tongue.

She typed in the required access code, her father's full name—Robert Thomas Archer—accepted the terms and conditions of the digital visit, acknowledged it would be recorded, and waited.

As his face filled the screen, he looked thin and frail, a fraction of the robust man she remembered. Immediately, a timer appeared in the right-hand corner of her computer screen, showing nearly 30 seconds already gone from the allotted ten minutes for their visit.

Tears filled her eyes, and she couldn't stop the endearing term from leaving her mouth. "Daddy," she began. "It's me, Abby."

"You look so much like your Mother, Bebee. You're so beautiful." His gruff voice cracked. "I had no hope of ever seeing you again."

When she didn't respond, he sat straighter in his chair, no doubt seeing the intense look in her eye and understanding she wasn't here to reconcile. "I can't thank you enough," he added.

"Yes. Well, we don't have a lot of time, and I have some questions I hope you'll answer."

"Of course, Abby. Ask me whatever you like." The tenderness in his eyes pierced her heart, even through the computer screen, and caused a flutter in her stomach she didn't expect.

"I need you to tell me why you're in prison." She cleared her throat. "The truth, from your side of the story." Her pulse raced, and she was spitting out words faster than a high-speed train. She took a deep breath and tried to slow her pace. "I read the court transcripts but want to hear from you. Why did you leave us?"

"I never meant to leave you, Abby. Any of you. I love you all to this day."

"Before you continue, you need to know I'm a cop now. I'm a sergeant at the Adams County Sheriff's Office. But I'm asking as your daughter, not in an official capacity. I need to know why you quit on us."

He stared at her for a moment, collecting his thoughts about that long-ago night. "After our movie night, I met your Uncle Rol at the bar for a nightcap. A guy named Joey Simon came up to us. He and Rol had been fighting over a girl for, I don't know, a couple of months. Joey's anger was a new level of eruptive, and he got Rol in a head-lock before I knew what happened. He was punching his face over and over, screaming, 'I'm gonna kill you this time!' Rol's blood was everywhere, and I snapped. I drew my gun and fired."

"Then it wasn't self-defense like you claimed in court."

"No. My lawyer drew up the self-defense strategy. He knew it was a long shot since the guy had no weapon, and the prosecutors made sure to educate the jurors about the law."

Abby studied his face. The story was believable. Her father seemed to be telling her the truth about what happened.

Robert sighed. "The whole fight stirred up the demons I'd car-ried for years. Our own father abused Rol and nearly beat him to death one night. I was his protector. I'm the one who stepped in and saved him. That night at the bar, I slipped right back into protector mode and made a split decision that came with consequences I will always regret."

Abby's voice was nearly a whisper. "You had to have known that you'd never come home to us if you took that shot."

"There was no time to think it through, Abby. It all happened in an instant. It was a reaction, not something I planned."

"The prosecutor said you'd threatened the victim before. That's why they charged you with first-degree murder."

"He was right. I did. About a month prior, Joey saw me when I was filling my bike at the gas station and started shouting out all the things he would do to Rol if he saw him alone. I told him he'd do no such thing if he valued his life. There were quite a few people who heard me say it. But I didn't plan to kill him."

Abby shook her head. "All these years, I felt like you quit on us. And now there's nothing left of the family we had. Mama worked herself so hard she got sick and died. Dahlia was murdered. And quite honestly, I've always believed Rol had something to do with that."

"What?" her father gasped. "Why would you think Rol would kill Dahlia?"

"There's a lot you don't know. The consequences of what you did that night go far deeper than you could ever imagine." She glanced at the on-screen clock. "We don't have time to get into all of that."

Her father's face was red with fury, a level of fierce anger she'd never seen from him before. "But Rol?" His eyes shifted, distracted by the thought of his own brother harming his daughter. "I hear things in here, Abby, about crimes that happen. I've never heard a murmur that it could have been him."

Abby was sorry she brought it up and did her best to change the subject. "Thank you for your honesty." The formality she heard in her voice sounded cold and uncaring, so unlike herself. But she wouldn't let him suck her in and start caring again. "It was such an abrupt change. We had such a great night together. You had two girls and a wife who adored you, and then you were just gone. It was like you'd vanished into thin air. Mama would never tell us what happened, and Dahl and I talked every day about when we thought you might come home."

"Believe me, there was nowhere else I wanted to be than at home with all of you. But the cops had me. I've been behind bars ever since." His eyes softened as he leaned toward the camera. "So you're a cop now? I can see why you'd choose that job. I'm proud of you, Abby."

"I love helping people. I guess I got that from Dahlia."

He smiled. "Yeah, she always was a helper, wasn't she? Will you come see me again, Abby? I've missed you, and I love—"

Her screen abruptly filled with the image of the Department of Corrections insignia. The online visit was over. Abby rubbed her temples and picked up her phone. Her mind was a swirl of thoughts and emotions. Hopefully, Mack could help her process it all.

CHAPTER 5

ABBY 2023

miss you! Call when you get this! Abby texted, knowing Mack was working the day shift and would be off soon.

Within minutes, the phone rang. Abby answered, "I talked to my dad."

"What? That's great! I hope it's great. What… how… I mean, what the heck, Abby? How did you work all that out from your couch?"

"I'd been praying about it since you were here, Mack, then I jumped online to find the details. Thanks to the pandemic, they're doing online visitations now. I had to wait a week for an appointment, and the anticipation was agony. I almost backed out, but I didn't. I could only talk to him for ten minutes, and it was all virtual, but I actually did it!"

"Tell me how it went?" Abby could hear road noise through the phone and could picture Mack's face as she drove.

"It went by so fast! I was all worked up to be furious with him, but when I saw him, I just couldn't be. He's so thin and looks so old. It was like I was looking at a shell of who I remember him to be. Then he got those big alligator tears in his eyes when he saw me."

"You say that all the time. What are alligator tears anyway?"

"They're fake. I thought his tears were fake at first, but it turns out he was genuinely happy to see me. I guess I didn't think he would be."

"So what'd he say?"

"I had to cut him off from the *'you're so beautiful'* kind of things and get straight to the point. I asked him to tell me his side of the story. Why he did what he did."

"Surely he denied it all, right? Hasn't he always maintained his innocence?"

"That's what the internet says about him, but with me, he didn't." Abby leaned back on the cushions and shifted her weight to get comfortable.

"I told him I've always felt like he quit on our family. That he made me think he was the best dad ever, and then he was gone. He said firing that gun was a split-second decision, and it was never about abandoning our family."

"I'm a little surprised. It sounds like he's being super straight with you. Did you tell him you're a cop now?"

"I did. And he said he was proud of me." Abby's voice cracked with emotion. "I've never heard him say that, Mack. Not ever. I wish I could say it didn't get to me, but it did. I didn't want to let him see that, though. I mean, he's my dad, but I don't know him at all, and I refuse to be manipulated by him."

Abby switched the call to speaker, laid the phone on the coffee table, and rearranged the sofa pillow to prop up her leg. Her gaze drifted through the window behind her sofa as she watched the leaves flutter in the breeze. "But here's the other thing. I asked him why he did it. He said a guy threatened Rol's life, and he snapped. He told me his father abused his brother, and he was always the protector—I never knew that. And when someone made a threat, he took care of the threat. I can't believe how fast the visit went. I feel like there's so much more to talk about!"

"Wow. Just wow. *I'm* proud of you, Abby. I can't believe you just up and scheduled a visit with him. That took so much courage! How do you feel about it after the fact?"

"Confused, liberated, full of energy, my emotions are surging. I'm feeling all the things. I just got off with him and haven't calmed down yet. I need to do something physical, but that's pretty hard these days!"

"Do you think you'll schedule with him again?"

"I don't know. I really don't. I may drop him a letter with some more questions. It might be easier to talk that way. Seriously, in ten minutes, there's hardly time to say anything meaningful.

"Oh, I almost forgot!" Abby exclaimed. "I've been cleared for light duty and can go back to work on Monday!"

"Well, this is a day of big wins!" Mack said. "Congrats!"

"They have a desk job waiting for me, and it doesn't sound *too* atrocious. It's a civilian position they're adding to the agency, but the sheriff said he wants me to get it all set up before they hire someone permanently."

"The sheriff himself asked for you?"

"Yeah, I'm a big deal around these parts," Abby teased.

Mack mentioned she'd arrived at the gym, but they spent the next 20 minutes chatting and cementing plans to get tickets to a concert that was coming to Denver. Gus Farmer, one of their favorite country artists, was sure to pack the house at Empower Field at Mile High.

After their farewells, Abby laid her head on the arm of the sofa, closing her eyes as dust particles invaded sunbeams filtering through the window. Her next call was to Auntie Beth, who she expected would have a more lukewarm reaction to the conversation with her dad.

Beth was supportive, and Abby felt bad for assuming anything less. She had always encouraged her in every way possible, even when she didn't fully agree with her decisions.

Auntie Beth applauded the courage it took for Abby to meet with her father. She, too, had reservations about the man who had abandoned her sister and their daughters, but appreciated the steps Abby was taking toward closure. Their talk was short, but they promised to connect again soon.

With her arm slung across the back of the couch, Abby stared through the window at the neighboring homes in her cul-de-sac. She could see her neighbor, Chris, setting a baseball on a tee for his 5-year-old son. Carefully showing him how to stand, hold the bat, and keep his eye on the ball didn't yield much by way of results, but Abby envied the memories they were building. From what she knew of Chris, he was a great dad, and she considered the father figures she'd had in her own life.

Her own father had missed opportunities like this. There were so few moments of wisdom shared between generations, virtually no celebrations over simple milestones like hitting a ball or acing a test at school. As she considered all she'd missed because of her absent father, gratitude swelled for the men who had stepped into her life.

The way Uncle David and Auntie Beth had taken her in after her mother passed away still brought a comforting glow that spread through her chest, even all these years later. They'd opened both their home and their hearts.

Uncle David often surprised her by sharing parts of himself he could have easily kept tucked away, mentoring Abby as a biological father would with love and unhurried gentleness. Standing 6'4, Uncle David was exactly one foot taller than Abby. David often reached down to hold her hand. His large paws swallowed her own, but the gesture helped Abby feel protected and secure.

He was the adventurous spirit in the family, and when he'd suggested a hiking trip to the Grand Mesa National Forest, just the two of them, she couldn't refuse. One summer morning, they'd packed their backpacks with sandwiches, bug spray, and water bottles, and David had loaded the camping gear into the bed of his pickup.

As they set off, the sun was just beginning to cast its golden glow on the horizon. The air was crisp, and as they entered the forest, it was filled with the earthy scent of pine trees.

Uncle David shared his knowledge of the wilderness with Abby, a passion Auntie Beth supported but never fully embraced. He'd taught her to identify different types of trees and plants and recognize wildlife tracks. She'd listen with rapt attention, absorbing everything he shared with her like a sponge.

They'd set up camp by the lake, and as night fell, Abby marveled at the starry sky stretching out before them like a wondrous tapestry. The absence of city lights, crisp, thin air and high elevation allowed the stars to shine with a brilliance and clarity that felt almost otherworldly.

Around the crackling campfire, they'd roasted marshmallows as Uncle David shared tales of his own youthful adventures, filling Abby with a longing for more exploration.

The next morning, they'd hiked to a breathtaking overlook. Abby felt on top of the world, both figuratively and literally. The panoramic view of the forested mountains below had captivated her, and she'd felt a sense of accomplishment that words couldn't capture. The world seemed to spread infinitely in every direction, and the possibilities for her life, all at once, had felt just as boundless.

Abby still remembered the wisdom Uncle David shared. "Abby," he'd begun, "always believe in yourself. You conquered this peak today. You have the strength and determination to overcome any obstacle that comes your way. The heights you can reach are unimaginable, and the world is waiting for you to explore it."

As they descended back to civilization, Abby knew this trip with her Uncle David had left a lasting mark on her. It'd been more than just a hike; it was a journey of discovery, bonding, and growth. She'd returned home full of gratitude for her uncle and a newfound appreciation for the Colorado wilderness.

Her thoughts shifted, and she considered another man, Detective Turo Torres, and his staunch support throughout the years. He'd checked in on their family monthly for the first two years after Dahlia's murder. He seemed to know how it hurt to hear there were no new leads in the investigation and made sure he told them personally.

Turo never shied away from the direct questions Abby posed; in fact, he seemed to appreciate how she considered the few details he could share and offered a perspective outside his own lens. Over time, their conversations swelled to topics outside of Dahlia, and he took an interest in Abby's dreams for the future. Without his presence in her life, she doubted she would have pursued law enforcement and found the career that brought her such a profound sense of purpose.

Staring out the window at the crystal blue sky with her knee elevated by a pillow, Abby thanked God for the myriad of surprises and blessings He brought to her life. Her father's absence left a void that had been filled by the love and guidance of others who had stepped in to nurture her growth.

It was their influence, their unwavering support, that had molded her into the woman she was today—resilient, determined, and ready to face unexpected challenges that lay ahead. Abby steeled herself, hoping that no matter what the future held, she could meet it head-on, armed with strength and wisdom.

CHAPTER 6

ABBY, 2023

eturning to work after eight weeks of medical leave brought a curious mix of emotions—anticipation, eagerness, and just a hint of trepidation. Abby had always been passionate about her job in law enforcement, and this hiatus had felt interminable. The community, the cases, and the camaraderie all beckoned to her like old friends she hadn't seen in ages. But she knew that coming back on limited duty would be a challenge unlike any other she'd faced in her career.

A wave of nostalgia washed over her as she entered Sheriff's Office headquarters. She breathed in the familiar scent of coffee that mingled with the low hum of conversations and the distant clatter of keyboards. It was as if she had never left, yet it felt as if everything had changed in her absence.

Colleagues she hadn't seen in weeks greeted her with a mix of surprise and relief, and Abby couldn't help but feel a renewed sense of purpose.

The transition from leading a shift of deputies to helping the records department was not going to be easy. Still, Abby intentionally pointed her mind away from fear and toward gratitude, happy to still have a job at all.

The records supervisor had cleared a small desk for her where she could review crime statistics and work to predict trends. Adding a crime analytics process was a project Sheriff Micah Adler was keen to implement, and he met Abby on her first day back to give her a pep talk.

She'd never met one-on-one with *the* sheriff before. Meeting the top brass was intimidating, but she looked him in the eye and focused on every word.

"Abby, I'm pleased you're here. I did some time on light duty, and I know the mind games it can start to play." He leaned forward in his chair. "I've wanted to add a crime analyst position for a couple of years now. We had one in the agency a few years back but didn't set the program up for success, and eventually, the position was absorbed by more pressing tasks. This is an important role, and I want to do things right this time."

"You can count on it, sir," Abby replied, the glint from the row of four stars embellishing each side of his collar catching her eye. They symbolized his authority and responsibility to the county's residents and the troops who worked under his command. His chest was decorated with two rows of medals, hard-earned recognition from decades of service.

"The process of analyzing and interpreting crime data will help us serve our community well," he went on. "When we can discover patterns in illegal activities, we can begin to predict them and prevent them from happening at all.

"Lieutenant MacDonald has given you glowing reviews, and Captain Torres says the entire detective bureau wishes you were back in their ranks. You're a great cop, and this assignment will utilize the skills you've worked so hard to develop. We're counting on you to create new strategies that will help keep our neighborhoods safe."

"I'm happy to help any way I can." Abby couldn't bring herself to say she was looking forward to the assignment but did appreciate the importance the sheriff was giving it.

"I personally asked for your help here," he continued. "I want you to establish the protocol to get this crime analyst program off the ground. We're already accepting applications for a new civilian position, but with all the background checks and red tape, new hires take weeks to bring on board. The position will be non-certified, but I'm thrilled to have a person with your background and skills setting the foundation."

Sheriff Adler motioned for Abby to follow him as he began walking toward his spacious corner office. "While you're in this role, you'll report directly to me, and together, we'll stand the program up. If you need software, I want to know. If you need personnel, I want to know that, too. Let's set this program up the right way so it will carry us well into the future."

"What's the best way to reach you, sir?" Abby asked.

He stepped around his desk and reached into a drawer, his hands hidden by a large bowl of hard cinnamon candies that sat atop his workstation. Behind him, a wide credenza sat beneath a window overlooking a small grassy area that abutted the guest parking lot. Several family pictures were professionally framed and carefully positioned: the sheriff and a young bride she presumed was his daughter, him posing with a young man in a cap and gown, likely his son, and one that must be his wife, laughing and sitting on horseback.

"Here's my business card. Text me whenever you'd like. I've already asked my assistant to add a meeting to my calendar every Tuesday at 9:30 am. You and I can talk through your progress during that weekly slot, so at the very least, you'll have my full attention once a week. But don't hesitate to reach out to me if you need me between Tuesdays."

She took the card from him and said, "That sounds great, sir. Will we meet tomorrow at 9:30?"

"Yes. Here in my office, please. I'll see you then." Abby turned to leave, and the sheriff escorted her down the hallway. She stopped when he continued. "And Abby, you can call me 'sir' if it makes you more comfortable, but I'm a pretty informal guy. You can call me Micah."

She responded with a nod, but as she stepped back to her own workstation, Abby gave a wide-eyed look of astonishment to Lisa

Keeper, the longtime records supervisor who'd overheard the exchange. "Did that really just happen?" she asked.

"It did," Lisa chuckled. "Micah is easy to work with, and you'll get along great. This will all be fine. You'll see."

Still, respect for the chain of command was a pillar of the organization's culture, a tradition rooted in discipline. Abby understood the importance of upholding this tradition, and it was ingrained in her from her earliest days on the job.

The sheriff, a figure of authority and leadership, had earned his position through years of service and experience and was elected by the community. Calling him by his first name, something he had generously offered, felt like a breach of well-established protocol. In law enforcement, the use of titles such as "sheriff," "captain," or "sir" symbolized not just the rank but also a demonstration of respect.

Even though the sheriff's demeanor might have suggested a more relaxed atmosphere, she'd continue to use his title and maintain the boundaries of the chain of command.

⁓

The enjoyment she received through several weeks of the administrative project surprised Abby. In fact, she was so consumed by the process that she barely missed the action and adrenaline she'd experienced on the street. Working in close proximity to others instead of in a patrol car by herself was a welcome respite as she dealt with the heavy discouragement of her injury.

The addition of a new crime prevention method sparked the attention of local media and other elected officials in the county. Sheriff Adler allowed her to handle press inquiries and even an on-air interview with a local news outlet. It was work she was proud of, especially when she read the article published in the Denver Post. As a small-town Grand Junction girl, she'd never been quoted in the newspaper, but she found she enjoyed the temporary spotlight.

She carefully clipped the article from the newspaper and mailed it the old-fashioned way, through the Post Office, to Auntie Beth. Abby carefully highlighted a quote attributed to her. It read,

"Sergeant Abigail Carter of the Adams County Sheriff's Office, an experienced officer known for her dedication to community safety, offered her perspective on the initiative: 'In our line of work, being proactive is key to preventing crime and ensuring the safety of our community. The crime analyst position will provide us with valuable insights to stay ahead of emerging threats. It will shine new light on unsolved cases and protect Adams County.'"

Abby smiled as she imagined Auntie Beth's delight, knowing she would memorialize the clipping in a scrapbook somewhere.

CHAPTER 7

ABBY, 2023

Abby scrolled through her computer screen and saw an email from the sheriff. She opened it immediately and scanned the contents. He shared that two of the elected county commissioners wanted an overview of the crime analysis protocol to understand more about how it would help strengthen the safety of Adams County. He'd provided a phone number for Commissioner Jennings, so she called him and arranged for them to visit the Sheriff's Office for a tour and a brief presentation the following day.

With the interest the media had given the program, Abby felt as if she were repeating the same words to different groups and seriously considered preparing a formal presentation so she'd have a framework to follow. But for tomorrow's visit from Commissioner Jacob Jennings and Commissioner Jayne Wheatman, an ad-hoc conversation would have to do.

The commissioners stopped by late in the day and met in the smaller of two conference rooms near her work area. The room had a panoramic view of the Rocky Mountain range, which interrupted the flat expanse of the cityscape. The mountains, clothed in lush blue-green hues, stood tall and imposing, with only the highest, faraway peaks still dotted with snow. She'd prepared the room with chilled bottles of water and a small dish of bite-sized chocolates at the center of the table.

"Thank you for coming," Abby began when Lisa escorted them into the room. "It's nice to see that you're so interested in crime analysis. I'm Sergeant Abby Carter, and I've been working with Sheriff Adler to launch this program."

She extended her arm to shake hands with each of them, who only introduced themselves by their first names. Jacob, she noticed, had a curious expression on his face. "You look familiar to me," he said. "Have we met before?"

"I believe we have, yes," Abby smiled. He was familiar to her as well. She remembered his pleasant looks and charming demeanor from an earlier encounter and appreciated the consideration he gave to neighborhood residents. "You were at a community meeting in District 2 that I attended. We weren't formally introduced, but I did share a few updates about neighborhood break-ins we were pursuing."

"That must be it," he replied. "And yes, we are very interested in the crime analysis program. First, because we approved the funding for the initiative, and second, because the safety of our community is always at the top of our minds."

Abby thought he had stated his priorities backward but left the observation unmentioned. Instead, she asked, "Do you have specific questions, or should I start from the top and share what I see as the most intriguing benefits?"

"You can give us the abbreviated version," Jayne answered. "To be clear, as county commissioners, we are elected to address constituent concerns and determine operating budgets for different county departments. We meet with the sheriff often, and he shared a formal presentation when he requested funding for this program. We want to see how it's going and if we can provide any additional support."

"I'm happy to fill you in," Abby smiled and inhaled deeply before she moved into presentation mode. "As you know, our crime analysis program is data-driven, but statistics are only part of the process. A computer can't always predict human tendencies. So, it's important to have a human decipher the data alongside statistical analytics.

"I can share more information with the two of you than I share with the media, so let me give you a specific example. Right now, I'm watching what looks to be a group of repeat offenders who are break-ing into garages and stealing cars, motorcycles, and even ATVs while residents are asleep. There are plenty of variables in the approach they use, so at face value, the incidents appear random. But when we look at the analytics, we see that all of the burglaries occur between 2:00 and 5:00 am, and always on weekdays.

"While we don't know where in the vast metro area the crime ring will strike next, we've increased our Adams County patrol pres-ence between 2:00 and 5:00 am and have pre-authorized the pursuit of stolen vehicles during that time window. Traffic is extremely light between those hours, and our command staff feels that reasonable ve-hicle pursuits will not put the community in harm's way."

Abby paused as Jacob reached for a small chocolate bar, un-wrapped it, and placed it in his mouth. "Analytical data is also easy to share between different law enforcement agencies, and we've learned that similar crimes are occurring all over Adams County in the cities of Brighton, Commerce City, Westminster, and Northglenn, as well as in Districts 1 and 2 of our unincorporated neighborhoods. So far, the city of Thornton isn't seeing this pattern of crimes, but I suspect they may soon.

"Collaboration will help all the involved agencies better utilize their manpower and resources. The crimes have been a puzzle for weeks, but we're confident we will make an arrest within days."

Jayne commented, "So the program is just becoming functional and already shows its value in policing efforts throughout the county." Jacob nodded in agreement and appeared pleased. The full-scale po-tential of the program was a great asset.

"Not only is this helping with crimes we see today," Abby con-tinued, "but it can benefit cold cases as we discover different habits of suspects and recognize their very human tendencies."

"How so?" Jacob asked.

"Habitual offenders often escalate their behaviors over time. Say, for example, someone commits abuse on an animal. That can grow over months and years and can, in some cases, lead to physical abuse toward people. Eventually, their behaviors may develop into more heinous crimes. That doesn't always happen, of course, but with crime analysis, other agencies in the U.S. are finding success predicting devolving behaviors and preventing crimes before they occur."

"Fascinating!" Jacob enthusiastically swung his arm and tipped his water bottle, leaving a wet splotch on his white dress shirt. He looked embarrassed, and Abby moved quickly toward a stash of napkins to hand him.

Jacob began blotting his shirt dry and asked, "How many cold cases do we have in Adams County?"

"I don't have an exact number. Not long ago, when I served as a detective, we had six unsolved homicides and a handful of other assaults where suspects had never been prosecuted."

Before serving as a sergeant, Abby was a detective who'd seen her fair share of grim cases, but one memory came rushing back—the day she'd helped reunite Brittany Russo, a kidnapped child, back with her family. The case had tested her skills, her resolve, and her empathy in ways she had never imagined. The joy and relief on the Russo family's faces when they embraced their little girl made every challenge worth it.

Abby returned her attention to Jacob Jennings and said, "It's exciting to know this kind of analysis can breathe new life into cases that may have previously seemed unsolvable."

"Exciting doesn't begin to describe it," he said. "Jayne, I believe we've taken enough of Sergeant Carter's time. Shall we move along?"

Jayne stood and gathered her things. "Before we go, I'd like to ask for a comprehensive update at our next Board meeting. Will you ask Sheriff Adler to call me to discuss the details?" She pulled her key fob from her purse. "Adams County is modernizing our crime management, and we need to celebrate it more officially."

"Yes, ma'am, I'll ask Sheriff Adler to connect with you about that." Abby rose from her seat and opened the conference room door for her guests.

As Jacob neared, she noticed he was staring at her again. "Sergeant Carter, I'm sure we've met before, and I don't think it's work-related." He reached out to shake her hand. "It will come to me, I'm sure. By the way, I hope your knee is healing nicely."

She hoped so, too. Her recovery had stalled. She worked hard at physical therapy, but her mobility seemed to plateau. At her last appointment, Dr. Patrick mentioned the possible need for a knee replacement. That would mean another surgery, many more weeks of medical leave, and starting the recovery process all over again. Returning to full duty felt miles away. She suppressed a sigh as she watched the commissioners leave.

The new civilian crime analyst, Michelle Luckett, was now hired, officially on staff, and had worked alongside Abby for the past two weeks. She was ready to take over the position, which meant Abby had worked herself out of her temporary assignment before her body was ready to return to patrol operations.

The Sheriff's Office was under no obligation to retain her when she couldn't physically perform the duties she was hired to perform. Doubts about her longevity as a deputy assaulted her in full force.

Abby knew she had no reason to be afraid, but the feelings of anxiety threatened to smother her. Her counselor encouraged her to create a plan, so she made a mental note to schedule an appointment with the HR Director to discuss the options and benefits available to her.

As she prepared to leave for the day, she could hear Sheriff Adler and Captain Torres having a conversation just outside the records office.

As she took her first step toward the exit, Sheriff Adler said, "Abby! You're exactly who we're here to see. I know it's the end of the day, but are you able to stay for a few minutes?"

"Yes, sir," she replied, mustering a smile as her stomach churned. With her knee injury still lingering and without her doctor's release for full duty, she feared he might want to address the end of her career.

CHAPTER 8

ABBY, 2023

The sun inched closer to the horizon, wisps of clouds collecting at the peaks of the Rockies to contribute to another magnificent sunset along the front range. Abby didn't notice. She followed Sheriff Adler and Captain Turo Torres into the sheriff's corner office, her stomach knotted with anxiety.

Sheriff Adler moved behind his desk and settled into his chair. "I'm sorry this conversation is so delayed," he said. "We've been meaning to talk to you about your work assignment but couldn't solidify our plans until today."

He took a long sip that drained a plastic water bottle, collapsed the empty bottle between his hands, screwed the lid back on, then shot it like a basketball across the room into a recycle bin.

He seemed relaxed, which unnerved Abby. She realized she'd crossed her arms across her chest—a defensive posture she hadn't wanted to portray, but defensive is exactly how she felt. Dropping her hands to her lap, she silently wished he'd get to the point.

"Tell me. How did you like setting up the crime analyst protocol?"

She wondered why the sheriff was making small talk. If her job were ending, she'd prefer he just drop the bombshell so she could get out of there. "I enjoyed it very much." She hoped her anxiety didn't show in her tone and decided to try opening up.

"Actually, I was surprised at how rewarding I found it. Setting up a new process brought challenges I liked working through. Your vision for the project is contagious, and I appreciate its potential. I'm sure it will help the agency. I'm happy to be a part of it."

"We have another project we'd like you to help with," Captain Torres blurted out the words as if he wanted to end the suspense and Abby's apparent tension.

Torres was much more than a supervisor to her. Yet they'd drifted over the last few years, as friendships sometimes do. When she'd transferred out of the detective division for her promotion to sergeant in patrol, their schedules were nearly opposite. Until recently, they hadn't shared more than a few professional comments in months.

Her mind reeled, trying to make sense of his comment. She couldn't conceive a project he would need her help with. The team of detectives at the Sheriff's Office was well-staffed, highly regarded, and tremendously skilled, so he had plenty of talent to draw from. Why would he need her?

"This will surprise you, Abby, but Sheriff Adler and I have been discussing creating a cold case unit."

The color drained from Abby's face. The tips of her fingers tingled. Instead of terminating her, he was asking her for the one thing she did not have the mental strength to do. Was offering her a cold case position his way of manipulating her to resign? She reminded herself that neither the sheriff nor Captain Torres had ever been anything but forthcoming, so she brushed aside any thoughts of dishonesty buried in their motives.

Her mouth felt bone dry as she said, "You know I'd have a personal conflict with an assignment like that."

"Let me level with you, Abby," Sheriff Adler said. "You've worked for this agency for a dozen years or so, is that right?"

"Yes, sir. Twelve years last October."

"We've thrown a lot of different challenges at you through those years, and you've excelled in each one."

Abby wanted to run. Receiving praise was uncomfortable for her, and she sensed his words were leading her toward an insurmountable hurdle. She gripped the seat of her chair and willed herself to sit still.

As if he could visibly see her insecurities, the sheriff continued. "Hear my words, Abby. Receive what I'm saying. It's more than me telling you that you do a good job. We've built a talented team of personnel in the S.O. who tackle any challenge that comes up. You are different; your tenure here is unrivaled." His compliment hit its mark and swelled somewhere inside her chest even as she tried to push it away. She had to stay focused.

"We're well aware of the personal conflict for you in a cold case unit. Captain Torres and I have talked at length about the unsolved murder of your sister. If there's anyone we'd trust with such a high emotional attachment, it's you. And I'm sure you realize your sister's case is *one* of our top priorities. But it's not the only priority."

Abby's stomach rolled, and she continued to stare at him as if waiting for a punchline.

"We haven't come upon this decision lightly. It's been an ongoing conversation for months. Not just between Captain Torres and me but among the entire executive leadership team. We'd like to appoint you as sergeant of the cold case unit."

Silence hung in the air for several seconds, then Captain Torres said, "I've known you since you were a teenager, Abby. I remember the day I had to tell you your sister was found dead. Since then, you and I have had countless conversations about your law enforcement dreams. I've had the privilege of walking with you through what I believe has become a rewarding career for you."

Abby nodded. Not only was the career rewarding, but her connection to Turo and his wife, Kerri, had become like family. She'd missed their camaraderie over the past months. "I've given a lot of thought to whether this is a smart move and whether or not I thought you could handle it. So has the sheriff. There will be nothing easy about this assignment, but we have every confidence that you are the right person for the job."

Abby felt a twinge of lightheadedness and realized she'd been holding her breath. She nearly gasped for air before speaking at last.

"This is personal, Captain. It's blurring the boundary between my private and professional worlds. I'm not ashamed to say this assignment terrifies me."

"I understand. And I'd like you to take a long weekend and give it some thought. Pray about it. Talk to your counselor, your friend Mack, your Aunt Beth. Gather opinions from people who know you best."

Abby glanced at the sheriff to gauge his reaction to Turo's words. Obviously, they'd already talked through some personal details of Abby's life. She trusted Turo and knew he would have guarded her vulnerabilities and only shared details on a need-to-know basis.

"Even when you were in high school," Captain Torres continued, "I could see a mountain of potential in you. At a young age, you'd already experienced more trauma than most people see in a lifetime. Yet you found a way to remain poised and positive." He didn't break eye contact, somehow sensing it was a lifeline to Abby.

Abby thought back to the few months of bliss when all was right in the world. Dahlia was home from rehab and could finally be a sister without the responsibilities of looking after her. They'd shared stolen moments late at night, quiet whispers where no topic was off limits. They'd cried together as Dahlia slowly shared all the ugliness that had transpired with Uncle Rol.

Later, they'd laughed through cherished stories, shared nail polish, and dozens upon dozens of homemade cookies. Abby preferred chocolate chip; Dahlia loved oatmeal, so Auntie Beth concocted a chocolate chip oatmeal recipe worthy of a Mayberry County fair.

More than the struggles they'd navigated, the echoes of laughter and silly moments filled her mind. Two sisters unwrapping a lifetime of happiness that had always been just out of reach. They'd lived through the collateral damage of their circumstances where life threatened to destroy them both. But when they were finally together, they'd set aside all that was missing to relish the present—hearts knit together with similar dreams and a future without limits.

More than best friends, they were sisters who'd assumed they had a lifetime of memories yet to be enjoyed. They'd had everything—an untraditional but perfect family, a beautiful home, and, best of all, each other. This was the life they'd always wanted, with Dahlia growing healthier by the day.

Then, Dahlia was gone.

Captain Torres' voice snapped her back to the present. "You won't go through this alone. We're not going to toss you onto an island by yourself. I'm still here for you. I trust you'll be open and vulnerable with me about the emotional and professional struggles. You can choose your teammate. Michelle Luckett will be a huge asset to you, and you can choose one of our Crimes Against Persons detectives to partner with you in the new unit."

He leaned forward in his chair and rested his elbows on his knees. "We have six unsolved murders and three unresolved sexual assault cases. The one that personally haunts me is your sister's. Selfishly, as I look into the sunset years of my career, I'd like to see it solved before I retire. But there are other families awaiting justice as well. If you're up for it, I believe you're our best hope at closing the cold cases of Adams County. You know the stakes better than anyone. I believe with you at the helm, we can finally get the cases solved."

The sheriff stood, signaling the impromptu meeting was drawing to a close. "We're giving you two days off, Abby. They'll be admin days, so you won't need to use your sick or vacation time. Plus you'll have the weekend. Take the time to talk with the people closest to you. If you need more time, just ask. But we'd like your decision as soon as possible."

Relieved she had a say in the matter, Abby asked the obvious: "If I turn the assignment down?"

"It goes without saying that we'll be disappointed," the sheriff answered. "The harder truth is that we don't have many desk assignments to utilize your skills and training like this one. Until you're cleared for full duty, you'd be pushing paper that's better suited to civilians than certified personnel, particularly a supervisor. I wish we had different options, but right now, that's how it is."

"Thank you for considering me." Abby pushed herself from her chair to stand on weak legs. "Both of you. You know I'd jump at this opportunity, except for one enormous obstacle." Abby paused and bit her lip. "In your long careers, have either of you known of a case investigated by a family member?"

"Not in our area, no. But I have heard of it happening from time to time. It's rare." Captain Torres said. "The right circumstances have to fall in line. And in our situation, we believe they have."

~

Abby stared through the computer screen into the deep brown eyes of her counselor, Dr. Williams, appreciating the years of trust that had developed between them. "Is there anything about this assignment that excites you, Abby? Any part of it that you look forward to?"

"All of it," Abby replied. "Except for the one obviously terrifying case."

"When it comes to Dahlia's case, what are you most anxious about?"

"Stirring up all of the emotions. I'm afraid it will feel like experiencing her death again. Like losing her again." Her voice cracked. "I'm not sure I can go there."

"Those are very real potentials. Remember, though, how we build up events and anticipate the unknown often escalates matters in our minds." Dr. Williams tilted her head slightly. "Remind me, how long ago was her murder?"

"It's been almost twenty years."

"Tell me about the coping strategies you've learned in those twenty years." Dr. Williams wiggled her pencil between her fingers.

Abby considered her question and answered slowly, "I've learned to talk more openly, to journal, and to pray through my emotions. When I feel grief, I allow myself room to feel that grief without letting it consume me."

She rested on the back of the sofa and then realized she'd moved out of camera view, so she adjusted her laptop. "I've learned to lean more on God and trust myself to navigate my emotions carefully. I've also learned to recognize some of my triggers and prepare for them ahead of time." She looked squarely at her webcam. "Working Dahlia's case feels like I would be stepping into a never-ending triggering event."

"That may be, but you've also developed coping skills you didn't have when you first learned of her murder," Dr. Williams observed. "What benefits can you foresee from working the case?"

"Well, I could solve it. I could finally find her killer and put a stop to the endless wondering that my family and I still experience." The cadence of Abby's words increased, and her voice intensified. "It would mean finding justice for Dahlia and making sure her killer reaps the consequences of his actions. That would feel fantastic."

"Have you talked about this with your Aunt Beth or Mack? What are their feelings about it?"

Abby chuckled. "Mack just screamed, '*hell yeah*,' and said she wants to come work it with me. For her, there's nothing to consider. She wants me to accept the position immediately."

Abby fidgeted in her seat and reached for her glass of ice water. "Auntie Beth is protective of me. She doesn't want to see me hurt, and if she had her way, I wouldn't work on Dahlia's case. But, like me, she'd love to see it solved. Both of us want to see the case handled professionally, and with the new technology available to help find the killer, we hope for a resolution. She's all for moving forward—she'd just like someone other than me to investigate."

Dr. Williams smiled. "And do you feel that's a fair assessment?"

"I do, yes. Deep down, it's exactly how I feel. But the perfectionist side of me wants to know it's done right. And if I want something done right, I know I have to be willing to do it myself."

"Ah, there's the tension, isn't it? You know you're not the only one who can do this job well." Familiar elements of the office where she'd received hours of therapy dotted the wall behind Dr. Williams. A long credenza was centered beneath a large clock and framed certificates, and Abby could see the trio of succulents she'd given Dr. Williams for Christmas.

"That's true, but I've been hand-picked. Pride is spurring me forward more than I want to admit. Maybe I shouldn't doubt myself if my bosses believe in me so strongly."

"What can you do to balance your personal connection with the unusual demands that come up?"

"If I do this, I think talking with you more often would be a good idea. We've pared down to twice a month recently, but what if we switch back to weekly again? Do you have time in your schedule for that?"

"You know I do, Abby. We have a long history together, and I'm always available for you."

"Captain Torres told me the same thing. He said whenever I need to talk through personal and professional challenges, I should just reach out."

"He's been a good and trusted mentor for you. I'm happy to hear he's supportive." Dr. Williams jotted a note in her electronic notebook before she added, "Physical exertion has also been a great outlet for you. Since your injury, how are you keeping up with that?"

"These days, I walk instead of run. I've built my upper body strength, but my knee is still weak and tender. PT has been a bear, but I'm up for it."

"How would you describe your motives, whether you accept or decline the assignment?

"My reasons to decline feel selfish, and when I take a step back and look at them, I can see they're centered on fear—fear of failure, fear of facing the truth I'll discover, fear of the unknown. You know I don't like letting fear hold me back from anything. I'd rather press into it when I can."

Abby ran her fingers up her scalp and scratched the back of her head. "And if I accept it, it would be to use the skills I've developed. I'm not just a deputy; I'm part of the community, too. One case would be self-serving but good for our county at the same time." She paused to collect her thoughts. "If you asked me what the next right thing to do was, I would say accept the position. It feels right, but it also feels scary."

"You've faced many fears before, Abby. What has the outcome been in the past?"

"I'm always glad I mustered the courage and did the thing I was afraid to do."

"And how do you feel right now?"

"Like I should accept the position."

"We're not motivated by 'shoulds.'" Dr. Williams reminded Abby of a principle she often repeated in their sessions.

"You're right. Let me say that differently. Accepting the assignment will ultimately be best for me, for my family, for my deceased sister, and for my community." Abby quietly quoted her favorite Bible verse, saying it more to herself than to her therapist. "I can do all things through Him who gives me strength."

"Yes, you can, Abby," Dr. Williams said. "This is a good place to end our session today. Should I plan to see you next week?"

"Yes, please. Virtually again, until I ease into my new schedule."

CHAPTER 9

DAHLIA, 1997

The front door of the small apartment slammed hard, and Dahlia could hear Uncle Rol's heavy boots move across the floor, each step a thunderous warning of his approach. Knowing he was looking for her, she retreated to the darkest corner of her closet, behind a bathrobe that smelled of sweat and mildew, her heart pounding in her chest like a caged bird desperate for escape.

"Dahl?" his voice boomed. "Dahlia! Where y'at?"

Her bedroom door crashed open, and the smell of liquor instantly filled the air, the stench of his breath a sickening reminder of the monster he became when he was drunk. She heard him rummage through the worn blanket on her bed, not bright pink as she wished, but a dull gray like the rest of her room, stained and stretched from overuse. She heard the soft thud of her teddy bear as it hit the floor, a small casualty in his rampage.

His knees cracked and popped as he bent to look beneath the squeaky bed frame. Dahlia's body trembled as she willed her breath to stay steady and silent, hoping to the heavens that he wouldn't find her hiding place.

All at once, the closet light flashed on, a single bulb swinging from a cord in the ceiling illuminating her cowering form. He stared down at her, his face contorted with volcanic anger, eyes burning with a fury that promised pain and suffering. With an unyielding grip, he grabbed her by the hair and yanked her from her hiding place, lifting her face to his.

"When I call you, you answer, got that? I got a guy waiting. He's paid double the normal rate, so get movin'!" His words were a hissed threat, each syllable dripping with venom.

He dropped her then, and her knees felt the sting of impact on the hard floor, a minor pain compared to the anguish that consumed her soul. She was glad Bebee wasn't home to see this exchange or risk becoming part of it—a small mercy in a world devoid of kindness.

Since Daddy left, their next-door neighbor, Mrs. Martinez, often entertained Bebee after school. Dahlia wished she'd accepted the invitation to join them this afternoon.

Instead, she faced the terror that was yet another outcome of her father's absence. Uncle Rol bartered with her, just as the man, Jerry, had in Walmart that day with the school supplies. More than anything, Dahlia wanted to know where her Daddy was and why he'd left. Uncle Rol promised to share details in exchange for a kiss.

When he'd finally shared the story, she thought she saw tears in his eyes. "Your dad killed a man, and he's locked up in prison." The moment of tenderness evaporated like a wisp of steam, and his familiar, spiteful demeanor returned. "You don't need to know why he fired that gun. Just get used to the idea he's never coming home. And because he's gone, *I'm* in charge, so you'd better do as I say." Things had devolved quickly since that day.

Uncle Rol now pushed her roughly through the kitchen, barely big enough for the two of them, and toward the front door. "But my shoes—" Dahlia protested in a small voice.

"You won't need 'em." He grunted back.

She had to move her feet quickly to keep up as he hurried down the apartment staircase and into his red El Camino parked on the street. Not waiting for her to belt in, Rol hit the accelerator. Her feet barely touched the floor, so she reached for the door handle, holding on tight as his tires squealed and he sped around the corner.

Dahlia knew the route well. It would be years before she would be old enough to drive on her own, but she paid careful attention to directions. Mama taught her to stay mindful of where she was so she could always find her way home.

If Mama knew anything about what Uncle Rol was doing, surely she'd put a stop to it. Dahlia believed that with her whole heart. She wanted to tell her but was too afraid to share what was happening.

"If you ever tell," Rol had threatened, "I'll make sure everyone you love—especially your mama—will see an early grave. But not before I sell Bebee to the highest bidder and get all I can for her." His horrifying words rolled over and over in Dahlia's thoughts. She carefully held her tongue to protect their secret. Bebee's innocence and her very life depended on it.

The red El Camino followed its normal path in a pattern of twos. Up two blocks, then a left at the light. After about two minutes on the interstate, there were two quick right turns. Next to the Dairy Queen was an old, empty building, which Uncle Rol accessed by punching numbers into a keypad next to the door handle. A musty, stained mattress covered the floor in a small back room with no windows. That's where the man was waiting.

Dahlia's imagination was her only refuge, a fragile sanctuary from the nightmare that was her life. She'd learned to disconnect from the harsh reality around her as if it were happening to a stranger and not to the shell of a girl she'd become. As the men loomed over her, their shadows casting a black-hearted cloud, she closed her eyes and ventured far away, seeking solace in the vivid landscapes of her mind. It was her desperate attempt to escape the inescapable.

In her mind, Dahlia pictured herself on a warm beach, like those she had seen in her school books. She imagined how it would feel to walk along the shoreline, her bare feet leaving delicate imprints in the wet sand. Rhythmic sounds of waves crashed against the shore like a soothing lullaby to drown out the harsh voices haunting her waking hours.

She imagined seagulls soaring overhead, their cries filling the air with a sense of freedom she longed for. The salty breeze brushed against her skin, carrying the promise of a life untouched by the stench of men and their cruelty. She was safe and cherished in this made-up world, surrounded by people who loved and protected her.

As Uncle Rol's *clients,* as he called them, carried out their deeds, Dahlia held tight to this daydream, allowing it to take her to a world far from the darkness of her reality. Someday, somehow, she would escape the clutches of those who tormented her. She would find her way to that sandy beach, where revolting men were forbidden, and she could finally know peace and happiness.

In the depths of her imagination, Dahlia found the strength to endure, to survive, and to hold onto the hope that one day, her dreams would come true.

Each time it was over, she tried hard just to be Dahlia again—the girl who liked school and loved to draw, who protected Bebee from knowing how vile Uncle Rol truly was, helped her with homework, and warmed up soup while Mama finished her night job.

But today, things felt different. Her neck hurt from when Uncle Rol pulled her by the hair, and her stomach felt tight. Emotion welled up inside her, but she pushed it away. She knew what would happen if she let herself cry.

Not long after Daddy went to prison, Uncle Rol had come to Mama and said he'd take care of everything. He promised to pay for rent and groceries—it was the least he could do for his brother's family, he'd said. Mama thanked him with hugs and tears. Dahlia guessed Mama had said thank you at least a hundred times.

Dahlia quickly discovered that Uncle Rol's offer came with certain conditions. When it first started happening, she'd cried a lot. He'd slap her face, screaming at her to shut up while counting the money in front of her, promising to share it if she'd be a big girl and take care of his clients without any of those crybaby tears. Because she did what Uncle Rol said, their small family always had a modest place to live and some food to eat. It was a high price to pay, but she didn't let herself think about that.

She didn't want his money for herself but for her little sister, Bebee. Dahlia had taught herself not to cry to make sure Bebee had clothes that fit, shoes that looked almost new, and folders that weren't bent and crinkled.

Today, after she watched the man zip his pants while leaving the room, Dahlia sat on the mattress for a few minutes and waited for the muffled conversation to finish before stepping into the hallway. Uncle Rol was there with that menacing grin on his face. She squared her shoulders, pushed the hair out of her eyes, and met his gaze, the only way she knew to signal that he hadn't broken her.

He whistled cheerful notes through his teeth as they made their way to his car, parked in a lot close enough to I-25 to hear the cars rushing by on the major commercial corridor. Rol pulled the door closed and pushed a few numbers on the keypad to lock it behind them.

Dahlia noticed for the first time that the license plate on the El Camino said, "RED DEMON." She didn't know much about demons but thought Uncle Rol must be one, even though he said she should be grateful he was helping their family survive. Most girls didn't have a job at such a young age. He reminded her of that often.

The ride home went quickly. His brakes screeched in front of her four-story apartment building, triggering Uncle Rol's routine grunt through his scruffy, reddish blonde beard that reached to the midpoint of his throat, "Get out." She knew what to do. He didn't need to tell her twice.

She cast her gaze toward the apartment building, an indistinguishable structure sandwiched between its identical neighbors. It bore the wear and tear of time, with green paint that flaked and peeled from the doors, exposing the weathered wood beneath. Once sturdy and gleaming, the metal railings were wobbly and rusted, marred by Colorado's intense sunlight and wild weather swings, a fitting metaphor for the decay that had taken root in her own life.

Debris collected in the corners of the balconies that protruded from the building. Discarded wrappers, crumpled newspapers, and errant plastic bags huddled together, forming unkempt, transient communities. The apartment complex exuded an air of neglect, mirroring how Dahlia often felt, as though she had been forgotten.

Dahlia reached for the car door handle to let herself out of the car truck, as she called it in her mind. She was surprised when Rol stopped her. "Wait a second," he said, handing her a few rolled-up bills. She behaved well enough to receive pay for her work today. "There's something wrapped up in there for you. I know that guy was rough on you. It will help you feel better."

The guy wasn't nearly as rough on her as Uncle Rol had been, but Dahlia would never say such a thing. His voice interrupted her thoughts. "Remember, don't say a word. I'd hate to have to put you in a shallow grave and go after your little sister."

She got out and stood on the sidewalk, suppressing a shiver that had nothing to do with the weather. Rol drove away without looking back, the low rumble of the El Camino reverberating through the neighborhood.

Inside the apartment, she followed the sound of the television and found Bebee resting on Mama's bed, mesmerized by a Sponge-Bob cartoon. Bebee's smile lit a fire in her heart, and she vowed to do whatever it took to protect her. Dahlia would die inside if Uncle Rol dragged her little sister into this, too.

She put on a smile, hoping Bebee wouldn't sense her inner turmoil, leaned across the bed, and kissed the top of her head. "I don't feel good, and I'm going to lie down. Should I warm up some soup for you first?"

"Nah," Bebee said. "Mrs. Martinez made me a sandwich a little while ago. And I already finished my homework." Dahlia silently thanked their neighbor as she muttered, "Good girl." Mrs. Martinez's cat purred and lay in a tight ball under Bebee's chin. "She let you bring Mr. Miyagi home?"

"She didn't want me to be alone," Bebee smiled. They weren't allowed a pet of their own, but this was the next best thing. Mama never minded a visit from the gentle tabby, especially because she could send him home to eat.

Dahlia's still bare feet padded against the floor as she took the few steps to her room, gingerly closed the door, and pulled the money out of the pocket of her jeans. She studied the pill that slipped out—a white, oval-shaped tablet. She wondered if she should take it or how much cash she could get if she sold it. Lifting a sock from the small cardboard box that served as her dresser, she tucked the small pill deep inside the toe where she could find it later.

As she stood at the foot of her bed, her strength felt like a flickering candle, burned to the end and about to be snuffed out. She reached for a hairbrush and worked the tangles out of her long locks, then went across the hall to pour a bath.

She couldn't imagine a way to escape from Uncle Rol's control; she was trapped like a rabbit in a snare of hopelessness, the wire digging deeper with each desperate struggle. But when she thought of Bebee, she found a spark of endurance, a tiny flame flickering in the darkness. Dahlia knew she could find the strength to persevere if only to protect Bebee from Rol's terrifying grasp—even if it meant sacrificing her own soul in the process.

CHAPTER 10

DAHLIA, 2004

Three months had passed since Mama had come home with a nasty cough and started missing work for the first time Dahlia could remember. Uncle Rol left her alone anytime Mama was home. But Mama struggled to get better, her cough getting deeper and more frequent every day. The doctors at the clinic sent her for tests that she never explained to Dahlia or Bebee.

Dahlia vividly remembered the day she was sorting their laundry in the basement of the building and found a washcloth covered with spots of blood. That was the day she'd begun to prepare for the worst.

Bebee had asked a million questions about Mama, none of which Dahlia could answer. So they'd cried together and spent hours sitting near Mama's bed. As time passed, Mama was awake less and less, so they'd glued themselves to the television in her room and watched countless sitcoms and cartoons. Sometimes, they'd read books aloud so Mama could hear, but she never stayed awake long enough to hear the fairytale endings. It was just as well. It didn't seem they'd ever enjoy a happy ending of their own.

On the worst days, Mama had yelled when Bebee momentarily left the room. She'd asked why Dahlia wasn't a better daughter, why she didn't do better in school, and why she didn't help Bebee keep up with her studies.

Mama's criticisms started coming more often, always directed at Dahlia as the oldest daughter. She'd complained about dirty sheets on the bed and food that didn't taste good. She'd wanted something other than soup. Why couldn't Dahlia get her some chocolate and peanuts?

The hurtful words had broken her heart, and Dahlia couldn't understand the sudden mean spirit that was nothing like the Mama she'd known and loved. She'd tried harder to be all Mama expected and hated the thought of disappointing her. Every day, she'd tried to do more, to make things more comfortable and pleasant for Mama, but it was never enough. Mama's kindness seemed to have disappeared.

Soon after Mama began lashing out, a nurse named Carly started dropping by the apartment a couple of times each week. Dahlia had no idea why the nurse appeared or who could have been paying for her services. Nothing came for free.

Carly had tried to explain away Mama's harsh words. Her body was very sick, she told the girls, and that meant she would say things she didn't mean. She loved them very much, but her mind was jumbled up. Dahlia had tried to believe Carly's words, but it was hard to know if they were true.

One day, Carly left several bottles of pills she said would help keep Mama more comfortable. She'd explained to Dahlia when to give them to her, even though they both knew she wasn't supposed to leave them with a child. But there simply was no one else helping Mama. "Somebody's got to do something humane for you girls," Carly had muttered, shaking her head.

That night, Dahlia made a long-distance call to her Auntie Beth, Mama's sister. Between Dahlia's sobs, Auntie had explained that Carly was a hospice nurse and, yes, she and Uncle David had arranged for her visits. She was surprised Mama hadn't explained all of that to her. Dahlia told Auntie Beth that Mama wasn't much like herself anymore.

Auntie had promised to drive to Denver the next day and said she would arrive before bedtime. Dahlia was to use care with the drugs and give them to Mama exactly as Carly instructed. Most importantly, she was not to tell anyone else they were in the house. They were narcotics and very dangerous.

Dahlia had heard the emotion in her voice when Auntie explained, "Your Mama doesn't have much time left, Dahlia. She'll be with Jesus soon."

"I don't even know what that means," Dahlia remembered sighing with frustration.

"She's going to be with God. He's getting ready to take her to heaven because her time here on Earth is nearly finished."

"You mean she's dying, just like we thought, right?" Dahlia's voice cracked.

"That's right, Dahlia. I'm so sorry. I'll be there tomorrow, hon, and we'll work everything out together. Don't worry, baby. "

Her sister's eyes widened, and her mouth fell open when Dahlia suggested Bebee go to the Western Slope to live with Auntie Beth and Uncle David. As they tidied the small apartment kitchen, Bebee complained loudly, making it clear she didn't want to go.

"I've already lost Mama," she'd cried. "I don't want to lose you too, Dally!"

Dahlia held Bebee tightly and tried to soothe the hurt. This wasn't the same as comforting Bebee as a child. She was nearly fifteen, and there was little Dahlia could do to ease her heartache. She'd released her embrace and continued sorting through the clutter on the countertop. "You're not losing me, Beebs. We'll always be sisters. We'll always be the most important person in each other's lives."

"But I won't see you! How can we talk? I don't want to go without you!"

"Auntie Beth and Uncle David will give you a much better life than I possibly can. You'll go to a better school and have more friends." Abby picked up an empty can of soup and tossed it in the garbage can. "You won't have to eat so much of this stuff," she said. "It will be great!"

"Then come with us, and everything can be great for both of us!"

Dahlia had looked away and said, "I'm too close to graduating." Lies were becoming more frequent and easier to manufacture. Like most things in Dahlia's life, the truth about what she experienced stood in sharp contrast to the lies she told everyone.

At Mama's funeral, the way Uncle Rol had looked at Bebee sent a chill up Dahlia's spine. It was easy to perceive his aspirations of bringing Bebee into his operation. With both sisters working, he could double his income. Dahlia couldn't bear the thought of Uncle Rol kicking her little sister or threatening to kill her. She remembered the time he held a sharp knife to her own throat after she refused to get into his car. She'd do anything to keep Bebee from being exploited and abused by him.

If Dahlia and Bebee *both* moved to Grand Junction, Uncle Rol would surely come after them, latching onto Bebee, too. There was no way he'd give up the income from the services Dahlia provided, and a four-hour drive wasn't enough to keep him at bay. But if she stayed behind and sent Bebee away, she hoped she could keep Uncle Rol satisfied enough to leave Bebee alone. It was the only way she knew to protect her little sister.

Auntie Beth, wearing a pair of rubber gloves as she'd removed expired condiments and cleaned spills from inside the refrigerator, had been quietly listening to her two young nieces talk about very grown-up matters. At last, she'd joined in the conversation. "Bebee," she started. "I think Dahlia's right. And Uncle David and I would love to have you."

Bebee's face was as crimson as Dahlia had ever seen it. An inner dam burst, and her sapphire eyes released a deluge of tears. "Don't I have any say in this? I just have to say goodbye to another person I love? First, Daddy left us, then Mama passed away, and now you just want me to move away and leave Dally. I *can't!*"

"Lovely One," Auntie Beth stood, gathered Bebee into her arms and stroked her blonde locks. "It's not goodbye. Dally can come and visit us in Grand Junction. And the drive isn't all that far. We can come back to Denver as often as we like, provided you and I don't miss too much school."

"But you'll be away working all the time, just like Mama was," Bebee said.

"No, Love. My job at the University means I work during school hours. Most of the time, when you're home from school, I'll be home, too. Not every single time, but almost always. And guess what? We have a big black, furry dog named Hugo, who you're going to love, and Uncle David is tons of fun to live with. He likes to play games, watch funny shows, and tell horrible jokes. I could use a partner like you who hasn't heard them all hundreds of times."

Auntie Beth had a calm tone that drew Bebee in and soothed the sting in Dahlia's heart at the same time. Dahlia reasoned that this was the best option for everyone but struggled to keep her emotions hidden as they shouted in protest. How would she survive all alone?

The more they coaxed, the more Bebee warmed to the idea of moving to Grand Junction. Trying new experiences wasn't comfortable for either of the sisters, but Auntie Beth painted a welcoming picture where comfort could meet adventure.

In her new home, Bebee could borrow from Auntie's large collection of books any time she pleased. She could learn to cook and could choose new decor for her room. By the time Auntie mentioned internet service and a laptop computer Bebee could use, she was becoming excited. When she mentioned getting her a cell phone, the deal was done.

The following morning, Auntie Beth brought a large cardboard box up to the apartment so the sisters could pack Bebee's meager belongings: a few sentimental toys she'd held on to, favorite notebooks and folders, the pink, glittery pen Dahlia gave as a present on her birthday, and select pieces of clothing that were worth saving.

The three women had walked together to Auntie's Toyota Land Cruiser, parked at the curb. Dahlia made sure Bebee's favorite pillow and the baby blanket Auntie Beth crocheted when she was an infant were within reach. Bebee still kept the blanket, now stretched and faded from years of use, on the foot of her bed. Dahlia knew it would offer a cozy measure of sentimental comfort on the drive through the winding mountain roads.

"Remember, we'll see each other again as soon as we can," Dahlia said before kissing the top of Bebee's head. "I'll miss you like crazy." Her voice quivered with emotion.

Dahlia was older and the protector of the family, but Bebee was the one everyone loved. Every neighbor, every teacher, and even the clerks at the grocery store all adored Bebee and how she lit up a dark room with her glistening blue eyes and enormous smile. Dahlia was the serious one. Her melancholy demeanor seemed to carry a gray cloud wherever she went.

How, Dahlia wondered, *am I going to survive without the sister who breathes life into my bleak and dreary days?* She feared the heavy cloud of sadness would never lift, wondering what she'd have left to live for. But she held to her decision to stay behind, knowing the only way she could keep Bebee safe was to ensure Uncle Rol had everything he needed to get whatever he was after. Was it power? Money? Or control? Dahlia could only guess.

By allowing Uncle Rol to believe he controlled Dahlia, he'd keep his focus off of Bebee. That was all the motivation Dahlia needed to endure.

Still, as Dahlia watched Auntie Beth's car pull away from the curb, she felt as if her heart were being ripped from her chest, every breath a laborious chore. Even compared to losing Mama, she'd never experienced a pain so intense or grief so consuming.

CHAPTER 11

DAHLIA, 2004

Back in the apartment, after watching Bebee drive away with Auntie Beth, she'd thrown herself on the bed Mama and Bebee had shared. Her hands searched for something to hold, but there was nothing left. Dahlia buried her face into the bedding, working to capture any residual scents they left behind. As hard as she tried to quell her emotions, tears flowed ceaselessly, borne from the profound ache of her shattered heart.

The apartment, once filled with laughter and shared secrets, now felt desolate and empty. The oppressive silence left Dahlia with nothing but the echoes of memories to fill the void. As the days passed, her depression deepened, and she retreated into the confines of her room like a wounded animal seeking refuge.

She numbly responded to Uncle Rol. The world outside felt gray and empty of color, with nothing left to look forward to, and her surge of feelings felt bigger than her body could process. Her thoughts turned to Mama and the way she pressed through such agony as the sickness took over. Nurse Carly had given her pills to help, pills Dahlia now recognized as Morphine and Fentanyl.

Carly believed Dahlia had given back all of the unused pills so they could be destroyed, but she'd hidden some away, thinking she could sell them to some of Uncle Rol's clients. The pills had eased Mama's pain. Could they help her now as she wrestled her own soul-weary anguish?

Dahlia knew those pills weren't for her. Auntie Beth warned her about the danger of narcotics, yet she'd discovered the white pills Uncle Rol gave her—Vikes, he'd called them—were narcotics, too. She'd been taking them for years now, and they didn't seem dangerous. The hospice medicine was stronger. Maybe it could bring the comfort she so desperately craved. If nothing else, they'd at least help her sleep so she could set her heartache and loneliness aside.

Just once, to help get through the night, she reasoned. Besides, there was no one she could disappoint. No one would ever know or care.

One dose of pills turned into many. Living alone in the apartment was nearly unbearable, even on days when she knocked on Mrs. Martinez's door and asked if Mr. Miyagi the cat could visit. Reason and self-control were no match for the promise of a euphoric haze that beckoned her to the secret stash of pills. Control spiraled away, and Dahlia was helpless to fight against it.

Once, her hands came within inches of dropping the pills into the toilet, but she urgently snatched them back and held them to her chest as if clinging to a life raft. Each day, she struggled anew until she could no longer bear the ripping anguish of her grief and the addiction that now consumed her. With each new day, she succumbed to temptation and floated into the blissful detachment that followed.

The pills became her solace when helping Uncle Rol's clients. Imaginative thoughts of faraway places used to sustain her through each violation. Now, her own body betrayed her, and dissociating herself from the sensory assault was no longer possible.

Men were crude, unkind, and offensive. Narcotics were a numbing friend and became Dahlia's constant companion. She stopped trying to resist and embraced their comforting effect.

"Is there anything else, sir?" she asked mechanically one day. Uncle Rol now required that she close each session with this question.

The man startled her by saying, "Actually, yes. One more thing."

He was a regular. Dahlia never learned his name—she never learned any of their names—but he said people called him "Doc" because he could give them the cure they wanted.

"Rol told me he's been giving you Vikes," he said. "The way those pills work, you're probably wishing you had more. I can give you something better. If you want some, call me." He slipped her a paper bearing a barely legible phone number.

She crumpled the note into the palm of her hand, holding it carefully until she dressed, then tucked it into her bra before heading out of the room to find Uncle Rol. Later, the note joined the collection of secrets she hid inside her socks at home in her room.

A week went by, and then another. Dahlia saw Doc three or four times, but he never mentioned his offer again. She noticed as they met together he moved slower than before and more tenderly than any of the other clients. Sometimes, he looked her in the eye, which no one else ever did. Once, he said something funny and made her laugh. It was hard to remember the last time she'd laughed.

When Mama's pills ran out, Dahlia tried to make herself stop. She didn't need them anymore, she told herself, but her body physically revolted. Her muscles felt tight and painful. Her stomach cramped; she battled the urge to run to the bathroom and lose what little she'd eaten down the toilet. As hard as she tried, she couldn't sleep her cravings away. Her mind thought of nothing other than her desire for the drugs that had become her lifeline.

After laying awake all night fighting what felt like sickness, her body dripping with sweat, Dahlia stepped into the kitchen and reached for the wall phone. She was unsure if it still worked and was surprised when she heard a familiar dial tone. She paused with one final consideration. Uncle Rol's temper was irrational enough that he could easily kill both she and Doc if he ever found out they'd talked. But need domineered over reason, and she pressed in Doc's phone number, just as she'd memorized from the note.

Dahlia shifted her weight on the hard bleachers. The Northglenn High School baseball game reached mid-inning, and players on both teams switched sides of the field.

She rarely attended high school sporting events but wanted time to talk with Alex Anderson, her best friend since middle school. "Today was my last day of school." Dahlia almost whispered the words. "I'm not coming back."

Their friendship had weathered the storms of adolescence. They'd first crossed paths in seventh grade during a chaotic school experiment gone wrong. While their classmates panicked, Dahlia and Alex laughed when an explosion of vinegar and baking soda went awry in the science lab. That laughter had sparked a friendship carrying them through the awkward years of feeling bewildered and self-conscious.

Alex was a free-spirited force. With unruly dark curls and a contagious zest for life, she drew Dahlia out of her quiet shell and had a knack for turning even the most boring days into exciting adventures. She grew up with four siblings in a bustling household and had a way of making everyone feel like family. She carried that warmth into their friendship.

"What do you mean?" Alex asked, holding her hand to her forehead and shielding her eyes from the sun. "I know we talked about this before, but I didn't think you were serious. You can't just just drop out of school!"

Dahlia turned toward the ball field. "Everything's a mess. Since Mama died and Bebee went off to live with Auntie Beth, things have gone even more haywire."

"I thought you said sending Bebee away would make things easier. And now you tell me it isn't? What's going on, Dahlia? I feel like there's something you're not telling me." Dahlia could feel her friend's frustration but couldn't bring herself to unravel the whole complicated story.

Dahlia thought back to the first year of middle school. Students had been asked to draw out a timeline of their lives, noting some of the significant events that shaped who they were. Other kids' timelines included the birth of siblings, trips to Disneyland, dance recitals, and moving to new homes.

Her own timeline was much darker. Bringing a baby sister home was a highlight, but it was surrounded by traumatic milestones: the day her dad didn't come home, moving from a house with a yard to a dingy apartment, and watching someone give Mama a handful of cash before loading her bedroom furniture into a truck and driving away.

Alex was the only friend Dahlia had ever invited to come home with her. She and Bebee connected quickly, and while Dahlia often wondered what Alex thought of the meager existence that was their apartment, the obvious scarcity went completely unmentioned, as if it were exactly like being in her own house.

Alex had the ideal family with parents who lived together and laughed at funny things. She had a real dresser and a bed with matching sheets and covers. When Alex invited Dahlia to stay for dinner, they feasted on homemade food, followed by ice cream and whipped cream. These were luxuries Dahlia rarely enjoyed.

There was no way Alex could understand. No one could understand how twisted and chaotic things felt inside of her.

Dahlia turned to face her best friend, who sat beside her on the bleachers. "You know how much school I missed when Mama was sick. I can't catch up, and to be honest, I don't want to. I can make all the money I need working for my Uncle Rol, so why do I need school?"

"Because you might want to do something else someday. You might want to go to college." Alex sighed and took a sip of her Dr. Pepper. "What do you do for him anyway? You've never really told me," she quizzed.

"I go to his office building and help his clients. I just make sure they have what they need." She couldn't believe how easily the lie slipped out of her mouth. But what else could she say?

Alex shrugged her shoulders, still not fully comprehending. "Please think about it. Dahlia. Don't drop out of school. The teachers will help you catch up." Alex pleaded. "I just want what's best for you.

Even though I don't see you very often anymore, you'll always be my closest friend. I'm not sure dropping out is the right thing to do."

"Trust me, Alex. This is the best thing." Dahlia wrapped her arms around her friend and gave a gentle squeeze. "Speak of the devil. There's Uncle Rol now. He's picking me up for work." They could hear Metallica blaring through the open windows before the red El Camino appeared, rounding the block and into the parking lot near the baseball diamond.

"Love you, girl," Alex said. It seemed she didn't want to release the hand she still held in her own. "Take care of yourself. Promise?"

"I promise. Believe me, okay? I'll see you soon." Dahlia jumped from the bleachers and hurried toward Uncle Rol. When she got into the car, he had a cold can of Pepsi and two small white pills waiting for her.

"One for now and one for later," Rol said. "Your medicine for the day."

CHAPTER 12

BETH, 2004

The night was cold. A thin layer of frost dusted the city streets. Beth Lane ran to the apartment's front door with frantic urgency as her breath misted in the chilly air. Her loud, banging knocks reverberated through the dimly lit hallway, creating an unsettling disruption of anxiety and anticipation. Beside her, her husband David's usually composed face was etched with concern.

The seconds felt like hours, but there was no response from within the apartment. Panic clawed at Beth's chest as she imagined the worst. She had never experienced a feeling of dread quite like this, a gnawing fear that something terrible had happened to her niece, Dahlia. She couldn't bear the thought of it, not after all Dahlia had been through. Little did she know things were far worse than they appeared on the surface.

After several loud, adrenaline-fueled knocks, David took charge. He placed a hand on each of Beth's shoulders and gently guided her toward the opposite side of the hallway. She watched in awe as he braced himself, then, in a move that seemed straight out of an action movie, smashed his shoulder into the apartment's door. The wood splintered and groaned under the force, finally giving way.

Beth could barely register what was happening before David stepped back, rubbing his shoulder, his face twisted with pain from the collision. He nodded at her, and she wasted no time maneuvering around him to enter the cold, seemingly abandoned apartment.

The scene that greeted her was a nightmare, and Beth was glad Abby was safe with a friend in Grand Junction and not here to see it.

The only light in the living room filtered in from the flickering fluorescent tubes in the kitchen. The oppressive silence felt weighty, and the apartment seemed abandoned, as if the very walls held their breath, waiting for a tragedy to unfold. With a racing heart, Beth called out Dahlia's name, her voice quivering with fear.

She found her niece in the bedroom, lying face down on the bed, disheveled and oblivious to the world around her. Her head was turned to the side, her usually vibrant and expressive eyes dull and half-lidded, as if lost in a deep and troubling dream. Her chest rose and fell in shallow, irregular breaths, and Beth wondered how she was getting any oxygen at all. Her lips were taking on a bluish hue, and the skin on her face was pallid, drained of its usual warmth.

Panic surged through Beth as she rushed to Dahlia's side, tapping her cheeks gently at first, then with increasing force. "Dahlia, sweetheart, wake up!" she pleaded, her voice trembling with desperation. But there was no response from her niece, no flicker of recognition in her eyes.

Beth looked up at David, who was already dialing 911. She turned her attention back to Dahlia's seemingly lifeless form, her mind racing with fear and uncertainty. As she heard David speak to the emergency dispatcher, his voice trembled, struggling to overcome the urgency of the situation to relay the pertinent details.

"Please," he implored the dispatcher, "you have to send help. Something's happened to our niece. She's not responding, and we don't know what to do."

Beth couldn't tear her eyes away from Dahlia, who lay motionless on the bed, a fragile figure in the dreary room.

When the ambulance finally arrived, paramedics rushed into the apartment, a team of young faces with fierce determination in their eyes. Beth couldn't help but notice how youthful and full of life they all looked, especially the one who seemed to be in charge. His short, dark hair framed a face that seemed barely out of adolescence, but his brown eyes held a depth of confidence, contradicting his youthful appearance.

All at once, every light in the room was on, and the team worked with well-practiced efficiency to assess Dahlia's condition. Beth anxiously hovered as they examined her niece, checking for visible injuries and monitoring her vital signs. Their swift and coordinated efforts were both reassuring and unsettling, emphasizing the fragility of human life.

The paramedics exchanged rapid-fire questions and observations, their voices loud and commanding in organized urgency. Beth strained to listen over the sound of her heart pounding in her chest. "Do you see any signs of drug use?" one of them asked, his voice cutting through the tension like a blade.

The word *drugs* hung in the air, a chilling possibility Beth had never considered. She couldn't fathom how Dahlia, a bright and vibrant young woman, could be involved with drugs. Her mind raced, searching for answers, but there were none to be found.

"I didn't see any bottles in the room or evidence of injectables," a young paramedic with a black, braided ponytail replied. "But her breathing is shallow, and her pupils are pinpoint." She ground her knuckles into Dahlia's chest, trying to trigger a response. "What's her name?" She asked.

David answered, happy to be of any help at all. "Dahlia! Her name is Dahlia!"

The paramedic began repeating Dahlia's name, moving her knuckles from her sternum to her upper lip, still without causing a reaction. She shouted, "I'm giving her a dose of Naloxone."

Then, talking to Dahlia with exaggerated volume, she said, "I'm going to spray something in your nose, Dahlia, and it may feel unpleasant." A quick squirt later, Dahlia became agitated but did not wake up. Her breaths grew deeper, and her color rapidly improved.

Beth stood by, her world spinning as the paramedics worked to stabilize her niece. She desperately wanted to reach out and hold Dahlia's hand, to reassure her everything would be okay, but she knew she had to step aside and let the professionals do their job.

"The Naloxone won't last long. Let's get the oxygen flowing and load her up." In a flash, Dahlia was fitted with a mask and lifted onto a gurney.

As they wheeled Dahlia out of the bedroom and toward the apartment door, Beth couldn't help but notice the absence of any evidence that Dahlia's uncle, Rol Archer, lived in the apartment. There were no men's shoes scattered about, no personal belongings hinting at his presence. It struck her as odd, but in the moment's confusion, she had little time to dwell on it.

"I'm Gary," the paramedic in charge said to Beth and David as they prepared to leave. His hands clutched a clipboard, and his brow was furrowed with concern. "Who are you both?"

"I'm Dahlia's Aunt, Beth," she replied, her voice shaky with emotion, "and this is my husband, David Lane."

"Dahlia is the patient?"

"Yes, Dahlia Archer."

"Do you live here, Ma'am?"

"No, we live on the Western Slope. We've been calling since last night, but she didn't answer the phone, so we drove over to make sure she was okay."

Gary's gaze swept over the apartment, taking in the disarray and the eerie stillness. "Who lives here with her?" he asked, his voice steady and measured.

"Her uncle, Rol Archer," Beth answered, but her voice faltered. Gary, too, had noticed there was no sign that a man lived in the apartment with Dahlia.

"Do you have a phone number for Mr. Archer?"

"I did… but it seems it's been disconnected," Beth replied, a sense of unease settling in the pit of her stomach.

"We're taking Dahlia to St. Joseph's Hospital," Gary informed them. "We suspect she's overdosed on narcotics."

The words hit Beth like a sledgehammer to the gut, and she felt the ground shift beneath her feet. "Dahlia doesn't do drugs," she protested, her voice filled with a mixture of anger and disbelief.

"That's what all the parents say, Ma'am," Gary replied, his tone sympathetic but resigned. "I'm sorry you had to find out like this. You're welcome to meet us at the hospital. Hopefully, the doctors can tell you more when they've examined her."

He glanced at his clipboard before asking, "How old is Dahlia, Ma'am?"

"She'll turn 18 in a few months."

"She's small for her age. I would have guessed sixteen. Either way, she's a minor. Social Services will likely get involved. I'd expect a lot more questions when you get to the hospital. And I'd suggest you reach her uncle any way you can."

Beth nodded. Her thoughts became a whirlwind of fear and uncertainty. As the paramedics wheeled Dahlia out of the apartment, she couldn't tear her eyes away from her niece's motionless form. The cold, unforgiving night had cast a shadow over their lives, and she wondered how they had arrived in this horror.

CHAPTER 13

DAHLIA, 2004

Dahlia had nearly no memory of the paramedic activity at the apartment. But she did recall that earlier in the day, she'd felt awful. After finishing the appointments Rol had lined up, he'd dropped her off alone. Her heart had pounded hard enough to escape her chest. Painful aches permeated every cell of her body, and she'd felt empty, as if a part of her was missing.

Her energy had been totally depleted. The refrigerator and cupboards in the apartment were completely bare, and Rol had, once again, refused to stop for food. It had been two days since she'd eaten more than a few chips. Sleep brought her the best relief, so she'd taken a few extra pills to quell her hunger and calm her jitters. They were the last of her stash from Uncle Rol and Doc. As she'd swallowed, she felt the heaviness lift almost immediately.

From what Auntie Beth told her, she'd nearly died that day, but strangely, it didn't scare her. As she lay in the hospital and considered the possibility of death, the more it intrigued her, especially during the wee morning hours as loneliness threatened to consume her. It was in those quiet moments that Dahlia's thoughts turned to Bebee and the life her sister was building with Auntie Beth.

After being discharged from the hospital, coming to Auntie Beth's showed firsthand how Bebee was thriving. Though Dahlia still felt weak and sick, Bebee's incessant talking felt like a soothing balm to her soul. How she'd missed her sister's company, her lack of personal boundaries, and her quirky humor. Bebee chatted freely about her excitement over new school, new friends, the sleepovers she enjoyed, and the tricks the furry dog Hugo would do for her when she promised him a treat.

Hearing Bebee describe her new life was a double-edged sword. She was thrilled for her sister but felt the sting of failure with each glowing remark. All of her work and everything she'd tried to do to give Bebee the best possible life just wasn't enough. Moving away delivered all that Dahlia dreamed for her sister but couldn't provide herself. Auntie Beth had succeeded in all the ways Dahlia had fallen short.

Although Auntie Beth offered Dahlia her own room, Bebee insisted they share her big queen-sized bed, covered in a bright, cheerful duvet with more pillows than they could lay their heads on. They snuggled as tightly as spoons in a drawer throughout the night.

When Bebee returned home from school each afternoon, the sisters spent hours trying new hairstyles, applying makeup and nail polish, and finding creative inspiration by leafing through magazines together. Bebee had acquired what seemed like a full library of books since moving west, and the girls often stayed up past bedtime, getting lost in an imaginary world of fiction stories.

Her sister never realized the intensity of the nausea and headaches Dahlia battled. She didn't seem to notice the tremor in her hands and arms or how hard it was for Dahlia to finish most of her sentences. When Dahlia looked in the mirror, an unhealthy pallor replaced her once rosy complexion. Her clothes had become loose and baggy. The long hair that was once so beautiful was brittle and broke easily, so she avoided brushing it as much as possible. Somehow, Bebee was able to overlook how her appearance had changed completely.

She slept late into the mornings, feeling warm and comfortable in the big bed after Bebee left for school. She was surprised when Auntie woke her early one morning. "I thought you'd be at work," Dahlia said through a yawn.

"I took the day off. You and I have some things to talk through." Beth saw every physical change in Dahlia's small body and struggled to reconcile the vibrant, lively niece she knew with the pale, lethargic girl before her. She sat on the edge of the bed and propped the pillows against the headboard as Dahlia sat up.

"I'm so sorry, Auntie. I'm embarrassed. I know I've disappointed you."

"Disappointment has nothing to do with it, Dahlia. I nearly lost you. We all nearly lost you. And to vile *drugs* of all things." Auntie Beth reached out and touched her leg gently. "I want to know what happened. When did it start? Where did you find drugs at all?"

Dahlia stared at Auntie Beth for several minutes, unsure of how much to share. If she told the truth, everything in her life would change. It wasn't the greatest life, but it was the one she knew. She knew how to keep Uncle Rol happy without taking a beating or being cut off from the meager finances he shared with her. But if she guarded all her secrets, she knew she would crumble from the inside out. Her life was shattering into thousands of pieces. She didn't know what would come next and sensed a pervasive level of danger that threatened to swallow her.

"There's a friend at school," Dahlia started before nearly choking on her own lie. No more words would come. She buried her face into the pillows and shook with racking sobs.

Beth sat quietly on the side of the bed, stroking Dahlia's back as she released the overload of emotions she'd clearly held in for far too long.

"Dahlia, I'm not trying to get anyone in trouble. I just want to understand how you got to this place, how it got this bad. We saw you just a couple of months ago, and today, a completely different person is here in my home. It's heartbreaking. You don't look like you've eaten, your skin is gray, and the paramedics had to revive you, for heaven's sake. The *paramedics,* Dahlia! Do you know how terrified I was?"

Dahlia sat up and turned to face Auntie Beth, only to wrap her arms around her neck and press her face into her shoulder with a torrent of tears.

"I don't know how to tell you. I just can't do it." Several more minutes passed before she blurted out, "Things are more horrible than you can imagine, and I promised I'd never tell anyone. He said he'd come after Bebee if I tell."

Auntie Beth placed a hand on each of Dahlia's shoulders and pushed her back to look her in the eye. "Who did you promise? Who will come after Bebee?"

It would be so easy to spill it all out right now in this safe place, Dahlia thought. She longed to unwrap the entire story and let out all the secrets she'd spent her lifetime trying to hide. But she knew being just four hours away from Uncle Rol wasn't enough distance. He'd surely find her—He knew Auntie Beth, knew she lived in Grand Junction. She didn't want to face the beatings and other forms of cruelty he'd surely inflict.

"I did it all to keep Bebee safe, Auntie Beth. I had to keep Uncle Rol satisfied so he'd leave her alone."

Beth felt the bile rise in her throat as she prepared for what this precious young woman would share. "Dahlia, you and Bebee are both safe. You're in a new place, and no one here will hurt you." Her voice cracked as she spoke into the growing silence. "You're terrifying me. Please tell me what you're talking about."

Dahlia ran from the bed and slammed the bathroom door behind her, barely reaching the toilet before emptying her stomach. She soon felt Auntie's gentle caress on her back and scalp as she knelt before the commode. She rested her head on the seat, finding relief as the cool of the porcelain calmed her clammy skin. Then suddenly, the stillness in the bathroom felt suffocating.

"I need to go outside and get some air, " she gasped.

"Do you think you can go that far from the bathroom?"

"I think so," she mustered the strength to stand and took a few steps toward the bedroom. Stepping into a pair of fleece pants Auntie Beth bought for her, Dahlia took a few deep breaths.

"How about some tea and toast?"

"I'll try," she nodded.

"I'll go fix it up and meet you on the back porch. It's shady back there, and we'll have a comfortable place to talk."

Dahlia gingerly navigated down the long stairway and moved through the large family room with walls covered with family photos. She paused to look at a picture of herself with Bebee and Mama. The three of them smiled and laughed together as if they could take on the world. Those days felt a lifetime away. Dahlia could barely remember feeling so carefree.

Once outside, she curled herself into a thickly padded patio chair. Filtered sunlight wound itself through the leaves of a peach tree and bathed her skin in warmth. Her body still quivered, but her mind seemed to clear. Her resolve strengthened. All at once, she knew what she had to do.

She could smell the sweet orange tea as Auntie placed the cup next to a plate of dry toast on the patio table.

Beth turned around and quickly returned with black coffee for herself. "Dahlia," she began thoughtfully, "Do you mind if I pray for you?"

Dahlia shrugged, her eyes filling with tears she didn't understand. "No one's ever asked me that, but okay. What do I need to do?"

"Sometimes people close their eyes, but you can do whatever you're comfortable doing."

Dahlia kept her eyes open to watch her aunt pray, curious about the practice that seemed so foreign. Auntie closed her eyes and tenderly held Dahlia's hands in her own.

"Father God," Beth prayed. "We need you. Dahlia is hurting. She doesn't know who to trust. Show her that You're near and that You care for her. Help her see she's safe here and that You love her more than she knows. Guide her words this morning so she knows just what she should say. And God, please prepare me for what I will hear. In Jesus's name, amen."

When Auntie opened her eyes, Dahlia saw a single tear escape and roll down her cheek. "Sorry," Beth apologized. "This isn't about me. It's about you. I don't want my emotions to get in the middle of all this."

Dahlia's lips curved into a slight smile for the first time in months. Something about Auntie Beth's prayer made her feel lighter. "I have enough emotions already interfering, Auntie Beth. Mixing yours in won't hurt anything." The girl raised her chin toward the sky and basked in the sunlight. She already felt more peaceful. She did feel safe here. Her body was stiff and sore, and she still felt sick, but she felt comfort for the first time in ages.

She looked in Beth's direction and said, "I don't know how I'll explain all this, but I'll try."

"I'm ready," Auntie Beth said, inhaling deeply, trying to steady herself.

Dahlia talked for over an hour, sharing every detail of her childhood, the truth about the job with Uncle Rol, where she got the drugs, even the ones from Mama and one of Rol's clients. Beth's tears started falling with the first words, and trying to hold them back was no use as Dahlia unwrapped every grisly detail.

But as each word left her lips, Dahlia felt increasing freedom. With each piece of ugly truth she shared, she felt more of the invisible burden lift from her shoulders. Nothing had changed, really, but uncovering the truth for Auntie Beth gave her an ally.

When Dahlia stopped talking, Auntie Beth was quiet for several minutes, seemingly sorting each thread of the story in her mind. Dahlia wondered if her aunt believed her—as if she could make up such an unimaginable tale.

There were piles of tissue around the patio, a result of Auntie Beth's tears. With nervous energy magnified by the silence, Dahlia stood from her chair and began gathering them all, carrying them to the kitchen receptacle.

From inside the house, she stood watching Auntie Beth through the patio doors, wondering if she should go back outside. Auntie hadn't moved other than to dab her eyes occasionally. As if sensing her presence, Beth peered over her shoulder at her. Catching Dahlia's eyes, she waved for her to come back out.

As Dahlia stepped onto the patio, Beth met her and wrapped her in a warm embrace. "I'm so, so sorry," she cried. "I'm sorry I wasn't there for you, not just since your mom died, but even while she was alive. I knew what a rough time she had trying to raise you girls, and instead of helping, I—I *judged her* for marrying such an awful man. I'm sorry to say negative things about your father, Dahlia, but our entire family warned your mom about marrying him. We told her it was a terrible idea, that he was nothing but trouble. But she said she loved him, and they eloped before we could intervene. When he went to prison, we were more concerned about being right than helping her manage. And look what's happened. This could have so easily been avoided."

Now, it was Dahlia's turn for silence. She had no idea what to say. She hadn't expected this response. Saying it was okay felt shallow, even untrue. It really wasn't all right. But at the same time, she knew it wasn't Auntie's fault. Dahlia had her own feelings of resentment toward Mama, who should have seen what was going on and stopped it. But she'd been so absorbed with work and trying to provide the best life she could, and there had been little time left to deal with family issues.

Dahlia had been too young to have felt responsible for raising her sister. But she'd stepped into the role naturally, from a depth of love she could never wrap into words. Bebee was everything to her. Her only cherished possession. And if she had to choose, she'd go through it all again to make sure Bebee was spared the agony she'd experienced.

"For a long time, I've known something felt wrong, but I couldn't quite put my finger on it. I think I'm starting to understand now," Auntie continued. "Dahlia, I have something to share that won't be easy, but believe me, it's the best thing. And the only reason for it is to help you get better."

Dahlia stared at her, wondering what to expect.

"I've been talking with officials in Adams County and the Colorado Department of Human Services. They've entrusted you to me as a biological family member. I don't know how to say this, but one of the conditions of bringing you home with me to Mesa County is that we get you into rehabilitative therapy."

Dahlia felt her eyes grow wide as her mouth went bone dry. "I can't leave you, Auntie. He'll find me. I'm sure he knows where I've come."

"That's one of the many reasons I think inpatient therapy is such a good idea. There's a facility here in town—the Gunnison River Rehabilitation and Treatment Center. It's private, and they don't let anyone know you're there. You'll have to stay there, of course, but I can visit. And they'll keep you safe. While you're there, I can keep working with the police, and we can get a restraining order for Rol." She let out a heavy sigh. "I can't bring myself to call him your uncle."

"How long will I have to stay?"

"That depends on your doctors and mentors and how well you recover. They say a month to up to six months." Seeing the fear cross Dahlia's face, she said quickly, "I know that sounds long, but we need to make sure you're free of this evil addiction that's grabbed hold of you."

Dahlia plopped into the patio chair, staring blankly at the backyard. "I don't know, Auntie," her voice was almost a whisper. "I'm not strong enough. If you knew how badly I want those pills right now—"

"You can overcome this, Dahlia. You *are* strong enough, and now you have your family behind you. I know you've done a lot of things alone, but you don't have to do that anymore. We're here for you. And even bigger than that, I hope you know God is on your side."

"I don't know how to rely on anyone for help." Dahlia's voice cracked with emotion. "I've always had to do everything myself."

"I'll help you, love. You don't know how it feels to have someone stand by your side. I hope I can show you that there are some people in this world you can trust."

CHAPTER 14

DAHLIA, 2004

Dahlia knew her Auntie Beth cared about her but wished she hadn't sent her to this place. She was alone again, and after spending the last few days reunited with Bebee, she felt the sting of solitude even more.

The days were long, and the nights seemed endless. In her second week of rehabilitation, Dahlia's body remained a battleground, where the cravings for narcotics waged a relentless war against her determination. The pull of addiction was like a tenacious shadow, a hunger clawing at her very core.

Yet, amidst this fierce internal struggle, a transformation was unfolding. With each day that passed, she gathered fragments of newfound strength, piecing them together like a mosaic of resilience.

She could begin to envision the future through a lens of hope. Auntie Beth's steadfast support helped the world, somehow, appear more conquerable. For the first time since she could remember, she knew she wasn't alone inside the loneliness that plagued her.

Slowly, after settling in, she found living in the rehabilitation facility was not as dreadful as she'd imagined. One thing she loved was the nearly unlimited supply of brand-new notebooks, pens, and art supplies they provided. Dahlia, like all the residents, was encouraged to keep a journal. She didn't mind writing. The release she found when expressing her thoughts methodically, recording them with a pen, surprised her. She learned bewildering things about herself and how she navigated challenges. She was shocked to view her addiction from a distance and see how quickly it took hold.

Journaling helped her sense who she was deep inside and how she could feel without the drugs. She thought back to the first pill she took, which was supposed to make her feel better. She hadn't expected it to make her feel free from the burdens and responsibilities she carried every day. She could begin to see why she continually wanted more. She never dreamed taking just a few pills could create such a rapid spiral into the pit of addiction.

Instead of her mind constantly replaying the paralysis and struggles of today, her counselor suggested she start telling her own story inside her journal. It would help her evaluate her decisions, the emotions that led to them and the actions that followed.

Dahlia was learning a lot about herself and seeing her family life for what it truly was: a mess. She loved Mama with her whole heart, but now, looking back, she wondered if all of Mama's work was necessary. Uncle Rol had promised to provide for them. If she'd accepted more of his help, maybe she could have stayed home more and prevented some of the heartache.

Caught in a cycle of looking back, Dahlia dissected the choices she had made and scrutinized the moments where things had gone awry. Regret weighed heavy on her heart, a constant companion in the emptiness of the facility. She couldn't help but replay scenes from her past, wishing she had done things differently, made better decisions, or simply chosen another path.

But there was a glimmer of something else, too—hope. It was a fragile, delicate thing, barely visible on the horizon of Dahlia's consciousness. Some of the residents, those who had been in treatment longer, spoke of how regret could transform over time. It could evolve, they said, into a driving force for change, a catalyst for growth.

Dahlia couldn't quite imagine how that shift could occur, how regret could morph into something positive. To her, the path ahead seemed daunting and uncertain, and the journey forward felt impossible. Yet, somewhere within her, a tiny ember of optimism remained, waiting for the right moment to ignite and light her way forward.

Dahlia enjoyed time in the warm and inviting common areas of the facility. Decorated in soft, soothing colors, each room had wide windows bathing it in natural light. It was a fresh change after the dank, dark apartment she knew. Still, she cringed at the thought of staying in rehab for six months. By working hard and doing everything the counselors suggested, she hoped for the best shot at getting out soon.

The worst thing about the facility, aside from the hard beds and lack of privacy, was the prohibition of visiting minors. She yearned to see Bebee, to look her in the eye and know her younger sister still believed in her for all she could be—not all she'd been. Knowing she was so near but too young to visit was enough to tear Dahlia in two.

Dahlia physically hugged a photo of Bebee framed in beautiful wood that Auntie had brought. The protective glass had been removed as a treatment center requirement so no one would be tempted to break it and use it to bring self-harm. She'd received it as a cherished gift and placed it beside her bed so she could see it as she went to sleep and as soon as she opened her eyes in the morning.

One day, Auntie carried a digital camera into the facility but was stopped abruptly by the receptionist. "No photos in here, ma'am," she said sternly. Dahlia could hear the woman's shrill voice all the way from the rec room.

She recognized her aunt's even tone, speaking louder than normal. "I won't take photos of anyone but my niece, I promise. I just need a photo for her sister to have."

"I'm sure you have other pictures at home that would suffice—"

"Actually, we don't, if you must know." Dahlia had never heard her aunt sound so angry. "This is a very difficult family situation, and I'm trying to mitigate as much heartache as possible. If I can't bring the camera in, can Dahlia come outdoors so I can take her photo outside?"

After a long pause, Dahlia heard her name through the overhead speaker. "Dahlia Archer, please come to the front desk. Dahlia Archer to the front desk."

It made her smile to know Auntie held her ground. She made her way to the building entrance and followed Auntie outside, where they took several photos to share with Bebee.

Then, for the next hour, the two ladies sat adjacent to one another on a sofa awash in sunlight in the building lobby. The warmth felt glorious.

Funny. Dahlia sat on this sofa often, choosing it for the filtered sunlight. But she'd never felt as calm and relaxed as she did in this moment with Auntie Beth. Maybe she was starting to recognize how it felt to trust someone.

"How are things going for you, Hon?" Auntie Beth asked, resting her hand on Dahlia's knee.

Dahlia paused and shrugged. "Pretty okay, actually. But my body isn't cooperating. It still shakes and quivers and keeps me up at night because it craves the drugs. I don't know how long it will take or if I'll ever get over it. I hate it."

"Don't get discouraged. I've been reading a lot, and recovery timelines vary a lot from person to person. One positive is your age. The older you are, the harder it is to fight it off, but for younger people, the recovery seems to go more quickly."

"Let's hope it starts soon." Dahlia's hand trembled as she pushed a strand of hair from her eyes. "I've been doing a lot of drawing. It helps to focus on the lines and colors I put on a page. When I do, it takes my mind off how hard everything else feels." Art therapy offered a sense of freedom. Because there was no right or wrong way to create, there was no judgment when she put her paintbrush on paper. Dahlia found it liberating and a way to find release from the confines of verbal communication.

"That's wonderful!" Auntie said, "Can I see some of what you've done?"

"Oh, Auntie, my pictures are awful!" Dahlia shared a quiet chuckle. "But they're here inside my journal." She never went anywhere without her journal. Her thoughts and memories were so private she couldn't bear the thought of anyone else reading them.

Once, in the room where she slept with three other women in bunk beds, she'd found a woman digging through another resident's assigned drawers. When Dahlia asked what she was doing, she'd given a mischievous grin and said, "Looking for her journal, of course." From that moment, she'd vowed never to leave her journal unattended. She even tucked it under her pillow while she slept for safekeeping.

Now, sitting with Auntie, who felt more and more like a trusted friend, she flipped through the pages and found a pencil sketch of a long-haired dog. She turned the book and watched Auntie's lips transform into a wide grin that would put the Cheshire Cat to shame. "It's beautiful, Dahlia," she said with melodic laughter. "You've got some real talent!"

"You think so?" It felt odd to have someone compliment her. "I was just messing around, really. My counselor said art could feel like a friend if I let myself become absorbed in it. I'm starting to think she's right."

Dahlia handed her journal to Auntie Beth. She'd already bared her soul to the woman. There was nothing written between its covers that would surprise her. Without reading a single word, Auntie Beth flipped through each page, looking for sketches. She recognized drawings of the large maple tree outside the building, a bluejay, and several dogs. One happy pooch was painted in abstract watercolor, with pink and purple ears, a yellow nose, and a bright blue face.

"That one's my favorite," Dahlia said as Auntie Beth examined it. "It makes me smile every time I look at it. All the colors are cheery. And I'd love to have a dog someday. For now, he's mine."

"Then art truly is becoming a friend. I'm proud of you, Dahlia!"

The young woman turned her face slightly away as a sudden swell of emotion filled her eyes, catching her off guard. Her voice quivered with vulnerability as she whispered, "Thank you, Auntie." Her words hung in the air, fragile and raw. Dahlia blinked away the tears that threatened to fall, trying to hold back the flood of emotions surging within her.

After a pause that felt like an eternity, Dahlia spoke again, her voice softer this time, carrying with it the weight of a lifetime of longing and unspoken pain. "No one's ever said that to me before, at least not that I can remember." Her words were tinged with a mix of astonishment and gratitude. Each syllable seemed to release a little piece of the heavy burden she had carried for so long.

With her simple expression, Auntie Beth had unknowingly woven a thread of acceptance and love into the fabric of her wounded teenage heart. The rare instance made Dahlia feel seen and valued for who she was, scars and all. Their tender exchange allowed the healing power of love and acceptance to begin its quiet work, mending the fragile pieces of Dahlia's spirit and allowing her to consider that perhaps she deserved happiness and belonging after all.

CHAPTER 15

DAHLIA, 2004

Dahlia longed for her stay in the facility to be over, to be free from the nagging reminders of the choices that led to this place of recovery.

The food was bland, and she found she could enjoy it only when paired with the comforting carbonation of a Pepsi on ice. Padding through the hallway in her slipper socks, Dahlia returned from breakfast to the cramped bedroom she shared with three other women. The room offered just enough space for two bunk beds and a few personal belongings.

Her eyes were drawn to one of her roommates, still in bed with covers pulled tightly around her. Dahlia's heart ached as she realized her roommate was silently sobbing, her shoulders shaking with each tearful breath.

Dahlia's feet drew her hesitantly closer to Caitlin's bed, her own personal struggles momentarily forgotten as she focused on comforting her roommate. Sitting down gently on the edge of the mattress, she offered a silent presence, a gesture that felt natural and almost healing to her nurturing soul.

With a gentle hand on Caitlin's back, Dahlia softly asked, "You okay, Caitlin?" Her voice was filled with genuine concern. She hoped that by being there for Caitlin, she could provide the same kind of support and understanding that she had always tried to give to Bebee. Dahlia felt a glimmer of the sisterly bond she so deeply cherished, and it brought a sense of warmth and healing.

Caitlin pulled the covers over her head and said, "Go away, Dahlia."

"Yeah, okay," Dahlia started. "But can I bring you something to eat? They're going to close the cafeteria soon, and you won't be able to get any food until lunchtime."

Caitlin peeked out from under her blanket. "That's nice of you, but I'm okay."

"You don't look okay. Do you want to talk for a while?" After a few beats of silence, she added, "We don't have to talk about what's bugging you." Dahlia hadn't seen anyone come to visit Caitlin, and she knew how comforting it had been to sit with Auntie Beth. "Sometimes it helps just to chat like a normal person who has normal friends," Dahlia released a quiet, nearly unnoticeable laugh.

"As if that would ever be true," Caitlin replied.

"Well, maybe it can be. We'll be here together for a while. Why don't we get to know each other?" Dahlia missed Bebee deeply, and the act of connecting with Caitlin seemed to fill a small part of the void left by their separation. It was in Dahlia's nature to care for others, and reaching out to Caitlin felt like a way to express the part of herself that had always found solace in offering comfort.

Caitlin scooted herself to a near-sitting position with her head resting on the wall behind her bed. Her face was red from crying. Her eyes looked sunken, the dark rings beneath them adding to the effect. Blemishes covered her face, and several cold sores lined the edge of her upper lip.

"It's nice out. Why don't we go sit outside?" Dahlia suggested.

Caitlin didn't reply but reached for a pair of jeans and pulled them on. They walked in single file, Caitlin behind Dahlia, who led the way down the long hallway, still in her slipper socks, toward the back patio.

They chose a small table beneath a tree that offered shade and a modicum of privacy. "I'm dying for another Pepsi," Dahlia said before sitting down. "Can I get you one? Or some coffee?"

"Coffee, please," Caitlin answered. "With four sugars."

"Oh, so that's how you choke it down—maybe I'd like it better that way."

When Dahlia returned with the drinks, she found Caitlin staring off into space. She blinked and shook her head as she reached her trembling hands up for the warm cup, nearly spilling it as she placed it on the table. "I don't think it's worth it. Feeling this sick, I mean. It's so much easier to stay high."

"Yeah, but the highs come with challenges, too." Dahlia sipped her Pepsi and hoped Caitlin would respond. When she didn't, she asked, "Why are you here?"

"Me?" Caitlin said. "My mom dragged me in. I fought her tooth and nail. Literally. I've never bitten and scratched anyone before, but I did a number on her." The deep sadness in Caitlin's eyes stirred something in Dahlia's heart.

"I get it. My aunt found me after a near overdose, and here I am. It's made us closer, though. For some crazy reason, I feel she's genuinely looking out for me."

"Not me," said Caitlin. "My mom just wants to torture me and keep me away from her credit cards." A small frown crossed her lips before she took a large gulp of her coffee.

Caitlin sighed, her voice tinged with regret as she leaned in closer to Dahlia. "You know, Dahlia, I did some messed up things to get a fix." Her eyes darted around as if she expected judgment from the trees and birds. "I mean, *really* messed up."

Dahlia gave Caitlin her full attention. Sharing demons was part of the healing process in rehab, and at some point, she realized maybe she'd want to share her past with someone, too. For now, it was a carefully guarded secret. With wide eyes, Dahlia nodded, signaling Caitlin to continue.

Caitlin swallowed hard, her gaze fixed on a distant memory. "I started stealing from my mom," she began, her voice trembling. "I stole money from her purse, from her dresser drawers, her car. Anywhere she hid cash, I would find it. Just a little at first, but then it got worse. I took her credit cards, too, and maxed them out without her knowing. All to buy drugs, to feel that high. Then, I didn't feel the rush anymore. I just needed the drugs to function. Like I couldn't be a real person without them, it was like they'd become part of who I was."

Dahlia nodded in understanding. She had her own dark secrets, and she knew how addiction could drive a person to do things they never thought possible.

Caitlin angrily wiped the tears from her eyes. "When she finally found out, she—she came to get me. She was hysterical, begging me to get help. But I fought her, Dahlia. I bit her. Scratched her. I didn't want to come here again, I didn't want to be forced to face my addiction. I didn't—*don't* want to live without the drugs."

Dahlia could see the pain etched on Caitlin's face, the weight of shame and remorse. She reached out and gently touched Caitlin's hand, offering silent support.

"Sometimes, I can't help but think about the hurt I caused her. She kept screaming at me, saying my choices were rehab or jail." Caitlin wiped her nose with the sleeve of her shirt. "It's my third time here, and I just can't break free. I want to make it right with my mom. I want to get my life straight, but I don't even know where to begin." She finished the coffee in her cup and Dahlia was amazed she could down the hot liquid so quickly. "Mostly, I'm scared. Scared I'll end up in jail. That's the only place I can imagine that would be worse than here."

Dahlia squeezed Caitlin's hand reassuringly. "My counselor, Dr. Nguyen, keeps telling me to take a step at a time. She says it's possible to rebuild our lives and start to fix some of the relationships we've damaged. It just feels so hard." Dahlia turned toward the small yard. A light swirling breeze carried several leaves from the peach tree and scattered them into the lawn. "I hope she's right."

They sat together quietly in the quiet corner of the patio. Dahlia and Caitlin—two souls on the path to recovery, trying to muster the courage to face their pasts so they could fill the emptiness inside of themselves with something other than drugs.

"How old are you?" Dahlia asked.

"I'm 25. You look about 12. All of us have been wondering how old you are."

"Who's all of you?" Dahlia queried.

"Just the roommates. But I've seen the other ladies staring at you, too. I think it breaks everyone's hearts to see how young you are and know the long road you have ahead of you. You got a cigarette?"

"No, I don't smoke, believe it or not. And I'm 17. If I don't go home soon, I'll turn 18 right here in the facility."

"What a milestone," Caitlin said, her voice laced with sarcasm. "Have you met many people yet?"

"Only a few. How long have you been here?"

"A little over a month. So I know almost everyone's names, except for the newest girls. But I've never had a conversation like this with anyone. Not the other times I was here, either."

She paused, seeming to study Dahlia's face. "I've seen you drawing and writing in your journal. Did you do that before you came here?"

"No," Dahlia said. "It's new to me, but it's actually really helping." Caitlin's piercing stare started to feel uncomfortable. "What do you do with your free time?"

"Ha. It will sound strange, but I like to sit in the room where the prayer group meets. Their voices are soothing, and sometimes I fall asleep. I don't sleep at night, so I love to be close when they pray. It almost feels like a different kind of drug. One that calms my demons somehow."

"I didn't know there was a group like that. When do they do it?"

"Every day. Right after lunch. Honestly, I think they're wacko. Some of them really get going, but listening makes me feel warm inside. Want to go with me today?"

"Sure. It's not like I have a lot on my calendar."

CHAPTER 16

DAHLIA, 2004

Auntie Beth's frequent visits to the rehab center had become a lifeline to them both. Beth was delighted by Dahlia's growth and improvement. Dahlia cherished the deepening relationship. Knowing she wasn't alone and had an ally in her corner fueled her desire to get clean and pursue a life far different from the one she'd left behind.

They sat near one another in their favorite spot, on a sofa in the atrium of the rehab facility. Though it was a common area, there was little commotion, and they could gaze out the floor-to-ceiling windows at the scenery outside.

After Dahlia had shared the art she was completing in her journal, Beth often asked to see her new sketches and paintings. She pointed out details Dahlia thought were too subtle for anyone to notice, and they talked of taking an art class together once Dahlia was released.

"Tell me what home feels like, Auntie Beth."

"What would you like to know?" Beth coaxed her gently.

"What's the routine? How has Bebee adjusted to life with you? I got to spend a few days there, but what's it like normally?"

"Well, we're in a pretty good rhythm," Beth smiled. "I drop Bebee off at school before work, and she catches a ride home with a friend every day. Uncle David normally cooks dinner—which I love, by the way—and Bebee is starting to cook more often, too. After dinner, we sometimes play cards or watch something on television before bed. Once in a while, we'll pull out a jigsaw puzzle. On Saturdays, I get up early while the house is quiet, but Bebee and Uncle David sleep late. Sundays, we go to church, then hike along the river."

Beth paused to watch the snow as it fell outside the window. A thin layer had accumulated on the grass. "We're eager for you to come home. We talk about it every day. Bebee's helping me pick out some new decorations for your room."

"I'm so excited to be part of all that. Even the church part, I think."

Beth chuckled. "What interests you about church?"

"I've gone to a few prayer meetings here. I know that sounds crazy, but I really like going to them. At first, all I would do was lie in the back of the room with Caitlin. Most times, I'd fall asleep, but then I started listening more. I wonder if there is really a God and if there is, why He lets all of this stuff happen to us. I guess I have a lot of questions, and I thought going to church might help me figure some of them out."

"I can imagine the questions you might have. We don't have to wait for church, though. If you'd ever like to ask me, I'll do my best to answer."

Dahlia sipped her Pepsi. "The big one is why I lost both my parents. Why does God let things like that happen?"

Beth studied Dahlia's face, fringed by blonde bangs that complimented her wide, steel-blue eyes. In the way her lips curved and how she held them when she talked, Beth saw her sister, Lydia, Dahlia's mom. The weight of grief washed over her. "There's no black-and-white answer for questions like that, I'm afraid. But dying is a part of living. Before we're born, God knows the number of days we'll have on the earth. And your mom lived her full life, just as God intended." Seeing the look of confusion cross Dahlia's face, Beth continued.

"Every answer I give you will sound trite. Maybe even superficial. The truth is, even though we may not understand, He knows what's best. Our world is a sinful place, and while God doesn't stop every awful thing from happening, He does promise to redeem it."

"What does that mean?"

"To redeem something? There are some very deep meanings, but think of it as turning something negative into something positive. God works everything, even the most horrendous things, into good. It doesn't end the hurt, but it gives us hope for a brighter future. When we watch for the way He moves us and provides for us when things are hard, we'll see Him at work."

"The prayer ladies say God is always with us. Is that true?"

"He is, but we don't always feel it or notice it. The Bible says God never leaves us. That's how we know He hears our prayers and is always nearby to help us."

The color drained from Dahlia's face. "Even when men do the things they do to us?"

Beth couldn't hold back her tears and wrapped Dahlia in an embrace. "Yes, even then, my love." She took a deep breath. "There are a lot of ways God protects us. It's not only physically. Sometimes, He allows awful things to happen to our bodies, but that's because He knows it's what's inside of us that lives on in heaven, not our bodies."

Beth loosened her grasp as Dahlia leaned back but held tightly to her hands. "He protects our hearts and our minds, and He gives us the strength to go through those awful things because He has plans to redeem them. God is redeeming you right now, Dahlia. Right here in this facility. He's helping you become a brand new person."

"I guess that's why I'm interested in church. I don't understand all of that, but I'd sure like to. I hope it's true."

They let a comfortable silence fall, and Dahlia asked, "Auntie, what does it mean to follow God?"

"It means to admit to Him that we need His help. That we need Him as our Savior and want to do things His way."

"Do you follow God?"

"I do. I don't always follow Him perfectly, but I like to think of Jesus as the Lord and leader of my life. When I follow His ways, things work out better. In the long run, that is." She smiled at her niece. "When I follow God, I feel a lot more joy."

"Joy. I think that's what I see in the faces of the prayer ladies. It's not like they're happy all the time, but they do seem to have joy somehow."

"That's how joy works. It's not about circumstances. It's something that comes from following God."

Dahlia stood and stretched. "We've been sitting here a long time! But I was wondering something else. Would you teach me one of those card games you play at home?"

"I'd love to! Do you think you can round up two decks? I'll teach you a game called Hand and Foot."

They spent the next hour playing a competitive game of cards. Dahlia raised her hands in celebration and cheered when she won the final hand. It was time for Auntie Beth to head home, but she promised to visit again soon.

Almost as an afterthought, Beth remembered to tell Dahlia that a detective from the Denver area was coming to interview her. She was still working on getting a restraining order against Rol and had reported Dahlia's story to the Sheriff's Office. They needed to hear the story first-hand from Dahlia.

"Do you think you can talk to the detective when he gets here?"

"I'm sure I can," she answered. "Telling you has made me ready to finally let the story out. In fact, I wonder when I should tell Bebee. Maybe we can talk that through the next time you visit."

"Yes, let's do that," Auntie Beth said.

Dahlia removed a letter she'd written from inside the cover of her journal and asked Auntie to deliver it to Abby. They hugged and fought to hold back tears as they said goodbye.

The next day, Dahlia heard her name over the intercom, asking her to report to the front desk. There, she saw a tall, middle-aged man with a kind but serious expression. He introduced himself as Detective Warren Sullivan from the Adams County Sheriff's Office.

"Good morning, Dahlia," he said, his voice gentle yet professional. "Your aunt said she'd let you know I was coming. I'm here to investigate allegations against Rolyn Archer. Will you talk with me about what happened?"

Dahlia felt both apprehension and relief wash over her. She had been carrying the burden of her trauma for so long, and now, finally, someone was here to listen and take action. The receptionist led them to a small, quiet room where they both took a seat.

Over the next two hours, Dahlia recounted every detail she could remember about the assaults she had endured. She spoke of the fear, the pain, and the shame that had haunted her for years. Detective Sullivan listened attentively, taking notes and offering words of support and encouragement.

As Dahlia shared her story, she felt a weight gradually lifting from her shoulders. It wasn't easy to relive the dark moments, but there was something cathartic about finally giving voice to her experiences. Detective Sullivan's presence was comforting, and his assurances that she had done the right thing by coming forward helped ease some of her anxieties.

By the end of their conversation, Dahlia felt emotionally drained and simultaneously hopeful. She knew the road ahead would be difficult, but with the promise of justice on the horizon, Dahlia allowed herself to believe that maybe, just maybe, she could begin to heal and become that new person Auntie Beth spoke about.

CHAPTER 17

DAHLIA, 2005

February in Colorado teases spring's coming arrival. Songbirds reverse their migratory patterns, flocking from the south to established breeding grounds. Winter chills flee from longer spans of sunlight. The slightest hint of green returns to trees that prefer to leaf out early. But February is also fickle, and snowfall can blow in on the heels of spring-like temperatures.

Dahlia basked in the warm sunlight of the now-familiar courtyard behind the rehab facility. She considered switching into a pair of shorts. She did have a pair buried under jeans and sweaters in her room. But soon, the sun would fade, and the air would become crisp and chilly once more. She decided to stick with jeans and wait it out.

Sitting at a courtyard table, she leafed through the pages of her journal while sipping a Pepsi from a paper cup. Months before, she'd selected a separate sketchbook for her art. Still, her notes filled all but the few remaining pages of the spiral notebook. Looking back on her journey filled her with a myriad of feelings and insights—she'd come a long way and was finally able to confidently say she felt clean.

She'd scaled a mountain she once thought insurmountable. Getting to this point had been grueling, marked by moments of intense self-discovery and painful confrontation with her past. Yet, she had persevered. She had faced demons, battled addictions, and felt stronger than ever.

Now that her stay in rehab was nearly over, she let herself imagine a new frontier. A home life filled with laughter and lighthearted banter. Building a new friendship with her sister. Looking for a real job where she could use her abilities and feel worthy of legitimate wages. She'd get her driver's license and a cell phone. Maybe she and Bebee could go on a shopping spree and splurge on some new outfits that could help her feel confident.

In just two days, her release from the facility would be final. She had one last appointment with Dr. Nguyen, who had already said it would be just a formality. They could continue their sessions on an outpatient basis at an office within walking distance from Auntie Beth's house.

She stopped herself—it wasn't just Auntie Beth's house, but her house, too.

She lived here in Grand Junction now, away from the destructive lifestyle Rol demanded. She was sure by now he'd given up looking for her.

Now that she was free from the abuse she'd endured, a new life and a new level of hope awaited her. For the first time ever, she believed she could pursue any dream imaginable. Even college, if she got her G.E.D.

The clouds began to darken, and the sky turned overcast. Dahlia collected her things and carried them inside the building just as the first gust of wind carried a patio chair across the greenway. A storm was brewing.

As she ducked her head and ran through the doorway, she missed the low rumble of Rol's red El Camino as he slowly drove past the facility. He was still searching the streets of Grand Junction for Dahlia. He knew she was somewhere in this Western Slope town but did not know exactly where to look.

———

Several weeks later, at precisely 1:45 pm, Dahlia left her house, as she did every Wednesday and Friday afternoon, to walk to her appointment with Dr. Nguyen. They now met in a newly renovated office building rather than the rehab facility. The doctor said it was to maintain safety and anonymity for the other patients. Dahlia didn't mind. The office was only seven blocks from home, and she enjoyed the walk there—just two blocks along the tree-lined sidewalks of their neighborhood, a casual stroll along the shops on 7th Street, then another three blocks toward the west on Main Street.

Their sessions had become less formal, talking through more upbeat topics—like feeling genuinely happy and how the tug of temptation that nearly paralyzed her just months ago was all but gone. Dahlia felt the twisted disorder in her mind had gradually untangled itself. A new level of peace had replaced the inner turmoil she'd experienced for most of her life. She shared her new goals of revisiting her education and looking for a job. Their talk felt more like a conversation over coffee than a therapy session.

Surprisingly, Dr. Nguyen suggested they drop Dahlia's sessions from twice a week to once. This would be the final Wednesday session, and Fridays would be their only day to meet. Dahlia felt nearly weightless as she rode the mirror-paneled elevator down from the fourth-floor counselor's office into the building lobby.

There was a coffee shop just up the street, and after today's session, she felt a celebratory latte was in order. While ordering from the barista, her mind raced with the possibility of jobs she could feel proud of. Working in a coffee shop like this one might be nice. But Dahlia could think of little else than the front desk position that would open soon in Dr. Nguyen's office. The doctor encouraged Dahlia to apply and said she'd be strongly considered.

The instant she stepped outside the coffee shop, she heard a low, familiar rumble that stopped her in her tracks. She willed her feet to run back inside, but they felt as if they were mired in concrete. Uncle Rol, in his red El Camino, screeched up to the curb, inches from where she stood. He slammed the gear shift into park and was out of the car, grabbing her by the shoulders before she could react. The vanilla latte fell to the sidewalk, light brown liquid flowing into a large puddle next to the parking curb.

He forced her into the passenger seat and slammed the door without saying a word, but once he was behind the wheel, the cursing and relentless questions started. *Who did she think she was to abandon him and run off with Beth and Bebee? They had clients to think about, and she'd eluded him for months! Now, most of those clients might never come back. He'd driven every street of this God-forsaken town searching for her. Where had she been? Why was she so hard to find?*

Dahlia stared straight ahead and held her tongue, knowing that any explanation would only further ignite his fury. It was clear he had no idea she'd nearly overdosed or that she'd been in rehab. His finding her was nothing more than a coincidence, even though her routine had been well-established over the last several weeks.

Speeding through streets of Grand Junction, racing around corners, and nearly flying through intersections was unpleasant enough. But when they reached the Interstate, Dahlia wondered if they'd arrive in Denver in one piece. Uncle Rol stopped yelling but drove manically, passing semi trucks on the narrow shoulders of I-70, pressing too fast through the curves, and tailgating the cars in front of him. Dahlia held on to the door handle with white knuckles. She was afraid they'd crash, but at the same time, she knew that if they did, she may have another chance of going back to Auntie Beth's. Or, if she didn't survive the crash, she could join Mama in heaven. Either would be a much better option than what she knew was coming when they got back to Denver.

For the first hour of the long drive, Rol let his anger vent by sneering at his niece, giving her piercing glances conveying the trash he thought she was. Then, without notice, the verbal assault began again. He screamed profanities at her, accusing her of stealing what was rightfully his and sneaking away behind his back.

Dahlia rubbed the back of her neck and hugged her knees to her chest. She used some of the resilience exercises she'd learned in rehab. Focusing her eyes on the keyhole of the glove box before her, she noticed every scratch and blemish on the chrome fixture and imagined the shape of the key that could breach the lock. Inhaling deeply, she held her breath for a count of four before slowly exhaling.

Gradually, she tuned out his words. When he saw they weren't having the desired effect, Rol went quiet for a few moments, seemingly puzzled by her lack of reaction. He'd always been able to control her with a verbal outburst.

Dahlia tried hard to relax the muscles in her shoulders. Her toes clenched inside her shoes, and the palms of her hand were sore from squeezing her fingers into a tight fist.

Without warning, Rol launched his fist at the side of her face. With one mighty blow, Dahlia's head snapped, nearly colliding with the glass on the passenger side door. She was immediately dizzy and fought to remain conscious through the sudden explosion of pain.

The man's hand seemed enormous, as if he'd covered her entire head with his balled-up fingers. The skin around her eye felt tight, throbbing in rhythm with her heart. She blinked several times to try to clear the sparks she saw in the air. Moving her jaw from side to side made her wince in pain, raising suspicion that it was broken. She fought to hide her emotions, and before she could react, she heard Rol swear under his breath.

"Now look what you made me do," he snarled. "The clients won't like your face all bruised up. I'll pull over when I can and get you some ice." Minutes later, he pulled off at an exit near Eagle and found a service station.

"Stay in the car. I mean it," he warned as he opened the door and climbed out.

She eyed the door handle, but her legs felt like jelly. She knew she didn't possess the strength or stamina to escape before he'd return. Convulsive breaths overtook the meditative breathing she'd used just moments earlier to remain calm. Tears streamed uncontrollably. As her face contorted, it brought even more pain to her jaw.

"I can't go back," she said aloud to herself. "I can't do this."

Dahlia did the only thing she knew to do and whispered, "Jesus, help me." The prayer was simple, but for the first time beyond the walls of the prayer room at the rehab facility, she felt the Lord's presence. Her breathing started to calm, and her emotions slowly followed.

She glanced at the door handle again and extended her arm to grip the lever. Just as she was about to squeeze it and push the door open, Rol threw the driver's door open and sat back down in his seat. He held out a cup of ice for her.

"You weren't doing what I think you were doing, were you?" He asked, eyeing her outstretched hand. "Don't make me hit you again, girl. That's not good for either of us. You're coming home with me, and you're going back to work. No more running away."

Tires squealed as he cut off several cars, bringing angry shouts from the drivers. Rol seemed oblivious to anyone else and drove as if his car was the only one on the road. Dahlia felt as if she were being carried away by a sudden, violent storm, ripping her away from everything she loved. Time seemed to stand still as if her entire world shifted on its axis, leaving utter devastation in its wake.

She considered opening the door and jumping out onto the highway. She might be run over by a passing car or suffer severe injuries from her impact on the road. If she waited until he was in the right lane, close to the shoulder, maybe she'd have fewer injuries. As if he could read her thoughts, he hovered between the center and left lanes on the three-lane stretch of interstate. The risk of death was worth the hope of escape. She just had to make the bold move and jump.

Rol abruptly pulled the El Camino to a stop on the left shoulder of the highway. He reached behind the passenger seat and pulled out a length of rope. "I thought I might need this," he said as he wrapped it around Dahlia's torso, securely tying her to the seat back.

Her tears flowed freely now. Between the pain and emotional anguish, there was no holding them back. She was tied to the seat of the car, bruised, battered, and devastated. The rope brushed against her arms, rough and abrasive to the touch, dissolving any hope for freedom.

Exhausted from the blow to her head, she dozed off and on for another hour before they parked in front of an apartment building Dahlia hadn't remembered seeing before. "This is my place," Rol said, seeing her wide eyes. "I stopped paying for your apartment while you were off on vacation. Sorry I didn't get any of your stuff out, but I figured you'd have taken what you wanted."

Vacation. A fire of rage began to burn inside Dahlia. The man fed her drugs and then called it a *vacation* while she fought to recover from addiction. Life with Rol—in captivity and prostitution—wasn't something she could go back to. She'd worked too hard to break free.

After feeling a genuine family connection, after truly being a sister rather than a caregiver to Bebee, and after forming a deepening friendship with Auntie Beth, how could she go back to isolation? Just hours ago, she was on top of the world. Now, she felt suffocated in a sea of hopelessness.

Uncle Rol was barking at her, loosening the rope as he yelled at her. "This is where you live, Dahlia, and it's the only place you live. I've had the house phone disconnected, so you can't call anyone. Now give me your purse."

When Dahlia hesitated, he reached over and yanked it from her. "Give it to me!"

Uncle Rol rummaged through every pocket and every cavity of her wallet, removing all the cash and loose change he found. "You won't be needing any of this. I'll drop off some groceries every day or two, and I'll come pick you up when it's time for work. Since I can't call and let you know I'm coming, you better be ready whenever I arrive."

He tossed her bag back to her and said, "One more thing."

Rol handed her a small white pill and a bottle of water. "Take it right now while I'm watching."

"Please, Uncle Rol, no! I don't want to take it. I just got clean!" Dahlia's emotions ran rampant, her thoughts teetering between fighting against him and giving up. She was frantic.

"You think I don't know that? If I can keep you hooked, I can keep you here. Now take it!"

His eyes turned dark, and he ground his teeth together. Dahlia knew he was on the verge of more physical violence and would watch her actions carefully. She placed the pill carefully between her upper and lower molars, took a small sip of water, and swallowed.

"Good." He continued. "Now, if you don't do what I say, I'll lock you inside that apartment. No more monkey business, got it? Go up to unit 5B. The door's unlocked. Get on up there. I've got somewhere to be. Lock the door behind you, and I'll see you in a couple of days once I have some clients lined up. There's food in the fridge."

Dahlia nodded, stepped out of the car toward the apartment, and scurried up the stairs, feeling every muscle in her body as she climbed. Once inside, she closed and locked the door behind her, then sprinted to the kitchen sink, where she spat out the pill and turned on the faucet so the water would wash it down the drain.

The electricity in the apartment worked, but there was no TV service and no dial tone on the phone.

She peeked into the fridge to see three partially filled Chinese food containers. A sleeve of bagels that looked new lay on the top shelf next to a container of cream cheese. When she took off the lid, she saw it was covered with mold. Two nearly empty bags of chips lay on the counter next to a six-pack of Pepsi.

Maybe he'd bring more food when he picked her up for the next job. She could wait it out. She'd done it before.

She thought hard about how to get out of this predicament, and as she did, her mind wandered back to the short prayer she'd said in the car. How comforting it felt, even in the midst of danger, to know God was near. She hungered for more of Him, instinctively knowing He was the only way she could truly feel whole.

With nothing but her prayers, she curled into a ball on the bed and whispered her needs to God, who knew them all. Sleep came quickly, but she woke a few hours later with a start.

The apartment was dark except for the street lamp shining through the bedroom window. She gazed outside, and about half a block up the street, she could see a payphone. It almost glowed against the pitch-black sky. Dahlia reached into the front pocket of her blue jeans, suddenly remembering she'd stuffed the change from her vanilla latte there. Two dollar bills and two quarters were more than enough to make a phone call—if only she could get there unnoticed.

She raced from the apartment, down the sidewalk, and into the plexiglass booth. She dropped a quarter into the slot above the phone. Her finger hovered over the buttons, her heart racing in sync with the rhythmic tapping of her fingers. It was a leap into the unknown, and there would be no turning back. Her eyes closed briefly, summoning the strength to make the decision. The memories of long-ago laughter seemed to guide her.

She dialed a number that her memory recalled in an instant. When the sleepy voice answered, she said, "Doc! I need your help!"

PART

TWO

CHAPTER 18

TURO, 2005

Turo Torres forced his eyes open, rolled over in the bed, and slapped his nightstand until he found his Blackberry. 12:14 am. The digital message read, "Deceased fem, probable homicide. 123rd Dr & Newport Cir."

He hated calls like this, yet they were the very reason he loved his work. He silently recited his personal motto as he often did when sleep was shattered for the job: *faithfully protect the innocent; relentlessly pursue the offenders.*

Dressing quickly in yesterday's suit—a brown Joseph Abboud he'd found on clearance—he kissed his wife on the cheek and tenderly caressed her bulging belly. His life was about to change in ways he could never imagine, and he was excited to welcome a new life into their hearts and home. Together as a small family, he hoped they'd find a way to embark on adventures that didn't involve crime.

When he made it to the bottom of the stairs and was out of Kerri's earshot, he turned on his police radio to listen for updates. The dispatcher coordinating the radio traffic was maintaining calm in the midst of the chaos, keeping fractured conversations flowing like a well-oiled machine.

Within minutes, Turo pulled his county ride, a blue Chevy Impala, to a stop in the small cul-de-sac. The tight circle was already crowded with emergency vehicles. He stepped out of the car, easily located the patrol sergeant, and approached him for a recap.

"Detective Torres," The sergeant extended his arm to shake hands. "I'm Sergeant McNally. I was first on scene."

"What do we have?"

"Deceased female. She's young. At first, we thought it was a suicide, but I can't imagine how this would be self-inflicted. It looks as if she was shot once in the back of the head. Her hair is covering most of the wound, but the shot appears to have been execution-style. Looks like she was kneeling and then fell forward. She's fully clothed, including her sandals. The medical team has already pronounced her deceased." McNally pointed to where the coroner's van was parked. It was up a small hill on Newport Court, about a block and a half from where they were standing.

Turo looked in the opposite direction toward the deceased victim. He wanted to examine the area as quickly as possible. "Who called it in?"

"A married couple," McNally answered. "They're already at the substation being interviewed. Their initial statements corroborated one another—their dog started barking like crazy around 11:00 p.m. while they were watching TV. When he wouldn't calm down, they let him out to run in the open space at about 11:45. He led them right to the body behind those trees." McNally lifted his chin toward a stand of Russian Olives where two patrol deputies stood watch over the girl's remains.

"Where does the couple live?"

McNally motioned to the southwest. "There. Fourth house from the corner. You can see the lights on upstairs."

Turo nodded. He estimated the two-story home was about 75 yards from the body and backed up to the open space. There was a distinctive metal sculpture in the shape of a sea turtle mounted to the light-colored lap siding. A privacy fence lined the back of the property, which looked well-maintained. He could not see if a back gate accessed the open space.

"When Detective Burroughs arrives, let's have him start canvassing the neighborhood," he said. "Someone likely heard the gunshot."

Adams County, Colorado, once a sleepy agricultural community, now had segments that had spiraled into a hub of impropriety.

Stretching 80 miles wide from the Denver Metro area to the eastern plains, the county's population had exploded over the last decade. The influx of people naturally invited more crime and malfeasance. To meet the needs of the growing populace, the Sheriff's Office added a steady increase of certified deputies and support personnel who were doing their best to manage the uptick in crime.

Turo had served as a patrol deputy for five years, so he was well familiar with the intimate pocket of homes near the scene. This neighborhood and its adjacent open space were distinctive, as the area had never been annexed into the city of Thornton but was surrounded by property that had. It was a dot within unincorporated Adams County's District 7, where the Sheriff's Office handled calls for service rather than the Thornton Police Department.

Typically a safe, quiet community, it bordered large spans of farmland and remained nearly unaffected by development meant to keep up with Colorado's influx of new residents. The jurisdictional location kept police presence on an as-needed basis.

"McNally, one more thing," Turo said. "Contact Thornton PD to see if their officers saw or heard anything suspicious."

"Will do," McNally answered. He glanced at his watch, then spoke into his shoulder mic to connect with Thornton via AdCom, the 9-1-1 center that dispatched for police and fire.

Turo surveyed the large open space that wrapped around the cul-de-sac and gave the city streets a country feel. The terrain was hilly, not well suited to farming, and all but neglected by the property owner. Residents habitually let their dogs off-leash to run through the field. Small thickets of trees here and there provided cover for teens who wanted to make out or smoke weed.

He stepped through a small pedestrian opening in the split rail fence that bordered the neighborhood and led into the pasture. This was one of those moments when Turo disliked wearing business attire as a Detective. Walking downhill through a field was much better suited to tactical boots. He'd learned to shop carefully and purchase dress shoes with rubber soles, but trekking through the untended open space was still challenging. Twice as he traversed the incline, he felt his feet slip and grumbled under his breath.

By the time he approached the body, his shoes no longer concerned him. His mind zeroed in on details in the scene before him. A creek bed crossed the open space farther down the sloping landscape, but with the lack of rain so far this year, it was dry as a desert. He'd have to look carefully for footprints. Maybe the shooter followed the creek away from the crime scene and toward Quebec Street instead of risking a walk back through the neighborhood.

The copse of trees sheltered the girl's body from view from the street. Grass and weeds had grown quickly in the early spring and were now long but dry. As he walked, he could hear them crunch beneath his feet. The only footpath he could see began at the fence opening he'd just come through. If the shooter was looking for an easy way in and out, he would have used the same route.

Turo circled around the trees from a distance and then carefully moved in a straight line toward the girl. He knew his steps would set precedence, and the team of investigators would use his path as the only way in and out of the area. It was a way of minimizing contamination of the scene and ensuring the least amount of evidence was disturbed.

In cases like the one he gazed upon now, it was nearly impossible to remain emotionally distant. Looking at the victim, he knew this would be a tough case to work. By her petite features and youthful attire, he guessed she was somewhere around sixteen.

Approaching the young woman, it appeared someone had prepared her resting place. The glow of his flashlight revealed tall grass, flattened into a makeshift circle to form a clearing. It looked as if she'd knelt with her back to the gunman, awaiting her execution.

She was lying off-center, partially on her right side. Her knees were bent, one folded over the other. Small hands were pulled to her chest, and she did not appear to have defensive wounds. This was not a victim who'd fought her attacker. She rested on a pool of long, blonde hair beneath her right cheek. He saw a large bruise from her jawline, along her left eye, and across to her ear. From this vantage point, Turo couldn't see the bullet's exit wound. But with the burns he could see on her scalp, the shot appeared to be close contact.

To his trained but non-scientific eye, the time of death was recent. He didn't see signs of gravitational pooling of her blood but caught a light scent of gunpowder. Paired with the timing of the neighbor's nervous dog, she may have died within the last hour or two.

By all appearances, the shooting took place right here. The girl and her killer likely walked to this spot from the direction of the cul-de-sac that was now a cacophony of emergency vehicles and responders. Farther to the west, the incline into the open space was steeper. Walking in or out of the area from that direction wouldn't have been easy with the overgrown foliage.

Turo looked up the hill to the team of crime scene investigators that had arrived. Soon, they'd have the field lit up like the midday sun. The neighbors weren't going to get much sleep tonight, but the investigations team would get a good look at the evidence left by the shooter. To the detective, that was all that mattered.

—

Turo looked at the clock. He'd worked thirty-six hours straight, and leads were drying up. The mug on his desk had been filled and drained so many times if someone tried to draw his blood, they'd likely strike coffee.

The team had hit the investigation hard, but they still had few details. They interviewed neighbors and anyone else who was in the area; they'd searched missing person reports but could not yet identify their victim. The ballistics team was running tests on the single shell casing and the mangled bullet found at the scene. They knew the shot was fired from a 9mm weapon, but that was not much to build a case on.

Turo needed some shuteye. He'd been asleep only an hour when his Blackberry paged him to the scene early Friday morning and hadn't been home since. He'd eaten two slices of room-temperature pizza in the breakroom and downed as much caffeine as he could ingest. He and his colleagues were out of gas. Early stages of homicide investigations required full-out effort, digging for leads around the clock. The entire team was on overdrive.

As the media caught wind of the young victim, pressure mounted to find the killer. Even the brass was out for this case, but they could do little more than hope for a lucky break.

Turo was ready to call it a day, planning to come back to the office early tomorrow and take a fresh look at all the details. He'd need to apologize to his wife for losing yet another weekend to work. Somehow, Kerri seemed to understand his drive and the sacrifice his job required. He was passionate about his job and thought of it more as a calling, but with a baby on the way, he knew he'd have to find a better balance in his life. For now, he took it one case at a time.

His mind was spinning as he mentally ran through the case. Evidence at the scene was scarce. Only a few partial footprints were identified, although nothing along the creek bed. Two neighbors reported seeing a white Ford Maverick parked in the cul-de-sac around 10:30 pm Thursday. One neighbor noted there were no license plates on the car. They didn't see anyone with it, nor did they recall seeing it there before.

Patrol officers throughout the metro area were searching for the Maverick, adding a dollop of confidence to Turo's discouragement. He reminded himself that their network of support was large. They'd find this guy.

It appeared as though only one shot had been fired since only one shell casing had been located so far. Until they got the autopsy report, that's all they had to go on.

Turo grabbed his suit jacket, shut off the office light, and closed the door. Sleep was a necessary respite that would prove hard to come by until they could string some leads together. And if they wanted to catch a killer, that had better be soon.

CHAPTER 19

TURO, 2005

"Well, look who's here on a Sunday!" Detective Warren Sullivan, known to his friends as Sully, smiled at his old friend. He leaned his shoulder on the door frame of the office Turo shared with three other homicide investigators. He and Sully started their careers in the jail division, transferred to patrol at about the same time, and then became rookie detectives together.

Turo lifted his eyes from the report on his desk and gave his friend a weary nod. Sully's hair was as light as Turo's was dark, and his eyes carried the familiar weariness that Turo felt in his bones. This line of work nearly sucked the life out of most cops. They learned to rely on friendships with colleagues and slowly became skeptical of anyone who didn't understand the weighty burden of each case they carried.

The connection he felt with Sullivan came flooding back in an instant. "Where've you been hiding? I haven't seen you in weeks!"

"I'm working a child exploitation case that's pretty involved. What's all the weekend activity around here?"

"Just the trending uptick in homicide cases. We have a Jane Doe, between sixteen and twenty years old. She was found in a field early Friday morning, shot execution style. I finally got the preliminary report from the coroner and was just wading through the details."

"Not exactly light weekend reading," Sully approached Turo's desk and peered down at the document.

"All part of the job. What brings you in tonight?"

"I need to call a victim. I got word our deputies arrested the guy who assaulted her, and I want to let her know he's off the streets."

"Good for you, Sully! Nice job."

"I was just at the jail interviewing the suspect. Of course, he says all the accusations are false, and if we think we have a case, we should charge him. His attitude alone seems to validate the entire case. That, and nearly 100 Vikes they found in this guy's car."

"It's good to know our agency is still in the business of solving crimes. I feel like we've stalled out on this homicide." Turo absent-mindedly stretched his neck, feeling it pop as he lifted his chin toward the ceiling.

"I'll leave you to it, Turo. Is there anything you need?"

"Yeah, some fresh ideas would help. Since your case is all wrapped up, come on over and give us a hand."

"Whoa! You want a sex crimes detective to come help the big-time homicide team? Was there a sexual assault on the victim?"

"No sex assault. And stop selling yourself short. I'd take you on my team any day of the week." Turo laughed as Sully stood tall and straightened an imaginary necktie.

"You know, you've got one of the most emotionally taxing jobs in the agency." Turo leaned back in his desk chair. His eyes aligned with Sully's. "When I look at a victim, it's too late to help them. When you look at a victim, it's someone who needs a protector. Someone to believe what they say and champion their cause. You're a great detective with a big heart."

Nearly 15 years ago, the two had partnered in the jail book-in unit. The volume of arrestees coming through the back door made overnight shifts fly by in the blink of an eye. Housed in the county seat of Brighton, the detention facility averaged 500 inmates, accepting arrestees from nine different jurisdictions. Since those days, a jail expansion allowed the inmate population to more than double. Crime wasn't going away any time soon.

Detective Sullivan grinned, then glanced at his watch. "Let me go make my call. If I get this wrapped up, I'll make myself available until I get my next case."

"Don't make a promise you can't keep." Turo returned his gaze to the report on his desk.

As he flipped through the pages, there were no surprises. Pending toxicology findings, the cause of the victim's death was a single gunshot wound to the head. The manner of death was labeled a homicide. Evidence for the time of death was consistent with 11:00 pm on Thursday night when neighborhood activity was reported. No sexual assault was indicated. The young woman had been beaten on the left side of her face, but no facial bones were broken.

Turo tried to imagine the last moments of her life. She was punched, then shot. The punch could indicate anger. Rage. Although it could have been a method of gaining her submission to kneel in the circle flattened in the weeds. Without discovering who the girl was, Turo would never be able to develop her story and uncover the motive for taking her life.

They'd submitted biological evidence from the victim to the Combined DNA Index System (CODIS), a national database of DNA profiles to help identify convicted offenders and missing persons alike. There'd been no hits. Detectives canvassed the neighborhood surrounding the crime scene, but no one knew or admitted to seeing a young woman matching her description.

This girl was a genuine Jane Doe. Without a photograph to share with news outlets, they weren't likely to get any helpful tips about her identity. Turo considered reaching out to the Denver Police Department. They had a forensic artist who could develop a sketch that concealed her wounds and injuries. It would be helpful to share it with local news outlets and send out a plea for help in finding her identity.

By Monday morning, Turo was back at the crime scene looking for clues to point him in the right direction. He walked the neighborhood as the sun came up and talked to a middle-aged woman who was walking her dog. Next, he interrupted a young couple leaving for work and probed for details he felt desperate to uncover.

None of them had insights to share. They hadn't heard anything unusual Thursday night or early Friday morning. They'd never seen a girl in the neighborhood who matched the victim's description. They normally felt very safe in their homes, but this incident understandably had them on edge. They were anxious to see the case solved as soon as possible.

No one's more anxious than me, Turo thought.

As the sun lit the ground beneath his feet, he stepped back into the open space, moving slowly toward the crime scene, which remained cordoned with crime scene tape. A patrol deputy continued to monitor the area to keep the lookie-loos at bay and prevent any contamination of evidence. Turo waved and showed his badge but didn't initiate conversation. He wasn't here to chat.

The detective stood among the tall grass and imagined himself in the girl's shoes. *Why would there be a clearing that resembled a sort of nest? What would make her kneel for her killer? Was it fear? Blackmail? Hopelessness? Protection of someone she loved?* Jane Doe had a story, and it was up to him to uncover it.

He'd seen his share of crime scenes, but this one felt different. This victim was just a kid—maybe still in high school, with a future that should have been overflowing with hope and promise. Her life had been cut short, brutally ripped from her. And no one seemed to be looking for her.

Turo felt he was her only ally. Those who loved her didn't even realize she was dead. No one was fighting for her justice. He needed to be her champion, her voice in a world that let evil have its way.

They were four days into the investigation, and he knew that if they didn't catch a break soon, chances of solving this case would dry up like the Arizona desert. He'd dreamt about the case for the last two nights, waking in a cold sweat after envisioning himself searching frantically through a murky, dark swamp for the girl's identity.

There was nothing new to uncover, no hidden evidence suddenly made visible by the passage of time. K-9s searched the area over the weekend and picked up scents that ended back at the cul-de-sac, confirming the white Maverick was a primary clue. The entire case hinged on it, and they had to find it as quickly as possible.

Every white car he saw driving along the highway or through his neighborhood caught his eye, no matter if they were old models, new releases, SUVs, minivans, or even semi-trucks. His hypervigilance was on overdrive. He loved the rush of working a new case, but this one had an emotional connection and unleashed a simmering anger he rarely felt inside.

When he reached his desk, Turo controlled what he could. Finding order in chaos was helpful for him, so he went through his desk drawers, purging old messages, broken rubber bands, empty candy wrappers, and dried-out ink pens. He sorted his collection of business cards and leafed through the stacks of papers on his desk, separating them by case and filing them away. The task did little to clear his head or improve his mood.

The fluorescent bulbs in his office flickered, adding to a headache that started at the base of his neck and traveled up to his scalp. Turo stood, raised his hands toward the ceiling, and arched his back to stretch. He stepped out of the homicide office to track down his lieutenant to talk with him about his idea of sharing a composite sketch of the victim with the media. On his first step outside his doorway, he bumped smack into Sully, who nearly dropped his coffee because of the collision.

"What's the rush, Sully? Where you headed so fast?"

"To see you. About your Jane Doe. Turo," Sully's eyes were dark and turbulent, "my victim has gone missing. I just got off the phone with her aunt on the Western Slope. My victim matches the description of your victim. I think we could be talking about the same girl."

Turo felt his skin bristle and his heartbeat quicken. "Are you kidding me?"

"Grand Junction PD emailed her photo to me. I've forwarded it to you. Check your inbox."

Turo nearly leaped over his desk to view his computer screen. Scrolling through the morning's email messages, he double-clicked the one from Sully. The eyes of his victim stared back at him. "It's got to be her. Tell me everything you know."

"Let's get to the morgue first." Sully began walking toward the main office doors. "I interviewed my victim in person, Turo. If it's the same girl, I can ID her."

Turo grabbed his car keys and followed Sully to the parking lot, where they jumped into Turo's Impala. Morning traffic was heavy near the substation building in Commerce City, but they both knew the back roads and avoided the congested highway to the coroner's office in Brighton.

The two detectives remained quiet through the 20-minute drive, each weighing the possibilities of a shared victim and what it could mean to their investigations. For Turo, it was the lead he'd been hoping for. He could learn the name of Jane Doe and finally get some traction on solving the case. For Sully, the news was devastating. The thought that he may have lost a victim to murder weighed heavily on his mind. He believed she was safe 250 miles away in Grand Junction, yet it looked like darkness may have achieved a gut-punching victory.

As friends, they respected the silence. They didn't need words to know they were on the same page. Their wordless connection spoke volumes about the need to partner together, solve this case, and find justice.

Within minutes of parking the car in front of the unsightly brick and metal building that was the coroner's office, they had their answer. Sully was positive the deceased Jane Doe was Dahlia Archer.

They pulled out their cell phones and began making calls, barking out orders, and preparing to take the investigation in new directions.

Sully called the detention facility and talked with the platoon lieutenant. "If it looks like Rolyn Archer is about to bond out of jail, you need to call me immediately. We're looking at him for a recent homicide on top of the sexual assault warrant that you're holding him for now." He paced back and forth in the hallway, trying to keep some physical distance between the two phone conversations.

Turo simultaneously called the department's public information officer and told her he'd be sending an email image of Jane Doe, who was recently identified as Dahlia Archer. "Get ready to share the details I'll send over, but not till I say. We still need to notify the family and tie up a few loose ends. But the minute we can put the information out, I want to be ready."

They called Lieutenant MacDonald together and talked to him on speakerphone about the discovery. "Get over to Grand Junction *now*," MacDonald said, peppering the conversation with expletives, "and get as many details as you can from the family. You can make the death notification while you're driving or do it face to face, but we need their help if we're going to put this guy away. We need as much information as we can to tie Rolyn Archer to this murder. Take your time over there. Stay overnight if you have to and do it right."

"We're on it, L.T.," Turo ended the call, then pushed open the door to exit the building and gestured for Sully to go through. "I'll drop you at headquarters. We can grab the files we need, go home, pack a few things in case we stay overnight, and be ready to go in an hour." He glanced at his watch. "That puts us in Grand Junction at around 1:30, even if we grab a quick bite along the way."

CHAPTER 20

TURO, 2005

They rode up the I-70 corridor and through the Rocky Mountains. The lengthy drive allowed Sully plenty of time to brief Turo on Dahlia's case file.

"Here's what we know," he started. "Dahlia nearly overdosed in her apartment on September 10th. Her aunt and uncle couldn't reach her by phone, and Rolyn, Dahlia's supposed guardian, couldn't be bothered to answer his phone. So they jumped in the car and drove for four hours to check on her. When they knocked at the apartment door, there was no answer, so they essentially broke in and found Dahlia unconscious on the bed.

"The paramedics suspected a narcotics overdose, and Dahlia spent a couple of days in the hospital. Beth, her aunt, got busy with the State and received emergency guardianship, under the contingency that she put Dahlia in a rehab center for substance abuse."

Tapping his fingers on the steering wheel, Turo asked, "How does Beth fit into the picture?"

"She's Dahlia's mom's sister. The mom passed away last spring, and Abigail, Dahlia's younger sister—who they call Bebee—moved to Grand Junction to live with Beth. Dahlia said she was staying behind to finish school but ended up almost dying.

"When she was released from the hospital, Beth took Dahlia home to Grand Junction. They spent some time together as a family before checking her into rehab. Beth and Dahlia had a heart-to-heart, and Dahlia spilled her guts about everything. Beth called us, and that's when I got involved."

"Okay, I'm following," Turo said, "and I think I understand the players."

"Rolyn had been trafficking her to a bunch of johns who paid hefty money for underage sex. This started when Dahlia was very young, shortly after Dahlia's dad was put in prison for murder."

"Seriously? Dad's in prison for murder?"

"Yeah, and Rolyn promised him he'd take care of the family. Some care."

"That's rough, man."

"Tell me about it. Mom was never home, working multiple jobs and trying to make ends meet, and Dahlia took it upon herself to make sure her sister could be a good student and have a bright future. She believed Rolyn would leave Bebee alone if she cooperated with him. By some miracle, he did."

"And Rolyn was feeding her pills, right?"

"Right. He could control her when she was using. It started with Vikes. Then, Mom got sick and was in home hospice. The nurses loaded her up with hard-core narcotics, and when she passed away, Dahlia kept a bunch of the Morphine, Fentanyl, and Hydromorphone and spiraled deeper into the addiction Rol was feeding into—until she OD'd.

"Beth made sure to put her into inpatient rehab so Rolyn would have the least chance of finding her. The scumbag knew Beth lived on the Western Slope, and Beth knew if he wanted to find where she lived, he could. So they tucked Dahlia away in the rehab facility. It served a dual purpose.

"While she was there, Beth filed a restraining order against Rolyn and petitioned for permanent custody. Dahlia turned 18 in rehab. I went to the rehab facility and interviewed Dahlia there. She was still struggling hard with addiction recovery but was very open about her story.

"I secured the warrant for trafficking and distributing to a minor, but Rolyn vanished into thin air. No one could find him. Meanwhile, I've been searching for the johns. Dahlia gave me descriptions of the ones she could remember, the routines they followed when it all went down, and where it all happened. We got a warrant to search the building—a vacant three-story. On the main floor, there's a back room, about the size of a storage closet, with no windows and a seedy-looking mattress that we brought in as evidence. There were good fingerprints on the keypad on the back door. Now that we have Rolyn in custody, the lab is trying to link the prints as we speak."

Sully paused the story as Turo navigated a backup of cars on the climb to Evergreen.

"Okay, I'm listening again," Turo said.

"When Dahlia was released from inpatient rehab, her counselor wanted to keep seeing her on an outpatient basis. Her office is just a few blocks from where Dahlia lives with her Aunt Beth, Uncle David, and sister Bebee. Dahlia doesn't have a driver's license or a car, so she walked to therapy twice a week."

Sullivan shook his head in frustration. "This is the part where I can just kick myself. They all knew the restraining order was in place and somehow convinced themselves that Rolyn would play by the rules. Dahlia had said over and over she was afraid he'd kill her if he found out she told someone about his abuse. But I helped them build up a false sense of security, and she let her guard down."

"Sully, don't do that to yourself."

"It's too late," he said, holding the bridge of his nose between two fingers. "Man, I wish I'd known she was walking to therapy. I would have put a stop to that. She walks into her counselor's office Wednesday mid-morning, comes out on top of the world, feeling like she has a genuine shot at creating a new life, stops for coffee, and the SOB is outside waiting for her. Had he figured out her routine? It sure looks that way. My guess is he'd been in Grand Junction stalking Dahlia since Beth took her away."

"That's why you couldn't find him, then. Because he was on the Western Slope."

"Right. The owner of the coffee shop said she saw a guy get out of a red El Camino and shove Dahlia into his car. She said Dahlia looked terrified and dropped her coffee when Rolyn came up and squeezed the top of her shoulder."

"From there, I think I know the rest of the story," Turo said, reaching to turn down the car's air conditioning. "He's the guy you found and put in custody, right? The guy you interviewed before I saw you yesterday?"

"Right."

Turo was mentally assembling the timeline. "He kidnapped her on Wednesday, and we found her dead early Friday morning. Rolyn's got to be the triggerman. But he's in our jail?"

"That's the problem," Sully shifted in his seat and stretched out the shoulder strap of his seat belt, letting it snap against his chest. "He's been in our jail since Wednesday night. Unless Dahlia was in that field for more than 36 hours, it wasn't Rolyn who pulled the trigger."

Nodding, Turo said, "The coroner's report estimates her time of death as 11:00 pm on Thursday. Still, Rolyn's got to be involved. It's too much of a coincidence that he scooped her up, and she was killed almost immediately. He's a party to this somehow. It's way too close for comfort."

"We're in agreement there." Sully stared out the window as several miles of pine forests blurred by. "I literally want to puke. I'm sick over this case. She was under my watch."

"Don't beat yourself up, Sully. It's impossible to protect someone from almost 300 miles away. You did everything you could. Even if it was for a short time, you helped give her life back to her. She found hope. What's better than that?"

"It's hard to see it from that viewpoint," Sully countered. All I can see is a young girl whose life was torn away from her. She was a good person who was trying to turn things around. I lose sleep wondering what she could have become or where life would have taken her."

"Believe me, bro, she somehow left a beautiful mark on this world." Turo was pensive as his thoughts formed into words. "This is one of those cases where restoration is out there waiting for us to find. Nothing makes sense right now, but someday the people Dahlia loved are going to say, 'Look at the amazing impact she made during her short life.'"

Sully stared at his friend in disbelief. "That's crazy deep, dude. I didn't know you had it in you."

CHAPTER 21

TURO, 2005

When they arrived at the house on Ouray Street, a teenage girl they assumed was Bebee sat in a wicker chair on the covered front porch. She was writing in a notebook, her blonde hair hanging loose about her shoulders. She wore cut-off shorts and a baggy T-shirt.

"Hello there," Sully said, approaching her. "I'm Detective Warren Sullivan from Adams County. This is Detective Arturo Torres. Are you Abby?"

Bebee's face drained of color. "I am," she said, "let me get my Auntie Beth." Bebee disappeared behind the squeaky screen door.

"That's her sister, all right," Sully said. "Same blue eyes. Same dimples."

The front yard of the home was beautiful. A large maple tree stood in the center of the yard, surrounded by carefully trimmed bushes and a well-manicured lawn. An array of flower pots and the American flag that hung next to the front door gave the home a welcoming feeling. It looked like any normal home, but Sully knew nothing would ever be "normal" in this house again.

Afternoon shade fell over the front porch of Beth and David Lane's home, making it a perfect place to enjoy a summer afternoon. But with a missing sister, it was doubtful Bebee was enjoying her afternoon. Turo ached for her loss and the grief she'd already suffered. Learning of her sister's death was going to wreck this poor girl.

Beth came to the door, wiping her hands on a dish towel. "Detective Torres," she said, "I'm Beth. Detective Sullivan, it's nice to see you again. Please come in."

The two men stepped onto the porch and entered the home, which mirrored the yard in neatness and comfort. "Ma'am," Sully began. This was his first death notification. Turo had coached him during their drive, reminding him there was no good way to deliver the news. The best way, he'd said, was to get right to the point and not get lost in the details. The next of kin would ask the questions they felt ready to hear.

He took a deep breath. "We've located Dahlia's body. I'm afraid she was killed."

Beth's complexion went ashen. She dropped to her knees and buried her face in her hands. From behind him, Sully heard Bebee's long wail. "No!" When he turned to face her, she was holding her head in her hands, tears streaming down her reddened cheeks. "How could he do that to her? Why?" Bebee's words stopped, but her sobs did not. She collapsed into an armchair, gripping the arms firmly and rocking her body back and forth. "Why?" she demanded.

Turo had a small packet of tissues in his jacket pocket. He opened it and extended his arm to offer one to Bebee. She accepted it, but the thin paper did little to capture the flow of tears.

Beth was working to catch her breath and stand to her feet. Turo stepped toward her and offered his arm as support. "I'm so sorry. Is there anyone we can call for you? Anyone you'd like us to notify or ask to come over?"

"Could you call my husband David?" Beth asked, her voice cracking through each word as she pointed. "The phone is on the desk there. He's speed dial two."

Sully moved toward the desk and picked up the phone.

He could barely hear Beth as she whispered, "How was she killed? Where did you find her?"

Turo took a deep, silent breath. "She was found shot to death in a field in Adams County early Friday morning."

"And you're certain it's her?"

"She didn't have identification with her, so we did have trouble identifying her. When Detective Sullivan realized Dahlia was missing, he made a positive identification since he'd met with her in person. We came to Grand Junction as quickly as we could to notify you face to face."

"I can't believe this happened. Have you arrested Rol?"

"No, Ma'am. I'm afraid Rol has a solid alibi. He was in the Adams County Jail at the time the coroner report estimates Dahlia was murdered."

A bewildered look crossed Beth's face. She stepped backward toward a chair, grabbing the arm for balance before lowering her body into it. "Then who could have possibly done this? Do you think it was random?"

"We're doing all we can to find out, Ma'am."

"It had to be him," Bebee yelled from just a few feet away. "I don't care if he was in jail or not! He's to blame! Dahlia told me all about his evil ways. Who else would have killed her?!" Beth stood and moved toward her niece, gently embracing her as her shoulders racked with sobs.

Sully, who had been quietly speaking into the phone, placed the handset back onto the receiver and said, "David's on his way home."

"Thank you," Beth said, her chin quivering. "I'm not sure I can even say the words aloud right now."

"Ma'am, we have a lot of questions we'd like to ask you. Would you like us to give you some time before we begin?"

"If you don't mind, maybe you could sit on the porch for a few minutes so we can regroup a little. I'd like David to be here to answer your questions as well. His office isn't far, so he should be here soon."

"We'll be outside when you're ready."

As they sat on the patio furniture, Sully said, "Well, that wasn't fun."

"You did a good job. There are no 'right' words to say. It's best to blurt it out and end the anticipation of the bad news as fast as you can."

"Do death notifications ever get easier?"

"No. Not at all." Turo shook his head, looking down and studying the concrete beneath his feet. "Every single one of them is awful in its own way."

After a few minutes, a gray sedan pulled into the driveway. A man got out and walked to the front porch.

"Mr. Lane?" Sully said.

"Yes, call me David. You must be Detective Sullivan?"

"Yes, sir. This is my partner, Detective Torres. We're sorry to meet under these circumstances. We offer our condolences."

"Thank you. Can I go inside?"

"Yes, of course. We have several questions to ask you all and would like to begin as soon as you feel reasonably ready."

"All right," David said, stepping into the house. "We'll try not to be long."

"First," Turo began as everyone found a seat in the living room. He hoped his voice wouldn't crack with the emotion pent up inside him. "We're deeply sorry for your loss."

He was emotionally invested in this case but also understood the sudden and all-consuming grief from the loss of a family member. Nearly twenty years ago, Turo sat in a similar situation, talking to a detective about the death of his own brother. His hope with every surviving victim—because the survivors were victims too—was to be more personable and tactful than the detectives he'd encountered back then.

Turo made eye contact with Beth first, then David, and finally Bebee, hoping to convey his compassion where words failed him. "You know that Rolyn was in the Adams County Detention Facility the night Dahlia was killed, and that rules him out as her shooter. But we're working very hard to solve this case for Dahlia. This conversation won't be easy for you, but it will be very helpful for our investigation. We have to ask difficult questions. Pointed inquiries can spark certain memories or bring to mind comments and situations you may not have otherwise considered."

None of the family members responded, each sitting quietly as they braced for the impact of the coming conversation. He hoped he could portray some small measure of gentleness as they talked.

As was his habit, Turo removed the small notebook from his pocket and then switched on his audio recorder. "Let's ease into this a bit. What would you like me to know about Dahlia?"

Bebee was eager to share, even as she fought tears. "She was amazing. I know she struggled with drugs at the end, but with every-thing she told me Rol did to her, I don't judge her for that. Dahlia spent her life trying to make sure I had everything I needed to get a good education and become a good person." The young girl paused to gather her thoughts. Sharing wisdom that surpassed her youthful appearance, she said, "I want her to be remembered for her generosity and kindness, not for her drug addiction."

Bebee blew her nose into what was left of a tissue. "There was so much more to her than her mistakes. She genuinely cared about peo-ple and bent over backward to care for them—to care for me." Bebee stopped trying to hold back her downpour of tears.

Turo looked to Beth, who said, "I don't have much to add to that. Every word is true. The world has lost a truly beautiful person who gave all she could to help others."

David added, "We've known her all her life, and she's never been anything but selfless. I was always astonished at how she could think of others before herself at such a young age. It's beyond me why any-one would choose to harm her."

"What can you share with me about Rolyn Archer?"

Beth said, "I think I only met him once before my sister's funeral, and when I learned he'd stepped in to help after Robert was impris-oned, I thought he was wonderful. But it turns out all along he was destroying them." Anger burned in her eyes like molten lava. "He's nothing but a betrayer. I was shocked by all the ways he was harming Dahlia!"

"Why did the family need help from Rolyn?"

Beth and Bebee began talking at the same time; then Beth quieted to let Bebee share her story. "My dad was arrested for killing a man when we were little, and they said he'd never get out of jail. Uncle Rol is my dad's brother and promised he'd watch over our family and make sure we had everything we needed. That didn't work out so well. My mom worked hard until she died. And now Dahlia's gone too."

Turo knew the reality of her sister's murder was a bitter pill to swallow and could see Bebee struggling to process the sheer cruelty of it. In the midst of her pain, her life was irrevocably altered, and the road ahead was fraught with darkness and uncertainty.

He asked, "Did you ever meet any of Rolyn's friends or know if he had a steady job somewhere?"

"No," Bebee said. "Every time he came around, he was by himself driving his ugly red truck-car. He never talked about working but always seemed to have money."

"When was the last time any of you saw Rolyn?"

"It was the day of my sister's funeral," said Beth.

Bebee added, "He walked up to me that day and said, 'Well haven't you grown into a beautiful young lady?'" She mimicked his sinister tone. "I've never been looked at up and down the way he did that day. It was creepy. But I never suspected any of this. Dahlia was standing right next to me when he said that. And that same night, she started pushing for me to move here with Auntie Beth."

"Why didn't Dahlia come with you when you moved?"

"I begged her to," said Bebee as she, once again, fell into convulsive sobs.

"It's the biggest regret of my life," Beth said. "Dahlia said she was too close to graduation and didn't want to change high schools. She said Rol would watch over her, and she'd come visit as often as we could arrange it. I had no reason to doubt her, but when I walked into the apartment the day of the overdose, there was no sign that anyone lived with Dahlia. No sign of Rol whatsoever. The world turned upside down that day, and I knew I had to take action."

"Can you tell me where she was attending high school?"

"She was enrolled in Northglenn High School," Beth said, "but dropped out after Bebee moved here. She didn't share that decision with me until I brought her here to Grand Junction."

"When did you discover that Dahlia was involved with drugs?"

Beth answered first. "The day David and I went to the apartment and found her unconscious. I never dreamed she was using. The possibility never even crossed my mind."

"I thought I knew everything she did," Bebee added, "but I guess she kept a lot of secrets from me. I didn't know about the drugs until Auntie Beth told me she was in the hospital. I was surprised, too. Shocked, really."

"Can you tell me the names of Dahlia's friends? Who did she most often hang out with?"

"Alex Anderson was really the only friend who ever came around. Dahlia talked about her sometimes, but mostly, she kept to our family. She was home most evenings and weekends when she wasn't working—" Bebee cut off her sentence as the reality of the work Dahlia did for Rol filled her mind. "—When she wasn't with that monster. She never wanted me to be alone while Mama was at work."

"Is there anyone else?" Sully asked.

"There was a boy she was interested in for a while, but he moved away to Florida last summer. They never went out or anything."

"Do you remember his name?"

Bebee glanced through the window behind Turo to stretch her memory. "It was Charles. I don't know his last name. He had red hair. She thought it was adorable."

"Did either Alex or Charles experiment with illegal drugs?"

"Not that I ever knew. The crazy thing is, I don't think Dahlia would have put up with that from her friends." Bebee shook her head at the irony.

"Bebee, have you ever done drugs?" Sully asked.

"No, and I never will. I know a few kids who have tried pot, but when I found out, I stopped hanging around them. There's no way I could do that now that this has all happened."

"Do you know where Dahlia got her drugs?"

Beth nodded. "She told me she got them from Rol. That he kept her supplied because he knew how hard the work was for her. She also took narcotics prescribed to my sister during hospice. There was morphine, and I'm not sure what else."

"Does her cell phone happen to be here?" Turo asked.

"She didn't have one," Beth said, leaning back in her chair. "I know that's strange nowadays, but for Dahlia, it was a matter of priorities. She believed there were more important ways to spend money. Quite a selfless attitude for one so young, if you ask me."

Turo nodded. "Is there a computer in the house? Did Dahlia have a MySpace account?"

"We do have a laptop computer," Beth pointed down a hallway near the stairs, "but I never saw Dahlia use it. I don't believe I ever shared the password with her. She never asked for it."

Sully was now making a list on his own notepad. "We'll need to take the computer for forensic analysis. Did she have access to your phone?"

"No, I didn't share my phone with her."

"Did Dahlia have any conflicts with anyone? Anyone she'd consider an enemy?"

"No!" Bebee's voice raised to a higher pitch as she choked back another sob. "Everyone loved her. They watched how she took care of me and told me all the time how lucky I was to have a sister like her."

Turo paused, careful not to speak over Bebee's mild outburst. "You were lucky to have each other. She seemed like a great sister." When he felt sure she was finished, he went on. "Did Dahlia keep a journal?"

"She did," Beth stood from her chair and moved into what Turo could see was the dining room. He watched as she opened a drawer in the china hutch and removed a spiral notebook.

Holding the notebook out to Turo, Beth said, "This is the journal she kept at the rehab facility. She was always afraid someone would steal it. Theft was a problem in the facility from time to time, and Dahlia was terrified someone would learn about what Rol had been doing to her. She kept it tucked into the front of her jeans so no one could find it. That's why it's so bent up. When she was at the facility, she wrote in it a lot and also did some of her art in it. It's special to us. I assume you'll have to take it, but we'd sure love to get it back."

"Have you read it?" Turo asked.

"She showed me large portions of it when I visited her in the rehab center. It was hard for her to say much out loud, but it seemed easier for her when I could read her thoughts and memories. There are some disturbing details in that journal. What we'd really like to look back on are the entries about her growth and the gratitude she was beginning to develop. You'll see her artwork at first was dark, kind of foreboding, then transitioned over time to sketches with color that were bright and beautiful."

"I'm sure it means a lot." Turo accepted the notebook and set it beside him on the sofa. "You'll get this back, but it may be a long time before we can make that happen."

Sully asked, "Can you give me the name and contact information of her counselor?"

David rose to retrieve a business card from the desk, then handed it to Turo. "This should have everything you need."

"Is there anything else you think would be helpful to us?"

Beth answered, "She wrote some letters to Bebee. Will you please go get those, Bebee? It's important that the detectives have everything we can share."

Turo noticed Bebee's pained expression as she left the room, understanding how hard it would be to hand over such a treasured piece of her sister.

Her chin quivered as she handed them over. "Thank you, Bebee," Turo stood to collect the small stack of folded papers held together by a paperclip. Suddenly, Bebee rushed toward him, buried her face in his chest, and wrapped her arms around him. As he loosely returned her embrace, she said between sobs, "I need you to find who did this. We need to know."

"We'll do everything we possibly can." A second or two ticked by before he awkwardly stepped back. "We'll need to search through Dahlia's room. Can you show us where it is?"

Beth led the way to the second floor and said, "Second door on the right."

Turo and Sully meticulously searched her bedroom, looking underneath dresser drawers, between the mattress and box spring, under and around the table and small chair, and every nook and cranny they discovered. Aside from the small assortment of clothes in the closet, there was nothing to suggest a teenage girl lived in the room at all.

The two detectives exchanged glances, knowing they weren't uncovering many details that would help the investigation. They bagged and labeled the items they needed as evidence and thanked the family for their time, again mentioning how sorry they were for their loss. Then they walked to the car in silence.

Before strapping on his seatbelt, Turo took the business card for Dr. Lynn Nguyen, Dahlia's counselor, and pushed the numbers into his phone. He was surprised when she answered the phone herself.

"Dr. Nguyen, I'm Detective Arturo Torres from Adams County, Colorado. I'm handling an investigation involving Dahlia Archer, and I believe you saw her as a patient. I'm in Grand Junction now with my partner. We'd like to come by in a few minutes to ask some questions."

"I do not have another patient appointment for two hours. I am available to see you now. Is Dahlia all right?" the doctor asked.

"I'm sorry to tell you this, but Dahlia is no longer with us. She was killed." After several seconds of silence ticked by, he said, "We'll be there soon, Dr. Nguyen."

With a determined nod, Sully urged his partner forward. "Time to move," he said, his voice tinged with the weariness of a detective who had seen too much.

CHAPTER 22

TURO, 2005

"Dr. Nguyen," Turo offered his hand as he entered her office, and she responded with a professional handshake. Her dark hair was collected into a neat bun atop her head, exposing the redness in her eyes and the flush of her cheeks. She'd been crying. "Thank you for taking the time to see us. I'm Detective Torres; this is my partner, Detective Sullivan."

"Whatever I can do to help, detectives." Her tone was formal, and she used careful enunciation of each syllable. She situated herself behind her desk, sliding into the high-backed swivel chair. "I've never lost a patient like this before. Dahlia had so much potential. I genuinely believed she could make a new life for herself."

The office, nestled amidst the quaint streets of a sleepy college town, spoke volumes about Dr. Nguyen's success. Its meticulous organization could make even the most troubled soul feel a sense of order in the bedlam of their lives. It was a place where secrets were laid bare, emotions untangled, and often where healing began.

In his penchant for unraveling the most intricate mysteries, Turo perched on the edge of his chair. To his right, Sullivan leaned forward in a seat identical to his own. Dr. Nguyen sat behind her desk, a symbol of her authority and professionalism. Her eyes were shrouded in the sorrow of the inexplicable loss of a young patient.

"I know this is difficult for you," Turo began, "and we're sorry for your loss. We're also aware of your doctor-patient privilege." It was a delicate dance, this exchange of words between the law and gentleness, and Turo approached it with the finesse of a seasoned investigator.

Dr. Nguyen, her posture the embodiment of poise, met his gaze with steadfast resolve. She understood the gravity of the situation and the need for cooperation. "I will let you know if there is information I cannot share," she replied, revealing her unwavering commitment to her patients.

"As you can probably assume," Turo continued, his voice gentle yet resolute, "we're trying to catch Dahlia's killer." The air seemed to thicken as the weight of those words settled between them. He watched as her shoulders shuddered at the mention of her patient's name, the memory of loss casting a shadow over the room. "Any information you can provide will be helpful."

With practiced ease, Turo retrieved his notebook and pen, placing them on the desk like long, trusted tools. Then, he positioned the audio recorder.

"Do we have your consent to record this conversation?" Detective Torres asked.

"Yes, of course."

He pressed the record button, then began. "This is Detective Arturo Torres and Detective Warren Sullivan interviewing Dr. Lynn Nguyen on June 12, 2005, at—" he glanced at his watch, "4:25 pm." Turo paused to gather his thoughts. "First, tell us how you know Dahlia Archer."

With that, they began the back-and-forth of a murder investigation.

"I see a number of patients as they work through recovery from substance abuse. I met Dahlia in August of last year at the Gunnison River Rehabilitation and Treatment Center. I served as her therapist during her inpatient treatment. After she was released from the facility, I began seeing her here in my office for outpatient therapy."

"What was the nature of Dahlia's addiction?"

"She was addicted to narcotics, specifically prescription painkillers."

"To your knowledge, did she have legitimate prescriptions for the medications she took?"

"No," the doctor answered. "They were illicitly obtained."

"When you met with Dahlia, I assume you talked about her life circumstances in addition to her drug use. Is that right?"

"Yes, we work on treating the whole person and delve into many levels of personal matters."

"Did Dahlia talk to you about abusive situations she faced?"

"Yes, from her Uncle Rol, specifically. During her inpatient treatment, we talked at length about her childhood and the ongoing trauma she experienced under his care. She told me that she and her aunt, Beth Lane, had reported all of the details to law enforcement officials. I assume you have that information."

"We do." Sully nodded. "Did Dahlia ever indicate that she felt afraid of Rolyn Archer?"

"Yes, she did. She told me that she was afraid he would kill her if he found out she told someone about the 'work' they did together." Dr. Nguyen lifted her fingers to make air quotes, folded her hands on the desk, and shook her head in disbelief. "The prostitution."

"To your knowledge, did Rol abuse her physically?"

"Yes, she told me of many instances where he hit her, pulled her hair, and used force against her."

"Did she ever mention that he threatened her with a weapon of any sort?"

"I recall a time when she said he held a knife to her throat."

Sully shifted uncomfortably in a crisp leather chair across from Dr. Nguyen's polished mahogany desk. A question had been gnawing at him, festering like an infected splinter. He was a detective known for keeping his cool and maintaining a stoic facade even when the stakes were high. But this was different, personal.

"Aside from his threats, did she feel Rolyn was capable—I mean, was he capable of killing?" Sullivan's voice wavered slightly, a crack in his otherwise steady demeanor. The words hung in the air as if daring the doctor to confirm his darkest suspicions.

Dr. Nguyen, a seasoned psychologist with eyes that had peered into the depths of human despair, studied Detective Sullivan's face.

She paused and appeared to read the lines etched by sleepless nights and the weight of his badge. She seemed to know the detective was on the precipice of something he couldn't walk away from.

"Her level of fear," she began carefully, her voice now the calming balm in the tense room, "led me to believe she felt he was capable."

He nodded with reluctant acceptance, struggling to contain the swell of anger and frustration that welled up in him.

"Did she disclose if Rolyn had any partners or anyone who worked closely with him? Anyone he trusted?"

"She did not say."

"What other acquaintances did she talk about in your sessions?"

"She shared about a few of her fellow patients at the rehabilitation center." Dr. Nguyen absentmindedly reached for a stray paper clip on her desk and twisted it between her fingers. "I cannot share those details with you, but I will say she did not seem afraid or cautious toward any of them. She did not lead me to believe anyone had threatened her there or that she had disagreements with any of the other patients."

"Did Dahlia indicate she confided in her fellow patients? About her addiction? Or the abuse she endured?"

"I am unaware of such confidences. Mentions of fellow patients were casual and superficial. She never referred to anyone as a friend." Dr. Nguyen took a sip of water and continued. "Dahlia doted over her sister, Bebee. In fact, Bebee is the reason Dahlia persevered through so much abuse from Rol. She was highly motivated to protect her younger sister from him."

"As far as you know, did she successfully protect her sister?" Turo asked.

"That was not discussed. But because Bebee is here in Grand Junction, I have always assumed she was spared Rol's abuse. That is only an assumption."

"Are you aware that Dahlia was kidnapped after leaving your office last Wednesday?"

"Yes. I knew she had gone missing," she admitted, her voice laden with sadness. "The police came and talked to me." Her pained expression hinted that the news of the kidnapping had struck her like a personal blow.

"We haven't located Dahlia's personal belongings from the day of the kidnapping," Sully stated. "Do you know if she normally carried a purse or had a cell phone?"

Dr. Nguyen closed her eyes as she tried to remember the details. "She began carrying a purse to our outpatient sessions. It was light brown, about 10 inches wide, with a southwestern tapestry-style fabric on the front flap. She had it with her for every appointment. As for a cell phone, she said she didn't have one."

Sully nodded as Dr. Nguyen's statement aligned with Beth's. "Did she say why she didn't have a phone?"

"It was a financial decision. Money was tight. She received money from Rol for her prostitution but wanted to provide as much as she could for Bebee. A cell phone felt frivolous to her."

Turo wrote on his notepad. He pondered briefly, then asked, "Did she ever mention any close friends? Any confidants?"

"Dahlia is—was—" Dr. Nguyen corrected herself, "a very private person. Next to her sister, Bebee, I don't know of any close friends or anyone she genuinely shared herself with. Her life was guarded. She frequently said no one could understand what she'd experienced, so she chose to keep to herself."

Turo nodded and jotted a few words in his notepad. "Did she talk with you about her drug use?"

"Naturally. That was the primary reason she was in my care." Dr. Nguyen's eyes glistened, and her lips quivered. "She worked so hard to confront her condition head-on. Her bravery was inspiring. Her death is a tremendous shame."

"We're hoping she talked to you about where she obtained the drugs."

She nodded and glanced above Turo's head as she collected her thoughts. "From Rol. And from her mother's supply of hospice medications. She ensured I knew she did not deny her mother what she needed. She took what was left of the drug supply only after her passing. It was important to her that I understood that."

"That makes sense. From what I've learned about Dahlia, she took great care of those she loved." He tapped his pen on his notepad, considering other angles.

"Did you notice any changes in her demeanor or mindset in the last few weeks?"

The doctor stared out the window with a faraway gaze as she answered. "She was happier, more hopeful. We'd begun to discuss future plans, which can be a good indication of recovery. Dahlia seemed more comfortable, as if she knew our sessions together were helpful. It seemed they'd become a resource for her. A way to progress and become healthier."

The doctor's words painted a picture of Dahlia's emotional journey, and Turo found himself silently piecing together the fragments of the young woman's life. "What future plans did she share with you?"

"She talked about finishing high school or getting a G.E.D." She turned to face him. "And since her aunt works at the university, she felt higher education might be a possibility. In our last session, we talked about a job at the front desk that's available here in our practice. Dahlia was hopeful she might compete for the position."

"Do you believe Dahlia could have left with Rol voluntarily?" Turo saw Sully shift in his seat from the corner of his eye. It wasn't a comfortable question, and he trusted his partner knew the question had to be asked.

"No. I do not believe that at all. She genuinely seemed repulsed by Rol and all he represented. I would be shocked to learn that she had coordinated an escape with him."

Sully asked, "Based on your professional assessment, do you believe her death might be related to her mental health or circumstances discussed in therapy?"

"Suicide is nearly always a concern with patients recovering from addiction. The physical symptoms are quite difficult to endure, and life situations that led to drug use are often disturbing, as they were with Dahlia. But she was beginning a new life here in Grand Junction. Of all my patients, I was less concerned about Dahlia harming herself than anyone else. Are you hinting she may have committed suicide?"

"It does not appear so, but the question bears asking," Turo answered. "Is there any other information or insights from your sessions that you believe could be relevant to the investigation?"

"No, I do not believe so."

"Is there anyone else you feel we should talk to?"

"I assume you have already talked with her family." Dr. Nguyen reached for a tissue and dabbed her eyes. "There is no one else I can recommend."

Turo wrote a few notes on his pad and then stood to leave. "Thank you, Dr. Nguyen. I appreciate your careful attention to our questions. If anything else comes to mind, please give me a call. No details are too small or insignificant." Turo handed her his business card. "Call me any time, day or night."

"Thank you for the work you do. Both of you. I pray you can find whoever did this."

Turo followed Sully out of the office and into the elevator. "Let's walk a bit," he said. "I want to see the route Dahlia followed after leaving here."

CHAPTER 23

TURO, 2005

It was the end of the business day, and Main Street was quiet. Merchant shops were almost empty. As he peered through the windows, Turo saw staff members sweeping up and reorganizing inventory. A new flood of visitors for the dinner rush would soon fill the local pubs and restaurants.

As he and Sully stepped onto 7th Street, not far from the medical building, they saw the shop where Dahlia stopped for coffee. Turo motioned with his head that he'd like to stop in. They found a middle-aged woman behind the counter, alone in the small cafe. Her salt and pepper hair, disheveled from a long work day, enhanced her gentle brown eyes. Her name, 'Dani,' was embroidered in bright yellow letters onto her dark blue apron.

They both recognized Danielle's name from the Grand Junction Police Department's case reports. She was the shop owner and the one who reported seeing the man in the red El Camino.

"Hi, Dani. I'm Detective Torres from the Denver area. I believe you talked to my colleague here, Detective Sullivan, about Dahlia Archer?"

"The girl who was kidnapped out front," she nodded. "Yes. Nice to meet you in person," she said to Sully while wiping her hands on her apron. "What can I do for you?"

"We'd like to hear firsthand what you saw that day. Do you have a few minutes to talk?" Sullivan asked.

"I do. In fact, I'd love to get off my feet for a few minutes. Pick a table, and I'll meet you there. Can I get either of you a coffee? Or water?"

"Coffee," they said in unison. Sully shared the last detail, "Black for both of us, please."

Dani quickly gathered two coffees and a bottle of spring water for herself. Turo let her get situated, then asked, "Did the girl get into his car of her own will?"

"Heavens, no! I would have never thought it was a kidnapping if that were the case. He nearly shoved her into the passenger seat. She obviously didn't want to get in. I called 9-1-1, but he sped away. The police said they never found him."

"And the guy who shoved her into the car?" Turo asked. "Was he a short, stocky guy with a bald head?" He deliberately provided an inaccurate description to test Dani's memory and consistency.

"No," Dani shook her head, the confusion evident on her face. "That's not how I remember it. He was on the taller side with a long, strawberry-blonde beard and a ponytail. He looked pretty question-able to me. Like a biker, maybe, but not dressed like one. He had on a dark t-shirt and jeans."

Dani's recollections were spot-on with the details she'd original-ly reported and described Rolyn to a tee. As he sat across from her, listening to her account, Turo admired her clarity and attention to de-tail. These were qualities that could make her an exceptional asset if and when this case ever made its way into a courtroom.

"Did you notice if Dahlia was carrying anything when he ap-proached her?"

"She'd just been here in the shop. She'd ordered an iced vanilla latte, so she was carrying that, and her purse hung from her shoulder. I believe it was light brown. I really didn't study it, though."

"Did both of those items make it into the car with her?"

"The latte didn't. She dropped it, and it spilled all over the side-walk. But I'm sure her purse was with her. I didn't see it anywhere when I ran out to the street."

"How was she acting when she came in for the coffee?"

"She was pleasant, smiling a little. She just seemed like a nice girl having a good day."

"So you didn't notice any nervousness or anxiety?"

"No, not at all. She seemed relaxed. Unhurried. I remember wishing all my customers would be as calm and nice as she was. I messed up her order and gave her a hot latte at first. She smiled and reminded me she'd ordered it iced. Some of my customers get pretty crabby when I make a mistake like that. This girl was happy to wait for me to remake her drink as if she didn't have a care in the world."

"Thanks so much, Dani. We appreciate your help." Turo had been eyeing the pastry display to the right of the cash register. "Can I have one of your chocolate croissants and a bottle of water to go, please?"

He stood from the table and reached for his wallet. "Anything for you, Sully? I'm buying."

"That sounds great. I'll have the same, please."

"Coming right up!" Dani smiled. "So I'm guessing you haven't found the girl yet?"

"The case is still developing. Thanks again for everything. You've been a big help." Turo smiled slightly, accepted the croissants and water bottles, and stepped out to the sidewalk before he was pressed for more details.

Ten minutes later, they were back on I-70 eastbound, headed for Denver.

Turo's frustration was palpable as he sat in the driver's seat of his unmarked police car. He clenched his jaw, feeling as though they were right back where they started, and it was a maddeningly familiar place.

He banged his hand on the steering wheel, a futile outlet for his mounting exasperation. The case had taken so many twists and turns, yet the core remained baffling, like a puzzle missing its most crucial piece. Dahlia Archer, a young woman with few friends and no known enemies, seemed to have been plucked from the world without rhyme or reason.

His partner shared his frustration but remained ever-pragmatic. "We can't rule out the possibility that Rol hired someone to kill her," he offered, his voice steady.

"Yeah. I'm starting to think that's our likely scenario."

"What a scumbag. Pimping out his niece and supplying her with drugs. Who does that?!" Sully's voice was animated, his pitch elevated.

"This is why we do what we do, man. Sometimes, I wonder, when I'm an old, fat, retired detective, will I be able to turn off all the images I've stored in my head all these years? Of course, they're countered by the convictions we've won, but from where I sit, darkness seems to be ahead in this game."

"Remember what they say. In a pitch-black room, the light of a single match can illuminate the whole area. We're making a difference, Turo. I tell myself that every day. Some days, I even believe it."

"Today isn't one of those days," Turo said. "I feel like we're getting nowhere. Meeting with the family is always hard for me. I could easily lose objectivity and become a bull in a china shop." He tapped his thumbnail against his teeth. "I'm glad you came over here with me. Thanks a lot for that, by the way."

"This is the worst possible way to partner, but I think it will take both of us to solve this one."

"Pull out your notebook, will you? Let's talk through some next steps."

CHAPTER 24

ABBY, 2023

Abby and Michelle spent Thursday morning pulling boxes of reports and evidence from various detective offices. Each case had gone cold. Leads had been exhausted. There were no new details coming in. Investigations had stalled.

For these detectives, clutching their case files held a deeper meaning—a show of unwavering respect for the victims and their grieving families. Each served as a tangible symbol, a promise to never give up, even when progress seemed mired in mud.

The rub Abby knew from her earlier detective assignments was that unsolved cases never truly leave a detective's thoughts. It isn't necessary to keep a reminder that a family still needs justice. *It's almost impossible to forget.*

As they carried data away from assigned detectives, Abby noticed the look of gratitude that crossed each face. It fueled Abby's resolve to give herself fully to this assignment. She felt honored to step in and offer a new source of strength that could bring an old case to fruition.

Captain Turo Torres' office was the last they entered. In the back corner of his office, Abby saw two white cardboard banker's boxes with *Dahlia Archer, 2005* penned on the front. She'd seen the boxes numerous times before, but as they captured her attention now, she felt the blood drain from her face. Her palms felt clammy, and her feet were heavy as clay.

Turo rose to his feet. "Can I move those for you?" he asked.

"I've got it, but thanks," Abby said, unsure whether she could will her feet to step closer to the recorded facts of her sister's murder.

"You know, there's almost nothing in here you haven't seen or heard before."

Abby appreciated Turo's kind attempt at encouragement. She made eye contact as a show of thanks but left his office without responding, reminding herself to breathe as she walked. The lightheadedness was replaced by a wave of nausea, and she wondered if she should step outside for some fresh air. Instead, she set the boxes on the floor of her office and took several gulps from the Stanley cup positioned at her desk, grateful this morning's ice had survived the day. The cold, refreshing water helped refocus her thoughts.

Michelle stood from her desk and leaned on the door jam to Abby's makeshift office. "You okay?" she asked.

"Sure. Of course. Why wouldn't I be?" Abby attempted a lighthearted laugh that fell flat. "The secrets of my sister's killer are nested somewhere in those boxes." Her words were filled with personal angst and emotion that she preferred to keep out of the workplace. She knew this assignment would be difficult but didn't expect boxes of cold data to nearly knock her to her knees.

Michelle extended a warm smile. Her dark hair was pulled into a side bun. She wore smart capri slacks beneath an olive green blazer. While new to the agency, she was a veteran of law enforcement operations in other agencies and understood the atypical mindsets.

In the few weeks they'd worked together, Abby already considered her a trusted ally and felt they were well on the way to developing a friendship. She'd openly shared her concerns about working on Dahlia's case, knowing there was no way such a blatant elephant in the room could stay hidden. Michelle took the news in stride and promised to help Abby face the challenge any way she could.

Michelle's next comment proved she meant it. She pulled the focus from Abby's tension and put it back on the task at hand. "Let's get a recap on each case, then decide where to start."

"Good plan," Abby tried to shake off her anxiety and was thankful for teamwork. She'd asked for Detective Wayne Finch to be assigned to their small unit. He was serving as an advisory witness and would be in court for another week before he could report to her in cold cases. Until then, she and Michelle could gather facts and prioritize their focus.

After they'd worked for several hours, Abby stood to stretch, scanned the collection of papers spread about, and glanced at her watch. "Let's call it a day and finish reviewing the last two cases next week."

"Speaking of next week, Lieutenant MacDonald wants me to analyze data from a few convenience store thefts they think are connected. It may take a couple of days."

"Good to know. I'll move through the last two files on my own." She was inwardly grateful to have a few days to sift through Dahlia's case alone.

If she could muster the courage, she would crack Dahlia's files open first thing Monday morning. For a fleeting moment, Abby considered taking the case files home with her but decided against it. She knew she'd push her PT workouts aside if the boxes were within reach. It was best to strengthen her body and try to give her mind the break it needed.

On the drive home, she let herself think through the details she knew about Dahlia's case. Deep down, she still believed her Uncle Rol was responsible. When Captain Torres had been a detective all those years ago, he'd meticulously investigated the case and assured her and Auntie Beth that Rol couldn't have pulled the trigger. His alibi was airtight since he was in the county jail at the time of the shooting. Still, anger toward him built up inside of her as she wondered about the myriad of ways he could have orchestrated her death.

Dahlia had told the family all about the abuse Rol was inflicting on her. It didn't take a rocket scientist to see that Rol had an unquestioned motive to get her out of the picture. Her sister's testimony would have put him away for a long time. Yet even without it, he was locked in prison for the crimes he'd admitted to Detective Torres.

Abby slept late on Saturday morning. It was cool and cloudy, perfect for spending some extra time in bed. She'd moved back to her primary bedroom upstairs a few weeks ago and was hitting new strides in refreshing sleep. Letting herself linger was a rare treat, and she savored the slow, relaxed moments.

Soon, her thoughts turned to coffee. Out of habit, she skipped down the stairs and into the kitchen toward the new Nespresso machine that Auntie Beth had sent for her birthday. It was an ideal gift for her single lifestyle and gave her a nearly perfect cup of coffee.

Before inserting the espresso pod, she realized she'd bounded down the stairs without any struggle with her knee. Her healing journey had been slow, but she was gaining strength and stamina. "Thank you, Lord," she said aloud and opened the refrigerator to reach for the small container of half and half.

She planned a morning workout and considered a short run, unsure if she should push the limits of her knee quite that far. Her journey down the stairs bolstered her confidence, and she decided to go for it. A half a bagel and a cup of coffee later, her shoes were laced. She pressed the lock button on her front door keypad and stepped off her front porch.

She loved running, the way the air felt on her face, and the meditative cadence of her breath syncing with her footfalls. It was easy to tune out her environment, but she knew better. *Safety first,* she could almost hear Auntie Beth say, and she made sure to stay aware of her surroundings.

As she prepared to step into the crosswalk, a blue Chevrolet truck pulled up beside her. The driver rolled the passenger window down and said, "Abby? I thought that was you!"

Abby looked up to see Jacob Jennings, the Adams County Commissioner who had taken such an interest in the crime analyst position.

"Commissioner Jennings! You startled me, but it's great to see you!"

"I should have guessed you were a runner with the great shape you're in," his smile was pleasant. "And please, call me Jacob."

Abby nodded. "Jacob, it is. This is my first time out in a long while. I decided to test my knee today to see what it's made of."

"Do you live nearby?"

Abby pointed to her house. "Just a few doors from here."

"I won't keep you," he said. "Hope you have a great outing. Maybe I'll see you at work in the next week or two. I hear you're the chosen one to start our county's cold case unit. I'd love to hear how it's going."

"Stop in any time, sir," Abby said. "And have a great Saturday!"

He motioned for her to cross in front of his truck, and she noticed he didn't drive on till she was well out of view. The attention felt nice, and Abby realized her social tank was a bit depleted. *It may be time to get together with a few friends,* she thought to herself.

Abby smiled, noticing that her knee felt strong, but her lungs were another story. It had been months since she'd done cardio of any sort, and she needed to build up her breath again. She knew it would come in time. For now, she was glad this would be a short jog.

By the time she circled back to her front door, her thoughts were filled with Rol and a mental replay of Dahlia's long-ago kidnapping.

I don't want to think about Rol this weekend, she reminded herself. She punched her combination into the front door keypad, stepped inside the house, and then locked the door behind her. Her nervous energy hinted she may need some time out of the house. Since she wasn't all that sweaty, she grabbed her keys and headed to the grocery store. Restocking her pantry was a situation she could easily control.

"Pastor Luke! How nice to hear from you!" Abby picked up her phone while putting a salad together for dinner.

"Abby, you've been on my mind today, and I finally decided to call. I've been meaning to check in. How are things going?"

Over the years of learning techniques for keeping her psyche as strong as her body, Abby had long ago let go of pretense. If someone asked how she was, she answered honestly. "Great, physically. I went for a run today, which felt amazing. But emotionally, I'm afraid things are a bit more complicated."

She spent a few minutes bringing her pastor up to speed with her new work assignment. He listened intently before responding. "God is good, Abby. This is why He's brought you to mind. I can see the struggle you're up against. Quite honestly, I'm surprised you've been given this assignment."

"I am, too. But to be fair, I did have a choice. My bosses gave me time to consider it all and talk to my support people before I made a decision. They even gave me a couple of paid days off to think it through. All that to say, *I* made the ultimate decision, not them. I prayed about it a ton and stepped into the assignment with my eyes wide open. But that sure doesn't make it easy!"

"No, I imagine it wouldn't. Do you mind if I ask you a few questions?"

"You have all the all-access pass, Pastor." Abby smiled. "If I can't be an open book with you, then who would it be?"

Pastor Luke's warm laughter was contagious. "Well, not everyone feels that way toward their pastor. I'm glad you do."

"Give me a second, though. I'm going to switch to my air pods." Abby despised holding the flat phone to her face for more than a few seconds and quickly connected the buds she placed in her ears. "Okay, I'm ready. I'd love to hear your thoughts."

"I was just wondering what you hope to gain through this assignment."

Abby chopped and sliced as they talked. "Well, obviously, there are more cold cases than just Dahlia's. But equally as obvious is that hers is the one I'm pressuring myself to solve. It feels crazy that I haven't brought myself to glance at her case file yet. I nearly go numb when I think of looking at the details."

"I'm well aware of the way you pursue perfection in everything you do. I mean that kindly, of course, and I'm not trying to criticize. Here's my real question—is it possible you agreed to investigate your sister's murder because you feel that you owe her something?"

Abby paused. "That's certainly something to think about." She moved from the kitchen into the living room and sat rigidly on the edge of an armchair. "There's no question I feel that I owe her. You and I have talked before about the guilt I feel. Dahlia allowed our uncle to abuse her so she could protect me from the same fate. *Of course* I owe her. She gave me my life at the cost of her own."

"I want to caution you against that kind of thinking, Abby. You've been given an immense opportunity, and it goes well beyond solving your sister's crime."

"Do tell." Abby feared her comment may have sounded sarcastic, but Pastor Luke didn't seem to take offense.

"Keep in mind that God is the ultimate source of justice. Whether or not you discover your sister's killer, He knows exactly who that person is. He will administer eternal justice. So, I hope you'll consider that this assignment could have little to do with solving the crime. As counter-intuitive as that sounds, perhaps it's as much about finding your own freedom as it is about putting the killer in prison."

"That brings a lot of perspective. Maybe there *is* more to accomplish than putting a killer behind bars."

"I sense that's what's happening. God's plan is always bigger than what we can perceive. I believe keeping His view in mind will prevent you from getting tangled in the weeds of the case while staying open to your own healing."

"I wasn't looking at it like that, Pastor. But you've given me a lot to think about. Thanks for sharing your wisdom with such a gentle delivery!"

"I'll be praying for you, Abby. Please reach out if you ever need to talk. I'm here for you."

"I know you are, and I thank you for that. Give Julie my best. I'll see you at church tomorrow."

CHAPTER 25

ABBY, 2023

***H**ope you're having a nice weekend. Come see me in my office as soon as you get in tomorrow.* Captain Turo's text lit up her phone during church on Sunday.

Her confirmed reply did little to quell her curiosity. Turo's tone seemed frustrated, but she knew better than to interpret his mood through a text message. It wasn't his favorite form of communication, so he was direct and refused to use emojis. To gauge how he felt, a playful smile or thumbs up from him would be helpful once in a while.

Monday morning, while carrying her belongings into her office, she wondered what he'd want to discuss. She'd reviewed most of the unsolved cases but hadn't begun dissecting them in an investigative role. He couldn't be expecting any illuminating updates at this point.

Turo looked up from his computer screen when she gently knocked on the doorframe of his office. "Morning, Abby. Come have a seat." His lips curved into a smile. "Kerri said you were probably up all night worrying about why I wanted to talk with you. She said my texts always sound grouchy, and I should learn to use emojis from time to time."

"She's not wrong." Abby returned her boss's smile, amazed at how she and Kerri were so like-minded. "But I've learned to stop thinking I can discern your mood when you send a short text like that."

"Good for you. Some of our commanders are still learning that."

"Well, I've known you for a while. And Kerri has helped me stop taking you quite so seriously."

"Speaking of Kerri, she asked me to make sure we schedule dinner at our house sometime soon."

"I'd love that. Why don't you have her text me a few dates? It may be easier than going through you," Abby teased.

"Not necessarily easier, but certainly faster." Turo swallowed the last of the coffee in his mug, then stood. "I'm going to get a refill before we talk. Can I bring you some?"

"No, I'm okay, thanks." Abby raised her Stanley to indicate she'd switched to water already this morning.

"Those crazy cups. They're oversized and clumsy, and I can't for the life of me understand why you'd want to lug that thing around."

"They keep a cold drink cold, and I don't have to keep filling it. And it's better for the environment than plastic bottles." She hugged the cup and held it to her chest. "They make tiny purses to attach to them, you know. Be glad I haven't gone that far."

"I didn't know that, and frankly, I didn't want to."

Turo was in an amicable mood, which comforted Abby. She hated the thought of disappointing him. He was a friend, mentor, and also her boss. At times, the relational lines could blur, especially because she also considered his wife, Kerri, a close friend.

As she waited for him to return to his office, Abby coated her lips with a layer of lip balm and pressed them together. She could almost hear her lips thanking her for the moisture.

"I was here over the weekend," Turo began as he stepped back into his office and closed the door behind him. "I noticed Dahlia's boxes are still exactly where you set them."

Abby nodded. "I haven't cracked them open yet."

"I know. And I can't blame you. I've been thinking long and hard about how difficult this must be for you." Turo walked around his desk and settled into his chair. "Abby, have I put you into an unconscionable position?"

Captain Torres' fatherly side was showing. "You haven't put me into any sort of position," she began. "You and Sheriff Adler offered an opportunity, and I accepted."

"I get that, but I'm seriously questioning the wisdom in offering this assignment to you."

"If it helps, I had a fairly long talk with my pastor on Saturday. He offered a new perspective that I hadn't considered."

"And that is?"

"He thinks this assignment may be about finding my own freedom, even more than about solving Dahlia's case. He suggested that I avoid pressuring myself to find answers. Instead, I should use this journey to let go of some of the guilt and the mess of other emotions I carry all the time."

"That's a unique perspective. Do you think he's right?"

"I do, actually. Do you?"

"It doesn't matter what I think," Turo leaned back in his chair.

"All right." Abby shifted in her chair and leaned toward him. "But your opinion has always mattered to me, even outside of work."

"I was going to offer similar encouragement. So, yes, I'd say I think he's right. Your emotional freedom is something I'd truly love to see."

Abby's face relaxed, and the intensity of her gaze softened. "That means a lot to me, sir."

"I'm afraid I put some pressure on you by saying I want Dahlia's case solved before I retire." Turo took a sip of coffee and shuddered as the scalding liquid touched his lips. "Ouch! That's still really hot!"

He pressed his lips together before continuing. "Of course, I want it solved, but more than anything, I wanted to give one of our best detectives—that's you, by the way—a look at the case before we file it away for good. The community needs to know we're still seeking justice. They need to know we're still working for the benefit of their safety. But some cases are unsolvable, and this may be one of them. I want to apologize if it feels like I've shrugged off the burden and put it on you."

"I don't feel that way, sir. Honestly, I feel like you and I have carried this burden together since the murder happened. Somehow, I always felt I'd have a role in solving the mystery. I guess back then, I thought it would be something I'd remember, some memory that could break the case open. It's hard to explain, but I've always felt as if finding her killer is up to me."

"You've never told me that before."

"I know. I guess it sounds kind of pretentious, especially to feel that way as a kid when you and Sully made such a great team."

Turo sighed. "Yeah, we did. I still miss that guy."

Abby tilted her head, surprised by the statement. "Where is he? He's still alive, isn't he?"

Turn chuckled. "Yes, still alive and well." He blew on his cup, then tried his coffee again. "Dahlia's case drove him out of law enforcement."

"What? I didn't know that."

"He felt like Dahlia was under his care. He was investigating Rol's abuse, and Sully is a guy who takes his role seriously. It was his job to protect her. When she was killed, it completely devastated him. Then, when we couldn't find the killer, he couldn't let it go. He almost lost his family because he was so obsessed. For him, finding a new profession was the right thing to do."

Abby felt her stomach fall as if she'd just ridden the long drop of a roller coaster. "I had no idea. Did his marriage make it?"

"Yes, they're still together, and they seem happier than ever. Sully became an insurance agent. He's my agent, actually, so I do see him sometimes. He was a heck of an investigator. I miss his partnership."

"You know what, sir? I'm not exactly looking forward to losing *your* partnership. If I leave Dahlia's case unsolved, does it mean you'll postpone retirement?" Abby smiled as she rose from her chair. "I mean, there's no pressure, right?"

"Go get to work, Sergeant. And leave the door open on your way out."

Abby stood and stepped around the large table that served as her desk. She stretched her arms above her head and heard her spine pop as she tried to relieve the tension between her shoulder blades. It had already been a long morning. With Michelle away, she'd taken several deep breaths and pulled the top of the first of Dahlia's boxes. She'd spent the last three hours reading reports and visualizing the details of the case.

It was good to get started, and she realized the anticipation had been worse than actually diving in. Captain Torres was right; there weren't many details that she hadn't heard before.

One new revelation was the physical location of Dahlia's shooting. Abby made a mental note to visit the site as soon as she could. As the lunch hour approached, she considered driving in that direction.

"Knock, knock," a male voice said from behind her. Abby turned toward the doorway and saw Commissioner Jennings dressed in a light-colored suit and tie that flattered his trim build. "You said to stop by any time," his grin widened as he saw the look of surprise on her face.

"That I did," Abby replied. "Come on in." Today was not a day she wanted to receive guests.

Abby mustered a smile that she hoped disguised her twinge of frustration. She'd been deep in thought, and her heart carried the heaviness of revisiting an excruciating event. Jacob was approaching an invisible boundary in her personal space; at the very least, it was emotionally personal. She felt torn, happy to see him but acutely aware of her mental space. She motioned for him to come in and reminded herself she was more on edge than normal.

Jacob carefully stepped into her office, watching where his feet landed to avoid stepping on a pile of data. "So," he glanced around the room with wide eyes. "This is where the magic happens? Looks a little chaotic in here."

"If I could wave a sparkly wand and understand all the details of these cases, it would be magical," she laughed. "But in reality, it's more tedious than anything."

"Then maybe you need a break," Jacob suggested. "Can I buy you lunch and hear about all you're doing? Maybe you could use a sympathetic ear."

Abby glanced at her watch, trying to think of a polite way to decline, but Jacob's expectant gaze—not to mention his role as a county leader—made it difficult. Reluctantly, she found herself agreeing. "A quick lunch would be nice, I suppose."

"Your chariot awaits, milady," Jacob said with a dramatic bow. "Follow me."

Abby's mind drifted to her Uncle Rol, considering how hard Dahlia worked to keep her away from him as a child. Still, there were pleasant moments buried in her memories. She recalled how Uncle Rol used to call her 'milady' and refer to his shiny red car as her chariot.

She studied Jacob as they walked and noticed his hair was graying around the temples. Wrinkles were forming at the corners of his eyes. She guessed he was twenty years her senior. There was no doubt she found him attractive. Still, there was something unconventional about him that she couldn't quite put her finger on. It might be nice to spend some time learning what drives him.

After staring at files all morning, the bright sun overpowered Abby's eyes. She held her hand above her eyebrows to shield its rays as she glanced around the parking lot for the blue truck she had seen him drive over the weekend. As they approached the Chevy pickup, he opened the door for her, and she climbed inside.

"Are you familiar with Mickey's Steakhouse?" he asked while getting into the driver's seat. "It's not far from here."

"I've heard of it but have never been there. Should we choose something a little quicker? My lunch breaks aren't long."

"They treat me like a king there; they'll get us in and out in no time!"

It was a short drive along 70th Avenue, and when they arrived, he hurried to her side of the truck to help her with the long step to the ground. "I don't want you jumping down on that knee," he said, then led her inside the cafe-style restaurant where the host referred to him by name.

Abby suddenly felt uneasy, sensing a personal motive behind his lunch invitation. She reminded herself he was interested in her work. Jacob was surprisingly warm and attentive, holding comfortable eye contact as he listened to Abby explain the process she and Michelle were following. He seemed genuinely interested, and once she relaxed, she found him easy to talk to.

"I'm confused about something," he said while slicing his steak. "You were a detective, then you weren't, and now you are again. I'm afraid I don't get the career path of a sheriff's deputy. Help me understand."

"The roadmap is fairly typical," she explained, "but it's not exactly the same for everyone. We move from division to division as positions or promotion opportunities become available. I started working as a deputy in the jail division, and then when I felt ready, I put in for a transfer to the patrol division. I knew that to be a detective. I needed the street experience. When an opening in the detective division presented itself, I jumped at the chance and was thrilled to get the assignment. I worked property crimes, then eventually moved to crimes against persons. Captain Torres, who is my mentor, suggested I was ready for a promotion to sergeant, so I competed and 'got my stripes,' as they say." Abby wiped her lips and returned her napkin to her lap.

"And with the promotion, you had to change divisions again?" Jacob asked.

"The only sergeant's opening was in patrol, so I left detectives and started leading a shift. I loved it, but that's where I got hurt. Because I'm on limited duty, the sheriff thought it was a perfect time to start the cold case unit he'd wanted to implement. And now, I'm temporarily back in the detective division."

"That's interesting. I never knew cops moved around in their roles like that," Jacob said. "But it makes sense." He waved his finger, signaling the waiter that he was ready for the check. When Abby reached for her purse, he said, "I've got it. Lunch is on me."

"Thank you," Abby said, surprised at how much calmer she'd become over the last hour. Lunch was over as quickly as he'd promised, and she felt silly for feeling such angst.

He drove her back to the substation and dropped her in front of the headquarters building to go back to work. There was something specific she wanted to find in Dahlia's case files.

CHAPTER 26

TURO, 2005

Turo and Sully met at the Adams County Detention Facility, primed to confront Rolyn Archer. As the middle-aged man shuffled into the interrogation chamber, he sported an orange and white striped jumpsuit paired with grimy white socks and rubber sandals. With hands cuffed and feet shackled, his eyes appeared sunken, shrouded by dark circles, and the pungent scent of body odor hung about him. His greasy, reddish blonde hair formed a ponytail that barely surpassed the length of his unkempt beard.

Turo pressed the record button on his audio recorder, setting it on the small table. The room was bathed in depressing half-light, with a pair of overhead fluorescent tubes casting a weak glow. A faint, persistent buzz accompanied their intermittent flickers.

"It's June 13, 2005. I'm Detective Arturo Torres. Detective Warren Sullivan is with me, and we're talking to Rolyn Archer at the Adams County Detention Facility." After the formalities, Turo turned to the suspect.

"We've got some new developments and need to have a conversation. I need to know first, Rolyn, if you're willing to talk to us without an attorney."

"I'm clean," Rol gave a sarcastic sneer. "Ready to talk. What do you want to know?"

Turo read him the formal Miranda Advisement that informed Rol of his constitutional rights during the interview. The inmate signed a document confirming his consent to a recorded interview without an attorney present.

Keyed up with the energy and wishing there was room to pace instead of sitting and staring at this suspect, Turo began. "I know you had an earlier conversation with Detective Sullivan, but we know you didn't share the truth about everything."

"What are you talking about? I'm no liar, man."

"Okay, good. I'm glad to hear that." Turo gave him a wide, exaggerated grin and nodded. "This conversation should go smoothly then. Tell me, Rolyn, why are you in jail today?"

"I went out on Wednesday night to get some food for my niece and got pulled over in my car. I thought I must have run a stop sign or something, but instead of getting a ticket, I was put in handcuffs and brought here."

"Where were you Wednesday night? What was going on?"

"I had just brought my niece home from Grand Junction, and she was starving. I was just a block or so away from my apartment when I was stopped."

"What's your niece's name?"

"Dahlia. Archer."

"Have you contacted Dahlia or anyone else since you've been here? To try to get bonded out of jail?"

"No, I don't know anyone with that kind of clout. And I can't call Dahlia. The phone's disconnected at my place." Rol tried to sling his elbow over the back of his chair, but the handcuffs stopped him mid-motion. He set his hands on the table.

"You said you brought your niece home from Grand Junction. Tell me about that."

"She just got out of rehab over there. She called me and said she wanted to come home, so I went to get her."

"Okay." Turo's sarcastic tone nearly reverberated off the cinder block walls. "Rol, do you know the charges you're facing?"

"They said something about child exploitation, which is ridiculous, by the way."

"Right. And what's your relationship with Dahlia?"

"I told you she's my niece." Turo stared him down, waiting for more. "She's my brother's daughter."

"How did you come to be her caregiver?"

"I'm not her caregiver. My brother is in prison, and his wife passed away. I promised to take care of his family for him." Rol's face reddened, and his eyes became intense. "I can't believe the little—" He glanced in Sullivan's direction and stopped himself before saying something derogatory about Dahlia. "I can't believe, after all I've done, she'd accuse me of something like this."

"We've got solid evidence, Rol." Sully could no longer stay silent.

"What evidence? I never touched the girl."

"It's not about *you* touching her. She said you brought a string of other men to abuse her, but that will all play itself out."

"That's a lie!"

"Is it?" Sully pressed. "Dahlia told us where it all happened. You know the place, right Rol? Next to the Dairy Queen on 84th Avenue? The one with a thin, stained mattress on the floor of the back room— which is a hotbed of DNA, by the way. Oh, and the building keypad is covered with your fingerprints."

Rol turned his head away.

"We have another problem, Rol," Sully said. "Now we've got you for kidnapping Dahlia, too."

Rol jumped to his feet, his shackles rattling. "No way," he roared, slamming the table. "Dahlia wanted to come with me. She was so excited, she nearly jumped into my car!"

"We have a witness with a different story."

Turo said, "You kidnapped her, Rol. And as we continue to investigate this case—I'm sure you're aware of this—we've also got you for murder."

He expected Rol to come unglued at the accusation, but instead, Rol leaned back in his chair and looked amused. "Now that's just stupid. I've never murdered anyone. Who would I murder?"

"You murdered Dahlia."

Rol's eyes grew wide. "But that's impossible. She's at my apartment. Have you looked for her there?"

"We don't need to look for her, Rol. We know exactly where she is. She's in the morgue."

"The last time I saw her—" he rifled through his brain to remember which day that was, "—Wednesday night, she was in my apartment. If she's dead, which is impossible, then it's because *you* all wouldn't let me get food for her."

Sully said, "Grand Junction PD says you kidnapped her on Wednesday, then Dahlia was killed in a field the very next night. Who else would have done it?"

"I don't believe a word of that," Rol's countenance began to shift as if he were seeing the gravity of the situation. He began rubbing his thumb with his fingers.

"I don't care if you believe it or not," Turo said. "Guess who's going down for her murder? The one who shoved her into his car after selling her services and feeding her narcotics like they were candy. You're the only one with a motive. She told Detective Sullivan here that she was afraid you'd kill her if she told your secrets. Well, she did tell. There's a restraining order against you, and for good reason. Because look what's happened."

"Prove it, buddy. The girl's alive and well in my apartment."

"I don't need to prove it to you, Rolyn." Turo slid a stapled packet of paper from a manila file. He laid an image of Dahlia at the crime scene on the table before him. Rol recoiled from what he saw and turned his face from the photo.

"Detective Sullivan personally identified her corpse, and you are our number one suspect. I've got a solid case to put you away for life." Turo stepped around the table to look into Rol's face. "My guess is the district attorney will pursue the death penalty."

Turo's words began to tumble out in quick succession. "You did horrible things to that young girl, and you're going to pay for it. The question is, are you going to tell us what happened, or are you just going to slip away and spend your life in prison as the cold-hearted monster you are?"

The room grew silent as Rol's tough facade wore thin. "Look," he said, trying to mask his emotions. "I've done a lot of things, and you can think what you want, but I didn't kill my niece!" The chains jingled as he slammed his fists on the table. "Are you legitimately telling me she's dead?"

"Yes, Rol. The girl you trafficked, got addicted to drugs, made money off of, kidnapped, the one you wanted to keep quiet, the one who can no longer testify against you? She's dead."

"She's my brother's daughter, man." He grew pensive. "I would never kill her."

"You would never," Turo scoffed. "If you're trying to convince me you care for her, you're talking to the wrong person. If it wasn't you, Rol, then who was it? How did Dahlia wind up dead beneath a tree? I'm sure you can see why I'm coming after you for the murder. If I can put the weapon in your hand, I'll put you away for good. If not, I'll put you in prison for a very, very long time as an accessory to murder. You kidnapped her, and if you didn't kill her, you brought her back to Denver so one of your cronies could do it."

"She wanted to come back to Denver!"

"She did not want to come to Denver. Stop *that* lie right now! We know better. You're going away for trafficking and distributing drugs to a minor. Sully won't have any problems filing those charges against you and winning the case in a court of law. You need to consider how much time you'll spend behind bars. We have Dahlia's statements to her family members, to the Grand Junction PD, to us, and the notes from her journal. I have a witness who saw you shove her in your car and can perfectly describe how terrorized Dahlia was to see you."

"What do you want from me? I didn't kill her!"

"I'm looking for the scumbags you hang out with. Who were the johns, Rol? If you're telling the truth and didn't kill her, chances are good it was one of them. It's time to name some names. Who did you sell your brother's daughter to?"

"Dahlia's a liar. I'm no pimp." Rol turned his body like a toddler throwing a tantrum and stared at the blank wall.

Turo continued to push Dahlia's mortality, seeing how it was escalating Rol's emotions. "You're telling me that your niece, who's dead, by the way, made all this up before she died?"

"Yes, she did. That's the thanks I get for providing for her and her sister."

Turo had enough of the man's lies and spoke slowly through clenched teeth. "I promise you I will do everything in my power to make sure you never see the light of day."

"What do you want me to tell you? I don't know how any of this came about!"

"I want you to start by telling me the truth! Who killed Dahlia if it wasn't you?"

"Do your job and figure it out!" Rol's neck and face were beet red, and beads of sweat formed on his hairline.

"You can't convince me you weren't involved in this. And you'll have to come up with a better defense than *I didn't do it.* When you deny everything we can already convict you on—the trafficking, the drugs, the kidnapping—and also deny the murder, why would I believe a single word you say? If you were truly innocent and cared for Dahlia or her sister, you'd do everything in your power to lead us to who did this."

"I was *here* on Thursday! It wasn't me! How could I have killed her from jail!?" He wiped the sweat off his forehead with the back of his hand.

"It looks to me like you orchestrated the entire event. It's why you went to Grand Junction to get her. She was starting a new life. She finally got away from you, Rol, and started to thrive. She was finally putting her life together, feeling like she was part of a family with a promising future. But she told your secret. So you went to get her, drive her back here, and have her killed so she can't testify against you in court."

Rol stared at the detective as if trying to make sense of all he was saying. "She's really dead?"

"Cold and in the morgue because of you. Your brother's going to love receiving that piece of news."

Rol's demeanor softened at the mention of his brother. "How did it happen?"

"You tell me, Rol. How did it happen?"

"I'm telling you, I DON'T KNOW."

Sully said, "Tell us about the johns, Rol. Dahlia told me one guy sent a driver in a fancy car to pick her up. She said the rear windows were completely darkened, and she couldn't see out from the back seat. Who was that? Would that john have the means to hire this out? To keep the girl quiet?"

Rol turned and stared blankly at the metal door. "I remember that guy," he nearly whispered. As soon as the words left his mouth, Turo watched Rol's face stiffen. His body tensed as if preparing for the impact of words he should have never let escape. He tried to back-pedal. "I-I-I haven't seen him for a long time. It probably wasn't him."

"Let us figure out those answers. What do you know about him?" Turo knew they'd turned a corner and pelted questions in quick succession.

"He had a ton of money. I never met him and never knew his name. Everything was coordinated through the driver."

Sully forced his voice to calm. "What do you know about the driver?"

"He was massive. Had to be a bodyguard. Bald head. Probably stood six-four. Wild eyes. No one I'd mess with. He talked with a foreign accent and I could barely understand the guy."

"Did he have any tattoos? Scars? Distinguishing marks that you noticed?"

"No, nothing like that, but he was always dressed in a suit with long sleeves."

"What did he drive?"

"A silver Porsche. I asked if I could take it for a spin one time. That was a no-go." Rol nearly laughed at the memory, then seemed to remember what was at stake.

"What direction did he head when he left with Dahlia?"

"He wouldn't leave until I went back in the building. I never saw which way he went."

"You better not be pulling our chain here, Rol," Turo interjected. "We'll look into this, and if it's a bogus lead, it won't be good for your case."

"I'm just answering questions. I'm not trying to accuse anyone. You already knew about this guy. I didn't snitch him out."

"You haven't proven yourself all that trustworthy so far, so we'll see where this takes us. Tell me about the other johns."

"That's all I got." Rol folded his hands and sat back in his chair, his lips pursed together.

"Come on, Rol. You know as well as I do there were others. Give me something to work with here. You're protecting people who can implicate you, but we will get to the bottom of this."

"I'm no snitch. Why don't you go do what you get paid to do."

"I'm done with this conversation," Turo said. "I can't believe a word that you say, so you go on back to your cozy jail cell, and if you want to tell me the truth, you know how to get a hold of me. I'll reach out to your brother to make sure he's in the loop. I'm sure he'll love hearing how you took care of his little girl. I'll see you in 45 days at the preliminary court hearing."

Turo gathered his files and stormed out of the cramped, cold room. He wanted to punch something. More specifically, he wanted to punch Rol but mustered enough control to leave the interview room without incident.

"That is one evil man," he said to Sully as soon as he heard the door click closed behind him. "But it's hard to fight an alibi as airtight as his. And as surprised as he was to learn of Dahlia's death, it doesn't look like he hired anyone to shoot her. Maybe he's really clean when it comes to her murder."

"It's hard to wrap my head around." Sully wasn't ready to give up on Rol's guilt. "We'll keep digging and see where the evidence takes us. And Rol all but admitted to the sexual assault charges we've got against him. He may not be the killer, but he just strengthened my case on everything else."

"With no victim to testify, it will still be a tough conviction. Getting her out of the way is motive enough for murder. I'll work on a warrant to go through Rol's phone. And I'll have the jail detectives monitor his phone calls from here. Let's see who this dirtbag is talking to. With any luck, he'll lead us to the killer."

"We're gonna need to catch a big break," Sully surmised.

But a big break never came.

CHAPTER 27

ABBY, 2023

Abby slid the first of Dahlia's boxes to the center of the table and carefully removed the lid. She was looking for something specific.

Years ago, when Dahlia had been going through rehab in Grand Junction, she'd written a series of letters to Abby. Abby hadn't seen the letters for ages since the day she'd tearfully turned them over to Detective Torres during the initial investigation. Placing those letters in his hands had felt like ripping out another piece of her heart.

For years, she'd replayed the memory of her sister's words in her mind. But over time, the memories faded until she struggled to remember what Dahlia had written.

Those very letters were somewhere in the collection of reports and evidence. Abby thumbed through the volumes of paper, searching one file folder and then another. At last, she found the four letters.

Her eyes grew moist as she stood to close her office door. Then, she privately devoured the words her sister had shared.

Dear Bebee,

I got some free time before dinner, and even though I was gonna paint, I couldn't stop thinking about you. So, here I am, writing you a letter instead.

I miss you like crazy, Bebee. I'm so sorry for letting all this happen. It's like I was swimming in the ocean, and this giant whale snuck up on me and swallowed me whole. I should have paid more attention; maybe then I could've gotten away.

How's school going? You must be close to summer break, huh? Remember those lazy days at the pool, munching on frozen Snickers and downing a whole box of Wheat Thins? Mama always said our big toes barely had to touch the water before we started hollering about being hungry. Those were simpler times, back when Daddy was still around and Mama was home more.

So, I checked out this prayer room here at the facility. A bunch of ladies were in there talking to God or something. This new girl, Caitlin, asked me to go with her. Said it helps her relax. It was a bit weird, but those ladies seemed to be into it. Not sure if I'll go back, maybe if Caitlin asks me again.

I'm really trying to get better while I'm here, Bebee. I can't wait to get out and come live with you and Auntie. I should've moved with you when you asked, but I had too much going on, too much I was trying to fix. One day, I'll explain everything, but for now, just know that every choice I made was to give you a better life.

Well, that's not entirely true. I didn't start taking drugs for you. That was me trying to help myself. Some really messed up stuff was happening, things I pray you never have to know about. Sometimes, it just got too heavy. Uncle Rol, he gave me my first pill. If he ever tries to give you anything, you run, Bebee. Run as fast and as far as you can. Don't do a single thing, he says, you hear me?

When we were little, he seemed like our hero, remember? Playing with us, bringing us toys, sneaking us candy when Mama wasn't looking. But it was all a lie. He just wanted to use us for his own sick reasons. I only did what he asked to keep him away from you.

Maybe I shouldn't be telling you all this, but I gotta stop treating you like a little girl. You've grown up so much since you've been with Auntie. You're so tall now and so beautiful. Having you ask me to sleep with you after I got out of the hospital, that meant the world to me. Best sleep I'd had in months. You made me feel loved and important again. I almost forgot how that felt.

I can't send this in the mail, something about not wanting people to know the facility's address. So, I'll give it to Auntie Beth next time she visits. Don't know if it's allowed, but I'm doing it anyway. Write back, okay?

Love you to the moon and back, sis.

Dally

—

Bebee,

You have no idea how happy I was to get your letter! Hearing about school and that book you're reading made my day. Don't even worry about giving away too much of the story. I want to know everything! I mean, I'd rather hear about what's going on with YOU, but just seeing your handwriting and knowing you were thinking of me while you wrote, it's like a warm hug. So, write about whatever you want, okay?

Remember I told you about that prayer thing? Well, I've been going back with Caitlin. She was right; it's really peaceful and relaxing. We just chill on the floor at the back of the room while the women sit in a circle and take turns talking to God. Sometimes, they read from the Bible. I don't always get the words, but it's like love just pours out of them, you know?

They're always talking about this guy Jesus, even at dinner and stuff. They say he's helping them stay clean and giving them strength to make better choices. I could definitely use some of that in my life.

I'm still feeling sick all the time, Bebee. It's crazy how hard it is to kick those stupid pills. The worst part? I still want them every single day. But I don't tell Dr. Nguyen, my counselor. She might never let me out if she knew.

You won't believe what happened to Caitlin. Someone actually broke into her stuff and read her journal! How messed up is that? I'd be so mad if someone read mine, so I keep it tucked in my pants all the time and pull my shirt over it. My clothes are baggy enough that no one even knows it's there. And at night, I sleep with it under my pillow. Privacy is like the one thing I can call my own in here.

When Caitlin found out about her journal, she cried for a day and a half. She cries so much it breaks my heart. She's miserable all the time. I want to help, but I don't really know how. I try to talk about stuff outside of this place, just to distract her for a bit, you know?

Auntie Beth gave me a picture of you, and I put it right by my bed. I fall asleep looking at it every night. You're my reason for fighting, Bebee. They say we all need a reason to get clean. Well, you're mine.

I'll write again soon. Never forget how much I love you.

Dally

~

Hey Beebs,

Something really weird happened. I went to that prayer meeting again, and as those ladies were praying, I just started bawling my eyes out. Like, out of nowhere. I wasn't even sad or anything before I went in, but then it just hit me. It was full-on "ugly cry" mode. It felt like all this pain was just pouring out of me, and I couldn't stop it.

It went on for a while, and I guess I was pretty loud about it because one of the ladies asked me to join their prayer circle. Talk about being put on the spot! I didn't want to be rude, so I walked over, feeling all awkward. Then they all stood up and put their hands on me. It wasn't creepy or any-thing, just unexpected, you know?

They started praying for something called redemption. Auntie Beth mentioned it to me once, but I couldn't remember what it meant. So, I looked it up in the dictionary. It said, "the action of saving or being saved from sin, error, or evil." Crazy, right? I mean, there's nothing I want more than to be saved from all the evil I've seen, but how could they know that? They don't know anything about me.

Then, one of them said that Jesus is my Redeemer. He's the one who can save me. She asked if I wanted that from Him. I mean, who wouldn't? So, I said yes. Then she asked me to pray, which was super embarrassing, but she told me what to say, so I just repeated it. Something about asking Jesus into my heart and forgiving me.

I actually felt pretty good after. But it didn't last long. I still want the drugs just as much as ever. One of the ladies told me to keep talking to Jesus about it. But since that day with them, it just feels like I'm talking to the air. They said I'll be able to "feel" him if I keep praying. I would love to "feel him," but I don't. I just feel empty.

Maybe they're all crazy, and I just joined some kind of cult. I really hope not.

Love you, Beebs. Keep those letters coming. I read them like 150 times a day. I hope I'll see you soon.

Love,
Dally

—

Hey Beebs,

Can you believe I've been here for almost four months? It feels like forever. Every day is the same boring routine. I don't know how they expect anyone to get better like this. But I guess some people do.

About your question, yeah, I'm still going to those prayer meetings. I even sit in the circle now. But I still can't seem to find this Jesus they keep talking about. They make him sound so amazing and tell me how much he loves me. I want to believe it so badly, but it just doesn't feel real to me. I wish I could have what they have.

When I'm in the room with them, and they're praying, it's so beautiful. I think I can feel him then. But as soon as I leave, it all disappears. When it happens, though, it's the most incredible feeling. I don't think about drugs or getting high or anything. I just want to be closer to Jesus. But why does it only happen in that room?

One of the ladies even let me borrow her Bible. But when I tried to read it, there were so many weird words, I couldn't understand a thing. So, I gave it back to her.

Remember when Mama was sick, and Auntie Beth told us that when she died, she'd go to heaven with Jesus? Maybe that's the only way to really find him—to die and leave this earth. I don't know.

But those prayer ladies, they love him so much. I think searching for him would be a good thing for us to do together when I get out. If you want to, I mean. And only if this isn't some crazy cult. Ha ha.

Oh, I almost forgot! Dr. Nguyen said I might get out soon! She told me I'm making progress, and she can see a real change in me. She said since I'm in a new place now and have such a strong support system, I can still see her but as an outpatient. I really hope she's telling the truth. It would be so cruel to say something like that if it wasn't real.

Caitlin left. She just checked herself out and walked out the door. She didn't even say goodbye, which was probably for the best because we both would have just cried more. I hope she's okay. I miss her.

I've been doing more art, and I drew a dog for you. I hope you like it. Dogs are my favorite thing to draw. Maybe we can get a dog someday. Wouldn't that be awesome? We could name him Mr. Miyagi, like Mrs. Martinez's cat. Remember how he used to snuggle with us?

I love you, sis. Write back and tell me everything you're up to. I can't wait to hear all about it.

Love,

Dally

—

It was as if she could hear Dahlia's voice as she read her words. The letters were a bittersweet memory, an echo of a life cut short. Abby's vision blurred as tears welled up in her eyes. She brushed her fingers over Dahlia's handwriting, tracing the lines and curves as if they could connect her to her sister once more.

Knowing a part of Dahlia lived on through these words brought a weak smile to Abby's lips. With shaky breath, she smoothed out the creases, then carefully folded the letters, knowing these precious remnants of Dahlia were more valuable to her than any treasure in the world.

CHAPTER 28

ABBY, 2023

Captain, I'm going by Dahlia's crime scene on the way in. Not sure what time I'll get to the office. Just wanted you to know I'm not missing. LOL. (See what I did there?)

Abby pulled her Ford Edge into the cul-de-sac and parked in the exact location she believed the white Maverick had parked in 2005. Just beyond a split rail fence was the field where Dahlia lost her life. Abby reached into the backseat and grabbed the cane she had kept handy for uneven terrain. She used it to support her on the 100-yard walk.

She'd looked through the crime scene photos and thought she might clear her head by seeing how the earth had renewed itself over the years. Crime is horrible to look at on a regular day. When it's inflicted on someone you love and recorded in full-color images, it's nearly unbearable. She knew the shooting happened beneath a group of Russian Olive trees just down the hill from where she stood.

The field remained practically untouched. The footpath looked just as it did in the photos. The grass was still neglected and wild. Abby wondered if the neighbors and school kids stopped visiting this area, knowing it was where a young, beautiful girl lost her life.

She took determined strides, each step bringing a growing sense of dread tearing at her very soul. The death scene drew her closer with an eerie magnetism as if the once blood-soaked ground were calling to her, yet there was no indication it ever existed at all.

As she reached the trees that had sheltered Dahlia's body, sorrow engulfed her, threatening to consume her from the inside out. With the sun filtering through the branches, she could recall the sound of her laugh and the sparkle of her blue eyes. She thought back to the cheese sandwiches and blue Kool-Aid Mama had let them eat outdoors in the summertime.

She sank to her knees, the native grass bending beneath her. For the first time in years, she allowed herself to fully surrender to her grief. Convulsive sobs wracked her body, helping her release years of pent-up emotions: anger, uncertainty, grief, and the unending confusion that had haunted her.

In the midst of her anguish, a newfound determination ignited. This agonizing release fueled her inner strength and her unwavering resolve—a promise to her sister's memory that she would stop at nothing to unearth the truth and bring her killer to justice.

Last night, after arriving home from work, she'd torn into the old journals she'd written after losing Dahlia. As a youth, she'd recorded every feeling she'd experienced within those pages—the happy memories, the gut-wrenching guilt, and the devastating sadness. With each written word, she'd found a way to cling to the long, tumultuous path toward healing. Right there on her kitchen table, turning page after page of the journals, she'd found what she was looking for.

After Dahlia was released, and before Rol took her away, she'd spent hours alone at Auntie Beth's. While Abby was away at school, Dahlia would choose random notebooks and leave hidden notes and sketches for her. It was a joyful surprise when one surfaced, and often, the messages were so playful and random that even Dahlia didn't remember what they'd said or where they were tucked away.

Abby came across them one by one until she realized there was a whole collection. After Dahlia died, she'd torn through every page of every notebook she owned, looking for any scribbles her sister left behind. The collection was now taped inside Abby's journals, mementos of innocent moments, random silliness, and bits of wisdom from her older sister.

Some of the messages made little sense to her now, but each note and drawing was preserved. To Abby from Dahlia, written by her hand. They were priceless.

Never forget I'm the Phase 10 Champion. You can't beat me.

Love you, my sis.

Dahlia is Abby's biggest fan.

Cling to Jesus, Beebs. He adores you more than I do!

The Parent Trap = Best Movie Ever.

Ephesians 1:7 says God is so rich in kindness and grace that he purchased our freedom with the blood of His Son and forgave our sins.

Abby makes yummy popcorn!

Don't worry, be happy!

Uno! You Know!

The Doc has the cure.

Don't forget your PE uniform!!!!!!!!!!!!!!!!

Live like you're dying.

Next time, I get the last cookie!

Always here for you!

Dahlia Loves Bebee.

You're something I'll never give up!

Dahlia's words played their way through Abby's thoughts. Now, she felt as if her sister were near. It was as if she could feel the anguish of her last moments beneath the thorny trees. She wiped the flow of tears from her cheeks and stared upward toward heaven. *"Help me, Lord. Give me Your wisdom and show me who did this to Dahlia. For Your glory."*

Abby took an extra half hour to return home and refresh her makeup before driving to work. The rims of her eyes remained red and slightly swollen. It would be obvious to almost anyone she'd been crying, but who could blame her?

Michelle greeted her when she entered the building. Her lips curved gently upward, showing a blend of warmth and understanding. Abby made her way to her office and invited Michelle with a motion to follow.

"How would you feel about starting with Dahlia?" Abby asked.

"Well, that's a new plan. Are you sure you're up for it?"

"I've dug into her case a little. It's not pleasant. Part of me is afraid if we don't attack it head-on, I may close it up and never go back to it." She opened the door to her office and was delighted to see Detective Wayne Finch sitting across the table from her chair.

"Wayne! I didn't expect you until next week. Did you win your court case?" Abby wrapped him in a warm hug.

"We did! Now we're just awaiting the sentencing hearing."

"Great! And it means our small cold case team is complete! Thanks so much for agreeing to join us. I personally asked for you, you know."

"I do know, and I'm ready to move. I hope you don't mind," he said. "I thought I'd start thumbing through the files and getting up to speed."

"Of course," Abby said. "I'm happy to see you—but I guess I expected you to work from your own office." A blank look crossed his face, and she tried to rebound. "It makes a lot of sense that you'd share the conference room with me." Looking around at the stacks and piles, she said, "I only wish I'd tidied it up a bit."

Wayne followed her gaze around the room. "It's going to take more than a quick tidy!" he laughed.

"No doubt," Abby said, moving toward her chair and taking a seat. "I was just saying to Michelle that we should start with Dahlia's case. Let's tackle it head-on and tackle my propensity to procrastinate."

"That's reasonable," Michelle said, scooting a stack of files off a chair so she could sit down. "I say we go for it."

Giving her a sideways glance, Wayne asked, "You sure, Sarge? That's diving into the deep end of the pool."

"You're not wrong," Abby tried to bring a smile to her face. "I spent a lot of time the last two days reviewing my sister's case, and I feel ready. If we delay—" Getting nods from her team, she said,

"Thanks for understanding. I know it's a different tactic from what Michelle and I planned. But it feels right. Hey, can I grab some coffee for either of you before we roll up our sleeves and get to work?"

"Sure. I'll take one more cup with extra creamer," said Michelle.

"I'm good, thanks," said Wayne, gesturing with his hand.

The team spent what was left of the morning tearing into the records and reviewing the timeline that started with Dahlia's stop at the coffee shop and ended with Turo arriving at the crime scene.

Next, they examined physical evidence stored in the evidence locker. In Dahlia's case, there were three precious pieces of physical evidence: a shell casing, a photo of a partial shoe print, and the ammunition round found with the help of a metal detector at the crime scene.

Technology had vastly improved over the last 18 years, so Abby directed Wayne to send the shell casing to the lab for reanalysis. It had been carefully preserved, so they'd score a win with a little luck and a ballistics match. The lab staff was as busy as ever, but she asked him to request expedited analysis.

Next, she asked Michelle to research the shoe print to see if she could learn the make of the shoe and locations where it may have been purchased locally. That was a long shot, but when clues were scarce, every potential lead could be important.

Abby fingered the spent bullet through the clear plastic evidence bag. She immediately felt a wave of nausea assault her gut. The bullet was covered in blood, evidence that would yield DNA similar to her own if it were tested. She marveled at its size and how such a tiny instrument could rob the world of indescribable joy.

They'd send the spent bullet to the lab as well and have the striations compared through ATF's National Integrated Ballistic Information Network, a national database to track weapons used in multiple crimes. Separate shooting incidents could be connected through its 3D technology and aid in suspect identification.

As she talked through the timeline with Michelle and Wayne, they examined it from multiple angles, staying alert to information that wasn't obvious or may not have seemed significant in 2005. Abby took notes on her tablet about people to contact, questions to ask, and scenarios to verify.

Cold cases were often solved through circumstantial evidence, so she knew she couldn't pin her hopes on DNA analysis or other physical evidence. By asking witnesses to share their stories again and comparing them to the original statements, Abby knew they might find important details that could bring new answers.

The hours melted away like snow in the sun. Just before packing her things to go home, Abby stopped to check in with Captain Torres. He wasn't at his desk, so she asked his assistant if he was due back today. "I sure hope so," she answered. "He just stepped out for a minute."

Abby gave her a knowing smile. "Do you mind if I wait in his office?"

"Be my guest," his assistant said, turning her attention back to the document she'd been typing.

Abby tumbled through her phone, catching up on accumulating email messages. After about ten minutes, she turned to leave Turo's office just as he was coming in.

"Abby! Good to see you," he greeted. "How are things going?"

"We made some good progress today. We pulled out the physical evidence from Dahlia's case and pushed it through to the lab for re-analysis. Hopefully, technology will prove its magic."

"That would be great! Who are you going to talk with first?"

"I want to go visit with Dr. Nguyen in Grand Junction. I gave her a call a few minutes ago, and she said she could see me tomorrow afternoon. Okay if I head to the Western Slope? I thought I'd take my personal car so I could also visit with my aunt."

"Yes, of course. But take an unmarked county car. You can still visit with Beth. I assume you'll stay overnight with her?"

"That would be best, yes. I don't enjoy driving there and back on the same day. Thank you, sir. I'll let you know how things progress."

"Please do. Did my wife reach out to you?"

"She did. We have dinner scheduled for Sunday. She asked me to bring my broccoli salad."

"Great. We're long overdue. Drive safe, Abby."

"Will do, sir."

CHAPTER 29

ABBY, 2023

Bright and early the next morning, Abby tossed her overnight bag into her Edge, drove to the substation to change to a white Explorer that was part of the county fleet, and spent a few minutes syncing her devices before hitting the road.

Her appointment with Dr. Nguyen wasn't until 2 pm, which allowed time for lunch with Auntie Beth. She'd missed her and looked forward to visiting. She hadn't seen her since before the bar fight, which seemed like another lifetime ago. Beth had traveled for work the week of Abby's surgery but called and FaceTimed numerous times to check-in.

After her mother passed away, Abby remembered feeling afraid and somewhat betrayed when Dahlia suggested she move to Grand Junction to live with Auntie Beth. But once she'd settled into her new surroundings, she'd adored her new life.

Auntie Beth and Uncle David never had children of their own, yet they had provided a home filled with unconditional support, love, and abundant laughter. They'd made themselves accessible to her in the fullest measure, sharing shoulders to cry on through moments of grief, friendship when she'd felt most alone, and safe boundaries when she'd pushed the limits of obedience. When her heart began to turn to God, they shared unquestioned encouragement.

Abby adored them both, and her heart felt the overflow of gratitude when she thought about all they'd sacrificed for her. Considering how her life could have looked without both Dahlia's protection and their involvement was unbearable. Rather than replicating the life of abuse and bondage Dahlia had experienced, Abby had enjoyed security, freedom, and comfort.

Auntie's role at the University had opened doors for education she would never have seen otherwise. The professional side of Auntie Beth provided an example of balancing a rewarding career with a fulfilling family life.

As she steered the SUV away from the metro area and began the climb into the foothills, she could see hints of autumn colors growing more vibrant the deeper into the mountains she drove. To Abby, it was like stepping into a canvas of nature's most glorious hues. Each curve and twist of the road brought a new, breathtaking view. She turned up the volume of her stereo, inflated the seat's lumbar support, and enjoyed the drive.

Just a few minutes past noon, she parked the SUV on 7th Street and walked two blocks to the Rockslide Brew Pub, where Auntie Beth was waiting at a patio table. They shared a long embrace before sitting down to look through the menu.

Auntie Beth looked fantastic. She was dressed in a flattering sundress and sandals. Her hair fell loosely around her shoulders, a shift from her normal professional up-do. She'd updated her prescription sunglasses since Abby saw them last and had a rested, youthful glow about her. Abby adored this woman, and leaving her was the worst part of moving back to Denver.

Beth extended her arm across the table and squeezed Abby's hands. "I can't believe you're sitting close enough for me to reach out and touch you. It's been far too long." She unwrapped the paper napkin from around her silverware and dabbed her eyes with a corner. "I feel horrible that I haven't come to see you since your accident. I'm so sorry, Abby. But it looks like you're doing well."

"Oh, Auntie," Abby said. "Please don't worry about that. I completely understand. And Mack made sure I had all the help I needed."

"We did enjoy the conference on the East Coast, and I was happy David could join me. I just wish the timing had been different."

The server stopped by the table and, without missing a beat in the conversation, each ordered unsweetened iced tea with lemon. "Now tell me how you're handling the emotions of working cold cases. I'm more than a little concerned about you, Abby."

"I think we should save most of that conversation for tonight when we can talk into the wee hours of 10:00 pm," Abby smiled. "For now, I'll tell you that it's been hard, but not as hard as I imagined it would be."

"I'm sorry. I know this isn't easy for you." Talking through Dahlia's case wouldn't be a good mealtime discussion. And seeing Abby across the table had already put her mind at ease. The topic shifted naturally to springtime in New England. Beth pulled her phone from her purse and shared pictures of breathtaking scenery and a few selfies with David. "Selfies are such a wonderful idea, but we're horrible at taking them. Our facial expressions are so awkward," she laughed, "and we can never agree on where we're supposed to look into the lens!"

Abby laughed and pointed to a spot on her own phone, showing her where to look in selfie mode. "I can't wait to see Uncle David. I've missed you both so much."

"Well, he's saved a collection of silly stories for you, so be prepared for that."

Just then, the server stopped at their table to collect their orders. The food at the pub never disappointed, and the atmosphere was among Abby's favorites. She loved sitting beneath the large elm and maple trees along Main Street, where pedestrians ambled by and furry companions often enjoyed the cool, shady seating with their humans.

Abby was a sucker for their French Dip sandwich, and her first bite confirmed it was the best she'd ever tasted. The bread was toasted, the meat sliced paper thin, and it was served with fries and a side of creamy horseradish. Sometimes, she thought she could eat here every day.

From the restaurant, Abby walked to Dr. Nguyen's office, arriving promptly at 1:55, and checked in with her receptionist. She took a seat on a black leather sofa that was functional but lacked warmth and comfort. A philodendron was positioned on the corner of a small marble coffee table, and two frameless canvas prints adorned the walls. The minimalist decor didn't leave much to focus on.

Abby was second-guessing her casual work attire and wondering if she should have worn slacks and a jacket for this meeting when Dr. Nguyen appeared in the doorway. *Too late now,* she thought as she stood to greet her, portraying as much confidence as she could muster.

"I'm Sergeant Abigail Carter," she introduced herself. "Thank you for seeing me."

Leading Abby into her office and closing the door securely, Dr. Nguyen said, "It's been a long time since anyone has asked about Dahlia Archer. But I still think about her every day. How can I help the investigation?"

"Dr. Nguyen, I am investigating Dahlia's case on behalf of the Adams County Sheriff's Office. But I also want to disclose to you that I am Dahlia's sister. I lived here in Grand Junction when she was killed but have spent the last 12 years in law enforcement in the Denver area."

There was a slight twitch in the doctor's eyebrows. "That's quite surprising. I question the wisdom in trying to solve the murder of someone so close to you."

Abby couldn't discern the meaning behind the doctor's statement. Was it meant to scold or reprimand? "It's highly unusual, I agree. But a lot of factors came together to create this opportunity, and as you can imagine, I couldn't turn it down."

"Yes, I can see why you would not want to. Please sit down, and I will share whatever I can." The doctor sat behind her desk and motioned for Abby to sit in an armless guest chair.

Abby's chair was equally as uncomfortable as the sofa in the waiting room. She pulled a notebook from her leather tote bag and pressed the Axon Capture app on her phone. The software would record and transcribe the interview and then upload it directly into the county's evidence system. "This interview is being recorded," She began. "It's 2:00 pm on October 7, 2023. I'm Sergeant Abigail Carter, and I'm interviewing Dr. Lynn Nguyen. Dr. Nguyen, I'd like for you to start at the beginning. Please tell me how you met Dahlia Archer."

"She became a patient of mine at the Gunnison River Rehabilitation and Treatment Center. She was a resident patient, so her identity and presence in the facility were carefully guarded. I reviewed her file before you arrived and have my notes here so I can be as accurate as possible with the information I share with you."

"Thank you for your diligence. Can you give me a recap of why Dahlia was in the rehab facility?

"Certainly. She was admitted so we could help her overcome an addiction to narcotics. She nearly overdosed prior to her intake. Her physical symptoms of withdrawal were severe and took some time to overcome. She was in the facility for just over four months. After her release, I continued to see her as an outpatient until the day of her kidnapping."

"Did Dahlia share the circumstances that led to her addiction?"

"She did." Dr. Nguyen didn't elaborate. Her expression implied she was uncomfortable talking to a family member about a patient. Abby could understand how difficult this could be.

"What were those circumstances?" she pressed.

"She had been exploited by her uncle, who trafficked her to other men as a prostitute. Dahlia said that her uncle began giving her Vikes when she was about 11 years old."

"What was that uncle's name?"

The doctor looked at her notes. "Dahlia told me it was her Uncle Rolyn Archer. He was her father's brother."

"Thank you. Was Rol her only source for controlled substances?"

"No, he wasn't. Dahlia also obtained narcotics by stealing morphine and fentanyl from her mother's hospice medications. And when that supply ran out, a man she knew only as 'Doc' supplied her with Hydromorphone, an opioid she used in addition to the Vikes Rol was giving her. It was a dangerous combination that led to her overdose."

"Did she ever share more information about 'Doc'?"

"She did not. She said she memorized his phone number and called him when she wanted more drugs than Rol had shared. That is all I know."

"How often did Dahlia meet with you as an outpatient?"

"We met twice weekly. She would walk to my office from where she was living, about seven or eight blocks away."

"Was she still taking illicit drugs at the time of her disappearance?"

"No, Dahlia had been clean for more than six months. It was enough time that I believe she'd turned a corner and could successfully beat her addiction. Of course, no recovery is guaranteed, but Dahlia had a great support system in place. She'd moved away from her drug sources, had a supportive and understanding family unit, and was faithful about meeting with me."

Dr. Nguyen rested her head on the back of her chair. "I believe Dahlia could have made a new life for herself. Her disappearance, her death, was a heartbreaking loss. I often think about her and what she could have become."

"Me too, Dr. Nguyen. Me too." Abby rested in the momentary silence that followed, then asked, "Is there any more information you think will be helpful to the case?"

Dr. Nguyen paused to think. "Dahlia was on the path to freedom. When I first met her, she was heavily burdened and tragically addicted. In our last meeting, she was happy and lighthearted. She could finally begin to imagine a different path for her life than what she'd previously experienced. We never had a session where she didn't mention you, Bebee, and the precious gift you were to her. She loved you more than life itself."

Hearing the endearing nickname stirred emotions that threatened to overpower her. Abby pinched the top of her nose between her thumb and middle finger in an attempt to hold in her emotions. "Thank you, Doctor," she said, her voice a hoarse whisper.

As she gathered her things to go, Dr. Nguyen stood and said to Abby, "This would have made her proud, Abby, seeing you like this. In law enforcement, helping victims and their families. You are an echo of the redemption she didn't have the chance to experience herself."

"She's been gone for 18 years. I've literally lived without her longer than I lived with her. And a short talk with someone who knew her ignites my grief all over again." Abby let her tears fall freely. She sat cross-legged on the bed in her old bedroom, squeezing a pillow into a tight ball. Auntie Beth had found her crying in the bedroom and now sat beside her at the foot of the bed.

"The fact that you're still grieving only shows that you're still loving, Abby. You miss your sister. That's natural, and honestly, it's precious to me."

"I loved her so much. I thought I'd let her go, but obviously, I haven't."

"That's the crazy thing about grief. It sneaks up on us at the most inconvenient times, and even years after a loss, it can nearly paralyze us with emotion."

"I'm supposed to be a professional, someone who can keep her emotions under wraps. Instead, I nearly came undone during an interview."

"Oh, Honey," Beth leaned in and wrapped Abby in her arms. "No one, including Dr. Nguyen, is judging you for the emotion you have for Dahlia. Your bosses and colleagues have gone into this with eyes wide open. There's no expectation that you'll walk through the work without exposing your feelings."

"My head knows that, but my pride believes I should do better."

"Think of it as honoring Dahlia. She deserves your love and the emotion you feel. It shows that her life mattered, that she was someone worthy of love."

Abby let Beth's words sink in. "I can't argue with that." Her eyes were swollen with makeup smeared into dark streaks and smudges on her cheeks. "Thanks, Auntie Beth. You always know just what to say." She blew her nose into a tissue and rested her chin on the pillow. "I'm afraid I've been focused more on myself than I should be. Thanks for helping me shift my attitude."

Beth gently lifted Abby's chin with her fingertips so she could look into her tearful blue eyes. With a weak smile, she said, "When you hurt, I hurt. That's because I love you. As you work on this case, you're going to hear all about Dahlia's hurts, and they're going to break your heart. You wouldn't be human if they didn't. Please know I'm here to listen anytime you need to talk, whether you're in Denver or right here in your bedroom."

"You know I'll take you up on that."

Beth nodded. "In the meantime, I made your favorite Greek pasta salad. Are you hungry?"

Abby gave a weary smile. Food didn't sound appealing at all, but she said, "Let me clean up a bit. I'll be down in a few minutes."

CHAPTER 30

ABBY, 2023

Abby stepped into First Watch Diner and scanned the room for Mack. Surely, she was here already. Mack was the more punctual of the two, and Abby was running uncharacteristically late. The morning's goodbye to Auntie Beth and Uncle David had drawn out longer than she'd expected. Their small family hadn't been together in months, and once they'd reconnected, walking away felt like tearing two pieces of velcro apart. She made a mental note to visit them more frequently for the good of all of them.

Spotting Mack in a corner booth, she weaved through the crowded tables. Mack met her halfway with a bear hug and a kiss on the cheek. "I ordered your coffee," Mack said as she slid back into the booth.

"I see you also took the rear seat," Abby teased.

"You know I did. First come, first dibs."

Cops develop certain quirks, and sitting with their backs to the wall was one of them. Finding a way to always face the public was a way to stay alert to their surroundings. When Abby and Mack had been together in the Academy, they'd vowed not to let their careers consume them, to leave work at work, as if it would be as easy as taking off a uniform. But reality had a funny way of melting away good intentions, and here they were, teasing each other about who sat against the back wall.

"Thanks for the coffee. Have you ordered yet?" Abby quickly scanned the front and back of the menu for any seasonal specials.

"No, I waited for you. Do you need the menu?"

"I knew what I wanted when I woke up this morning," Abby grinned as she set the menu aside. "Auntie Beth and Uncle David send their love, by the way."

"I almost called you a few times last night, but it's been so long since you've seen them, I decided to leave you alone."

"Thank you. We needed it. I was a hot mess last night. I met with Dahlia's counselor yesterday, and she nearly ripped my heart out."

"What? Was she a jerk?"

"No, just the opposite, actually. I could tell she genuinely cared for Dahlia." Abby started to tear up again as she continued. "She said Dahlia mentioned me at every visit. She even called me Bebee as she told me how much my sister loved me."

"Ouch." Mack nodded. "It had to be hard for you to hold it together."

"No kidding. It was a good conversation, but it threw me into emotions I thought I could control. I couldn't. By the time I got home to Auntie Beth's, I ran up to my room and slammed the door. Just like I was fourteen again."

"Oh, you threw a teenage fit, did you?"

Abby choked on her sip of coffee as she laughed. "It looked like that from the outside. On the inside, it felt like I never left the sadness behind."

"You probably haven't, Abby. That's going to be the awful part of this investigation, but you have to keep your eyes on the outcome. Did she share anything helpful?"

"She did, actually. I reviewed the report Turo wrote when he talked to her in 2005. She'd said then that Dahlia's only sources of drugs were Rol and Mama's hospice meds. When we talked yesterday, Dr. Nguyen said she'd recently reviewed her notes and told me about another person who supplied narcotics. Dahlia only knew him as 'Doc,' but that's definitely new information. She said he was one of the johns."

"How are you going to track down someone by only a nickname they had 18 years ago?" Mack asked.

"Great question. Do you have any brilliant ideas?"

"Not one. But I'll ask around the detective squad here."

Several minutes later, when their meals were delivered, Abby said, "I'm starving. I guess crying my eyes out burned a lot of calories." She dove into the house-made toast and jam, the first bites of which were melt-in-her-mouth delicious. "I have dreams about this stuff."

She wiped the corner of her mouth with a napkin. "On another note, how do you know if a guy is interested in you?"

Mack's eyes widened. "Well, that's a question I didn't see coming. Who do you think is interested?"

"He's one of our county commissioners. He's a lot older than me, so at first, I thought I was crazy to think he might have more than a professional interest. But I can't seem to shake him. He stops by the office, and we even crossed paths when I was out for a run a few days ago." She considered her words. "It's not what he says. It's more the way he looks at me."

"Are you interested in him?" Mack held a bite of waffle on her fork until Abby answered.

"I don't have a reason to be," she teased. "I mean, he's nice-looking, charming, and acts like a gentleman. But I don't know anything about him. I have no idea what he likes or even if he's married. He always wants to talk about my role in cold cases. He's almost insatiably curious."

"Maybe it's purely professional, then. Millions of people are interested in crime stories. Otherwise, true crime podcasts and TV shows wouldn't be so wildly popular. Maybe he just likes the elements of mystery."

"Maybe." Abby nodded and sipped her small glass of orange juice. "But like I said, it's more the look in his eyes. Maybe when you come to Denver for the Gus Farmer concert, you can meet him and see what you think."

"I cannot wait for that weekend!" Mack's enthusiasm steered the conversation in different directions, and before long, the check arrived.

"I could sit here all day and talk to you, Mack."

"Me too, but you've got a long drive ahead of you, and I need to go home and shower for work. Let me get the check this time."

"Are you kidding? I'll be forever trying to pay you back for the week of nursing you gave me. Let me get it!"

"No, you bought the concert tickets, which was way more than you should have. Besides, there's no payback needed, and I'm buying breakfast." Mack's lightning-fast reach pulled the check from Abby's fingertips, and she bolted to the register at the front of the restaurant.

Outside, Abby accepted Mack's farewell hug as she stepped into her car. She connected her phone to the sound system, selected her 'classic rock' playlist, and made her way out of the parking lot and onto eastbound I-70.

As she always did, Abby marveled at the grandeur of Glenwood Canyon. She counted it among the most beautiful settings in Colorado. Each journey offered a unique experience brought on by seasonal weather, the way the light filtered through the cliffs at different times of day, the amount of moisture over the past few months, and wildlife that occasionally chose to reveal itself.

She switched off her music and enjoyed the 12-mile stretch of magnificence that followed the Colorado River with nothing but road noise to play as a backdrop to her thoughts. Auntie Beth often said of the canyon, "God is just showing us what He's capable of." As she drove, Abby reflected on His power and creativity.

As she neared the last curve before passing the small town of Dotsero, her cell phone rang with an unknown number. Hoping her cell service would hold, she pressed "answer" on the dashboard of the Edge and said, "This is Sergeant Carter."

"Abby, Jacob Jennings here. How's your day going?"

Well, speak of the devil, Abby thought before she responded, "It's just fine, although hearing from you is a surprise. What can I do for you?"

"The better question is, can I do anything for you? Michelle mentioned you were driving back to Denver today. It's a long drive to take by yourself, so I thought I could keep you company for a few minutes."

Abby had no idea how to respond, but before the silence became too uncomfortable, Jacob continued. "I'm also driving, by the way. I'm headed to see my mom in Colorado Springs. A chat might do us both some good."

It seemed the perfect opportunity to learn more about this man. "Did you grow up in the Springs?"

"No, my mom moved there after my father passed away about five years ago. Housing was a little more affordable at that time, which helped her hold on to her independence. I go down to see her every month or so."

"Is it just you, or do you have siblings?" She hoped she didn't sound like an investigator.

"I have a brother who is somewhere in Denver, but we don't see or hear from him. He fell deep into drugs. Sadly, I wouldn't be surprised if he's among the homeless. I used to worry that his lifestyle may be a detriment to my career path. I'm not proud of it, but I changed my name before running for county commissioner to provide some distance." Another few seconds of silence ticked by, and he said, "Well, I can't believe I just told you that. Probably too much information for a casual chat."

Abby knew she needed to say something. "I'm surprised more than anything. I wouldn't think voters would elect someone who seemed to be hiding something." She filled the awkward pause that followed with, "Oh, maybe I shouldn't have said *that*."

Jacob laughed. "Most voters don't actually do much research. In our county, they vote primarily by party line, which has brought all kinds of questionable characters into government leadership. One of our elected sheriffs was even brought up on felony charges for fraud a ways back. If you're on the correct side of the ballot, it's almost easy to get elected."

Abby remembered hearing about that sheriff. Plummer was his name. He'd been charged before she was hired in Adams County.

"That's a sad state of affairs, but I'm pretty ignorant about politics," she said to Jacob. "It's not something I spend time thinking about."

"Just like most people. You're certainly not alone. Sometimes I wish I didn't have to pay attention to politics, either." Again, his pleasant laughter filled the speakers of her car.

"What do you like to do with your mom when you go see her?"

"It's more about what she likes to do. There's a Chinese buffet she loves to visit, so we go there for lunch. She loves to bake, so she loads me up with bread and cookies to bring home. And, of course, she asks if I'll ever give her grandchildren. I always allow time for that conversation. She can't understand why I've never married. I keep telling her I just haven't found the right one. Mom's generation doesn't think that way, but I believe in marrying for love, not convenience, don't you?"

No wife, no kids, treats his mom well. Abby made mental notes of the details Jacob felt so willing to share. "Oh, I'm not one to give advice or opinions about marriage. I don't have a great track record with relationships."

"That just means you haven't found the one either. No harm in that."

"I suppose you're right. Listen, Jacob. I need to pull off for a pit stop soon, so I'm going to let you go. Thanks for checking in. You were right. It was nice to chat for a few minutes."

"Before you go, I was wondering. Do you think I could take you to dinner sometime?"

"Like a date?" Abby couldn't believe she sounded so immature. Of course, it was like a date.

"Yes. Just like a date. I'd like to get to know you, Abby."

"I think I'd like that. Let's make plans when you get back."

"You can count on it," he said. "Drive safe."

CHAPTER 31

ABBY, 2023

Rolyn Archer swore like a sailor when he saw Abby waiting for him in the interview room. "You look just like your sister. It's like going back in time." He almost looked like he wanted to hug her. Abby squared her shoulders and held her professional posture.

Turo sat at a table about four feet wide that took up most of the cramped room. Abby glanced at him from the corner of her eye, then focused on the inmate before her. "We're not going back in time, Rol. We're here in prison where you've been for 18 years because of the awful things you did to my sister."

He looked smaller than she remembered. Abby considered how his age, his prison lifestyle, along with the striped jumpsuit and shackles contributed to his diminutive appearance. She and Captain Torres had driven 120 miles together to the Sterling Correctional Facility, the state prison where Rol was incarcerated. Here, they could conduct a face-to-face and fully videoed interview.

"You're a cop now?" Rol asked the obvious, but Abby didn't respond. "I didn't kill her, Bebee."

"I know that," Abby said, "But I think you know who did. That's what I want to talk to you about."

"I had nothing," Rol looked Abby straight in the eye and raised his voice, "*nothing* to do with Dahlia's death." His voice cracked, and he looked away, wiping at his eyes with hands bound by metal cuffs. He glanced at the hard plastic chair reserved for him in the matchbox-sized interview room, then lowered himself into it. "I've said all this before. Bebee, you gotta know I'm broken up. To this day, I can't believe it." His voice was almost a whisper now.

She wanted to tell him to stop calling her Bebee. That was a nickname reserved for people who loved her. Dahlia died trying to protect her from this man, and he had no right to use the term of endearment. But she held her tongue, knowing that giving him this small concession may work to her advantage. If nothing else, Rol saw her as family, which could help develop new leads in solving Dahlia's murder.

She slowly paced back and forth behind the table that separated them. "I believe you." She watched him react to her words and jerk his head back to face her. "We need you to help us." His clenched jaw relaxed, and his eyes transformed to display an evil, manipulative stance.

"You need me. That's new." Rol let out a deep, throaty cough, bringing both of his cuffed hands to his mouth. "What's in it for me?"

Abby chuckled under her breath. "That's the Rol I've come to know." She planted her hands on the table and leaned toward him until her face was inches from his. "There's nothing in it for you. Not one thing."

Standing straight once more, she offered a bargaining chip. "Except this. If you help us, I'll tell my dad that you are innocent of Dahlia's death. As for the other horrendous deeds you did to her, he'll know every detail. But he won't go to his grave believing his brother murdered his daughter."

Rol visibly shuddered, and Abby understood the yearning ache he carried for his brother's forgiveness. "I already told them who I thought coulda done it! That rich guy. The one I never met."

"Yeah, you said he owned a silver Porsche. That's not a clue we can easily track down. What else can you tell me about him?" The case file was placed carefully on the table in front of Turo. Abby had most of the details memorized, but Turo was at the ready if there were details they needed to verify. She reached for the file and thumbed through it.

"His driver was all high-and-mighty and an *I'm-better-than-you* kind of guy. I only put up with him because of the cash he delivered."

Right, Abby thought. That was the motivation for most of his decisions. She wondered how that attitude was serving him behind bars.

"A big guy?" she asked, keeping her eyes on the file. Abby led the questioning. Turo was there for protection and accountability. Should this interview ever be admitted inside a courtroom, they'd need both Turo's presence and a video of the meeting to avoid the appearance of coercion.

"Giant. The biggest human I've ever seen, even inside here. He had some kind of thick accent I could hardly follow. But he got his point across. He used to just point at the girl—" he corrected himself "—at *Dahlia* and point to the backseat of the car. She was such a champ. She'd just get in all brave, like she wasn't scared of nothing."

Abby diverted her thoughts to the man sitting before her. Imagining this story from Dahlia's viewpoint was more than she could deal with at the moment. There was no doubt she'd process it in the middle of the night while she lay awake on her bed. But right now, she had to fight the inner battle and find a way to stay emotionally detached.

"Tell me more about the car."

Rol's face took on a dream-like glow. "Just touching it, man. It made my heart beat all crazy. It was so clean, as if he had it detailed every day. I wondered how a guy that size could even fit inside, but when he got in, it was like the car was made just for him. The interior was dark with shiny buttons. It always had that rich leather smell. I loved it."

Abby was surprised Rol could genuinely love anything. "How do you know the driver didn't own it?"

"Oh, I could tell. He was afraid of it. If Dahl or me touched it, he'd bark at us, so we'd keep our hands off the thing. He'd say, 'Mr. W no like touches.'"

"Mr. W?" Abby asked.

"The license plates!" Rol exclaimed. "I remember now, they said MRWAZZ."

"Very good, Rol. That's helpful." Treating him like a child felt oddly satisfying. "Now, what else do you remember?"

Rol closed his eyes as if trying to envision a memory from the past. "A small tattoo. The driver had a tiny tat behind his right ear. It looked like letters. Like initials or something. I never could make it out. He had no hair, so I saw it when he closed Dahlia into the back seat of the car."

Abby waited in silence to allow Rol time to reflect. Several minutes passed before he said, "That's all I have."

"Who else? What other johns may have had access to Dahlia outside of what they paid you for?"

"None! I was careful about that."

Abby had no doubt that was true. To Rol, Dahlia was property. If anyone could contact her without going through him, it would mean he'd lost two of the most important things in his life: control and money. He'd never stand for it.

"Were there any johns who seemed nice to her?"

"Nice to her? No. They just wanted what she gave them." Rol turned his head and looked toward the right side of the room for several seconds as if lost in thought.

When Rol spoke again, Abby's eyes widened at the sudden intrusion into the silence. "I heard her laughing one time."

"Laughing?" Abby clarified.

"Yeah. I almost never saw the girl laugh. One time, from that back room, I heard it. There were low voices like they were whispering about something, and then she laughed."

"Who was she with?"

"I'm trying to remember!" He nearly shouted. "It was a long time ago, Bebee! Give me a minute."

Abby glanced at Turo, who almost indiscernibly shrugged his shoulders. She didn't feel as if she were pushing for details, but Rol was suddenly defensive as if he were still furious that one of the johns had more access to Dahlia than he wanted. She waited, and they sat in another period of silence.

"It was that 'Doc' guy," he finally said. "He was a young one. At least younger than any of the other johns. Somewhere around 30, I bet. I always wondered why he didn't just go get a date instead of coming to me. It was him. I'm sure. I remember telling him that it better not happen again. He wasn't here to make friends, and neither was the girl."

"Do you remember what he looked like?"

"Dark hair. A little pudgy. Not too tall. Dark eyes. He wore glasses, I think. He always wore sweatpants. Never jeans. I always thought he looked like a slob, and I wondered where he got the money to pay for his sex habit. He was a regular."

"You didn't know his name?"

"I never knew any names." With that, he looked both Turo and Abby in their faces and added, "For obvious reasons. He said to call him Doc. There was a beat-up white car that was always in the lot when he came. It had to be his."

"Is there any way it was a truck and not a car?" Abby asked.

"No, Bebee," his words were laced with sarcasm. "I know the difference between a car and a truck. I don't know what kind it was, but it was old and rusty."

Again, Abby looked at Turo, widening her eyes in silent frustration. "Did you ever notice a license plate?"

"I don't remember that."

"Do you remember anything else?"

"No," Rol murmured. "I don't have anything else for you. If I think up something, I can reach out, right?"

"Just let the guards know you have more to say. They'll get in touch with us."

"Bebee," Rol said, his demeanor softening. "I'm so sorry about all this." Abby closed the file, stood up, and turned her back on her uncle as she walked out of the room. It was small moment of satisfaction for her.

Approaching the parking lot, Abby said to Turo, "Let's stop for lunch. I'm starving." She realized she'd been saying that a lot lately.

Turo pressed the key fob to unlock the car doors. As Abby put her files in the back seat, he checked the map app on his phone and found a nearby cafe. They clicked in their seatbelts as he looked at her and said, "Abby, that was a beautiful interview! You mined some gold in there! Great job!"

She sat with her eyes closed and leaned against the headrest for several seconds. "You're right. It's so frustrating that the jerk has so much control over this. But he did give us some gems to work with, didn't he?"

"He did. And I don't think anyone else could have gotten him to open up the way you did. You have a couple of strong leads to follow. Having a license plate for the Porsche could be the break we've been looking for. Why don't you call Michelle with the plate number and have her start researching?"

Abby had already texted the details to Michelle, who replied that she'd get right on it.

CHAPTER 32

ABBY, 2023

It had been a week fraught with sentiment, one that had left Abby feeling weary and emotionally drained. She longed for a quiet evening alone to gather her thoughts and find the rest her body craved.

As she prepared for an evening with Jacob, the weight of the days behind her lingered in her thoughts. Echoes of conversations, moments of vulnerability, and endless hours of investigation were taking their toll. A date was hardly what she wanted tonight.

With a deep breath, she resolved to put on a brave face, hoping that, in some small way, it might offer a respite from the turmoil of the week. She knew that a night out with a new friend could bring the diversion and laughter she knew she needed.

They'd planned to meet for a simple dinner, and she'd found a way to wiggle out of his offer to pick her up. She preferred to control her situations and liked to drive herself whenever possible, a habit her Uncle David taught her as a high school student. *When you're the driver,* he'd said, *you can always control the sobriety of the driver.* She'd learned she could control a lot of other situations as well and carried his advice into adulthood.

After work, she stopped by her house to change. Rapidly rejecting the first three outfits and tossing them on her bedroom floor, she settled on capri slacks, topped by a light floral blouse and a simple gold necklace. She vacillated on the decision to wear her hair up or down, finally choosing down. Her curls didn't behave the way she'd wished, and she was tempted to pull her locks back, but the digital clock goaded her out the door. She'd rather be insecure about how her hair looked than arrive late.

They met downtown at a local Italian staple where he'd called ahead for seating. The entryway and bar area were loud and energetic, making conversation difficult. After a short wait, a host led them to a small, round table, which offered a more comfortable, if not intimate, setting.

The timeless charm of exposed brick walls adorned with vintage photographs reminded her of a warm family gathering. Tony Bennett's *The Best is Yet to Come* played in the background, and Jacob began quietly singing under his breath as the host presented the menus. When Abby smiled at him, he stopped abruptly.

"I'm sorry, I listen to this music all the time. It just comes out of me. I know it's old-fashioned." His dark hair was wavy, a stark contrast to his well-trimmed salt-and-pepper beard. For a moment, she wondered if it was dyed, but his graying temples suggested not.

"I have a crooners playlist as well. Most of the time, I dance around the kitchen to songs like this."

"It's too bad the dance floor is closed this evening."

Abby looked over her shoulder to see the dance floor, then realized there wasn't one. She laughed, "You got me. I don't dance in public, so I'm glad to know you won't try to persuade me."

"What do you do in public?" He removed his napkin from beneath the silverware and placed it on his lap.

"With my job, that's a loaded question," she said. "There's a lot I do in public that most people wouldn't dream of doing at all."

"Let me rephrase. What do you enjoy doing? Outside of work."

Abby sipped her water and selected a piece of bread from the basket at the center of the table. As she dipped it in olive oil, she said, "I enjoy cooking and dancing in the kitchen. I also love to read, and I spend a lot of time at church."

"Church? I didn't see that coming. I haven't been since I was a kid when I went with my grandma. What's the draw for you?"

Abby studied Jacob's face to discern the motive of his question. His tone of voice wasn't malicious, and there was nothing assertive about his expression. He didn't seem to be mocking her the way his words implied. "I enjoy knowing a powerful God cares for me and has a plan for my life. I like learning more about Him and following His lead through my circumstances."

"The last time I asked someone that question, they said they go to church because they feel guilty about the things they've done. Church helps them feel clean and forgiven."

"I'm sure there are many people at church who feel that way. But it's not why I go. I try to avoid things I'll need forgiveness for. I don't always succeed, but I do try."

"And what happens when you don't?" He raised his eyebrows and fixed his gaze on her face, making her a bit uncomfortable about where the conversation was heading.

"I talk to God about it like I'm having an honest conversation with Him."

Jacob considered what she'd said. "That sounds nice. You're saying guilt doesn't have to play a part in it."

"Not in my opinion. God knows we're going to make mistakes. I believe He's a Father who loves when we turn to Him for help."

"You make it sound like you have a connection with God. I've never heard anyone explain it like that." He raised a small chunk of bread to his mouth.

"You can come to church with me sometime if you're interested. No expectations or anything. Just come as a friend if you ever want to check it out."

"I may do that. I didn't have a great relationship with my dad, so seeing God as a Father would be a new perspective."

"I get it," she nodded. "My dad wasn't around much when I was growing up. I had to learn to trust that God wouldn't quit on me like he did."

"This was a serious start to our evening, wasn't it?" He tilted his head slightly and gave her a wide-eyed grin as the server approached.

She hadn't even glanced at the menu. Abby was happy she'd eaten here before. She had an entree in mind and ordered a pasta dish without reviewing the selections, then asked for a side salad and iced tea. Jacob ordered the same.

With the menus cleared, Jacob circled back to the topic at hand. "You were saying you didn't see much of your dad."

"I didn't. He left home when I was young, so my mom raised us. My dad's brother promised to help support us, but his idea of support was less than ideal. Still, my sister, my mom, and I made a good, strong team. Later, I moved away to live with my aunt. I'm still very close to her. She's wonderful."

"Someone raised you well. You seem like a genuinely kind and thoughtful person, Abby. That's why I wanted to get to know you more." He reached into the basket of fresh bread and continued nibbling. He turned his head toward her and asked, "Just to be sure, you're not with anyone, are you?"

"No," she smiled. "I'm better off as a loner, I'm afraid. Besides, a lot of men see a woman with a job in law enforcement as intimidating. Dates aren't always easy to come by."

"It's their loss," he said. "You don't seem like a threat to me." Seeing the server coming with their salads, he moved his bread plate aside. Abby followed suit.

"Give it time," she teased.

As the evening wore on, the tension that had knotted Abby's neck and shoulders gradually began to unwind. The unhurried pace of their meal gave room for easy conversation without the pressures and demands of her professional life. She found herself sharing stories and discovering common interests with Jacob. The world outside seemed to blur into the background, leaving only the two of them to enjoy this pause.

Jacob's wit and charm were evident, and he embodied the qualities of a true gentleman. She enjoyed watching his impeccable manners—the way he held his fork, his upright yet relaxed posture, and the way he seemed to hang on her every word. His maturity held a unique allure she hadn't anticipated.

Yet thoughts of her afternoon interview with Rol crept in, threatening to distract her from the lovely evening. He'd shared disturbing details about her sister's situation that she couldn't shake. As she drove home from work, she'd considered calling Dr. Williams for an impromptu counseling session but had run out of time. For now, she reminded herself to stay attentive to her conversation with Jacob.

"Why did you decide to run for county commissioner?" she asked, raising the last forkful of pasta to her lips and turning her focus to her companion.

He leaned back in his chair. "I've lived in Adams County for a long while and thought this was a good way to give back. I believe level-headed leaders are hard to come by and can make our communities a better place to live. Besides, politics fascinates me. I thrive in the cutthroat environment of campaigning. My ultimate goal is to run for Colorado governor in the next 10-12 years."

"Impressive goal," Abby raised her napkin to brush her lips. "I'm afraid I'm thinking week to week at this point in my career, hoping my body will get strong enough to do the job I love."

"From what I hear, you're very good at it."

Abby's eyebrows raised, her eyes holding a mix of curiosity and confusion. "From what you hear?"

"I've asked around. You're a well-respected law enforcement professional, Abby. And not just in your own agency. There are a lot of people anticipating great success in the cold cases you're working."

"Who knew?" she asked playfully. "But it's not going to be an easy road."

"What kind of progress are you making so far?"

Abby wondered how much to share. Most cops would understand the complexities of working a case involving a family member. But it involved intricacies that would be nearly impossible to convey to someone outside her field.

"I'm reviewing several cases. This week, I started reaching out to contacts from the most complicated of unsolved cases. That's why I went to Grand Junction." His face was fixed on her every expression, and she decided to keep details vague. No sense in letting emotions overtake the moment. "It's a heartbreaking story. Every story is heartbreaking when a life is lost, of course, but this case involved a young victim with a promising life ahead of her."

Jacob placed his hand on top of her own. "I don't know how you do it," he said, slowly shaking his head. "Do you feel like you're gaining ground?"

"I am," she answered. "Cold cases are interesting. When years pass, and you ask people to repeat their stories, new details often emerge. Maybe they didn't seem important when the crime was fresh. Sometimes, details are just missed when people deal with trauma, but they come to mind later.

"Going back to talk with the same people who were interviewed when the case was fresh can uncover new information that may develop into strong leads. That's what's happening now. But it's hard to hear the details of such a troubling story. It makes for long days. And long nights, if I'm honest. I'm not the best at turning off my job at the end of the day, and losing sleep over investigations takes its toll."

Okay, she said to herself, *time to lighten up here.* Attempting to change the subject, she said, "That's why it's so nice to have an evening like this. Thank you, Jacob."

"It's my pleasure. This has been a delight." His eyes held hers as he asked, "Can we finish with dessert and coffee?"

She put a hand on her stomach. "I'd love to, but I can't eat another bite."

"I was hoping you'd say that!" He laughed. "I'm stuffed to the gills."

Abby reached for her purse and was surprised when Jacob held her chair as she stood. No one had ever done that for her before. It was like being in a movie. "Your manners are ..." she searched for the right word, "*classic.* And unexpected. Where did you learn how to make a woman feel so special?"

"I treat others the way I'd like to be treated. And my mom enjoys being pampered. I suppose I learned it from her." They made their way to the exit, and just a few steps outside, Jacob touched her elbow and asked in a tender voice, "Can I see you again, Abby?"

She'd worried he'd ask to extend their night somehow, and she wanted nothing more than to close her eyes and try to sleep. His question signaled the end of their date yet left the door open for more connection in the future. It was the perfect bow to tie around a pleasant evening.

"I'd like that. You have my number." How could he make her feel so respected and childlike all at the same time? "My car's right here," she pointed to her Edge. "Let's talk soon."

Abby was out for a short run early Saturday evening when her phone rang. "Hello, Jacob." Even she could hear the smile in her voice.

"And what are you up to this evening?"

"I'm finishing a run. How was your day?"

"Uneventful, but good. I mowed my yard for what I hope will be the last time of the year."

"That sounds like cause for celebration!" She stopped near a park bench and willed her breath to slow.

She enjoyed the sound of his chuckle. "I don't want to keep you from your run. If I wanted to show up for church tomorrow, what would that look like?"

She gripped the side of the bench, her tentative smile building as the surprise set in. "It looks like 9:00 am at Flatirons Church in Lafayette. Are you familiar with it at all? Should I send you directions?"

"Directions would be great. And maybe a website so I can check it out a bit."

"Will do. It's a big church. Text me when you get there so we can find each other."

"Sounds good. I'll see you tomorrow. Have a wonderful night."

PART THREE

CHAPTER 33

ABBY, 2023

The next morning, as Abby descended the stairs for coffee, her knee felt annoyingly sore. The long periods of driving she'd endured last week weren't kind to her body, and she questioned the wisdom of yesterday's run. As the coffee brewed, she did some heel and calf raises and knee flexor stretches, trying to loosen the stiffness she felt.

She took her coffee cup outside and stood on her patio to see a breathtaking spectacle. The sun was just cresting the horizon toward the front of her house, golden rays kissing the edges of clouds that filled the western sky in her backyard. They caught the sunlight and cast a luminous glow that painted the sky in soft shades of amber, apricot, and rose.

She studied the beautiful display and silently thanked God for His creativity. Abby sat with her legs outstretched on the dewy lawn and prayed. *"Lead my day, Lord. If Jacob comes to church, show him You exist and that You care for him. Give me Your wisdom. I need it in this new relationship."*

She couldn't resist laying on her back to gaze heavenward. Her imagination identified shapes in the clouds, a game she used to play with Dahlia on summer days when they went to the park. There above her tree was a dog. And over the neighbor's roof was a smiling alligator.

A tear streamed from the corner of her eye into the grass. "I wish you were here, Dally. I still miss you so much," she whispered. She thought of all the moments she wished she had her sister to talk to.

Her first kiss, the challenges of the Police Academy, her failed marriage. She'd love to talk with her right now and get Dahlia's opinion of Jacob. Most of all, she'd ask who pulled the trigger of the gun that killed her.

Through the screened patio door, she heard her iPhone buzz in the kitchen, so Abby flipped over and got on all fours before standing on the lawn. By the time she reached the kitchen counter, Captain Torres' name appeared in her notifications as a missed call. She pressed his name on the display. He answered before she heard it ring.

"Good morning, Abby. I hope you're not in church just yet."

"No, sir. Just about to start getting ready."

"I wanted to ask you something. When you interviewed Rol on Friday, he said Doc drove a white rusty car, and you asked if it could have been a truck." She heard him take a slurp of what she assumed was coffee. "Why did you ask that?"

"The reports said there was a rusty white Maverick near the crime scene. I thought Rol could verify if Doc had that kind of truck."

"Truck?"

"Yes, sir. What's the confusion?"

"Abby, the Maverick parked on Newport Court was a car. Not a truck."

"What? I googled a Ford Maverick and saw dozens of images of pickup trucks. Then I noticed my neighbor drives a Maverick truck."

"Ah, that explains it," Turo said. "But here's a surprising fact. In the 1970's, the Ford Maverick was a *car*."

"Are you kidding me right now?" Abby's voice grew louder. "That makes Doc a more likely suspect than the rich Porsche owner! We've got to figure out who he is!"

"Yes. We do. I'm sorry to bother you on a Sunday with this, but I just couldn't quit thinking about it. You might as well have the details straight in your mind."

"I agree. Thanks so much for the call, Turo. That shines a different light on a man they called Doc. Now I just have to figure out how to find someone based on a nickname he had 18 years ago."

"See you tonight, Abby. Kerri and I are looking forward to seeing you."

———

After church service, Abby and Jacob walked out of the auditorium into the expansive lobby of the megachurch. "I feel like I was just at a concert," Jacob said.

"The music is one of the best parts about this place," Abby said.

"I could tell you were very moved by it."

"I may have shed a tear or two," she playfully bumped his hip with her own as they walked side by side through the double doors to the parking lot. "Oh my gosh. Jacob, will you excuse me for a minute? I see someone I don't want to miss. I'm so sorry. I'll be right back." She scurried off and hoped he'd wait for her.

"Alex! Alex, is that you?" The long-legged, dark-haired woman was hoisting a stroller from the trunk of her white Kia while balancing a toddler in her arm. She turned toward Abby with a confused look. "I'm sorry you probably don't remember. I'm Dahlia Archer's sister, Abby."

"Bebee?! Come here right now," the woman nearly shouted, then wrapped Abby in a hug, pressed against the messy face of a toddler who seemed to enjoy the embrace as much as she did. When she let go, Alex was visibly crying. "My word, Bebee. You look so much like her. How are you?"

She shifted her child, who Abby could now see was a little girl, to her other hip. Before Abby could respond, Alex said, "I'm sorry, I can't stop staring at you." Wiping her face on her sleeve, she said, "And apparently, I can't stop crying either."

Abby hugged Alex again. "I can't believe I bumped into you." She glanced at her watch and said, "You're probably getting ready for the next service. Can we have coffee soon?"

"I'd love that!" Alex said. "Hand me your cell phone so I can type in my number." Abby did and was amazed at how much a busy mom can accomplish with one hand.

The women hugged once more. "Soon. Let's make it soon." Alex said, and she hurried off toward the nursery.

Abby made her way quickly toward Jacob. "I'm so sorry. I haven't seen her since I was a kid, and I'd have kicked myself if I hadn't given her a hug. I got her number so we can talk without all this drama next time."

Jacob's demeanor had shifted. "She certainly had her hands full," his voice was nearly monotone.

"She was a good friend of my sister's," Abby explained. "I'm sorry to have left you standing alone on your first time here."

"I'm a big boy. I can handle it, Abby."

"Has something upset you? You don't seem your cheerful and encouraging self."

"I'm not *always* a cheerful and encouraging person. I just got a text, and I have a situation blowing up at work. I should go. I'll call you in a day or two?"

"Okay," Abby said, sensing that wasn't the true reason for the shift in his mood. "I hope you get everything worked out okay."

"Thanks," he said and walked briskly into the depths of the parking lot.

Abby stood for a moment, watching him go. She saw him stop and shake hands with a man who approached him near his car. The two talked for a few moments, and then Abby saw the man's wife get out of their car and approach the two men. She realized she knew the couple. It was her friends, Tim and Pasha Kline, who'd spent a lot of time with her in a small church group and brought her all those wonderful meals.

She waited near the entry doors, thumbing through her phone until the couple approached. "Hi guys," she smiled, then reached out to Pasha for a hug. "Thanks again for helping out after my surgery. Your casserole was incredible!"

"You're so welcome, Abby!" Pasha raised her lips and wrinkled her nose. "I hope it tasted okay. I tried a new recipe, and it's not always the best decision to give away a meal you've never tried yourself."

Abby laughed and said, "It was delicious! One of my favorites in the assortment, actually. I'd love the recipe if you still have it to share."

"I do. I'll text it to you when I get home."

"I'd love that!"

"Maybe Pash will cook it for me sometime," Tim chimed in. "It smelled amazing."

"Well, when she does, you won't be disappointed, I assure you. On another note, did I just see you talking to Jacob Jennings? He came to church with me this morning, and I was worried he might have felt out of place."

"Yes!" Tim said. "I've known him since my early rebellious days. I don't even like to think about the stories we could tell. I was shocked to see him here, actually. He said he came with a friend. How nice that it was you."

"He's dreamy, Abby. Is there something brewing here?" Pasha teased.

"That remains to be seen," Abby grinned. "We've spent a little time together recently."

"If things work out, the four of us will have to get together sometime." Pasha looked to Tim for confirmation.

"Hey, we better get in there, or we'll miss the start of service," his reply was abrupt and vague.

"It's a good one today," Abby offered. "Who am I kidding? All the services here are good."

They exchanged farewell hugs and promised to connect again soon. Abby turned to leave before seeing Tim hold his gaze on her for a split second, a dark cloud passing over his face.

—

Abby pulled her Edge into the Torres's driveway and nudged close enough to the garage door to capture what was left of the afternoon shade. She stepped out of her vehicle and walked around to the passenger side to collect the Pyrex bowl full of broccoli salad.

The way things dissolved with Jacob had replayed in her thoughts most of the day. She retraced her steps, mentally skimming through the morning as it unfolded. From her perspective, there was no reason he would become so agitated. She'd been tempted to call him, but he made it clear he'd reach out to her again at some point. Best to let things simmer, she supposed, and wait to see how they'd play out.

The Torres's ranch-style brick house was about 15 minutes from her own in a beautiful, older neighborhood. The homes were robust, with wide yards shaded by stately trees and surrounded by lush lawns. Abby could envision unending soccer games that moved from yard to yard and meaningful friendships that grew through decades of living along the same street.

She reached out to knock on the front door, freshly painted black and adorned with a hydrangea wreath to welcome visitors. A small placard that dissuaded solicitors was carefully placed below a glass pane, through which Abby could see a young woman bounding toward her. The door was thrown open before she could knock, and Cora wrapped her arms around Abby, nearly knocking the salad out of her hands.

"Nice to see you, Cora!" Abby adored time with the Torres girls. "Where's Camila?"

"She's out with her boyfriend. She wanted to stay, but he told her the warm weather was almost officially over and persuaded her to go to the amusement park."

"So she chose a date at an amusement park over dinner with me?"

Cora mimicked Abby's disgusted expression, then broke into a smile. "I get you all to myself." The energetic teen reached for the bowl and asked, "Is this your broccoli salad? Sweet! We'll have to eat it all. Camila will go berserk if she doesn't get any."

Kerri stepped around the corner to welcome her dinner guest with a warm hug. "So good to see you!" Her hand slid tenderly down Abby's arm and gripped her fingers in her own. She led her by the hand into the living room and sat beside her on a sofa that nearly swallowed them in its cushions.

Abby often noticed the striking resemblance between Kerri and Auntie Beth. It was as if they shared a similar warmth—kind, soft eyes adorned with smile lines, full lips, and chiseled cheekbones. Yet, there was a marked difference; while Kerri's hair was as dark as the night, Auntie Beth—like Mama, Dahlia, and herself—had flowing blonde locks that displayed the tapestry of their family's history.

"Turo says emotions have been heavy. I can't believe they're asking you to investigate Dahlia's cold case. How are you holding up?"

"It's minute to minute, honestly, and has a way of tossing me from despair to elation. At the same time, the process is exhilarating, and I'm getting some new leads that could lead us to answers."

"As much as I'd love to keep our conversation personal tonight, I know better. It will devolve into work before the dishes are cleared." Kerri looked over her shoulder and whispered, "So tell me all the good stuff before Turo comes in."

Abby laughed and reached to squeeze her friend's knee. "You've always been Turo's better half, you know that, right?!"

"Of course I do!" She tilted her chin upward and put on a proud, celebrity-style smile. "But let's talk about you." Kerri leaned closer and said, "I hear you might be seeing someone."

Kerri Torres knew more about her than many of her closest friends. She was a trusted confidante that, through many years of dinners like this one, had yet to breach a single layer of trust. Abby's face softened, and the corners of her eyes crinkled as she said, "I really have no idea." She gave the 45-second version of the weekend events, which left Kerri shrugging her shoulders as Turo's voice boomed from the kitchen.

"I see broccoli salad in here," he said. They heard the silverware drawer open and the sound of a fork sliding against a glass dish. He stepped toward the living room, and when he greeted his guest, she saw bits of green between his teeth.

Turo had on a black canvas apron with a blue-lined American flag embroidered into the chest pocket. "I'm pulling the Tri-Tip off the Traeger," he told Kerri. When he stepped back into the house with a plate full of meat, Abby's stomach rumbled in anticipation. Torres's Tri-Tip was the stuff of legends, coveted throughout the department. Soon, they were devouring meat tender enough to cut with a fork paired with roasted petite potatoes, Abby's salad, and a bottle of Cabernet.

As predicted, once the talk of autumn colors, school schedules, and college plans died down, Cora cleared the dishes and slid her Air-Pods into her ears as she loaded the dishwasher. Kerri was first to ask Abby about the cold case unit.

"I'm enjoying it far more than I thought," Abby admitted. "There are several cases where I believe we can apply new technology and get answers that have been just out of reach. I've sent several DNA samples for analysis in two of the older cases, and I'm hopeful we'll see some quick results on those." Abby fiddled with her napkin. "The others are going to take a lot of legwork, just like Dahlia's case."

"I've wondered," Kerri asked, "if the lead detectives on the unsolved cases feel threatened by the work you're doing or if they see it as a help."

"I can answer that," Turo chimed in. "We see it as help. There's not a detective among us who doesn't carry the burden of a case if it goes unsolved. No matter what other cases come up, the old ones still rest in the back of our minds. They never leave us. To have a new set of eyes looking at the details is like breathing new hope into our very core."

"It's helpful to talk to the lead investigators on each case," Abby said. "I've asked if there were witnesses they couldn't track down or leads that just didn't develop for them. That usually gives me some direction."

Turo refilled his glass of wine and held the bottle over Abby's glass to offer more. She waved her hand to indicate she'd had her fill.

Kerri stood and carried Abby's water glass to the kitchen for a refill. Abby looked at Turo. "I've never asked you those questions. Do you have some of those raw leads in Dahlia's case?"

Turo thought for a moment, then said, "I do. The couple who lived in the house closest to where the white Maverick was parked were traveling in Europe on the night of the murder. They had a house sitter who was coming by the house every couple of days to pick up their mail and water their plants. I could never track her down."

"I remember reading that. The report said she told the home-owners she didn't see anything that would help."

"She was a college student commuting to the Metro State campus. She worked near the crime scene, if I remember correctly. I had her contact information but could never get her to come in and talk to us. Some people just don't want to get involved, and we can't force them to without a subpoena."

"Small details like that can bring a big break in a case. It's worth trying to contact her." Abby made a mental note to do so.

"What happens when you get all the cold cases solved?" Kerri asked, stepping back into the dining room.

"I appreciate your faith in me," Abby laughed. "Unless I'm cleared for duty when our team solves all the cold cases, it's possible I could work myself out of a job."

CHAPTER 34

ABBY, 2023

Carrying three iced lattes into the office was no easy task. Deputies quickly opened the doors for her as she walked through but tried to negotiate one of the coffees for their efforts. The journey from the parking lot to her desk took more than the usual two minutes with all of the jokes and added conversations. Abby wondered if she'd ever make it.

She set one of the lattes on Michelle's desk, surprised to see she wasn't sitting in her chair. Stepping into her own office, she placed Wayne's latte near his chair, set her personal items down, and reached for her cell phone.

She found and reread an email she'd seen on her phone this morning with news that DNA tests results from the Davis investigation were in. The bad news was the test was inconclusive. Another dead end. She sipped her latte, then looked through the stack of case files, searching for the 2017 Tiffany Davis homicide.

The case involved a young woman who'd been found shot to death in her apartment. Her roommate had come home late one night and found her on her bed. She'd been shot in the head, and while it appeared she'd brought a man home from a night out, there was no evidence of sexual activity, consensual or otherwise.

Abby believed there might be a chance for some touch DNA from the doorknob and shell casing, but neither sample had yielded a profile.

She found the file and had spread its contents across her desk. Wayne had already interviewed the victim's family and co-workers, whose stories had remained consistent with earlier statements. Her sister hinted that Tiffany's roommate, Carolanne Geneaux, didn't respond well to men, so Abby agreed to contact her.

She'd just pressed Carolanne's number into her desk phone when Michelle poked her head in the door. She was holding her coffee and lifted it up in a "cheers" gesture. *Thank you,* she mouthed with a smile.

Knowing the Sheriff's Office would show up on caller identification, Abby was reasonably sure Carolanne would pick up her phone. She did. "Hello, can I speak with Carolanne, please?" Abby said while she waved off her new friend.

"This is she," the voice on the line answered.

"Carolanne, this is Sergeant Abigail Carter from the Adams County Sheriff's Office in Colorado. Thank you for answering my call. I'm taking a new look at the Tiffany Davis case. Can I ask you a few questions?"

"If you can hang on one minute, I'll tell my boss I need a break, and I'll be right with you."

Abby twirled a pen in her fingers and doodled the shape of a maple leaf on her notepad before Carolanne returned.

"Okay, I can talk now," she said.

"Again, thank you for answering my call. We're working to move Tiffany's investigation along and finally get a conviction for her murder. I'm hoping you'll tell me what you remember about March 17, 2017."

Abby heard Carolanne take a deep inhale before she started. "Of course. It was St. Patty's Day, so everything was green. I had a date with my boyfriend, and Tiff said she was seeing someone new that night."

"And your boyfriend at the time was Steven Hyatt, is that correct?"

"Yes, it was Steven. He was taking me to an Irish pub downtown, and we were in a hurry because the crowds were going to be fierce. He didn't want to wait all night for a table, so I took my makeup with me to put on while he drove. And I left Tiff there," Carolanne paused, "by herself." Abby could hear the quiver in her voice. "That's the last time I saw her alive."

"I'm very sorry to make you go through this again, but can you tell me what you saw when you arrived back at the apartment?"

Wayne Finch shuffled his way into his seat at the conference table, peering at the manila file in front of Abby so he could see which case she was working on. As he did, Carolanne relayed the story over speakerphone, and Abby reviewed her report from 2017 for any inconsistencies. Details were exactly the way she'd shared them on the night of the murder. She'd come home late, and Tiffany's car had been in the parking lot, so she'd expected the door to be unlocked. But it wasn't.

It had been cold outside, and she'd had to dig through her purse to find her key. By the time she'd found it, she and Steve were freezing, and Carolanne was yelling at Tiffany because she hadn't answered the door to let them in. When she'd gotten inside, the house had been completely quiet. No music was playing, which was strange. Tiffany always had music playing. No one was home.

Carolanne and Steven had moved to her bedroom, and when it was time for him to leave, there'd still been no sign of Tiffany. After he'd gone, Carolanne returned to her bedroom and started to hear a strange noise, as if something was dripping. She'd checked the bathroom first, then the kitchen, then opened Tiffany's bedroom door to see if anything was out of the ordinary. And that's when she saw Tiffany lying face down on her bed. She'd screamed so much the downstairs neighbor came up and she'd yelled at him to call 9-1-1.

"Did you know who she was seeing that night?"

"She never told me," Carolanne answered. "It was this big secret. She'd said he didn't want a bunch of people to know his name, so she had to keep it just between the two of them. I mean, how creepy is that? And she went out with him anyway. Sometimes, I get so mad at her for being so stupid. And then I get so sad because she's gone."

Carolanne was crying again. "You know what came to me the other day?"

"Please tell me," Abby said.

"Every time I listen to the radio and that KISS song comes on, Calling Dr. Love—" Carolanne went silent again.

"Yes?" Abby prodded.

"I have to turn the station. I do it every time. I can't stand that song, and I never quite knew why. Then, the other day, it hit me. When I asked Tiffany about the new guy she was seeing, she'd always sing that song. She said he wanted her to call him Doc, and he'd give her the cure she wanted. I never remembered that until a few days ago, and now it's so vivid it feels like yesterday."

Abby wrote furiously on her notepad and had to fight the knot that was growing in the pit of her stomach. "Caroleanne, do you know if Tiffany was involved in drugs?"

"We both were at that time. I've been clean since then. It's amazing how many changes something like this can bring to your life. Tiffany and I used prescription painkillers like Vikes and Oxycodone."

"Was this Doc person a dealer?"

"Not that I know of. Now that I think about that song, though, it would make sense if he was. I never bought from him. Maybe Tiffany did."

Abby made a note to re-check Tiffany's toxicology report from the autopsy. "This is all helpful, Carolanne," she said as calmly as she could. "Thank you. Is there anything else you remember? About that night or other memories that have stirred up since then?"

"That's it, I think. If I think of anything else, can I call you?"

"Of course you can. Use the number that came up on your cell phone and ask for Sergeant Carter."

"Are you getting close to catching the guy?"

"I hope so. The process runs slowly, but we're using new technology and trying to look at the case from a lot of different angles. We want to get justice for Tiffany, and I know you do, too. Please call me immediately if anything else comes to mind."

She ended the call and threw her hands in the air. "Holy Hannah. Wayne, I think we just caught a break."

Abby's adrenaline was still surging when she met with Dr. Patrick later in the day. He'd reviewed her newest x-rays, and the plan was to determine whether a knee replacement was needed. Waiting for him to enter the office felt like an eternity. The news of the morning still ricocheted through her mind like a piece of shrapnel. It tore at everything she thought she knew.

Could Dahlia's case be connected to Tiffany Davis? The cases were a dozen years apart, but they had to be. There was no probable way that both victims would have referred to someone by the nickname "Doc." Was there?

The random, playful notes Dahlia left for Abby had been running through her mind all day. One in particular. *The Doc has the cure.* She'd sketched musical notes alongside her words. Abby had always assumed they were lyrics to a song but never knew which one. After speaking to Carolanne, Abby googled the lyrics to *Calling Dr. Love* by KISS, and they were nearly verbatim. There was no way it could be coincidental.

After talking with Carolanne, she'd talked with Michelle and Wayne, then called Captain Torres. When he didn't answer, she texted him and asked to speak to him as soon as possible.

"I think he killed someone else, Captain," she said as soon as he called her back.

"Who has? Dahlia's killer?"

Abby ran through the details of what Carolanne had shared and the random notes Dahlia had written for her.

"That's a very specific crime signature. If he's committed two murders, there could very well be three. If three, then maybe four or more. I'm with the sheriff right now. When I wrap up with him, I'll call a meeting of the entire detective unit, and you can share what you learned today. Maybe someone with a solved case had a similar clue, and we already have this guy in jail."

Ninety minutes later, she'd stood at the head of a conference table in front of the detective squad. There was no time to get nervous or to feel insecure. The link in cases created a sense of urgency that made sharing with her colleagues feel like a normal, everyday occurrence.

"The guy goes by 'Doc' and likes to think of himself as having the cure people are looking for." Pushing a strand of hair out of her eyes, she had explained, "We've linked this moniker in two unsolved murders: Tiffany Davis from 2017 and Dahlia Archer from 2005, both of whom were shot in the head by a 9mm weapon. Both victims were known to use narcotics. Neither were sexually assaulted before they were killed. No fingerprints or DNA were found at Tiffany's crime scene. DNA results from the Archer case are still pending. Maybe we'll catch a break.

"There's a twelve-year span between victims that leaves a high probability there's another case—or several—we haven't yet connected.

"Detective Calvin Bissel, you worked the Tiffany Davis case." Abby scanned the room until she made eye contact with him. "Can you let me know when you have some time on your calendar? We have a lot to talk through. Everyone else, please review your cases and let me know if anything sparks your attention."

Abby continued, "Michelle, our new crime analyst, will be going through our records looking for case similarities. She'll also send an intel bulletin to statewide agencies today. He could have easily killed beyond the boundaries of Adams County or acted inside city limits where police departments would have handled the cases. Wayne has already reached out to the North Metro Drug Task Force to see if there's a 'Doc' on their radar. Let's get this guy!"

The meeting amplified the urgency and fueled the adrenaline of the detective squad. She'd left headquarters filled with optimism, and now, as Abby waited for Dr. Patrick, she couldn't keep still. She paced the medical room like a runner before a race, waiting for whatever he would say so she could hit the starting blocks and chase after a guy named Doc.

Getting cleared for full duty was no longer her chief concern. She needed to put her full focus on these two cases and let the others sit on the back burner for now. With Doc still out there somewhere, Adams County had a possible serial killer in their midst. More than anything, she wanted to leave this appointment and do whatever it took to get him off the street and into prison where he belonged.

She was mentally prepared for the news that she'd need a knee replacement. Certainly, Dr. Patrick would let her delay the surgery until these cases were wrapped up. She could get around easily enough in a detective role, even though her knee wasn't 100%. But there was no way she'd pass the fitness qualifications or be able to test her physical limitations out on the street.

Finding Dahlia's murderer and the man who also killed Tiffany Davis was paramount. Abby's optimism had been simmering, and she allowed it to boil over, imagining going through the trial as an advisory witness before going back for a second surgery.

The door to the examination room opened, and Dr. Patrick entered. "Good to see you, Abby," he said.

CHAPTER 35

ABBY, 2023

Sheriff Adler stopped in Abby's doorway. "Come on. Captain Torres and I are taking you to lunch."

"I'd love to, sir," she answered, "but—"

He cut her off as she fanned her arms over the stacks of paperwork on her desk. "You gotta eat, Abby. And we want to celebrate this break in the case with you."

"It's a little too early to celebrate, Sheriff. It's a link, but we're far from finding the whole chain."

Sheriff Adler smiled. He held his right arm out and began waving his left arm from the elbow to hurry her along, as a third base coach would wave a baseball player toward home plate. "I appreciate your focus, Abby. Now, let's go. Mental breaks are important. So is nourishment. It's the best thing you can do for the case right now. Besides, I'm hungry."

Abby shook her head in mock protest but knew the man was right. It would feel good to get out and talk for a while instead of keeping her head buried in reports. Besides, she had some of her own news to share, so she should seize the opportunity for uninterrupted time with her bosses.

The trio climbed into Sheriff Adler's Ford Expedition, and Captain Torres insisted on taking the rear seat. Her petite frame hardly required much legroom, but she conceded, gracefully slipping into the front passenger seat. Using the running board for a boost, she climbed aboard the formidable vehicle. The computer, firmly fixed in the middle console, extended into the passenger's seat, compelling her to nudge its swivel mount back toward the center.

Sheriff Adler suggested Mickey's Steakhouse, which surprised Abby. A month ago, she'd never been there, and this would be her second visit. She did enjoy the food there, and it was a more celebratory place than the sandwich shop up the street from Headquarters. If she took a break at all, it would have been to grab a sandwich and eat at her desk.

They pulled into the parking lot, and Abby recognized Jacob's blue truck parked in one of the front stalls near the building. *Well, this could be interesting,* she thought to herself. She hadn't seen or talked with Jacob since Sunday morning but was sure to have the opportunity now. Inside the open, airy restaurant, it would be hard to miss one another.

The host sat them at a booth near the restaurant entrance, and it was as if the three of them saw only two seats. Abby laughed as she realized what was happening. They all wanted to sit facing the front door. Trusting these two men would observe their surroundings enough for the three of them, she chose to try to let her guard down and relax through lunch. Captain Torres slid into the seat beside her. With a subtle nod, he whispered, "We'll let the sheriff stand watch this shift, what do you say?"

"Great minds think alike," she responded with a quick side glance.

After the drinks and entrees were ordered, Abby spoke up. "Before we get this celebration going," she said, "I have some news to share." She flushed with embarrassment over the emotion her voice revealed.

"I've been cleared for full duty. I saw my Orthopedic yesterday, and he gave me the news."

"Abby! Congratulations!" Captain Torres leaned over to give her a hug, made awkward by the tight space. His care was apparent. He wanted nothing but the best for her and understood the angst she'd felt knowing her body wasn't whole. But to Abby, this news was surprisingly bittersweet.

"Fantastic!" Sheriff Adler agreed. "That's got to feel so good for you to hear! You have no further physical restrictions?"

"No. Not one. I'll admit I'm shocked. I still feel pain and stiffness, but Dr. Patrick said that's nothing to worry about. Now it's all about building strength and stamina. I shared the paperwork with HR this morning." She looked each of the men in the face. The three of them stared at one another as a few seconds ticked by as Abby tried to find a steady, professional voice buried somewhere inside of herself.

"It *is* great news," she said. "I'm happy to have passed this milestone, but if I can be completely transparent, I cried all evening after receiving the news."

"Why in the world—" Sheriff Adler started.

Abby interrupted him. "It means I'll have to give up cold cases. I've made such amazing progress, and now I'll have to turn it all over for someone else to finish. What if no one else has time to give these cases the attention they deserve?"

"No," the sheriff said. "That's not how it's going to work. You'll stay and finish and take each of these cases to a clear and logical finish. We won't transfer you back to patrol until this assignment is complete."

"You mean it?" She didn't want to draw attention to the tears threatening to spill over but reached into her bag for a tissue.

"I mean it," he said. "I hear Deputy Brunson is still doing a great job as acting sergeant in your absence. In fact, he's proven himself ready to compete for a promotion with the next sergeant's opening. We need you right where you are until the work's finished."

"I thought it might be more budget-friendly to put a deputy or detective on this assignment."

"If this were a permanent role, maybe I would. But it's always been slated as temporary, and I'll keep you here as long as it makes sense for the project—and for you."

Abby stared wide-eyed at him before responding. She was almost giddy. "Thank you, sir! That just cleared a dump truck full of garbage from my head." She laughed, "I'm so relieved!"

"So tell me about the connection in these two cases," Sheriff Adler said.

Abby relayed Carolanne's story and how she'd connected the dots about Doc. Most of her salad sat uneaten while she filled him in on every detail she'd already shared with Captain Torres. The two men were fully engrossed in the way the story unfolded, but Abby noticed the sheriff's expression suddenly cooled. He was looking over her shoulder, and by reading his body language, she knew she'd lost his attention.

Glancing over her shoulder, she saw Jacob approaching their table, smiling pleasantly. "Hello, everyone," he said. "Sorry to interrupt, but I owe Sergeant Carter an apology. Our last meeting ended rather abruptly."

Abby appreciated his discretion in not calling it a 'date' in front of her bosses. "No harm, no foul," she replied. "I hope everything worked out the way it should."

"It did, indeed. Can I call you soon to reschedule?"

"Of course," she smiled.

"Then I'll leave you to your lunch."

Jacob nodded politely and casually walked toward the restaurant exit. He was out of earshot when the sheriff said, "There's something off about that guy."

Both Turo and Abby looked at him with wide eyes and raised eyebrows. "Sheriff, I've never heard you say a negative thing about anyone," Abby said.

"I'll say it when it's warranted. I can't put my finger on it, but something bothers me about him."

Sheriff Adler sliced his sirloin. When Abby and Turo continued to stare at him, he carried on with his rant. "We campaigned together before the last election, and I get a strong sense that his political goals have more to do with personal ambition than serving our community. There's no room for that in county government.

"I have to attend a lot of the commissioner board meetings, and from what I see, he misses more of them than he attends, like he can't be bothered to do the job the people elected him to do. Then he shows up and starts asking you all about the crime analyst position as if he's suddenly fascinated by all that we can accomplish through it. It just doesn't sit right."

"And now we know," Captain Torres said, making silent eye contact with Abby, who finally released the breath she'd been holding.

"Sir," she began, "I had dinner with Jacob Jennings last Saturday, and the 'meeting' that ended abruptly was him visiting church with me."

Sheriff Adler swore under his breath. "I apologize, Abby. I had no idea. I shouldn't have said any of those things."

"I'm happy you did, sir. You've reminded me to use caution." She dipped a crouton in her ranch dressing and popped it in her mouth. "He does have a lot of interest in the cold cases. Since he's an elected official, I've felt obligated to answer his questions. Without sharing confidential details, of course. Would you like me to respond to him differently going forward?"

"What I'd like you to do and what is professionally appropriate are two different things," he pursed his lips together and shook his head. "He *is* an elected official, so keep answering his questions, but don't give any case details. And since I already put my foot in my mouth, I'll go ahead and say more." Sheriff Adler held his water glass in his hand, shaking it toward Abby. "From what I've seen, he likes to control things and can be manipulative. Keep your guard up."

"Thanks, sir. Point taken." They ate in silence for a few minutes, then regained the earlier light-hearted mood. Abby enjoyed the banter of two men who had worked their whole careers side by side. They harbored more information about one another than most family members would know about their loved ones and had developed an uncommon bond of trust.

Abby couldn't help but reflect on the profound reasons she had grown to love law enforcement. It was more than just a job; it was a calling, a way of life. Beyond the satisfaction of helping people and the sense of purpose that came with her work, there was an intangible quality binding them all together—a brother and sisterhood forged through shared experiences, sacrifices, and an unbreakable trust.

In the tight-knit community of law enforcement, camaraderie ran deep. Somewhere along the line, Abby had realized that, yes, she was putting her life on the line every day, but she never doubted that her fellow officers would always have her back. They all understood the missed holiday celebrations, the absences from family gatherings, and the sacrifices made for the greater good. Few people outside the profession could truly comprehend it, but these shared sacrifices formed a connection that transcended words.

With these thoughts lingering in her mind, Abby leaned back in her seat. Her journey was far from over. She felt ready to face whatever challenges may come, but she had no way of knowing her resolve was about to be tested like never before.

CHAPTER 36

ABBY, 2023

Abby pulled Mack into a tight embrace as Mack removed her suitcase from her Kia Sonata. She slung a backpack over her shoulder, wheeled her luggage inside, and headed toward the downstairs bedroom. "I'd rather have the upstairs suite if it's all the same to you," she teased.

"Forget it. You got it last time while I was down here sleeping off the anesthesia and drooling into the pillows. Which have been replaced, by the way," she laughed.

"All right, all right, the downstairs room it is. At least you've made it delightfully comfy. And I'm closer to the coffee now, so that's a plus. What time is the concert tonight?"

"The opening band starts at 7:00 pm, but Gus Farmer probably won't come on stage till around nine. If you hurry and unpack, we can go grab a quick bite, enjoy the facials I scheduled—compliments of my patrol shift for my birthday—then come home to shower and change." Abby stared at Mack for a moment. "What a great day with a great friend. I'm so glad you're here!"

"Someday, I'm going to ask you to get me a job with Adams County so we can live closer together. For now, I'm climbing my own ladder in Mesa County. Did I tell you I just got transferred?"

"No, you did not! Where are you working now?"

"They officially moved me into investigations. I'm working in property crimes."

"No more shift work! That's the dream, but you'll still get called out a bunch at night, I'm sure."

"Not so much with property crimes. Later, when I move over to major crimes—because that's the goal, of course—I'll be a woman of little sleep." She hoisted her bright orange suitcase to the top of the bed and unzipped it. "For now, I'm taking advantage of full nights' rest and a lot of weekends off. I love it! I didn't even have to take a day off for the concert like I thought I would."

Mack unpacked her clothes and smiled when she saw a tiny pink resin duck she'd tucked in a dresser drawer during her post-surgery visit. She'd hidden dozens of them throughout the house and wondered how many she'd find still lingering about.

Abby sat on the bed and studied her friend. Since they last saw one another, Mack had restyled and colored her hair. The new look suited her and accentuated the green eyes Abby had always found stunning. Even without a smear of makeup, Mack had a natural beauty. What was most attractive about her friend was that she didn't realize it. She didn't even think about it. Mack was comfortable in her own skin, always true to her inner self. Her genuine warmth made her easy to be around.

"You know I watched a documentary about Gus Farmer," Mack said. "He grew up in Scotland and then moved to the States with his mom when he was a young teen. I guess that's why I love to listen to him talk. I wouldn't have guessed his accent is Scottish. I just know I could listen to him for days. He should narrate an audiobook or just marry me, and I'd be quiet for once in my life just so I could listen to his voice."

Abby rolled her eyes and said, "Okay, dreamer. That reminds me. I beefed up my playlist and added a bunch of his songs. We'll try to blow out my speakers as we're driving around today."

A few minutes later, the music played through Bluetooth, and country rock filled the car speakers. They rolled down their windows and sang at the top of their tone-deaf voices. They stopped for chile relleno nachos at a new restaurant that had opened since Mack had been in Denver, then took their full bellies to the spa for some proper pampering.

The rest of the night was flawless. The opening band at the concert was one they hadn't heard before but instantly loved. When Gus Farmer took the stage, they were thrilled to have premium seats. They sang along, danced, and let thoughts of the world slip away while they enjoyed a night of fun.

It was nearly 1:00 am when they pulled into Abby's driveway, the girls still chatting happily about their favorite songs, guitar riffs, and unexpected dance moves. Across the street, a blue truck was parked just outside the halo of the streetlight, its form melting into the darkness.

Abby pulled into the garage and stepped down from the SUV, nearly jumping out of her skin when Jacob spoke to her.

"I'm so sorry," he said. "I didn't mean to startle you." He'd walked across the street and was now standing inside her garage.

"What are you doing here?" Abby's greeting was less than cordial. Her hand was pressed against her chest. She took a deep breath, trying to get her heart rate to slow.

"I wanted to see if you enjoyed the concert and thought this would be a good time to meet Mack."

"Um, yes," Abby faltered. "We had a great time. Mack, this is Jacob. Jacob, Mack."

The two exchanged greetings and a hasty handshake. "Were you just waiting for us out there?" Mack asked pointedly.

A pertinent question, Abby thought to herself. She didn't remember mentioning the concert—or Mack's visit—to Jacob and was replaying their past conversations in her mind.

Jacob answered, "I took a chance. I was out late and thought the timing might be right for you to be getting home about now, so I popped over. And I was right. It was great I could catch you."

Abby tried to take the awkwardness out of the moment. "We were just going to open a bottle of wine. Do you want to come in for a nightcap?"

"That sounds great," Jacob said. "I would have thought you'd had your fill by this time."

"We're not beer drinkers, and we're much too cheap to pay concert prices for drinks anyway. Plus, when you wait until you get home, you can always get what you like," Mack said.

As Abby stepped up the stairs from the garage into her house, she said, "I'm a total lightweight, not to mention the drinking and driving thing. That's a no-go." The garage opened to the laundry room of her house, and she was grateful for its unusual tidiness. She set her small cross-body bag on the dryer, waited for Jacob and Mack to come in, then moved back onto the step to press the button and watch the garage door lower.

Minutes later, they were sprawled comfortably on the soft seating of her living room, each holding a glass of Cabernet. Mack and Jacob chatted about Abby's accident and her move to cold cases. "Isn't it a bit unusual for a sergeant to handle investigations?" Jacob asked.

"I think it's great they made room for her there," Mack said. "It speaks of the trust they have in her and the way they value her as an employee. Abby also has a ton of investigative experience. She was in the detective unit for, what, three years?"

"Five years, actually," Abby replied. "I was there until I was promoted to sergeant, then they moved me back to patrol."

"Still," Jacob said. "It would be very difficult to work a case where your sister is the victim."

Abby felt the back of her neck bristle. She was positive she hadn't shared that detail with Jacob. In fact, she'd intentionally kept it from him.

"Again, it just demonstrates Abby's professionalism." Mack was showing her friendly, chatty side. "It *is* highly unusual and would take the right set of circumstances—and the right detective—to be able to work a case like that. Captain Torres has guts, I'll give him that. And his choice in this assignment was stellar, in my opinion."

"I hear her work is exemplary," Jacob said. "I, for one, am very proud of the way Abby represents Adams County. We're lucky to have her."

Abby smiled but held her tongue. This was a strange side of Jacob. She wondered if he'd been drinking before dropping in on them.

"What role do you play in law enforcement, Mack?" Before she could answer, he added, "It feels strange to call you by your nickname when I don't know you well. What's your full name?"

"Macaylie Thomas," she answered. "I'm a detective with the Mesa County Sheriff's Office."

Abby excused herself to use the restroom while they talked. She was bone tired, and the wine had a sedative effect on her already weary body and mind. Maybe she was overreacting to Jacob's odd comments. She'd have a long talk with Mack about it in the morning over breakfast in their cozy pajamas, messy hair, and smeared makeup, just like they did as roommates in college.

For now, she wanted to clear the room so she could get some sleep. By the time she stepped out of the powder room, Jacob was already standing near the door.

"I need to let you ladies get some sleep," he said. "It's been a long day, and I didn't mean to interrupt your time together. I know Abby feels there's far too little of it." He unbolted the lock and pulled the door open. "When do you head home, Macaylie?"

"After lunch at some point," she answered.

"Maybe I'll see you again then." He said. "Abby, it was terrific to see you. I'll reach out again very soon." Jacob reached for her hand and raised it to his lips, brushing against it with a feather-light touch. His eyes met hers, and he extended a warm smile. Abby searched his face for any hint of insincerity or manipulation but could only see what looked like genuine appreciation.

This, she thought to herself, *is where he gets me.* His manners and old-world charm were nearly impossible to read and even more difficult to resist. She closed the door securely behind him and fastened the deadbolt but didn't turn to face Mack for several long seconds.

"Are you swooning?" Mack asked.

"Swooning? Now there's a vocabulary word," she laughed. "No, I'm not *swooning*. Just trying to figure out yet another mystery in my life. Is that guy for real? I can't tell. Help me, *Macaylie*." She mimicked Jacob's formal tone as she used her full name. She pressed her back against the door and slid down until she was sitting on the floor.

"He seems pleasant enough, but I do think he sat out there waiting for us for a time. It's still hot outside and I didn't hear the engine tinging as most cars do when they're cooling down." Mack stepped into the kitchen, removed a plastic water bottle out of the fridge, and gulped it down. "And to answer your question from weeks ago, the man is definitely interested in you."

They slept late. By the time Abby came down the stairs for coffee, Mack was already browning potatoes. "That smells divine," she said, lowering her face to the skillet.

"You have to cook the eggs, though," Mack said. "I still can't flip them without breaking the yolk, and you know I love 'em runny."

"Have you tried basting them? I'll show you. It will change your life." Abby set her coffee pod in the Nespresso machine and waited for it to brew. "Did you sleep okay?"

"Like a hibernating bear." Mack shook her body as if she were a bear coming out of its cave. The tight ponytail she wore on top of her head looked like it would break loose any second. "I hope you didn't hear me snoring from upstairs. You?"

"I don't think I moved all night. I was wiped out." She took her first sip of coffee and closed her eyes as it moved down her throat. "Coffee makes my whole self happier."

When the potatoes were crispy and the bacon fried, Abby showed Mack how to baste eggs. Then she removed the eggs with a slotted spatula and set them atop a pile of potatoes on Mack's plate.

"You're right, these are life-changing," Mack said. "Buttery texture, so much more flavor than fried." She took another bite, then said with her mouth full, "Where did you learn this?"

"Kevin's sister showed me. Game changer, right?" She was plating her own eggs and about to sit down when her phone vibrated. Glancing at the text message, she said, "Jacob wants to stop by. He thinks you'll enjoy seeing the car he's restoring."

"He's right, I'd love to. You know I love that kind of stuff."

"Okay. I'll tell him to give us an hour or so, then come by. I need a shower!" Abby hoped Jacob wouldn't insert himself into their day. They only had a few more hours of girl time left. She was sure he was just being friendly and trying to get to know Mack. But just in case, she texted him again and said they could take a quick look but had some errands to run before Mack got on the road.

Ninety minutes later, Abby heard the throaty growl of a car engine and peeked out the front window. "Here he is," she said to Mack, who followed her out the door.

Jacob had parked the car on the street in front of Abby's house. It was an old model red, two-door sedan. Mack went nuts. "Now that's a rare beast," she said, nearly sprinting to look inside. "What year is it?"

"It's a 1973. I've had a lot of bodywork done on it because it was pretty rusted out when I got it. Can I take you ladies for a ride?"

"We'd love to, but we have to stay on track," Abby said. "It is nice, though. I didn't know you were into cars."

"Isn't everyone?" He lifted his hand to emphasize his question. "I just got it back from the paint shop. Candy Apple Red. I don't have all of the insignias put on yet, but when I get the ones I ordered, it will be sharp!"

Abby peered into the window. It had bucket seats with what looked like leather trim, an automatic gear shifter on the floor, and an old-school AM/FM radio with turn knobs. Mack was gushing about its features with animated enthusiasm, while Jacob wore the smile of a proud father.

Without warning, a queasiness rippled through her body. She felt her head swirl and a heaviness in her throat as though she might heave. She gave a quiet, "Excuse me," then hurried into the house for a glass of cold water and stood beneath her ceiling fan for a moment. When she stepped back outside, she sat on her front doorstep and watched Mack admire the car as only she could.

Her friend picked up on her distance and cut the conversation with Jacob short, restating that they had several errands to run before she left town. He told Mack how nice it was to meet her, gave a friendly wave to Abby, and drove the car down the street.

"You okay?" Mack asked as she stepped onto the front porch.

"Yeah, I just felt queasy all of a sudden. Yesterday's heat and the hike to our seats must have really taken it out of me. I'll have to stay hydrated today. In fact, let me mix up some electrolytes in my Stanley, and we can get on our way. The outlet mall is calling!"

"Indeed it is," Mack said. "Let's do this. I'll drive today so you can shut your eyes whenever you need to."

"With you driving, I'll just keep them closed," Abby teased.

CHAPTER 37

ABBY, 2023

Abby had always imagined having an office with windows, and now that she had it, the glass panes were obstructed by the same information that consumed nearly all of her thoughts. Instead of blue skies and vibrant trees, she saw lists of suspects and details that needed uncovering. All this was to fulfill her lifelong purpose of bringing justice to victims and the families who loved them.

Without warning, Michelle jackrabbitted through her door. "I found it!" she nearly shouted.

Abby grinned at her excitement. "Do tell!"

"I found the Porsche!" Abby and Wayne were immediately on their feet and formed a small huddle around Michelle to avoid missing a word. "It's a '97 Boxster owned by a Tyler Watson. He's the original owner of the car and resides in Greeley. I started an intel sheet, so I have some facts for you."

Michelle referred to the printout she held in her hand. "Watson owns an auto shop, Watts Auto Repairs, near the college campus. His record is pretty clean outside of old marijuana charges and unpaid traffic tickets."

"Michelle, I could hug you. In fact, I think I will," she said, then squeezed her tight. "Great work!"

"I wish I could say it was hard work, but once you got the license plate number, there wasn't much to it."

"Sometimes it's not how hard something is, but the focus it takes to get a task done. We're creating a great team here," Wayne chimed in.

Abby put her hand on top of his head and messed up his closely cropped hair, a move she'd pulled on him numerous times over the years. Wayne was meticulous about neatness and never let his hair get too long or tousled out of place. He was good-natured with Abby and was always ready with a lighthearted payback.

Abby moved back to her desk chair and spun around on its swivel, thinking aloud. "The detective sergeant in Greeley is a friend of mine. We went to Reid together," she said, referencing the interview and interrogation course that nearly all new detectives attend.

Wayne said, "Can you give him a call and fill him in on the case? If Watson is our guy, he's the suspect in two Adams County homicides. On top of that, we've been told he pursues young girls for sexual favors. I doubt that's changed over the years, so the teams up north will likely be very interested in him."

"I'm looking for a connection with the 'Doc' moniker, but there's still a lot to sort through," Michelle said, nodding. "I'll keep knocking on those doors while you connect with the team up north."

Abby reached for her phone and looked up the phone number for the Greeley Police Department. She got through to her friend, Detective Sergeant Caleb Berkeley, and outlined her case. Berkeley agreed to try to spot Watson at his mechanic's shop and poke around for suspicious behaviors. He also promised to share the information with his captain.

The new discovery felt like taking a car out of park and shifting it into drive. With the gears in motion, she walked over to Captain Torres' office. He was at his desk and waved her in. She sat in a well-worn armchair and nervously picked at a frayed spot in the blue upholstery while he finished a phone conversation. "Good morning, Sergeant Carter," he said as he ended his call.

"Boss, we found the Porsche Rol told us about, and we had a flurry of activity this morning." She filled him in on the path she was following and watched his face light up with anticipation.

Turo picked up his desk phone and punched a few numbers. "Let me see if the sheriff's available. I have a feeling he'll want to talk personally with the sheriff from Weld County and possibly the chief at Greeley P.D."

Within seconds, Sheriff Adler was sitting beside her in Turo's office. After hearing the update, he said, "I'll call the two agency heads and make sure you have as much leeway as you need. We've always had a great working relationship with the teams in Weld County. But if you get anything other than a green light, call me directly—and immediately—and I'll take care of it."

For the next few hours, Abby's phone barely left her hands as she talked with detectives in Weld County. Wayne alerted task force teams so they could begin tracing and tracking Tyler Watson. Michelle was glued to her computer doing additional intel. When they came up for air and compared notes, Watson looked to be a viable suspect for Dahlia's murder and possibly that of Tiffany Davis as well.

They gathered in the detective division's main conference room, equipped with another set of mounted whiteboards to chart their notes. Wayne and Michelle sat at the oversized table, which was now covered in folders, sticky notes, and pens. Abby stood before the whiteboard, with a dry-erase marker in hand, and divided it into three sections by drawing two lines down the board. On the right side, she listed characteristics and circumstances that pointed to Watson as the killer. On the left were details that spurred doubt that he was involved. In the center, they kept notes about the next steps to take in the investigation.

Michelle had located Watson's Facebook account. Although he didn't post often, they printed an enlargement of his profile picture, taped it to the whiteboard, and listed the details they knew:

- Watson had been pointed out by Rol as a john who liked interactions with young girls.
- He still owned the Porsche Rol had described.
- Greeley PD was already watching his auto shop for potential drug activity.

- Their suspect had never been married and lived in an apartment close to the University of Northern Colorado campus.
- He'd grown up in Adams County.
- His mother still lived within two miles of Dahlia's murder scene.
- He would be very familiar with the area where the murders took place.

They plotted, charted, and talked 'what ifs' and 'how-comes.' As they did, several detectives popped in and out of the conference room to stare at the board and add their thoughts to the conversation.

Detective Tynlee Jones, who was on her way out of the building, stopped in, listening for several minutes. She suggested, "If he's running drugs out of the shop, he may also be running people. The shop may be a front for human trafficking. And maybe, like Dahlia, he's transported them in his cars. I'd check into his traffic tickets and see if there are any notations of passengers who might have been with him when he was pulled over, particularly kids." Abby nodded, gave her a silent fist bump, and added this to the 'next steps' section of the whiteboard.

"We need to get a pole camera on the building and start watching what really goes on at Watts Auto Repairs," Wayne said. He'd already contacted the North Metro Drug Task Force, a team of officers from various agencies who were equipped to coordinate surveillance operations. They could have a live-feed camera installed on a utility pole just outside the auto shop within hours. Because it was a public area and no inner privacies would be recorded, Wayne had given them the nod to move forward.

Abby replaced the lid and tapped the end of a dry-erase marker on her chin as she stared at the board. "It's a little odd that the address he's filed with the Secretary of State for his business is an apartment. Clearly, he has money. I'd think he'd have a house or two somewhere. Let's keep digging and see if he's named as an owner of any other real estate. Does he truly live in the apartment, or is he just using it for business activities, nefarious or otherwise?"

Just then, Detective Sergeant Enrique Rhys carried several files into the room and grabbed a seat at the table. He was considered one of the best dressers in the agency. While most detectives had switched to soft uniforms, Rhys still dressed in a suit and tie every day. He said it helped him feel more competent and professional.

"Mind if I poke my nose into the mystery?" Rhys asked.

"Heck no," Abby said. "The brainstorming has been fantastic. We'd love your input."

"The curiosity is killing me, so I brought a few files to review while keeping an eye on what's going on here."

"Make yourself at home," Abby said and turned her eyes back to the board.

They continued listing the knowns and unknowns about Watson, details that made him a viable suspect. They punched holes in their theories, knowing the district attorney could potentially reject the case if they didn't plug those holes. As was typical early on in most cases, what they didn't know outweighed what they did, but Abby was encouraged by what they'd gathered so far. Answers were on the horizon, and with the plans they were putting in place, they'd become more evident and easier to obtain.

"I'd love to see his unofficial financial records. Where is his money really coming from?" Abby plotted. "Twenty years ago, Watson had the means to buy a Porsche and hire a runner to do his bidding. He's got to have an income stream besides the small auto shop. What's he really doing?"

"His money didn't likely come from family," Michelle surmised. "In the area he grew up here in Adams County, they may have been comfortable, but not *Porsche* comfortable. What do you suppose his bank deposits look like?"

"Exactly my question. We need to establish his pattern of life— his habitual routines. We need to know his schedule, the people he commonly does business with, and his financial habits. What websites does he visit? What causes hiccups in his normal rhythms?"

"I was just thinking the same thing," Enrique said. "You ordered a pole cam, right?"

"We did," Wayne answered.

"Let's get as many eyes on him as we can. I've got two new detectives who would be great at tailing Watson for a week or so. Let's get as close as we can to him without being seen and just observe him."

"That's great," Abby said, appreciating the teamwork and the importance Rhys was giving the case. "We can see where he goes, who he's with, who he bosses around to do his bidding. That could give us enough probable cause to get warrants for his financial records and phone records."

"Which could get us closer to legal searches for the weapon or any mementos he collected from the murders," Michelle said.

"I like it. I like it a lot," Abby said. "When can the detectives move on this, Rhys?"

"I'll go talk to them now, and they can move in tomorrow morning."

CHAPTER 38

ABBY, 2023

Michelle pulled into the parking lot at the Adams County Sheriff's Office Headquarters just before Abby on Tuesday morning. Parking just a few spots from one another, they began their conversation while collecting their personal items.

"When I got home last night, I realized our day was so busy that I didn't even get to ask you about your weekend. Did you guys enjoy the concert?" Michelle asked.

Abby set a mug of brewed-at-home coffee on the roof of her car and peered her eyes over the Edge. "We had an incredible weekend. Gus Farmer was amazing. I'd see him live again any day of the week!"

"I'm glad one of us had fun," Michelle sighed. "I pulled weeds all weekend and finished up last night. Our hard-as-clay soil around here grabs hold of roots and doesn't want to let go. I grew up in Missouri, and yard care felt 1,000 times easier than it is here. But I wanted to get them all pulled before the snow flies."

"Speaking of the weekend," Abby interjected, "I wanted to ask. Has Jacob Jennings been talking to you?"

"He stopped by Friday after you left the office, and we talked for a while." Michelle gave a sideways glance. "Why do you ask?"

"He stopped by my house unexpectedly after the concert." Seeing the 'Are you kidding me' look on Michelle's face, she added, "Right. It was pretty much the middle of the night, but Mack and I were just getting home. Weird, but that's beside the point. He brought up two things that I can't figure out how he knew for the life of me."

"Oh, I hope I didn't say too much." Michelle's jaw softened, and her eyes went wide with concern. "What were the two things?" By now, they were walking side by side toward the building, stepping over parking curbs and a raised lip on the sidewalk that threatened to trip Abby almost daily.

"I don't remember mentioning my weekend plans to him at all. Not the concert, not Mack's visit."

Michelle dropped her chin and raised her palm in a wave. "Guilty," she said. "I'm so sorry. I absolutely told him what you were up to this weekend."

"I'm actually glad you did." Abby breathed a sigh of relief. "It feels a lot less creepy knowing where he got the info. He also mentioned how unusual it was for me to investigate my sister's case. Did that come up when you talked?"

"No!" Michelle said with a grimace and added volume. "I wouldn't share case details. Especially not something like that."

"Okay." Abby gazed into the parking lot. "It's just strange. I mean, it's not exactly a secret around here, but I wanted to avoid explaining it all to someone who may not understand all the complexities. Mack was her all-star self, though, and didn't give him any room to pass judgment."

"You'll have to let me meet her someday. She sounds like the kind of friend we all wish for."

"She definitely is."

They entered the building and were met with a few congratulatory comments from staff members who were getting the gist of the progress they were making. Abby was grateful but wanted to shy away from what she felt were unearned accolades. There was still a very long road ahead, and while Watson looked like he could be the killer, there was no physical evidence to support the theory. Today was a day to roll up their sleeves and dig deeper into finding probable cause.

Abby had already decided she'd drive the 45 miles to Greeley today and get eyes on Watts Auto Repair for herself. Maybe she'd pose as a customer and get a glimpse of the suspect. How he'd treat a female could be a small indication of his mindset.

She stood in the building's common area before entering her office, turned to Michelle, and said, "Could you look into Watson's mom for me? I was wondering about her health and if we could use her to get to him somehow."

"Happy to," Michelle replied as she rounded her desk and set her mug on her coaster and her tote bag on the floor.

Abby turned back to her office and saw a lovely bouquet of peonies set in the center of piles and stacks of paper covering the table. She paused to study the beauty—so out of place in the mess of paperwork and the tragedies it represented. The play of colors in each flower was gorgeous, with lighter shades of pink on the edges gradually deepening toward the center. They were lush, opulent flowers with layers of petals that seemed to embrace one another.

Peonies weren't easy to come by in Colorado. The gesture surprised her, and she immediately thought they must have been from Kerri Torres, who knew peonies were among her favorites. It was just the sort of encouraging gift Kerri would send.

She set down the items she carried and walked toward the bouquet to read the card. The smile it brought to her lips surprised her. "Looking forward to making you smile and spending some wonderful moments together. Can we start again? ~ Jacob." There were his chivalrous manners again, tugging at her heart.

Her phone chimed with a text message. She glanced down and saw Jacob's name.

Have you seen them?

Yes, they're divine. You shouldn't have, but thank you!

I haven't acted like myself lately. Can we take a fresh run at things? Dinner tonight?

I'm taking a short road trip for a case today. Can I let you know how things time out?

I'll anxiously wait to hear from you.

She wondered what she might be opening the door to. He had some characteristics she'd classify as unusual. But didn't everyone? She pondered the good she saw in him, his kindness, and how he made her feel special and properly cared for. She enjoyed those things. What could another dinner hurt? Over the last few weeks of work, she'd been surrounded by negativity. Today was a day to think positively, and that's what she'd do.

Abby changed into jeans and a t-shirt, which she kept in her locker, and collected the keys to one of the county's undercover cars. It was a taupe-colored sedan that hadn't seen a car wash for a while. Mud covered the wheel wells, and road grime collected over most of the paint. The inside was clean and didn't smell of smoke, so that was a plus. She could plug into the USB port and listen to her playlist as she drove. She selected her streaming service, plugged the address to Watts Auto Repairs into her GPS, and pointed the car north.

While she drove, she called Sergeant Rhys. "Enrique, I'm headed to Greeley to make a pop-in visit to Watts Auto Repair. I don't plan to be there long, but I want to poke around and see what I can learn about the place."

"Sounds like a good idea," he said.

"I know you sent detectives up there this morning. Who did you assign?"

"Dan Johns and Lilah Mason."

"Okay. Can you make sure they know I'm coming so I don't throw anyone off? And if I'm inside the shop for more than, say, 15 minutes or so, things have gone south, and I'm going to need some subtle cover."

"Copy that. You need someone to ride along with you?"

"No, I don't think so. Watson's been off the radar for decades, so he has no reason to suspect that someone will be digging into his business. I'm going to act like a civilian who has a car at home needing service."

"All right. Be safe, Carter."

"You know I'll do my best," she said, then silently prayed for God's protection and wisdom.

Driving on Highway 85 through Brighton and toward Greeley was always an adventure. It was the route of countless semi trucks hauling gravel, produce, and all manner of things carried over the road. The four-lane road bore numerous traffic lights, which made getting stuck behind an 18-wheeler all the more dreadful. But it was the most direct way to her destination, so she tolerated the slow-moving, stop-and-go traffic.

The county seat of Weld County, Greeley, is home to the University of Northern Colorado campus. Known for oil and natural gas production, the city has a reputation for one prominent negative quality—its stench. The assortment of stockyards, meat packing plants, and farms give the city a peculiar and unpleasant smell that is well-known and satirized throughout the Colorado front range.

About midway through the city limits, she pulled her car into the small and very tight parking lot of the auto repair shop. It was crowded with cars of every variety, all apparently waiting their turn for service. Seeing no available parking spaces, she did a three-point turn, drove back to the street, and parallel parked half a block from the garage. The closer she walked toward it, the more sediment she noticed covering the asphalt, cars, and even the structure.

The building was constructed of gray stucco adorned with an arched portico that covered a wooden deck-style floor. In one corner, just to the left of the entrance, a toilet sat on a flat piece of cardboard. It was covered in dust and cobwebs as if it had been there for some time. Its lid was open. Abby chose not to peek inside.

A residential-style screen door opened into the shop where an assortment of auto parts filled two long rows of shelving, separated in the middle to reveal an employee manning an appointment book and cash register. Abby was the only customer inside, so she approached the employee and waited until he looked up. He held a pen in his large, greasy hand as he scratched notes on a pad. The other hand held a phone covered in several layers of soot.

As he talked, she noticed the name "Dale" embroidered onto his gray mechanic's shirt. He was clean-shaven with a dark crew cut. A tattoo of something Abby couldn't identify was inked across the front of his neck and down his chest inside the buttons of his shirt.

At last, he hung up the phone and glanced her way. "Hi, I'm Nicole, here to see Doc," she picked a name out of thin air.

"We got no Doc."

"Oh, I'm sorry. I thought my friend said to ask for Doc. Really, I'm just here to get some car repairs." She grinned into his blank stare. "I have a classic Ford that needs a tune-up, probably a little more than a tune-up, actually. I'd like to get it running again."

Dale stared at her blankly.

"Do you all work on old cars?" she prompted.

"Yeah. My boss collects old cars. We work on 'em."

"Great. Would he be able to take a look at mine?"

"At your what?" he asked.

"At my old car. Should I talk to your boss about that? Is it better to talk to him? Because he likes old cars, I mean?"

"No. You need a tow?"

"I can have someone tow it here for me." She answered. "When's a good time? I'd rather not have it sit here for very long. You know, waiting for the work to be done. Can I schedule a time to bring it and have it looked at the same day?"

"We don't do it like that. Never know about parts and such."

"Oh, I see," Abby said. She tried to fill the silence. "I'd love to see your boss's collection. Are any of his cars here? I'm kind of learning to be a car geek. It's a new interest for me."

"No, they ain't here." His gaze lingered with subtle intensity. "He'd love to see you though. You're just his type."

"What type is that?" Abby gave him her best flirtatious smile and leaned on the counter toward Dale, hoping her coffee breath didn't break through the smell of sweat that emanated from him.

"Blonde." Dale studied her from the crown of her head to her waist as she stood at the counter. "Pretty. Young."

"I haven't been called young in a while," she forced a giggle. "What's your boss's name?"

"Goes by Ty. He ain't here today."

"Oh, *that's* the name my friend said. Too bad he's out. What steals him away from here on a day like today?"

"Who knows? He's got lots of …" Dale paused to think of the right word. "Interests."

"Well, I'm sorry I missed him," Abby said, twirling a strand of her hair with a finger. "Is he married? Kids? Maybe I'm his type, but, you know. I don't want to interfere with a family if he has one."

"Got a little girl. Adopted his niece." Dale said.

The blood drained from Abby's face. With Tyler Watson't history, she was sure a young girl in his grasp was no niece but a trafficking victim. She swallowed hard and steadied herself to keep up the act.

"Nice of him." She nearly spat the words from her mouth. "So it's just best to bring the car by whenever I can and leave it till you can get to it?"

"That's right."

"Can you keep it under cover or inside somewhere? I just had it painted. I'd hate for it to be out in the weather for a long time."

"Costs extra, but we can."

"Okay," Abby said. "I'll bring it by. When is Ty usually here? Maybe I can see him next time."

"He's in an' out. We never know."

"Thanks for your help, Dale." She tapped her hand on the counter. "I hope to see you when I come back."

Dale didn't respond but went back to writing something on his notepad. Abby paused for a brief second, then casually walked back to her car.

She noticed a public utility vehicle working on a light pole across the street from the garage. A worker in an orange vest was in a bucket truck. As she looked closely, she recognized him as one of the men from the task force. He was installing the pole camera they'd request-ed.

Abby reached for her phone and dialed Wayne Finch. "How'd it go?" he asked as he picked up.

"It went fine, and I'm back in my car. I didn't see Watson and I don't think his employee has any idea of the real reason I was there."

"Okay. That's disappointing, but we'll keep him on our radar. I talked with the Weld County detectives a few minutes ago, and they're uncovering piles of dirt on this guy. They won't want to take their eyes off him for a while."

———

Jacob picked Abby up at seven that evening, and they drove together to Hickory and Ash, an out-of-the-way restaurant with an easy, com-fortable ambiance. They chatted over a quiet table, and Jacob asked about Mack. It was an easy topic for Abby; she loved Mack as a sister and could talk about their friendship for hours. She had countless sto-ries to share, either from living as roommates, attending the Academy together, or the closeness they shared through FaceTime, calls, and texts while living 250 miles apart.

"She's become more like a sister to you than a friend," he ob-served. Abby responded with a nod while sipping iced tea.

"But no one can replace the sister you lost." This was the awk-ward side of getting to know someone new. The tenderness in Jacob's voice was endearing, but he seemed to commonly dive into topics Abby wasn't prepared to share with him. She felt a subtle nudge in her spirit but reasoned it away. Maybe she should feel flattered that he was interested enough in her to ask.

"Of course not." She fingered the rim of her glass while deciding how to respond. "Have you ever lost someone close to you, Jacob?"

"Certainly not by *murder*." His judgmental tone was unmistak-able.

Abby's face flushed, and she leaned away from the table as if she'd been slapped.

"I've done it again, haven't I?" he asked.

"Yes, I'm afraid you have." She turned and stared out the window to collect her thoughts. "You have a way of making me feel so valued for who I am. But it feels abrasive when you push too hard about personal things."

"I apologize, Abby." His eyes were soft and warm. He reached for her hand and said, "I guess I'm in a hurry to get to know you better. I think about you constantly. I'd love to take our relationship deeper."

"While there's a part of me that wants that, too," Abby spoke slowly, trying to choose her words carefully, "I'm not sure I'm ready for a relationship."

"You're a grown woman. Unattached. How ready do you need to be?"

"There is a lot you don't know about me, Jacob. There are deep reserves of very unflattering issues hidden deep inside. Things you won't hear through the grapevine of the Sheriff's Office." She gauged his expression to see if her comment had gone too far. His eyes still held a twinkle, and his hand hadn't left hers, so she went on.

"I went through a painful divorce recently. My earlier years were filled with more trauma than most people see in a lifetime. I'm finding my way through a few challenges at work and just happen to be investigating a murder that hits extremely close to home. I feel raw around the edges. Not quite myself, at least not the way I'd like to be. I'm not sure this is the best time to move into more vulnerability with someone."

"We can't control the timing of our affections." Jacob swallowed hard. "Or love," he said softly.

The server picked that moment to deliver the check to the table, but Jacob's eyes never left Abby's face. She gently pulled her hand from beneath his and reached for her glass. "Let me ask you something that's been rumbling around in my head." She didn't want to sound accusatory and tried to keep a gentle tone. "How did you know that one of the cases I'm working on involves the death of my sister? I don't recall mentioning that to you."

Now, it was Jacob's turn to pause. At last, he said, "Let's just say there are several employees of the Sheriff's Office who don't respect the sheriff the way you do. They're quick to bring information to the commissioners when they feel he's working outside the lines. Some have felt that putting you in a position to work a case involving a family member is just that—outside the lines."

He cleared his throat, and Abby sensed he was uncomfortable. "The reality is, and I hate to admit this, there's nothing the board of commissioners can do about it. The people elect the sheriff, and he is free to run law enforcement operations the way he sees fit. He works at the authority of the voters, not under our direction—"

She held up her hand and interrupted him. "My emotional ties to this case aren't a level of vulnerability I was ready to bring into our friendship. While I enjoy the time I spend with you, it's becoming obvious I'm not ready for something deeper. I'm sorry, Jacob. If I were ready, it wouldn't be so hard to be open, to share more of myself."

"And where does that leave us, Abby dear? Why did you come to dinner with me tonight?" His tone portrayed friendliness, but his defensiveness was rising.

Abby paused for a moment, still considering Jacob's words. She couldn't help but feel a pang of unease at the mention of employees going behind the sheriff's back to the commissioners. It was a bold reminder of the political games that often surfaced in their line of work. For the first time, she questioned the true nature of Jacob's interest in her case.

Pushing aside her concerns, she focused on the question at hand. She nodded as if to find a new resolve after sorting her feelings. "I like the idea of being with someone. And I enjoy your company. I'm here tonight to see if we're a fit. To discover whether I'm ready for more. I enjoy spending time with you, but I'm beginning to realize

I'm not emotionally solid enough for a deeper relationship right now. It wouldn't be fair to either of us to continue when I'm still processing so much."

As they sat in silence for several moments, Jacob's anger simmered. Abby caught movement from the corner of her eye. "Look," she said. "It's Tim and Pasha Kline. I believe you know them, right? I saw you talking to them after church that Sunday."

Jacob stood and reached to shake Tim's hand as the couple neared the table. Pasha stood near to Abby and gently caressed the back of her shoulder as a greeting. "It's so good to see you two. Are you having a date night?" Abby asked.

"We are! This is one of our favorite spots. Fancy meeting the two of you here! We don't want to interrupt, but we wanted to say hello." Tim's voice seemed strained, and Abby wondered if the couple were working through some tension. "Um, Abby, would you mind if I give you a call? I have a question about what could be a legal matter, and I'd love to pick your brain."

"Of course," she said. "No need to ask. You can call me any time. Let's talk soon."

Tim reached for Pasha's elbow, and they continued following the host to their table. "Such nice people," Abby said. "I adore them."

Jacob's face twisted, and he leaned back in his chair. "You adore Mack, you adore the Klines, but you're not sure you adore *me*," he said with a dark cloud falling over his demeanor. His comment was jarring and signaled the end of the evening. He rose from the table to look above the crowd, located their server, and waved her over. Then he pulled his wallet from his pocket and hastily dropped his credit card on top of the check.

"Jacob, I—"

"No, it's okay. Better to know now, I suppose, before I get even more attached. Let's just call it a night, shall we?"

CHAPTER 39

ABBY, 2023

Almost nothing troubled Abby more than disappointing people. Last night's debacle at Hickory and Ash led to yet another night of tossing and turning, but now there was a new reason to lie awake. She stewed over her actions, replayed her words, weighed her options, and wondered if a different approach might have led to an outcome where her date didn't end the evening barely speaking to her.

Somewhere around 3:00 am, she got up and showered, as if knowing that washing yesterday away would help her sleep. The warmth and steam helped her relax. She climbed back under the covers and slept soundly until her alarm sounded at 6:15.

Within minutes, her coffee mug was filled. She opened the door to the back patio and let the cool air wash over her. The morning wasn't as chilled as she thought it might be, and still in her pajamas, she soon found herself sitting cross-legged on the lawn as the sun's light began to touch the Colorado sky.

The morning air sparked her senses. As the world stirred from slumber, the air felt charged with a subtle, electric energy. She stretched out and felt her body awaken. The touch of the morning breeze and fresh dew on her skin carried the promise of a new day filled with new opportunities.

"Lord," she prayed. *"I need you. Things are swirling so fast around me. Guide my steps. Show me your wisdom so I can walk in it."* She sat quietly for a time, focusing on God and giving Him space to prompt

her heart and mind. Rarely did she feel a response, but this morning, she discerned a thought she knew was not her own: *I will show you.*

Her eyes darted open, and her heart beat with anticipation as if she'd just received a long-awaited gift. Those few simple words validated her journey and all she'd overcome to get to this point. She knew in an instant God was near, aligning her path and affirming her purpose.

Resisting the urge to rush through her morning routine and get to her desk, she willed herself to sit and be still. She embraced the moment, quietly noticing how her body reacted to His prompting, thanking God, and receiving His promise. Then, like an unleashed puppy, she bolted up the stairs to get ready for the day.

All of the thoughts and details from events that filled the last few days replayed in her mind as she drove to work, beating the morning rush hour with her early departure. She considered the progress they'd made identifying Tyler Watson and all that was underway to uncover his pattern of life. It would help in determining any crimes he was currently involved in and those from his past.

On other fronts, the digging she'd done into locating the house sitter from 2005 at the home near Dahlia's crime scene on Newport Court was unfruitful. The student's name was Sandra Winter. Her parents' phone number was in the case file and miraculously still in service. Late last week, before Abby uncovered Doc's name in the two cases, she'd called and talked to Sandra's mom.

The woman had remembered the news of the homicide as if it were last week and was still unnerved about her daughter being so close to something so heinous. She'd said Sandra had moved to Arizona and was working as a veterinarian in the Phoenix area. She had agreed to reach out to Sandra for permission to share her cell phone number but wasn't hopeful that her daughter had anything to share.

Now, Abby made a mental task list: *Get with the lab about DNA tests on Dahlia's case. Review pictures of Ford Maverick cars. Call the owner of a pot shop she'd driven by over the weekend called Doc's Apothecary. It would be worth at least asking the "Doc" question.*

The voice message light on her phone was blinking when she arrived at her desk, and she decided to listen before filling her coffee in the break room. There were two voicemails. The first was from a reporter asking for an update about a case Abby had nothing to do with. She forwarded it to the public information officer. The second was from Jamie Winter, Sandra's mother, who shared Sandra's cell phone number. Abby jotted it down and then quickly dialed.

After three rings, Sandra answered. "This is Dr. Winter."

"Sandra, my name is Sergeant Abigail Carter from the Adams County Sheriff's Office. We are taking a fresh look at a homicide that occurred in 2005."

"Yes, my mom said you'd be calling. I've told the police before I have nothing to share, and I don't want to get involved. I'm sorry that girl was killed, but I can't help you."

Wayne walked into the office, and Abby mouthed the words "house sitter" as she pointed at her phone. He sat quietly and listened with rapt attention.

"Would you mind if I ask a few brief questions, just in case?"

"Look, I'm pretty busy. I took your call just to tell you again that I have nothing for you and ask you not to contact me or my family again."

"Sandra, do you have a sister?" Sensing she was about to lose this lead, Abby decided to appeal to her emotions.

"I do, yes, but what does that matter?"

"I had a sister, too. Very few people know this, but in the case I want to talk to you about, it was my sister who was murdered. Any recollection that you can share may prove helpful. And it would mean the world to me personally."

With that, Abby pushed the speaker button on the phone so Wayne could listen in.

"Oh." A few seconds ticked by before she continued. "I'm very sorry to hear that, Sergeant. I suppose I have time for a few questions if we can keep it short."

"Thank you, Sandra. You were house-sitting for the Turners that evening. Is that correct?" She reached for a pen to scribble notes as she talked.

"I wouldn't call it house-sitting," Sandra said. "I wasn't staying there, but I stopped over after work a couple of times to check the mail, water the plants, and make sure their cat had enough food and water."

"Were you driving yourself, or was someone giving you a ride?"

"I had my own car."

"Can you describe your car for me?"

"It was a white Toyota, kind of old and beat up—you know, a college kid's car."

"Did you park on the street or in the driveway?" Perhaps her white Toyota could have been the old rusty car parked on the street.

"I always parked in the driveway. It was a lot easier than parking on the cul-de-sac."

"Did you see anyone on the night of the murder? Anyone walking or driving, maybe? I know it was a long time ago."

Abby heard Sandra let out a long breath. "I saw the victim that night. I guess it would have been your sister. When they showed the picture of her on the news, I recognized her as the girl I saw. The news report mentioned all the details I knew. I didn't want to have to think about someone getting murdered so close to where I was, and since I couldn't share new details, I decided to stay quiet."

A million questions were firing inside Abby's mind, and she wanted to ask them as quickly as they formed. But she tried to match the tone and rhythm of Sandra's words as she pressed in, hoping it would keep the witness engaged in dialog.

"What did you see her doing?"

"She was getting out of a car. It was also an old white car, which is why I remember. She was on the passenger side, and I saw her get out, shut the door, and then stand there for a minute like she was waiting for the driver to get out, too."

"Did you see the driver?"

"While I was standing at the Turners' mailbox, he got out of the car, and they started walking together toward the trees in the field below the neighborhood. I didn't see his face. Just the back of him."

"Did you notice anything about him? How tall he was? Hair color? How he was dressed?"

"He had on a ball cap, and I think his hair must have been dark. It was dark outside, but they were fairly close to a street lamp, so I could see them pretty well. It looked like she was smiling at him."

"I'm sorry. Did you say she was smiling?"

"Yes, like they were friends. So when she was found murdered, I wondered what happened to him and who would have come across them down by those trees."

"So you're saying it looked like they were supposed to be together? Like she wanted to be there?"

"She sure didn't seem scared or stressed or anything. Just an ordinary couple who walked into the field. I figured they were going to smoke pot or something. There was a lot of that in those days."

"Did you notice if they were carrying anything?"

"No, I didn't see anything."

"Could you hear any conversation?"

"No, I always had headphones on. I was attached to my iPod."

"Is there anything else you remember?"

"No, I just went in the house and took care of things there. When I came out, the car was still there, but I didn't see them."

"I don't suppose you remember what time that was?"

"No. It was so long ago, and I didn't pay much attention to time in those days."

"I understand." Abby wrote a few more notes on her notepad. "Sandra, this has been very helpful. I deeply appreciate your time and your willingness to share."

"I still don't see how any of that can help, but you're welcome. Take care, Sergeant."

Abby hung up her desk phone. One of the last people to see her sister alive said she was smiling, and it seemed as if she wanted to be with the driver of the Maverick. That was not at all the story Abby expected to hear.

Wayne was shaking his head. "I didn't see that coming."

"No, neither did I. What do you make of it?"

"The guy with her may not have been the killer. He could be a witness who's never come forward. Or an accessory. I don't really know what to make of it."

CHAPTER 40

ABBY, 2023

*A*re you working today? Abby texted Mack.
Yes.
I need to talk. When do you have a break?
Lunch-ish. Probably around 12:30.
I'll call you then.

The news she'd just received was perplexing, something she couldn't make sense of in her mind. She'd call Auntie Beth tonight to talk it through, but she also needed some investigative minds to help her sort it all out. Why would Dahlia have been at her final location voluntarily? Who could have taken her there? Maybe, as Wayne suggested, he was a friend of Dahlia's and not the killer at all.

Were all of her leads a dead end? Or was someone named Doc a suspect? He had to be, or else the 'Doc' in the Davis case was pure coincidence. That seemed almost impossible. Did the white car have anything at all to do with the crime? That could go either way.

She stopped by Captain Torres's office to talk it through, but he was out of the office for a meeting. Her next stop was the lab. "Melissa," she said. "Can I check the progress of the DNA testing on the Archer case?"

"Let me take a look." Sorting through reports, Melissa found it. "They finished the analysis on Friday afternoon, and it should hit your email soon. We didn't find enough DNA to run a profile. I'm sorry, Abby."

"Thanks for checking. Back to old-fashioned detective work!" She was headed back to her office to make a call to Doc's Apothecary when her cell phone rang with the *Friends* theme song.

"Hey, Mack!" She answered.

"I got an early break. I know things are a little tense for you, and I didn't want to keep you waiting."

Abby filled her in on the witness's statement that Dahlia didn't seem to be under duress just before her death. They talked through possible scenarios but didn't reach a solid explanation.

"Thanks, Mack. I just wanted your take on it. I'm sure I'll get to the bottom of it as the case unfolds, but I was hoping you'd have a brilliant insight."

"I'm sorry. I've really got nothing. How are you doing, by the way? Are you done being rude to Jacob?"

"What are you talking about? When was I rude to Jacob?"

"When he brought his Maverick over."

"What Maverick?"

"The red one. The car he's restoring. You were giving him the cold shoulder that day."

"How do you know it was a Maverick? And I told you, I got nauseous all of a sudden. I wasn't trying to be rude."

Concern etched Mack's voice. "My bigger question is, are you doing okay?"

Abby brought her friend up to speed with the way things ended the night before and said she wouldn't be seeing Jacob again any time soon.

"It's probably for the best," Mack said. "He doesn't really seem your type. Hey, I've got to take a report from a victim who's waiting. Let's talk more tonight."

"Thanks for calling, Mack. You're the best."

"I know," she teased as she ended the call.

Seconds later, Abby's cell phone rang again, and Tim Kline's face filled her screen.

"Hi, Tim!" She said cheerfully, walking through the corridor and turning to the left into an outdoor courtyard. "It was great to see you and Pasha at the restaurant the other night. How are things going?"

"Things are good, Abby. Listen, I have something I want to talk with you about, but I feel ridiculously awkward bringing it up."

"No need, Tim. What's on your mind?" She sat on a concrete picnic table and shielded her eyes from the bright sun.

"It's Jacob. I have no business stepping into this, but I feel I need to warn you about him." Tim went silent as if waiting for Abby's permission to continue.

"How so?" she asked.

"I mentioned I've known him for a long time. By that, I mean a very long time. We went to high school together and used to be good friends. He was Jacob Everett back then. We got into more than our share of trouble together."

Tim sighed into the phone. "Abby, I feel like I'm gossiping. I want you to know that's not my intent. Pasha and I consider you a close friend, and I'm genuinely concerned about you. Will you take what I'm about to say in that light?"

"Of course. Jacob told me he changed his name to put some distance between him and his brother's colorful past." It was getting hot in the autumn sun, so Abby moved to a shaded table.

"Wow. That's what he said? His brother is actually a stand-up guy. Jacob's the one who put us all up to mischief. And it just escalated over time. Here's what I know about Jacob—" he took a deep breath.

"He has a strong desire for success and achievement, or at least the appearance of success and achievement, and he doesn't care who he damages along the way. The Everett family was pretty well-to-do, but Jacob, even when we were young, wanted to be in the spotlight. He wanted to be known for his status, his possessions, and even his ability to get whatever he wanted."

Again, Tim paused. "I hate this conversation," he said, almost to himself.

"You're doing the right thing, Tim. I need to know."

"We got into the drug scene. I know I've shared that with you before. I have a past I'm not proud of, but I've tried to own what I've done. Jacob never did. He tried to get away with as much as he could, then found ways to avoid the consequences, like changing his name. He thought that would just push everything under the rug, and it did. I guess that works in the political realm, but I can't in good conscience sit by and watch you become collateral damage."

"I'm curious. What kinds of drugs did you use?" She asked. "With Jacob, I mean."

"We all started with pot, then found a way to get prescription painkillers. Jacob got tired of having to find suppliers, so he found a way to become one himself. I don't know the ins and outs of it, but he started dealing drugs, not just using."

"This was all in high school?"

"It was, but it carried beyond that, too. Jacob supplied my habit and made tons of money from a lot of people, including me. Over the years, Jacob developed a reputation for getting what people needed and calling them 'cures.'"

Abby's head began to spin, and she felt as if she were in a free fall. She grabbed hold of the side of the table to keep her balance. Her hands started to tremble, and sweat began to pool in her palms. "Tim, I need to stop you. Please."

"I'm so sorry, Abby—"

"No, don't be sorry. I may need to call you later. Would that be okay? I've had something urgent come up on a case I'm working." Abby stormed into the building and stopped at the first desk she approached to grab a sticky note and a pen.

She scribbled something on it as Tim asked, "You sure we're good?"

"One hundred percent sure, Tim. I appreciate everything you shared and the way you're looking out for me. Truly, it means a lot. I'll talk to you soon."

She ended the call and handed the note to Michelle as she passed by her desk on the way to Captain Torres' office. Seeing he was there, staring at his computer, she burst through his door and nearly collapsed into his armchair.

CHAPTER 41

ABBY, 2023

Turo looked up from his paperwork as Abby breathed, "Dahlia's killer isn't Tyler Watson."

Turo was already dialing Sheriff Adler's extension. "Micah, can you come down? I think Abby's had a significant break in the Archer and Davis cases."

Abby stood, pacing back and forth with frenzied energy. Her face felt flushed. She ripped off the jacket she wore over her blouse, dropped it on the back of an armchair, and began fanning her face with her hands, trying to cool her flushed skin.

"Sit down, Abby. Let me get you a glass of water. The sheriff will be right here."

With emotions boiling over, she was too unnerved to sit, so she continued to pace while taking deep breaths to try to keep her thoughts together. "How could I be so stupid?" she said aloud, just as Sheriff Adler stepped in.

"Well, you're far from stupid," the sheriff said. "And remember, this case has been cold for a long time. You're not the only one who couldn't see the outcome. So tell me, what's this breakthrough you've found?"

Turo stepped in and handed her a glass of water, then closed his office door.

"Does he want to get caught? Does he want me dead, too?" Abby tread a circular path around the small office, murmuring to herself.

The two men made eye contact in unspoken agreement to disrupt Abby's nearly imperceptible rant. Turo led Abby to a chair and pressed on her shoulders to make her sit. "Is there something you want to tell us?"

"Tyler Watson isn't our guy. He's slimy, but he doesn't go by 'Doc,' and he didn't kill Dahlia. A lot of stray threads came together today and have woven themselves into something substantial."

"What do you have?" Turo asked.

"It was Jacob Jennings. He's the killer."

"Now, Abby," the sheriff said, "That's a very strong accusation. He's an elected official, for heaven's sake. He's been background checked and has a clean record."

"He told me himself he changed his name before running for office. He told me it was to distance himself from his brother, but now I suspect there's a different reason."

There was a knock on the door, and Michelle poked her head in. "Sorry to interrupt, but can I share this background with you?"

Abby nodded and waved her in. "I've asked her to run a history on Jacob Everett." She explained. "That was his last name before he legally changed it to Jennings. Michelle, what did you find?"

"Felony charges for drug trafficking. He was convicted and served six years before being released on Parole in 2013.

"Okay," Sheriff Adler said. "That's definitely something we need to look into. You're saying Jacob Everett is now Jacob Jennings?"

"I talked to a friend who went to high school with Jacob and said he was Jacob Everett back then." Abby went back to murmuring as she processed her thoughts. "He told me he'd changed his name, and now it makes sense. If I believed it was for an innocuous reason like distancing himself from his brother, maybe it would keep me from digging deeper and finding out he had a record."

"But dealing drugs and murder are two different things," Turo said, pulling Abby back into the conversation.

"You know we're looking for someone with the moniker of 'Doc' in both the Archer and Davis cases." She stood and resumed her circular track, waving her hands in the air as her voice escalated. "My friend said Jacob had a reputation for finding cures. That fits with what Tiffany's roommate said. And get this. Jacob brought an old classic car by my house last weekend. He said he was restoring it and was painted a bright, shiny red. There were no make or model insignias on it, but my friend Mack told me today that she recognized it as a Ford Maverick. That's two strikes."

Sheriff Adler was pulling up the contacts on his cell phone. "Let's get a warrant to search that car." His voice trailed off as he left the room.

Abby continued to share witness information with Turo and Michelle. "I tracked down the house sitter today, the one you told me would never talk to police, Turo? She was trying to brush me off, so I pulled the emotion card and told her the victim was my sister, and it would mean a lot to me personally. It felt a little manipulative, but it was true, and it was effective. She told me she saw Dahlia standing beside the white Maverick on the day of the murder, and she looked happy to be there. She said she didn't seem afraid or stressed at all, which meant she knew the person who took her there."

Abby took too big a drink from her water glass and spent the next few seconds coughing and trying to catch her breath. "Sorry," she said, wiping her mouth on her sleeve. "I've gone through Dahlia's journal, the letters she wrote to me, and some random notes she used to leave for me in hidden places around the house when we were kids. In one of them, she references 'Doc' as having the cure."

"We don't have a motive," Turo said. Abby gave him a sideways glance, and he added, "I know. We're not required to show motive to prove guilt, but it's extremely helpful in a jury case."

"I need to bring my friend, Tim—Jacob's old high school friend—in for a formal interview. Maybe something will turn up. And we haven't interrogated the suspect yet, or searched any of his property, namely the Maverick. I'm sure we can find a motive."

She sat for a moment but popped right back to her feet. "Let's keep gathering what we can on Jacob Everett," she said, looking at Michelle. "And dig up the earliest photo you can of him so I can see if Rol recognizes him as a john."

"Show him a photo array, Abby. Don't show him just one picture. Group it others, or you'll be accused of leading the witness."

"Right." Abby nodded. "I'll send Wayne if that's okay."

The sheriff let himself back into Turo's office with good news. "We should have a warrant within a few hours. The DA will draw it up himself to protect confidentiality, and he'll walk it through for the Judge to sign it. That way, we can avoid leaks and keep this thing close to the vest."

Abby said, "Jacob's home address is public record, right? Because he's an elected official?"

Sheriff Adler answered, "Candidates have the option of redacting their addresses now, so it may or may not be in the public database."

"Well, let's hope it is. Or could we obtain it through county HR somehow? Without raising suspicions? My hope is that the Maverick is at his house."

Abby stood and stared out the window. "Michelle, see if you can find a storage facility listed in the drug cases for Everett. Perps are often creatures of habit, so maybe we'll find the Maverick in a unit he's had for a long time. We can list both addresses on the warrant if you can turn that around quickly."

"I'm on it," Michelle said while stepping toward her desk.

"Do you want to bring our PIO into the circle of trust just yet?" Turo asked.

"No," the sheriff said. "If the media somehow catches wind of this, I'll address them personally. I don't want the public information officer involved in this one."

CHAPTER 42

ABBY, 2023

After all the details were readied for the following day, which she hoped would end in Jacob's arrest, Abby left the office a little after 7:00 pm. A team of detectives would serve the search warrant to Jacob at his home at 6:00 the next morning. Abby was to be kept out of that confrontation, and rightly so. Her role would be to conduct a formal interview with Tim Kline while the forensics team searched the Maverick.

Having slept just a few hours the night before, she was beat and ready to head home. After her rant in Turo's office, they'd all sprung into action, leaving her no room to process the confusion and angst that threatened to overtake her.

On the drive home, her mind raced. *She was dating her sister's killer. How did she miss the signs? How could she have let him get so close to her?* With her thoughts spiraling into self-degradation, a sudden, grounding revelation emerged. *Dahlia trusted him, too.*

Jacob was a master manipulator who drew them both in. It was comforting to know she wasn't alone and that she could finally put a stop to his controlling ways. Jacob was an evil person who preyed on women, and he'd become skilled at making friends with nearly anyone.

When she got home, a soak in her sunken, oversized tub felt fabulous, and Epsom salts helped ease away the tension. She added hot water twice to extend the bath, then finally climbed out, donning her softest pajamas before moving downstairs and curling up on the sofa.

She flipped through channels on the television and landed on a classic game show. It was mindless, and before long, she was shouting out answers to the old Jeopardy rerun as if the contestants could hear her.

During a commercial break, she got up from the couch and stepped over to the fridge to open an individual portion of white wine. As she filled a stemless glass, she pressed Auntie Beth's contact on her cell phone.

It was too early to give her all of the updates on Dahlia's case, but she did want to talk about the witness's comments about Dahlia before the shooting. While it raised a lot of questions in Abby's mind, the knowledge also ushered some peace into the ugliness of her sister's death. It didn't seem that she'd suffered for a long period of time. She and her family had learned to embrace small wins like this to help them move past the hurt that was still overwhelming. And she needed to talk with someone who understood her grief.

They'd chatted through nearly an entire Jeopardy episode when Abby pulled the phone from her ear. She'd heard a loud noise outside her house.

"Everything okay?" Beth asked.

"Yeah." Abby pressed the phone back to her ear. "The wind must be blowing trash cans outside. It swirls around like crazy sometimes. How are things going now that school's back in session?"

"I'm starting to daydream about retiring." This was big news. Auntie Beth was a self-admitted workaholic who loved her job as a full professor of mathematics at the university.

"I never thought I'd hear those words from you!"

"I would just like to slow down and enjoy life a bit more. Visit you sometimes. Travel with Uncle David and see the world while I'm still young and vibrant." She laughed out loud.

"As well you should. You've worked hard and deserve some rest." Abby heard another bang. "Auntie, can I call you later? Something's really blowing around out there, and I'd better go see what it is. But I want to hear all about this daydream of yours!"

"Of course. I'll talk to you later. You be safe and have a good night's sleep!"

"Love you, Auntie. Good night."

Knowing the flashlight on her phone would come in handy, Abby carried it through the laundry room and into the garage. It was pitch black, and she didn't sense any movement but heard the noise again, louder this time. She reached across her body to push the door opener. The overhead light turned on, and the large garage door creaked and groaned as it lifted.

She couldn't see much and stepped out into the driveway, around the corner of her house, where she stored the trash cans. There they were, upright and intact. Abby noticed how still the night air was, completely absent of the wind she'd expected to feel.

Moving around in a full circle, Abby shined her light to see if anything was out of place. Nothing was amiss. She walked toward the street, looking toward the neighbor's houses for any unusual activity. All was quiet. Strange.

Without thinking, she moved into cop mode and began a perimeter check of her own house, forgetting she was in her pajamas and had nothing but a cell phone in her hands. She reached over the top of the privacy gate that led to her backyard, opened the latch from the inside, and walked around the entire house, not seeing anything out of place.

Returning to the front of the house, she stood in her driveway for a moment before deciding that whatever she'd heard had moved on. She switched off the flashlight and reversed her path back into the house, pressing the button to lower the garage door.

"Hello, Abby." His voice, low and menacing, sent a chill down her spine. He stood just a few feet away, and even in the dimly lit garage, she could see his eyes glinting with a dangerous intensity.

"Jacob! What are you doing here?" Abby's heart raced, her adrenaline surging.

"I came to talk wi' you," He slurred. "I had to see you."

Abby's eyes scanned Jacob's body. His jacket hung loosely on his frame, and she couldn't help but wonder if he was concealing something threatening beneath its folds. The uncertainty sent a new wave of fear surging through her veins.

"I don't think this is a good idea, Jacob," she said, her voice trembling slightly despite her efforts to keep it steady. "Let's talk tomorrow when you've sobered up."

Abby reached for the garage door opener, but his hand shot out, gripping her arm with surprising strength. "I need to be wi' you," He stammered, pushing her against the door so hard it rattled on its hinges.

She pressed her hand against his chest, trying to push him away, but he overpowered her easily, forcing his way into the laundry room. "Jacob, you need to leave," she said, her voice rising.

"And to that, I say 'no thank you,'" he sneered, his breath reeking of alcohol.

"We have nothing to talk about tonight. I'm very tired, and I want to go to sleep." Abby's mind raced, searching for a way out of this situation.

He was leaning into her, his lips brushing her ear. "I need you to like me, Abby. I need you t-t-to trust me."

Her left hand still clutched her iPhone. Discreetly, she felt for the buttons and squeezed five times, initiating a silent SOS call. She prayed the police would arrive in time.

"This isn't the way," she reasoned. "This isn't helping. Just go home, and we can have a nice long talk tomorrow."

Jacob's eyes were filled with a desperate intensity as he spoke. "Tomorrow won't work, Abby. This can't wait. There's so much I need you to understand." He reached out his fingers to touch her hair. "You look so much like her," he whispered. "I knew the minute I saw you that you were her sister. I need you to trust me like she did."

All at once, Abby understood it all. She knew why Jacob wanted to get close to her. In Jacob's twisted mind, earning Abby's trust was the ultimate conquest, a chance to relive the power he had once held over Dahlia. He had never dreamed that his carefully crafted facade would crumble, that the truth of his heinous crimes would be exposed.

But now, since she rejected him, his desperation had reached a fever pitch, the outpouring of his rage threatening to consume them both.

Trapped between the laundry appliances, Abby had little room to maneuver. His grasp was firm, and she couldn't break free, so she tried a different approach.

"You knew Dahlia?" She asked softly. "She trusted you, didn't she?"

"Yes," Jacob said, his touch lingering on her cheek. "She trusted me so easily, and you're s-so much like her. Why can't you trust me too?"

"I trust you, Jacob," Abby lied, her heart pounding. "You've never given me a reason not to, have you?"

"'Course not. You know that, Abby, don't you?"

"Is there something you want to tell me? Come in, Jacob. Let's sit down and talk. You have a lot on your mind." As she touched his arm, she felt his body relax and led him into the kitchen. It was a larger area that would give her a better tactical advantage.

"What do you want to tell me about Dahlia, Jacob?" She longed to turn on the voice recorder on her phone but knew it would only reignite his rage.

"I convinced her to l-like me. She thought I was her friend. That's why she called me."

"Were you her friend?" Abby asked, fighting to keep her tone steady.

"She thought I was." Jacob's voice trailed off, his eyes unfocused. "It took some doing, but I kept giving her what she wanted so she'd keep calling—" He paused, struggling to complete the sentence. "Sometimes I gave it to her for free! I wanted to see her, you know?"

He leaned his head on her shoulder, his words slurring togeth-er. "Sh-she, she was beautiful—just like you." His voice dropped to a whisper. "She looked just like you."

Abby's eyes darted to the block of knives on the kitchen counter, desperately searching for a way to defend herself.

"Now, *that's* not a good idea," he said, his eyes following her gaze. A sinister smile spread across his face as he tightened his grip on her arm.

"What's not?" She fought to keep her voice calm and steady.

Jacob's eyes lit with a dangerous glint as he pulled his jacket aside and reached toward the small of his back. He revealed a 9mm gun from the waistband of his jeans. "You, of all people, should know," he sneered. "Never bring a knife to a gunfight."

In an instant, he had Abby back in his grasp, his face flushed with anger. His eyes burned with determination. "I can tell what y-you're thinking, Abby."

"What are you talking about?" She asked, willing her voice to be slow and innocent.

"You think I'm the one who killed her."

"You'd never do such a thing." Abby's heart pounded. "You said she was your friend. You wouldn't hurt a friend."

Jacob blinked slowly, and his eyes closed for several heartbeats. His inebriation was slowing his motions, and Abby knew this was her chance.

With all her strength, she jerked hard three times to try to free herself from his grip. She managed to turn her back to him, urgent-ly reaching for a knife, but Jacob yanked her back, pressing the cold, hard steel of his gun against her temple.

"You don't want to do this, Jacob." Her voice was nearly a whis-per.

"You have no idea what I want!" he roared. "What I WANT is for you to listen to me, for you to be on my side, just like Dahlia was."

"Okay, Jacob. I'm listening. You have my full attention." As she spoke, Abby slowly shifted her legs to the left of his body, as much as his tight grip would allow. With a gun against her head, one false move could be her last.

Suddenly, a loud, authoritative knock reverberated through the house, sending shivers down Abby's spine. The floor seemed to quiver in response to the commanding force.

Jacob's head snapped toward the commotion at the door, giving Abby the diversion she needed. In one swift motion, she pressed her leg into the back of his knees and used the leverage to throw his body off balance. She reached down, wrapping her arms around his calves, and yanked his legs upward while slamming her shoulder into his torso.

Jacob fell backward, his head colliding with the corner of the kitchen counter as he squeezed the trigger. The explosive sound of gunfire and shattering glass filled the air.

Abby's instincts kept her from freezing in terror. The bullet had narrowly missed her, and the commotion gave her the second she needed to secure his gun. She gripped it with both hands and aimed it toward her captor. She planted one foot securely on his chest just as a pair of Thornton police officers kicked through her front door.

"I'm ACSO!" she yelled at the officers.

One officer, his weapon drawn and ready, studied Abby's face with a mixture of concern and caution. "I recognize you, Sergeant Carter," he said, his voice slicing through the chaos. "Are you hurt?"

Abby shook her head, her breath coming in short, ragged gasps as the adrenaline surged through her veins. "No, I'm okay," she managed, slowly lowering the gun as the officer approached. The second officer moved swiftly, rolling Jacob onto his stomach and securing his wrists with handcuffs.

Jacob groaned as his face pressed against the cold tile floor, a trickle of blood running from the gash on his head where he'd struck the counter.

"We received your SOS call," the first officer explained, holstering his weapon and gently removing the gun from Abby's trembling hands. "Dispatch tried to reach you, but when you didn't respond, we came as quickly as we could."

Abby nodded, her mind still reeling. She watched as the officers hauled Jacob to his feet, his eyes glazed and unfocused.

"You're under arrest," the second officer informed him, his voice commanding. "You have the right to remain silent. Anything you say can and will be used against you in a court of law."

As the officers led Jacob out of the house, Abby sagged against the counter, her legs suddenly weak. She took a deep, shuddering breath, the reality of her narrow escape slowly sinking in.

Captain Torres rushed into the doorway and scanned the room, searching for Abby with a look of concern on his face. When they made eye contact, her confusion was evident. *Why was he here?*

He answered her unspoken question, "I'm your iPhone emergency contact. I got a notification that you'd sent an SOS signal, and it displayed your location. I called dispatch, and officers were already responding. I came right over." The moisture in her eyes and the scrunched way she held her lips communicated the gratitude she felt for his support.

She moved toward her sofa and reached for the remote to turn the television off. There were a lot of questions she'd have to answer for Thornton PD and her own agency as well. It would be a long night, with hours of interviews at the police station ahead of her.

Jacob would be transported to the police department for processing. There, they'd interrogate him about the evening's incident, but this would remain a separate case from the two murder investigations. Because of his position with the county, the media would be all over this in a hurry. Still, the story would center around first-degree burglary and attempted homicide. Being suspected as a possible serial killer would hopefully stay under wraps for now.

Her house would be treated as a crime scene, and as she overheard conversations on the officer's radios, a detective team was already on the way. The shattered front door wouldn't keep out an elephant if it wanted to stroll through the place, so a different officer was assigned to stand watch until the CSI team had gathered all they needed.

Sitting on her couch, surrounded by noisy, invasive police activity in her own home, Abby wanted to curl up into a ball and push everything out of her mind. The last thing she wanted to do was talk about all that had happened. Would the officers believe her account? Would they judge her for her relationship with this man or her reactions?

Turo, she knew, would stay by her side. He'd offered to drive her to the PD, and just knowing he was near would help her work through the details she'd have to relive.

One troubling aspect of the criminal justice system is that victims are often re-victimized as their bodies, emotions, thoughts, and memories are treated as evidence. While detectives do their best to show empathy and compassion, their job is to extract the information they need from victims in order to pursue justice on their behalf. She knew it would not be an easy process and hoped she had the strength to press through.

CHAPTER 43

ABBY, 2023

Abby squinted through closed eyes as sunlight filtered in through the bedroom window. Fighting to raise her eyelids, unfamiliar surroundings momentarily startled her. As her mind caught up with her body, she remembered she was at the Torres' house at Kerri's insistence. If Abby wasn't nervous about staying alone, Kerri was anxious enough for both of them.

Fragments of the previous evening flashed through Abby's mind, some blurry and indistinct, others painfully vivid. Recalling Jacob's intrusion sent a surge of fury through her body. He admitted to a relationship with Dahlia, and she shuddered to think of how he treated her sister. Violating her sanctuary only added to her anger.

Had Thornton PD not responded at precisely the time they did, the outcome may have been grim. She'd been a breath away from being forced to shoot the man she once believed was becoming a friend. The man who killed her sister.

Last night, as she and Turo had pulled into the Thornton Police Department, she'd been overwhelmed by the way her law enforcement community rallied around her. A collection of upper-echelon leaders from the Sheriff's Office had gathered, their presence a testament to the gravity of the situation.

Her colleagues had gathered near the front doors of the building and offered support through gentle touches and understanding glances. It was a powerful display of unity in the face of an unprecedented betrayal. They championed her cause as one of their own, victimized by someone who portrayed himself as a pillar of the community.

As Abby had stepped inside the police department building to undergo her interview, she saw Turo and Sheriff Adler speaking in hushed tones, Turo no doubt giving him a full account of what had occurred.

The two cases—Abby's assault and Dahlia's murder were intertwined, so Turo would have to play a complicated straddling act. He'd serve as co-interviewer alongside Thornton detectives so he could share his own insight about the complexities of multiple cases—18 years in the making—that were now twisted together in a way no one could have predicted.

Pushing her legs out from beneath the bedcovers, Abby contemplated how her role in Dahlia's murder investigation had dramatically shifted from investigator to witness. Turo told her last night that he would retake the lead in Dahlia's case. That news was tough to hear, no matter how logical.

The forensics team was scheduled to search Jacob's Ford Maverick today. *Today!* Abby looked at her watch. It was 9:30 am, and she had to get moving. She sat up and glanced around the room for the pair of jeans she must have tossed somewhere.

Turo had the foresight to suggest she bring a soft uniform, probably still hanging on the clothes hook in his car. Somehow, without any of her bathroom essentials, she'd have to find a way to get ready for work. Her interview with Tim Kline was in two hours.

She tossed off the covers and entered the hallway. It was a part of the Torres house she'd never been in, and she guessed which closed door would likely be the bathroom. Choosing correctly, she stepped in. A quick glance in the mirror revealed that making herself presentable was going to take some work.

Kerri had placed a new toothbrush with a travel-sized toothpaste tube on the counter. Digging through the bathroom cabinets, Abby found a washcloth to use for a quick sponge bath. Then, glancing quickly through drawers, she found a hairbrush and clip, compliments of Cora, she presumed. She brushed and then pulled her hair into a bun, carefully twisting it upward and securing it with a claw clip.

Abby stepped back into the bedroom to finish dressing, slipped on her shoes, and scampered down the stairs to the main floor. The house was quiet, and she assumed everyone had gone to work or school. Then, out of nowhere, a voice broke the silence.

"Abby?"

Startled, Abby's heart leaped in her chest. She turned abruptly toward the source of the voice, her wide eyes searching the room in alarm. There, standing in the doorway that led to the kitchen, was her friend.

"Kerri!" Abby exclaimed, her initial shock at last giving way to laughter. "You scared the daylights out of me!"

"I'm so sorry, Abby. What horrible timing for such a thing! I thought you'd know I'd be home. I took the day off so I could drive you wherever you need to go."

"You did?! That's so nice of you, thank you!" Abby said, tears pricking her eyes again. "I do need to get to work as soon as possible."

"Turo said you'd say that, although I'm to persuade you to get more rest. He said he's got things handled, and you can postpone your 11:30 interview."

Abby laughed. "He does know me well, doesn't he?" She instinctively reached up to touch the clip in her hair. "I borrowed a few things from the bathroom. I hope that's okay?"

"Of course it is," Kerri said. "I was wondering how you could look so adorable after the night you had."

"I woke up like this," Abby again chuckled, glad to have a friend to banter with. "Did Turo happen to leave the uniform I put in his car?"

"Yes. It's in our bedroom. Let me get it, and we'll get you some food on the way to headquarters."

"Thanks, Kerri. You guys are going above and beyond. Really, thank you so much."

It was 11:15 when Kerri dropped her in front of department headquarters, and Abby rushed in, hoping to have a few minutes to review her notes before meeting with Tim. The extra minutes quickly evaporated as she was inundated with people wanting to check on her and wish her well.

Nearly half an hour later, she and Wayne reached the interview room. She apologized to Tim, who was scrolling on his phone. He was completely unaware of the way things unfolded after they'd talked yesterday, and she needed to keep those details from him for now.

"Tim, I'm sorry to keep you waiting. Things have all but blown up around here." She pulled a chair from beneath the table to sit down. Wayne, who'd been instructed by Turo to join Abby in the interview and monitor her emotional well-being, followed suit. "When you called me yesterday, you told me some things that were pertinent to a case we're investigating. That's why I called you back to schedule this interview. Thank you for coming in."

"I'm happy to help any way I can," he said.

"This interview is being video recorded. Are you ready to dive in?"

"I'm ready," Tim said.

For the next hour, Tim relayed stories about a long-ago friend and how he'd morphed from a kindhearted jokester to a drug dealer and pedophile. Most of the details were a repeat of what he'd shared in yesterday's phone conversation but were now documented so they could be used as evidence for obtaining warrants or presenting arguments in court proceedings.

As they talked, Abby convinced herself she'd kept the level of her rage masked but knew she'd missed the mark when Tim commented, "I'm so sorry if I have upset you, Abby."

Abby glanced at Wayne before answering. "You can see right through me, Tim. It does upset me a lot, actually. But you're not the one causing me to be upset. I'll be able to fill you in at some point, but for now, I'm really grateful you reached out to me. Let me shut down the video. We can stop the interview here."

Abby left the room momentarily to collect herself, then came back to say goodbye and lead Tim out of the building. She looked him in the eyes and said, "I appreciate this more than you know. I realize you called me as a friend yesterday, and things have moved well beyond what you intended. You did the right thing in speaking up. With your help, it looks like we're going to be able to put a horrible person behind bars for a very long time."

"Well, I don't know what Jacob's done, but if I've protected you from anything, I know I've done a good thing. I was afraid you wouldn't believe me, Abby. It means a lot that you did. As you know, there are parts of my past I'm not proud of. I mean, I ran in the same circles as Jacob and nearly crossed some of the same lines."

"But things are different for you now. You found a solid source of help, changed your ways, and made a good life for yourself. Every one of us is worthy of redemption. Even Jacob. But it's only available if we accept it. I'm glad you have." They walked through a maze of hallways, finally arriving at the exit near guest parking. "Give my best to Pasha, Tim. And thanks again." She gave him a quick hug, then turned to head back to her office.

Rounding the corner and passing Michelle's workstation, she saw Turo talking with Michelle and Wayne. "Abby," he said. "Good to see you! Can we talk?" He motioned toward his office, and she followed him there.

He stood near the door as she entered, then gently closed the door behind her. "A few logistical things first," he began. "Thornton PD has released your house, and I've arranged for a contractor to replace your front door, install a new lock system, and get it painted to match the old one. You don't want to change the color or anything, do you?"

"No, the color's fine," she said behind a weary smile. "Thank you. When does it look like that work will be done?"

"Hopefully tomorrow. For now, it's boarded up with a giant piece of plywood. It looks horrible, but no one can get in or out through the front door without breaking it down. I've also arranged for a cleaning crew to come in and thoroughly clean your place. They've sprayed luminal, dusted for prints, and generally created a much bigger mess than anyone would want to go home to. That should also be completed tomorrow. And the Sheriff's Office will cover the expenses, of course."

"So I shouldn't go home just yet?"

"No, I don't advise it. Kerri and I hope you'll come to stay the night. It helps Kerri know she's doing something that's supporting you." He scratched his head. "She's barely speaking to me right now, convinced I should have never given you this assignment."

"You didn't give me the assignment; I took it," Abby argued.

"I know, I know." He gave her a playful grin. "What I'm really saying is it will help my marriage if you'll just come stay the night."

"Okay," she laughed. "But can I at least go into my house and get some stuff?"

"The house has technically been released. We try to spare victims from seeing the mess until it's all cleaned up. But you've seen crime scenes before, and many of them were a lot worse than yours. You won't be shocked to go in, so yes. Go in through the garage and get what you need to stay over."

"Will do, sir," she stood to leave.

"Abby, there's more."

She turned to give him her full attention.

"The forensic team spent several hours this morning searching Jacob's house and the Maverick."

"What did they find?"

"Nothing in the house. Absolutely nothing. Of course, they'll still run tests and see if they can find scientific evidence."

"But in the Maverick?"

"In the trunk of the Maverick, under the spare tire, they found a hidden 9mm Glock and a small bag that matches the description of Dahlia's purse. The lab is processing both items as we speak."

CHAPTER 44

ABBY, 2023

Dahlia's purse. Both Dr. Nguyen and the coffee shop owner were certain Dahlia had her purse with her when she was kidnapped. So, if Jacob had kept it as a carefully guarded trophy, it neatly pinpointed the timeline of when he and Dahlia were together.

Rol had taken her on Wednesday just before he was arrested and booked into jail. Dahlia's slain body was found late Thursday night, within hours of her murder. Somehow, after Rol was hauled away, Jacob entered the picture, drove Dahlia to a secluded area, and ended her life.

The idea of Rol's involvement resurfaced. She'd nearly set the theory aside, but the timeline was too tight to ignore the possibilities. Rol and Jacob knew one another. Rol also said there was a john who had been nice to Dahlia and could even make her laugh. That had to have been Jacob. Was it possible that Rol called him to end the threat Dahlia posed to his trafficking operation?

Abby's mind raced as she stared blankly at Turo. "When can I interview Jacob?" she asked.

"You can't, Abby. There's no foreseeable scenario where the sheriff, or I for that matter, would put you in a room with him."

"But I—"

Turo interrupted, the volume and intensity of his voice ticking up slightly. "Abby, it's out of the question. You can observe from another room, but I'll interview him. You can share details and questions through text. We can do this as a team, but I'm not letting you within 50 feet of this monster. It's for your safety as well as for the integrity of the case. We don't need to stir up an emotional response from either one of you. It would ruin our conviction chances and possibly put you in harm's way. It's not worth it."

"Can I go show the photo array to Rol?"

"No, Abby! I let you interview Tim because you'd already interviewed him informally. You're friends, and he wasn't likely to trigger an outburst with you. But that's the end of the interviews you'll conduct in this case. We'll stick with the original plan, and Wayne will show Rol the photos."

She nearly stumbled into a chair behind her, overcome with swirling thoughts and escalating emotions. The urge to crumple to the floor and surrender to her tears was almost overpowering, but she refused to unravel. "Is Jacob still in jail, or has he bonded out?"

"He's still in jail. The DA petitioned the judge for a no-bond hold until his first court appearance. Our transport team is bringing him here to headquarters as we speak. We'll bring him in through the sally port with handcuffs and shackles. With any luck, this will all go down without media attention."

"How much time do we have?"

"He should arrive within 20 to 30 minutes. I need you to go grab the files. Give me the paperwork that will be most pertinent and keep the rest within reach so you can reference them in real-time."

From the closed circuit television in the detective division conference room, several investigators gathered to watch the interview as it happened. Sheriff Adler and District Attorney Potts sat around the large table with Michelle, Wayne, Rhys, and several other detectives. The Patrol Chief would join them any minute.

Wayne offered his chair, but Abby was too keyed up to sit. She stood near boxes of data she'd piled onto the table.

Through the screen, they could see a uniformed deputy escort Jacob into the room with leg shackles that limited his movement and jingled with each step. He had dark rings beneath his eyes and a new crop of whiskers covering his face. He sat in a hard, unpadded chair, and the deputy left the room.

Several minutes later, Turo entered. The two men sat on opposite sides of a table in the cramped room with cinder block walls that had been recently covered with fresh white paint. The lights shining from the ceiling seemed obnoxiously bright.

Turo took time to position himself, carefully setting a manila file folder before him. He flipped his iPhone into silent mode, placing it face down on the table.

"Jacob?" Turo started. "Everett, is it?"

"Jennings," the inmate corrected. "My name was legally changed several years ago."

"But it was Everett when you knew Dahlia Archer, correct? She called you 'Doc,' I believe."

"I'm sorry," Jacob answered, "when I knew who? What was the name again?"

Abby's stomach lurched, and a wide assortment of profanities ran through her mind. She knew he'd lie, of course. But denying he knew Dahlia after he'd so clearly told her they were friends felt like a punch to her gut.

"Dahlia Archer. We've verified that you knew her and played an unusual role in her life in the years prior to 2005."

A camera was trained on Jacob's face, his eyes fixed on Turo. Calculating. Considering what to say next and formulating a plan to somehow convince the detective he was mistaken.

"Let's start with something more recent. Are you familiar with Abigail Carter?"

"Of course I am," Jacob admitted. "You've personally seen us together. I stopped to talk with her at the steakhouse one afternoon when she was there with you and Sheriff Adler."

"I recall that interaction, yes. And you were arrested inside Abby's home last night after holding a gun to her head. Abby reported—and we established through your statement—that during the altercation, you stated you knew her sister, Dahlia. That the two of you were friends."

"Ah, yes, I recall that now. I did know Dahlia years ago. Her name slipped my mind. I believe she was murdered. Such a shame. She was a very nice girl."

Abby rubbed her forehead with the tips of her fingers. This was going to be a long, excruciating interview. She took a long draw of water from a plastic bottle.

"Was Dahlia ever in your car, Jacob? An old Ford Maverick?"

"I own a Ford Maverick, but I don't recall if Dahlia ever sat in it. I can't think of a reason why she would." Abby noticed a slight quiver in his lips as he spoke.

Turo pressed. "We've searched your Maverick, Jacob, and our team is processing it for DNA as we speak. Is there any reason we'll find Dahlia's DNA in that car?"

"Again, I don't recall if she was ever in the car, but I don't know why she would have been."

There it was again. The corners of his lips tremored almost imperceptibly. She realized she'd seen that tremor from Jacob before, on their first dinner out together. The subtle twitch lasted only a fraction of a second when he said he'd changed his name to distance himself from his brother.

"He's got a tell," Abby said aloud. She took several strides to the monitor and stared as if she were trying to decipher a hidden code. "It's right there in plain sight," she mused, her eyes locked on Jacob's face in the video footage.

Abby had always been a keen observer of people, but this new-found revelation sent a surge of adrenaline through her. That minuscule but telling quiver was illuminating the shadowy corners of his deceit.

Abby couldn't help but wonder how many times she had missed this subtle sign before. How many secrets had Jacob concealed behind that barely noticeable twitch? It was a disconcerting thought, and it fueled her determination to get to the truth no matter how well he thought he could hide it.

By now, all of the observers were standing, huddled around the screen. "The corners of his lips quiver when he's lying," Abby explained, using as few words as possible so they could hear the unfolding dialog. She grabbed her cell phone and typed in a message to Turo. Immediately, they watched him raise his cell phone to read her message.

The interview went on for several hours. Jacob was unwavering in his story: He didn't know of anyone named Rolyn Archer; he did appreciate younger girls but didn't recall a building on 84th Avenue where illegal sexual activities took place. He'd never heard of a Tiffany Davis. He didn't know any lyrics to any of KISS's songs. He'd had several nicknames in his younger years and didn't recall asking anyone to call him Doc.

At last, Turo called for a break. Jacob was escorted to the bathroom and offered a bottle of water. Turo made his way upstairs to the conference room, where the rest of the team was gathered.

"I don't know why he hasn't lawyered up," he said, stepping into the room. "This guy's just odd. And I've yet to see a tell." Turning to Abby, he said, "Explain to me what you see."

"Watch the corners of his mouth. They quiver just a little when he's lying, as if he's grappling with something beneath the surface. From what I can see, he hasn't been honest with you yet."

"When I go back in, I'm going to change my approach. Maybe offer him a hamburger or something to eat and play 'nice cop.' Maybe he'll see me as someone who wants to help protect his career."

Within the hour, Jacob ate a fast food hamburger and fries as a team of onlookers scrutinized his every move. Turo sat beside him, this time on the same side of the table as if he were an ally. He began making small talk about the changes they'd seen in the county since Jacob was elected to the board of county commissioners. "You've done a good job for us," Turo complimented.

Jacob was quick to jump into a tirade of how difficult his work was and how much he cared for the community. It was the opening Turo needed to approach the questioning from a different angle.

"You really care about people, don't you?" Turo asked. As Jacob nodded, he continued. "I can see it in you. And it makes me wonder how you got into this mess. Take the other night, for example. It sounds to me like you went to Abby's because you care for her and wanted to check and see if she was doing okay."

"That's exactly why I went over, but it wasn't portrayed that way at all. I'm very disappointed that she twisted the story around the way she did."

"Women will do that," Turo said. "They don't have the ability to see the big picture all the time. They just see things from their own perspective."

"Where's he going with this?" Michelle said aloud in the conference room, clearly offended by Turo's comments.

Abby gave her mentor the benefit of the doubt. "Give him a minute, and let's see," she coaxed.

"I know you don't remember Dahlia calling you Doc, but from the entries in her journal, it sounded like she saw you as a source of help. Even back then," Turo said, "you were doing all you could to help people." He let several moments pass before speaking again.

"You probably don't remember this, either, but Dahlia's Uncle Rol once told us you could make Dahlia laugh. He said he never heard the girl laugh, barely even saw her smile, but when she was with you, she seemed almost happy."

Jacob smiled as if remembering those days. His eyes darkened with a sinister glint flickering within their depths. "Yeah," he said. "I used to love seeing her smile. When I made her laugh, she'd do practically anything I asked."

Abby gasped. Jacob's lips hadn't twitched, and the look in his eye had transformed from domineering to diabolical.

"Her journal said you always had the cure she was looking for. She seemed fond of you. Just goes to show how much you cared for her, I guess."

"I'm a caring guy," Jacob said. "Always have been."

"So maybe," Turo went out on a limb with this question, "that night when you went to pick her up, you were just helping her find a way to leave Rol. She didn't want to live a life of prostitution anymore. Maybe you were just helping her escape. That would make sense to me."

Jacob tore a section from his paper cup and nervously wrapped it around his finger.

"Did you feel like you were helping her that night, Jacob?" Turo asked as sweat began to accumulate on Jacob's hairline.

Jacob held eye contact as if gauging Turo's sincerity. "You know what it's like to help people," he said at last. "It feels great."

Several excruciating seconds of silence ticked by before Jacob continued. "Dahlia had cried to me for months about how much she hated working for Rol. She said she needed a way out. I told her repeatedly she'd have to die to escape. But I knew she'd never find the courage to hurt herself."

Jacob leaned forward, his voice dropping to a whisper as if sharing a treasured secret. He looked straight into the camera as if looking Abby in the eye. "I'd been waiting for the moment for months, since Dahlia first confided in me about wanting to escape Rol's clutches. I knew she couldn't do it herself, but I also knew she trusted me implicitly."

Jacob swallowed hard. A twisted smile tugged at the corners of his lips. Abby felt a chill run down her spine as she watched the monitor. "I'd been grooming her," he continued, his voice projecting an air of pride. "I planted the seeds of self-destruction in her mind, making her believe the only way out was through the barrel of a gun. And not just any gun, but *my* gun."

Abby could see Turo fighting to keep his composure. His jaw clenched, his disgust barely contained.

"What happened that night, Jacob? The night you went to pick her up?"

In Jacob's eyes, Abby saw perverse satisfaction. "She called me like I knew she eventually would. When my phone rang, she asked me for the release she so desperately craved. Who was I to deny her final wish?"

Jacob stared blankly at the wall before him, his voice thick with a sickening nostalgia. "I savored every second. The look of confidence she gave me, the thrill of power I held over her, the smell of the gunpowder. It was everything I'd dreamed of."

"You pulled the trigger," Turo clarified.

"Yes, I pulled the trigger. And as I watched her lifeless body fall, I knew I had found my purpose. Dahlia was just the beginning, Detective. Just the beginning."

CHAPTER 45

ABBY, 2023

Abby pulled into the driveway of Auntie Beth and Uncle David's house, never so relieved to be home. They had much to talk through, many tears to shed, and decades of turmoil to finally put behind them.

Abby unfastened her seatbelt with trembling fingers and reached for the door handle. Auntie Beth ran out of the house and was already standing beside her SUV, tears flowing from her eyes. As her feet hit the ground, the two embraced in a long hug, finally giving themselves room to release emotions that threatened to overtake them. Beth was the first to pull back, looking into Abby's eyes and gently wiping her tears with her thumb.

She'd shared only a few details with her aunt. Jacob had confessed to shooting Dahlia. He claimed she'd asked him to assist her with suicide after he'd spent months planting the idea in her mind. At first, Abby thought the idea preposterous, but replaying the life Dahlia left behind when Rol kidnapped her and the life she'd be forced to return to, the concept didn't seem so absurd.

Arm in arm, the women crossed the threshold of the front door, reentering the very living room where Detective Arturo Torres had once stepped, bearing the grim news that had shattered their world— the news of Dahlia's death. Now, they gathered with Uncle David in this same room, forming a tight-knit circle of unity, ready to confront the fragmented pieces of their lives that had eluded them for far too long.

These fragments, like pieces of a jigsaw puzzle scattered haphazardly, held truths they yearned to discover. But with the revelation came a sobering reality—the completed picture might reveal a truth they were not entirely prepared to face.

They had long since reconciled themselves to Dahlia's passing, but the reasons behind her tragic end had remained hidden. With heavy hearts, they knew the time had come to talk as a family, weigh the new information, and come to terms with the full story.

Abby sat next to Auntie Beth on the floral sofa, a large box of tissue within reach on the coffee table. David found a seat in an armchair, facing the two most dearly loved women in his world. Trying several times to begin speaking but lacking the strength to share what she knew, Abby finally stood and began pacing back and forth across the floor.

"None of this is pretty," she said. "The more I learn, the more horrible things become. It's not going to be easy to share, so bear with me."

David spoke first. "Just tell us the truth, Abby. We need it so desperately, no matter how it hurts."

"Here's what we can put together," Abby began, taking a deep breath to steady her nerves. "Rol kidnapped Dahlia and, while he was driving, beat her to a pulp. That's why Dahlia's face was so bruised. Not from the killer, but from Rol." David's face reddened with murderous rage, and Abby sensed that had Rol not been in prison, he might be wise to fear for his life.

"He tied her up in the car, which explains the fibers of rope that covered her clothing and the small abrasions on her arms. Then, when they arrived at his apartment, he made her take a Vike. Rol confirmed these details himself when Turo went back to the prison for another interview.

"Dahlia begged him not to make her take the drug, but he didn't care. He said if he could keep her hooked, she wouldn't leave him again." Abby blew her nose and tried to quell the stream of tears.

"He took every bit of cash from inside her purse so she wouldn't have any way to leave him. He disconnected the phone in his apartment so she couldn't call anyone for help. Lord, help me. I have an unhealthy desire to hurt this man. He was awful to her. Pure evil. Naturally, he was going to put her back into a life of prostitution." Her chin quivered as she spoke, and she struggled to speak in a volume her family could hear.

"When our forensic team searched Jacob's Maverick, they found Dahlia's purse and the murder weapon in the trunk of the car. The items had been hidden there all these years, kept as trophies of his first kill. After the night Dahlia died, Jacob never drove the Maverick. He wanted to restore it so it would become a sort of shrine to her. He'd hidden it away until he had it painted just a few months ago. Then he brought it over to show me—taunt me—one weekend when Mack was in Denver."

Abby reached for her cell phone, which was in the back pocket of her jeans. "Inside Dahlia's purse, they found a letter written to me. In Dahlia's handwriting." Tearful sobs came in waves, rendering her utterly speechless.

She opened the images on her phone and zoomed into the one she needed. "They won't let me have the letter until the case is closed, but Turo did let me take a picture so I could share it with you. It was written on the inside of a Burger King bag." Working to regain her composure, she said, "Here's what she wrote:

'Beebs,
I'm so sorry. Please, please forgive me.
I let my guard down for just a moment, and Rol snatched me right off the street. I was only a few blocks from Auntie Beth's. I can't believe how stupid I was. He took all the cash from my purse, but I had some change left in my jeans pocket, so I ran to a pay phone and called the only number I could think of—Doc's.

He's coming to get me tomorrow, and we're going to take care of this once and for all. He's had this plan for a while now, and he's been trying to convince me it's the only way out. I think I finally see that he's right.

I can't go back to the life I had before, Beebs. Not after knowing what real happiness feels like. And that happiness is you. Being with you, spending time as your sister, not just your protector or provider, has shown me what true joy is.

You've always meant everything to me, but now, even more so. Because of you, Auntie Beth, and Uncle David, I know what love really is. And I can't live without it anymore.

All I can think about is being with Jesus. Ending this insanity and living with God forever. I wish I could tell you goodbye in person, but this note will have to do. I love you more than words can say, Bebee.

Please, promise me you'll live a long and happy life. I'll be waiting for you in eternity.

Love always,
Dahlia'"

Abby's fingers involuntarily released the phone, allowing it to tumble onto the soft carpeted floor with a muffled thud. She rushed toward Auntie Beth, whose arms opened wide to receive her. Falling to her knees, Abby found refuge in her long, gentle hug.

In the shelter of Beth's comforting presence, Abby buried her face in her own folded arms that rested on her aunt's lap. A torrent of tears and sobs wracked her entire body. Beth, with tears streaming down her cheeks, could do little more than offer a soothing touch, her fingers tenderly stroking Abby's hair.

David knelt beside them. They cried as a family, remembering the beautiful life they'd lost. It was a moment that cemented the unbreakable bonds that held them together, even in the face of life's harshest trials.

Early the next morning, Mack rapped gently on Abby's bedroom door. She wordlessly settled beside Abby on the bed, a reassuring presence as Abby began to recount the heartbreaking story of

Dahlia's life and death once more. Abby's voice, heavy with emotion, filled the room, and Mack listened attentively, allowing her friend to share the fullness of her sorrow.

Gradually and gently, Mack encouraged Abby to leave the confines of her room, steering her toward the comforting aroma of freshly brewed coffee wafting from the kitchen. Abby reluctantly complied, her steps heavy with grief. There was comfort in the warmth of her family, who gathered around the table.

To provide the closure they'd been longing for, they'd decided to visit Dahlia's final resting place later in the afternoon. Auntie Beth, with her customary grace, extended the invitation to Mack, offering her a place alongside the family during this deeply intimate moment. But Mack knew the family needed to find their strength within each other and declined.

As Mack rose from her seat, a familiar chime broke the silence in the room, and all eyes turned towards Abby's phone. Turo's face illuminated the screen.

Abby's heart raced as she answered the call, her voice trembling with a mixture of anticipation and trepidation. "Turo," she greeted, bracing herself for what was to come.

"Abby," Turo's voice was measured. "I'm sorry to interrupt, but there's something you need to know. Jacob confessed to Tiffany Davis's murder."

The room seemed to hold its breath as Abby absorbed this critical piece of information. Her eyes flicked to her family, each equally gripped by the gravity of the situation.

Turo continued. "The ballistics came back, and they matched the gun he had with him at your house to the one that killed Tiffany. We've got him pinned down, Abby. He's avoiding trial and has agreed to a plea deal for both murders."

Abby's mind raced, thoughts swirling in the wake of this revelation. She couldn't help but think of the lives that could have been saved had they uncovered this earlier. Her heart ached for the families who had endured the pain of loss, a pain she knew all too well.

The detective in Abby couldn't be silenced, even in the face of her own grief. "There were two different guns?"

"Yes, it looks like the gun in the Maverick has been there since Dahlia's murder, as if he never touched it again."

"Did you ask him if there are more victims?" her voice was laced with anger and determination.

Turo sighed, his weariness evident. "I did, Abby. He's not giving us any more information, but I strongly suspect there are more victims. Law enforcement agencies across the county are comparing some of their cold cases with the details we've uncovered—thanks to your tireless efforts."

Abby's eyes welled with tears, and she blinked them back, struggling to find words. She understood the magnitude of what she had achieved, yet the toll it had taken on her was immeasurable. "And your efforts, too, Turo," she finally managed, her voice steady despite her emotions. "I can't celebrate just yet. But maybe, someday."

In her heart, Abby knew she'd made a difference. It was a painful victory, but a victory nonetheless, one that would finally bring a tiny measure of closure. While it could never bring Dahlia or Tiffany back, over time, it would allow both families to find their own peace.

CHAPTER 46

ABBY, 2023

"Uncle David, can we go to the Grand Mesa for a day hike this weekend?" Abby asked over FaceTime while shoving her last bite of avocado toast into her mouth. The long winter had finally melted into spring, and as the days grew warm, she was eager to spend some time in nature.

"What about me?" Auntie Beth asked playfully, poking her face into the camera view.

"You've never enjoyed hiking, Auntie. But of course, you're welcome. We'd love to have you!"

"Speak for yourself," Uncle David teased. "She'll just slow us down, Abby." Abby chuckled at the banter between them.

Auntie Beth leaned further into the camera's view, her smile filled with affection. "Well, you know, I might surprise you both. Maybe I'll discover a hidden love of hiking while we're there."

Uncle David grinned, his eyes twinkling with mischief. The good-natured exchange continued for several minutes. Despite the challenges they'd faced in recent times, their spirits remained resilient, and the prospect of a family hiking trip had already become something to look forward to.

In the days following Jacob's confession, they'd become inseparable, their time together filled with bittersweet moments. Sifting through dusty photo albums, they felt as if each picture was like stepping into the past. Moments of laughter erupted as they reminisced about the antics Dahlia played. Their shared prayers felt like a lifeline of connection.

Every memory was tinged with the profound sense of loss that Dahlia's absence still brought, a loss even two decades couldn't heal. In their shared grief, it was as if they were trying to cling to every moment they'd spent with her.

Jacob's confession had shaken them to their core. It was a crushing, unexpected twist, one that brought a complex mix of unsettling emotions.

The initial shock had slowly given way to sadness and regret. Guilt gnawed at their hearts as they wondered if there was more they could have done, even when reason told them otherwise.

Abby had shared two virtual visitations with her father in prison since she'd come home. In the first, she tearfully shared so much information during the ten-minute appointment that all her dad could do was listen. She'd felt bad that she couldn't offer much comfort. Instead, it had been an information dump of the most painful kind.

A couple of weeks later, they talked again, and this time, it was Abby who listened. Her father had verbally processed his own emotions of grief and outrage. He was furious with Rol and the part he'd played in tearing their family to shreds. For once, through this display of emotions, Abby was able to see her father as a real person, not just a mythical figure who'd abandoned his daughters. A nearly imperceptible hint of fondness had sparked in her heart. She could only wonder where it might lead if she allowed it to grow.

The arrest of Adams County Commissioner Jacob Jennings reverberated far beyond the county's borders, sending shockwaves throughout the entire Denver metropolitan area. It was a harsh blow to the already shaky reputation of the community. While home to many upstanding members and local leaders, Adams County bore the scars of notorious leaders, a legacy that stretched back through generations.

There was satisfaction in knowing elected officials were not above the law. Jacob Jennings' arrest showed even those in positions of authority could and would be held accountable for their actions. It was a small but important victory.

Tyler Watson, once a suspect in Dahlia's murder, was arrested in neighboring Weld County. The closure of Watts Auto Repair marked the end of a nefarious operation that had lurked under the radar for far too long. The once-bustling garage had been nothing more than a cunning façade for Watson's unspeakable trafficking crimes. With the authorities closing in, the ring of crime was finally extinguished.

Still, this was just one small step in a much larger battle. The fight against sex trafficking was far from over, and countless more perpetrators were out there. The pursuit of justice was endless.

As the last details of Dahlia's case were finalized, Turo announced his retirement from the Adams County Sheriff's Office. It was a tear-filled occasion for Abby, but she'd never seen Kerri look so happy. The weight of the world was lifted from her shoulders, knowing she'd no longer have to share him with unending interruptions and midnight callouts. Abby would desperately miss Turo's mentorship at work but knew she would always think of his family as her own.

Turo and Sheriff Adler persuaded Abby to put in for promotion to lieutenant. She submitted the paperwork and competed well in the oral examination process, but ultimately, the promotion was awarded to Enrique Rhys. She was thrilled for him, and he'd specifically asked for her to take his place as detective sergeant.

The resolution of Dahlia's case had rekindled a fire within her. The heavy burden that had saddled her for so long had been removed, bringing the feeling of freedom, a sensation she hadn't experienced before. It reminded her of a conversation she'd had months ago with her pastor.

She'd had a long talk with Pastor Luke, her heart heavy with the news that Dahlia had wanted to die. She'd trusted her pastor to help her navigate her spiritual confusion. With wise words, he conveyed that only God knows a person's heart in their final moments. He is a loving and merciful God who extends His grace to everyone who seeks Him. Though evil exists in the world, and while God doesn't always stop it, He promises to ultimately redeem it.

Before she'd left him, she asked, "Do you remember what you said to me when I first accepted the cold case assignment?" His curious expression had led her to continue. "You told me finding Dahlia's killer might be just as much about finding my personal freedom as it was about putting someone in prison."

"I do recall that, yes." Pastor Luke smiled.

"I feel that freedom," Abby explained. "It's like my future holds new promise for making a lasting difference. Every doubt and insecurity to pursue my calling has been released, and, Pastor, it feels amazing!"

"I'm thrilled for you, Abby. You know I'll be praying for your safety. And for God's wisdom to lead you every step of the way."

As she planned to visit Grand Junction in a few days, she couldn't help but notice a difference in her emotions. In the past, thoughts of returning home were tinged with sadness. Every visit was a bittersweet reminder of the void left by Dahlia's absence.

But now, as she carefully mapped out the details of her trip, there was a newfound lightness in her heart, the anticipation of moments she could spend with loved ones.

She envisioned laughter, shared stories, and warmth, knowing Dahlia's memory would always be a part of their gatherings, but it wouldn't define them. And, she believed, that's just how Dahlia would have wanted it.

She knew the mountains would still be windy and cold, but she could think of nothing better than getting out where the air was clear and the sun was as bright as a thousand radiant smiles. From the peaks of the Grand Mesa, the sun painted the world in hues of gold, filling every corner with warmth and hope. That's where she wanted to be.

Ending her FaceTime, Abby heard a rustling sound behind her, followed by a clicking noise. She turned her head to look toward her living room, her eyes sparkling with delight.

Her new puppy, a black and brown Labrador Retriever mix, bounded toward her, nearly tripping over his disproportionately large paws. Abby crouched down, extending her hand and allowing him to nuzzle and lick her fingers. She scratched his soft, floppy ears, which seemed somehow connected to his tail, and caused it to wag furiously. His entire back end wiggled with infectious enthusiasm. "Mr. Miyagi," she said. "Are you ready for your breakfast?"

Just then, her phone chimed. "Good morning, Wayne," she answered.

"Sarge," his voice came through on speaker. "Westminster Police Department has tied another cold case to Jacob Jennings' gun."

If you or someone you know is considering suicide or self-harm, please get help now. Support is available for you.

Text: 741741

Call: 988

If you suspect trafficking or are being trafficked, please speak up. If you see something, say something. Contact the National Human Trafficking Hotline:

Text: 233733

Call: 1-888-373-7888

ACKNOWLEDGMENTS

Writing is a solitary process. But when a writer looks up from her computer screen, it's the supportive community around her who fuel the embers of creativity.

I'm blessed beyond measure to have steadfast encouragement from my family, friends, and those who have become friends along the way. This is my small way of saying thank you, although my words will always fall short of what's in my heart.

First, my truest friend and love of my life—my husband, Michael, was at my side when inspiration for this novel struck. From that moment on, he answered questions, bantered ideas, and fueled my passion to keep going. He's approaching four decades in law enforcement and once served our community as the elected Sheriff of Adams County.

This book would not be what it is without our endless brainstorming sessions, middle-of-the-night questions, and spur-of-the-moment road trips to help me find the exact settings I envisioned—close to home and in Grand Junction. His irrepressible support was my favorite part of the process.

My kids and their families stood steadfastly on the sidelines and cheered me on. They sometimes rolled up their sleeves and did the dirty work of reading rough material, planting ideas and creative twists, laughing at ridiculous mistakes and oversights, and being more enthusiastic than I could ever hope they'd be. My heart overflows with love for them all: Taylor (who read and reread my drafts and is the primary inspiration for Mack in the story), Chris, Nikki, Dean, and our beloved grandkids who have stolen our hearts: Calvin, Tynlee, Gus, Braxton, and Lilah.

Belinda Shipp, far away in Cornwall, England, has been a champion in my corner for years. When I stop believing in myself, she never does, and once a week, she breathes life into my weary heart. Many of the sticky notes on my computer monitor remind me of her words of wisdom, which often keep me pressing on.

When I got stuck on all the narcotics terminology and needed to know which street drugs were popular at various times in the storyline, Joel White answered every question and helped me maintain authenticity. He's become a good friend, always willing to listen to my stream of ideas and imagination.

Darwin and Doreen Ohlin are prayer warriors extraordinaire. They have never stopped seeking God's provision for everything I need during the writing journey. I adore this couple and want to be more like them. They also introduced me through their son, Pete, to Covered Colorado, a nonprofit that empowers sex trafficking survivors.

I've met with a group of women for weekly Bible study for over 15 years. Debbie Andrews, Tia Clark, Vicky McClure, and even Marilyn Bryan, who is new to our group, have covered me in prayer, cried, laughed, and celebrated with me throughout the journey of Redemption's Echo. I can't imagine my life without these friends.

Sarah Damaska, my copy editor, became nearly as attached to the characters in Redemption's Echo as I am and tried her best to teach me how to use a comma correctly. It's said there are no good writers, only good editors, and Sarah is living proof. I adore seeing her fingerprints throughout this book.

Julie Kranjcec, my dear friend whom I met on the first day of our junior year in high school, allowed me to use a few sentences from her life story. Mack also reveals some of her personality because she's a friend I love like a sister.

Some had temporary roles in this journey: Krissy Nelson was the first writing professional to hear my story idea and gave it an immediate, warm embrace. TJ Ray, the first of many editors to review my work, helped me overcome my imposter syndrome and believe I could. I'm grateful to them both.

The beta readers for Redemption's Echo—Amber Carvalho, Kaleigh Perez, Jenny McMillan, Joel White, Belinda Shipp, and Julie Kranjcec—were kind enough to read the manuscript in draft form and provide suggestions that strengthened the story. While you may not know it, if you enjoyed the book, it has much to do with their thoughtful feedback.

I'd be remiss if I didn't mention my mom, who once upon a time planted the seeds of my curiosity about writing fiction. We did it, Mom. I love you.

This book was God's idea in the very beginning, and He gave me a glimpse of it long before I was ready to receive it. His first prompting was to pay attention. That's not much to go on, but through countless hours of prayer, He revealed the plan an inch at a time until I could finally see the final destination. To Him be all the glory.

ABOUT THE AUTHOR

Cathy McIntosh spends her days as a uniquely positioned writing and marketing coach with a diverse author portfolio spanning multiple genres. Her debut novel, Redemption's Echo, is a heart-gripping tale that draws from nearly four decades as the wife of a law enforcement professional and offers readers an authentic glimpse into the world of crime and justice.

When Cathy isn't crafting compelling stories or guiding fellow writers to success, she is often delving into the latest crime podcasts, always eager to unravel a mystery. With an insatiable curiosity, she embraces the opportunity to learn new skills and embark on exciting adventures, rarely shying away from what lies around the next proverbial corner.

She and her husband relish the joys of living in Colorado, where they are surrounded by the laughter and love of their children and grandchildren.

Cathy is a supporter of Covered Colorado, a nonprofit empowering Colorado's sex trafficking survivors toward a life of self-sufficiency. A portion of proceeds from *Redemption's Echo* will support this crucial cause.

Follow Cathy on Instagram @cathymcintoshcoach

www.ingramcontent.com/pod-product-compliance
Lightning Source LLC
Chambersburg PA
CBHW022004310726
48972CB00006B/1512